## PRAISE FOR *IN THE CARDS*

"Infused with . . . fresh detail. Between the sweetness of the relationship and the summery beach setting, romance fans will find this a warming winter read."

—*Publishers Weekly*

"Fans will love the frank honesty of her characters. [Beck's] scenery is richly detailed and the story engaging."

—*RT Book Reviews*

"[A] realistic and heartwarming story of redemption and love . . . Beck's understanding of interpersonal relationships and her flawless prose make for a believable romance and an entertaining read."

—*Booklist*

## PRAISE FOR *WORTH THE WAIT*

"[A] poignant and heartwarming story of young love and redemption and will literally make your heart ache . . . Jamie Beck has a real talent for making the reader feel the sorrow, regret, and yearning of this young character."

—*Fresh Fiction*

## PRAISE FOR *WORTH THE TROUBLE*

"Beck takes readers on a journey of self-reinvention and risky investments, in love and in life . . . With strong family ties, loyalty, playful banter, and sexual tension, Beck has crafted a beautiful second-chances story."

—*Publishers Weekly* (starred review)

## PRAISE FOR *SECRETLY HERS*

"In Beck's ambitious, uplifting second Sterling Canyon contemporary . . . conflicting views and family drama lay the foundation for emotional development in this strong Colorado-set contemporary."

*—Publishers Weekly*

"Witty banter and the deepening of the characters and their relationship, along with some unexpected plot twists and a lovable supporting cast . . . will keep the reader hooked . . . A smart, fun, sexy, and very contemporary romance."

*—Kirkus Reviews*

## PRAISE FOR *WORTH THE RISK*

"An emotional read that will leave you reeling at times and hopeful at others."

*—Books and Boys Book Blog*

## PRAISE FOR *UNEXPECTEDLY HERS*

"Character-driven, sweet, and chock-full of interesting secondary characters."

*—Kirkus Reviews*

## PRAISE FOR *BEFORE I KNEW*

"A tender romance rises from the tragedy of two families—a must read!"

—Robyn Carr, #1 *New York Times* bestselling author

"Jamie Beck's deeply felt novel hits all the right notes, celebrating the power of forgiveness, the sweetness of second chances, and the heady joy of reaching for a dream. Don't miss this one!"
—Susan Wiggs, #1 *New York Times* bestselling author

"*Before I Knew* kept me totally enthralled as two compassionate, relatable characters, each in search of forgiveness and fulfillment, turn a recipe for heartache into a story of love, hope, and some really good menus!"
—Shelley Noble, *New York Times* bestselling author of *Whisper Beach*

## PRAISE FOR *ALL WE KNEW*

"A moving story about the flux of life and the steadfastness of family."
—*Publishers Weekly*

"An impressively crafted and deftly entertaining read from first page to last."
—*Midwest Book Review*

"*All We Knew* is compelling, heartbreaking, and emotional."
—*Harlequin Junkie*

## PRAISE FOR *JOYFULLY HIS*

"A quick and sweet read that is perfect for the holidays."
—*Harlequin Junkie*

## PRAISE FOR *WHEN YOU KNEW*

"[A]n opposites-attract romance with heart."
—*Harlequin Junkie*

## PRAISE FOR *THE MEMORY OF YOU*

"[Beck] deepens a typical story about first loves reuniting by exploring the aftermath of a violent act. Readers will root for an ending that repairs this couple's past hurt."

*—Booklist*

"Beck's portrayals of divorce and trauma are keen . . . Readers will be caught up in their journey toward healing and romance."

*—Publishers Weekly*

"*The Memory of You* is heartbreaking, emotional, entertaining, and a unique second-chance romance."

*—Harlequin Junkie*

## PRAISE FOR *THE PROMISE OF US*

"Beck's depiction of trauma, loss, friendship, and family resonates deeply. A low-key small-town romance unflinching in its portrayal of the complexities of friendship and family, and the joys and sorrows they bring."

*—Kirkus Reviews*

"A fully absorbing and unfailingly entertaining read."

*—Midwest Book Review*

## PRAISE FOR *THE WONDER OF NOW*

"*The Wonder of Now* is emotional, it is uplifting, it is heartbreaking, but ultimately shows the reader the best of humanity in a heartfelt story."

*—The Nerd Daily*

## PRAISE FOR *IF YOU MUST KNOW*

"Beck expertly captures the bickering between sisters, the pain of regret, and the thorny path to forgiveness. With well-realized secondary characters . . . and believable surprises peppered throughout, Beck's emotional tale rings true."

—*Publishers Weekly*

"[Beck's] heartwarming novel explores the sisterly bond with a touch of romance and mystery."

—*Booklist*

## PRAISE FOR *TRUTH OF THE MATTER*

"Beck spins a poignant, multigenerational coming-of-age tale as these three women navigate their identities, dreams, and love lives. Complex and introspective, this is by turns heart-wrenching and infectiously hopeful."

—*Publishers Weekly* (starred review)

"This is [a] sharp and graceful tale of mothers and daughters, secrets and tangled family histories. Jamie Beck brings her clear-eyed prose style and smart characterizations to the story of a mother and daughter doing their best—and often failing—to make their way to a new life after a divorce. A thoughtful, moving book from a writer stepping into the fullness of her talents."

—Barbara O'Neal, bestselling author of
*When We Believed in Mermaids*

# For All She Knows

# ALSO BY JAMIE BECK

In the Cards

## The St. James Novels

*Worth the Wait*

*Worth the Trouble*

*Worth the Risk*

## The Sterling Canyon Novels

*Accidentally Hers*

*Secretly Hers*

*Unexpectedly Hers*

*Joyfully His*

## The Cabot Novels

*Before I Knew*

*All We Knew*

*When You Knew*

## The Sanctuary Sound Novels

*The Memory of You*

*The Promise of Us*

*The Wonder of Now*

## The Potomac Point Novels

*If You Must Know*

*Truth of the Matter*

# For All She Knows

A Potomac Point Novel

# JAMIE BECK

Montlake

Published by Montlake, Seattle

www.apub.com

Amazon, the Amazon logo, and Montlake are trademarks of Amazon.com, Inc., or its affiliates.

ISBN-13: 9781542008754

ISBN-10: 1542008751

Cover design by David Drummond

Printed in the United States of America

*For all the parents who hold their breath and pray
for the wisdom, strength, and courage to guide their
children safely and happily into adulthood.*

# AUTHOR'S NOTE

Dear Reader,

Thank you for picking up *For All She Knows*, a story that is very dear to my heart as a mother of teens who are navigating the high school and college social scenes. In writing this tale, my goal was not to cast judgment on anyone's parenting style, but rather to start a conversation about how and why we make certain choices, and whom and what we might want to consider when doing so. Most of all, I hope that Grace's and Mimi's journeys of discovery—with each other and within themselves—will resonate with you.

It is also important to note that this book was written prior to the pandemic. During the editing process, we decided not to address COVID-19 in the context of this story because there were still too many uncertainties about what the world (and science) would look like by the time the story was released. We appreciate your acceptance of our omission in this case. As I write this note, I am very hopeful that by the time you read this story, we might all be able to safely move about and gather in groups again.

Happy reading!

Jamie Beck

# PROLOGUE

G RACE

*Sunday, January 10, 2021, 12:15 a.m.*
*Shock Trauma Center ER near Baltimore*

Everyone warned me that the day would come when I'd regret befriending Mimi Gillette. But despite our many differences, Mimi and I had
clicked from the moment we first met in our sons' toddler playgroup
years ago, when her earnestness cracked me open like an egg. After
fifteen minutes of chitchat, she'd grabbed my hand to say, *"I hope we
can be good friends,"* and I'd known she'd meant it. Sure, she could be
flamboyant, and our differing parenting styles had made for some interesting conversations, but she was all heart—even after her ex-husband
ground it beneath his bootheel and left her to raise their son alone. And
so I'd tuned out public opinion all these years.

Curling forward, I hugged my calves and buried my face in my
lap, each breath burning my lungs. The not-quite-sweet chemical odor
of hospital disinfectant wasn't helping. With my eyes closed, the recent
scene in Mimi's basement flickered like a horror film. The memory of
my son's terrified tears as he lay prone and immobile on the tile floor
sent a shiver down my back; I swallowed another bitter surge of bile.

"Excuse me." I grasped for the young nurse passing by the area where they'd left us after wheeling Carter off for tests. "My son, Carter Phillips, was taken for MRIs and other tests a while ago, but we haven't had any updates."

"Let me check for you." Despite being harried, he flashed a sympathetic smile before continuing his journey, his focus again glued to the iPad in his hand.

"Thank you," I called after him.

The clock read twelve fifteen. Every minute seemed an eternity.

Across the room, our daughter, Kim, lay sleeping in her pink-and-black leopard-print pj's and slippers, her lanky ten-year-old body strewn across my husband's lap. When we'd gotten Mimi's phone call, I'd charged across town to her house to catch the EMTs—still in my UGG slippers and yoga pants—while Sam had stayed behind, waiting for the girls at Kim's sleepover to be picked up by shocked parents. Now he was stroking her hair, staring into space, probably praying like me.

In between prayers, prior dreadful moments—like the blue lights flashing through my mom's living room window years ago when the cops came to tell us that my older sister, Margot, had died—revisited me. My mother's pitiful howl that evening struck a new chord now. My gaze drifted back to Sam.

Our eyes met, but I glanced away.

"Grace." Sam's deep voice quavered.

"Please, not now." Nothing he could say would settle the chaos in my brain. Sweat seeped from every pore. I crossed my arms and closed my eyes, wishing that when I opened them again, this would be nothing more than a terrible nightmare. That I could go back to yesterday morning—or even before the damn budget debate—and make different choices.

"Babe," Sam whispered loudly enough for me to hear, "I can see you spiraling. Try not to jump to the worst-case scenario. We could still get good news."

His soothing manner and optimism had always been appealing, but neither strategy worked for me tonight. I tugged hard at the roots of my hair, but no self-inflicted pain would reverse time. I didn't deserve peace of mind. Not when everything I'd done to protect my children had been undone by a single bad decision.

Each cough, creaky chair, and turn of a page in the waiting room reverberated in my head. The alcohol odor of the hand sanitizer I'd applied reminded me of the spilled drinks all over Mimi's home, making me nauseated and twitchy. I sprang from my chair and paced, envisioning my sweet boy in a wheelchair. What would that be like? How would we manage rehab and school, or make the house accessible?

I covered my mouth with both hands to hold in a scream about why this was happening to my baby.

My phone vibrated in my pocket. Mimi again. I couldn't listen to her apologies and concern now. All I wanted at this moment was for somebody to tell us that our son would recover and walk.

I collapsed back onto my seat.

Sam slid out from beneath Kim and stretched. "I'm going for coffee. Do you want one?"

"No thank you." Without meeting his gaze, I crossed the room to sit with Kim while he searched for caffeine. Was it only a week ago we'd been excitedly planning an August family biking tour of the Canadian Rockies?

I shook my head again, hoping to clear it, but the faint buzz of overhead lights drilled on.

That my daughter could sleep in this brightly lit, hardly peaceful waiting room astounded me. I toyed with a curl of her blonde hair, wanting to cradle her to my chest and squeeze her tight, as if my arms would keep her safe in a way that I'd failed to do for my son.

A thick tear rolled down my cheek while I tried to follow Sam's lead and grasp for positive thoughts. None came. Or if they did, they got crowded out by self-recriminations.

Then Mimi's splotchy face and the somber faces of those cops reappeared, and the agony of it all stuck in my throat like a bowling ball.

"Mrs. Phillips?" A doctor whose name I couldn't remember how to pronounce stared down at me as Sam returned. "I have an update."

# CHAPTER ONE

## GRACE

*The previous Monday, January 4*
*Stewart's Grocery Mart, Potomac Point*

"Oh, hey, Grace." Mimi flashed a smile while her knee-high leather boots, tight jeans, and fringed sweater drew looks from other shoppers perusing the produce aisle. Her blue-tipped curls were piled high on her head with a bohemian headband decorated with tiny pink cutout flowers.

My shallow leather loafers, gray slacks, and pearl studs wilted in comparison.

"Hey, I didn't expect to run into you." I smiled, remembering then that she closed her hair salon on Sundays and Mondays.

"Sorry about this morning's post in the group." She raised her hand like a witness testifying on the stand. "I swear, I had nothing to do with it."

"What post?" I never checked the Potomac Point Moms Facebook page as frequently as she did. She claimed it helped her engage with customers and organically grow her business. On the surface that seemed sound, but every week at least one comment would leave her feeling glum or excluded.

"Oh, you didn't see it?" She grimaced. "So this is awkward," she singsonged. "But the thing is, whatever happens tonight, we're friends. I get why you object to the budget, and you get why I support it. We both love our sons, so we can't hold fighting for them against each other. It isn't personal, right?" She lifted a cantaloupe and sniffed it before putting it in her cart.

"Of course not." Although in truth, it had already begun to affect us. For starters, this was the first time in a decade we were grappling with something we couldn't discuss with each other. It'd been odd to not be as candid as we normally were about everything from our sex lives to our kids' issues. Plus, Mimi's leadership role in the pro-budget group had won her respect from some women who'd previously been dismissive. She deserved that, so I didn't begrudge her, but I worried her expanding pool of friends might overshadow our relationship.

While my husband and children sustained me, life without Mimi would be lacking something—like a holiday table with an empty place setting. She brought easy laughter and adventure into my days: the Carrie Bradshaw to my Charlotte York. Whether dragging me to a psychic, organizing a meteor shower watch party with our kids years ago, or even making me take a hip-hop dance class one autumn, she made life a little more interesting.

Despite my uneasiness, I winked as we pushed our squeaky-wheeled carts around the bend. "That doesn't mean I'll wish you good luck, though."

She chuckled. "Me neither, but we're still on for coffee early Friday morning."

"Sugar Momma's?"

"Is there even a question?" Mimi blew me a kiss before we parted at the deli counter.

Meandering away, she idly swung her hips and hummed while pausing to scan the artisanal bread display. Like many of the other men in town did whenever she passed by, Leo—the guy working the deli counter—wore an appreciative grin as she wandered off.

Mimi showed no anxiety about the upcoming hearing. Why would she? The budget's nearly three-million-dollar proposal to modernize the turf and field house and create a new practice field would be difficult to overturn. As a VP of the school's booster club, she'd rallied all its alumni to show their support. The town hall auditorium would be packed with champions tonight, many of whom were longtime residents with deep ties in the community, unlike me.

When we were first married, Sam and I had lived in Baltimore, where he'd worked crazy hours at a national accounting firm while I'd put my fine arts degree to use teaching piano at a music studio near our condominium. A perfect job for me, since stage fright made concert performances impossible. I didn't regret that, though, because of my profound satisfaction in sharing the gift of music with children. Carter was not quite three, and we'd been discussing getting pregnant again when Sam received a junior-partnership offer from a regional firm based near this community. He loved being a father, so he jumped on the opportunity to achieve a better work-life balance.

We'd visited several nearby towns before falling for Potomac Point's town center, with its herringbone brick sidewalks and lampposts with hanging flower baskets. In addition to its sandy public beach, where kids would occasionally dig for fossilized sharks' teeth, it also boasted an array of restaurants and plenty of tourist shops chock-full of crab-themed snow globes, key chains, and holiday ornaments. The board-walk—which stretched north from the East Beach Café, its railing flower boxes overflowing with bright begonias—provided a terrific place to ride bikes in the sunshine and inhale the salty sea air, or to sit on its benches and enjoy ice cream as if on a perpetual vacation.

The quaint town seemed safer and more family oriented than our Baltimore neighborhood, and its high school was ranked sixth out of two hundred twenty-six in the state at the time, cinching our decision.

We'd bought a lovely yellow colonial on a flat half-acre lot and slid into this community as if we'd grown up here. But we weren't lifers, which made rocking the boat now feel a bit treacherous.

Like a concert performance, taking the mic tonight would require a colossal act of courage. Ironically, Mimi's can-do spirit had inspired me to stand up for my beliefs now. Throughout the years, she'd quit a job and started her own salon (without a college degree or any business training), and within days of her ex, Dirk, filing for divorce, she'd begun to pick up the pieces. The other motivation? Potomac High's statewide ranking had slipped from sixth to twenty-sixth since we'd moved to town. That affected the competitiveness of Carter's college applications compared with kids from Bethesda and Rockville, hurting his chances of acceptance in MIT's prestigious chemical engineering program. And if the downward trend continued—which seemed likely if millions got directed to sports facilities—where would that leave Kim?

After loading the groceries into my trunk, I opened the town moms' Facebook group—which normally featured complaints about school policies or requests for recommendations for glass installers, calculus tutors, and the like—to find the post Mimi had just mentioned.

> ATTENTION Tigers' fans and families. Y'all better show up at town hall tonight to "roar" in support of the proposed budget so the small but whiny group of disgruntled parents doesn't win. It's past time that our teams get a new practice field, scoreboard, and better equipment, so let's show the board that we Tigers' families approve of their plans!

Amid the supportive comments, I spied my friend and fellow protester Carrie Castle's response about ensuring a fair process. Some rabid budget supporters had already pummeled her with snide or bullying remarks. Those folks' kids must be the ones Carter had mentioned who'd been making trouble for him and others at school ever since an ugly argument about this budget broke out during the last PTC meeting.

Sighing, I tucked my phone into my purse and drove home. With only ten minutes remaining until my first piano lesson of the day began, I rushed to season the roasting chicken, put it in the oven, and clean myself up.

My phone rang. Mom again. Having already put her off once, I answered. "Hi, Mom. Everything okay?"

I peeked through the blinds to see if Keri Bertram was pulling up to the curb to drop off her daughter, Jasmine, a high school freshman who'd never been late for any lesson in three years. A dream student, although she preferred pop music to classical. We were currently working on Billy Joel's "New York State of Mind."

"Yes, honey. I'm fine, but I'm worried about you."

"Me?" I let the slats fall.

"Yes, you. Isn't tonight the big town meeting?"

"It is."

"And you're really going to speak?" The surprise in her tone irked me.

"That's the plan." I waited: one, two, three . . .

"Grace, nothing good comes from stirring the pot."

Her standard line. She'd preached some version of this throughout my life: *"Don't be like Margot, Gracie. There's nothing to gain from making waves. Discretion is the better part of valor."*

"I'm hardly starting a war."

In my mind, her bony shoulders rose briefly before falling while she blew dangling gray hairs from her eyes. "Maybe not, but life is easier when you accept what is and make the best of it."

Easier for whom, exactly?

From my perspective, that attitude had let Daddy run roughshod over us all and still come home to a clean house and a good meal. Maybe if she hadn't been so accepting—if she'd had the courage to take us to a domestic abuse shelter like the one I sewed dresses and drapes for—Margot might still be alive. This kind of thinking is why her attempts to make up for all the years she'd prioritized enabling and justifying my father's alcoholism and violent tendencies over protecting Margot and me fell flat.

Sometimes the urge to criticize her choices came on so strong I worried it'd leap right out of my mouth. But berating her for the past served no purpose now.

"Except that this budget isn't approved yet, so I don't have to accept it."

"Isn't it better to focus on keeping your family happy than to get political? Less chance of regrets."

Perhaps she meant to spare me the regrets she carried on her back like an invisible cross, so I didn't point out that *she'd* never managed to build a happy family.

"Mom, you're being overanxious. It's a hearing."

She tsk-tsked. "You know how people get when they fight about money or kids, and this deals with both."

"Well, I appreciate your concern, but it's my choice." I knew she was shaking her head despite her silence. A car engine idled out front. "Listen, my student just arrived, so I'll call you tomorrow, okay?"

"Think about what I said, honey." The parting shot. I pictured a grimace deepening her wrinkles. "Bye, dear."

"Goodbye, Mom." I hung up, turning away from my past, and then answered the door.

In an unusual move, Keri had walked Jasmine up to the house.

"Jasmine, go ahead and warm up for a minute. I'll be right there." I gestured toward the living room, where we kept my grandmother's Steinway. My grandmother had played for her church but left me the magnificent upright piano when she died fifteen years ago. Now my family enjoyed singing around it on holidays, and as always, playing remained my way of relieving stress and releasing my emotions without fear of reprisal.

When Jasmine left us, I turned to Keri. "Is there a problem with Jasmine's lessons?"

"Oh, no. I love listening to her practice. She's becoming so good." Keri's proud smile wrought one from me as well.

"She's a terrific student."

"Thank God she inherited my husband's discipline." Keri adjusted her purse strap. "I just wanted to wish you luck. Sorry I can't make the hearing, but Paul's working late and Jasmine is babysitting for the Singhs later, so I've got no one to watch my other two."

"No need to explain yourself, Keri. We'll have enough protesters to make our points."

She shrugged. "I don't know. That Mimi and the booster club are all whipped up."

I braced, fighting a scowl. Other women often referred to Mimi as *that Mimi*, especially when they didn't personally know her. Some of their contempt probably arose because many husbands flirted with her. Others might resent that she didn't change herself to make them more comfortable. But most of all, I think Mimi—like my mom years ago—got condemned for her former husband's bad behavior. Dirk had been something of a boor and a notorious cheater.

Having lived through my mom's defenses and rationalizations, I guessed that, deep down, Mimi had put up with it because she'd been hoping that he'd change back to the man she'd fallen in love with.

In any case, I'd grown tired of how some women justified harshly judging other women. When did it become the rule that we all had to conform to one standard and agree about every little thing? As long as a person wasn't out to hurt others, live and let live. Mimi never set out to hurt a soul.

With a firm but polite tone, I said, "Mimi's only supporting her kid like the rest of us are. Fingers crossed that the board members are persuaded by our arguments."

"You're right." Keri nodded, then checked her phone. "I'll be back in forty-five minutes to get Jasmine."

"Perfect." I waved goodbye, then put tonight's meeting out of my mind.

———

My kids came home from school shortly after Jasmine's lesson began. Usually they did their homework in the kitchen and then retreated to their rooms until my last lesson left for the evening. When I finally went to take the chicken from the oven, Carter was closing his textbooks. Although his sophomore workload had increased over last year's, the worry lines on his forehead surprised me.

"What's the matter, honey?" A glance at the clock told me only one hour remained in which to help him, serve dinner, do the dishes, and freshen up before racing to town hall for the seven o'clock hearing.

His shoulders fell. "Mom, please don't make a scene tonight."

"When have I ever made a scene about anything?" If Margot were here, she'd be laughing hysterically. I shoved my hands into the Christmas-themed oven mitts he'd decorated with fabric markers as a sixth grader.

He stuffed his school supplies into his backpack and heaved it over his slim shoulders. Poor kid inherited my lanky build. "I told you, kids at school are fired up. The football team will go off if they lose their field money."

I stiffened, resigned to the fact that high school remained a hier-archy where jocks ruled. Carter had Sam's bright blue eyes and ebony hair, nice sense of humor, gentle heart, and sharp mind, but because he wasn't athletic and extroverted, he remained on the fringes of school society. I'd watched helplessly as he sat alone many Saturday nights, reading dystopian novels or watching TV with Sam and me. But in truth, Mimi didn't have it easier, despite her son's popularity. If anything, maybe she had it harder because popularity brought its own set of risks—the parties and sex and peer pressure.

Perhaps there wasn't any parenting nirvana or perfect teen experience.

"Are they still giving you trouble?" My mitted hands rested on my hips.

"Just . . . Why are you making this a big deal?" He groaned.

When I was young, my sister was the only one to stand up to my father. Watching their vicious arguments convinced me to keep my head down to avoid getting caught in the cross fire. For a long time I thought myself smarter than my sister, although I loved her for trying to protect us. But by the time I turned twenty-one, the fallout from all she'd done had turned her into what she'd once hated. In our teens, I'd felt betrayed by her drinking and drug experimentation. As time went on, I ached for her pain and suffered with guilt for never once standing up to Dad with her.

On one anniversary of her death, I'd shared my feelings with Mimi, who suggested practicing taking a firm stand with something small. In her casual way, she'd also hinted that asserting myself might teach my kids to handle conflict better, sparing them my regrets. Although I didn't agree with all Mimi's parenting choices, some of her instincts were dead-on. I couldn't give in to teen bullies tonight if I intended to help my kids develop the backbone they'd need to stand up for themselves in the future.

"Because academics should be the school board's top priority, not sports. The science labs haven't been upgraded since before we moved here." I opened the oven and crouched to retrieve the roast chicken, freshly irked by the way athletics garnered so much attention in high schools and colleges.

"The labs are fine," he said. "So are my grades."

"We're very proud of you, honey." His summa cum laude average boded well for him, but Potomac High needed to do better by all the taxpayers' kids, not simply the ones who played sports. "But this isn't about only you. Other kids and parents care. And your sister will be coming up behind you in a few years. By the way, call her to dinner, please."

"Whatever." He took his backpack to the mudroom and called up the back stairs, "Kim, dinner!"

If I'd wanted to hear yelling, I would've called her myself.

Kim came skipping into the kitchen and then scowled at us both. "Dinner's not ready."

That one was almost ten but going on twenty, with a personality like my sister's. Brash. Confident. Taking no guff. It was as if she had rejected my DNA in the womb.

"Help your brother set the table." I mashed the lumps in the gravy and turned off the burner beneath the pot of rice.

I heard Sam enter the house before I saw him. He came into the kitchen, loosening his tie and then unbuttoning the top button of his shirt. At forty-three, he retained a youthful charm and playful smile, with only fine wrinkles at the edges of his twinkling eyes.

After giving Kim a kiss on top of her head, he swerved around the island to give me one on the cheek. "Smells delicious."

"Too bad we don't have much time to enjoy it tonight." I wanted to practice my speech once or twice more before the hearing.

Standing before a packed town hall to argue against the proposed budget could draw boos or cutting remarks from ramped-up parents. That claustrophobic feeling I'd always gotten while trying to make myself invisible during my father's public drunkenness could return as quickly as the memories of my sister's long stare and my mother's muttered apologies and prayers. I rubbed my chest to ease the tightness.

Sam narrowed his gaze. "Relax, babe. Your speech is great. No one can squeeze more facts into sixty seconds than you." His light chuckle loosened my shoulder and neck muscles. Sam's faith always helped me relax. He was made for me, with his easy affection and attentiveness, his homebody ways, and even his love for music.

When Carter slumped with a pout, Sam mouthed, "What's his problem?"

"Carter, lots of parents will be speaking out tonight, not just me."

"Like Mrs. Gillette." Carter looked up at me. "Is this really worth fighting with your best friend?"

"Grown-ups don't make this stuff personal. In fact, she and I have plans to get together on Friday." I handed Sam a carving knife, set a bowl of rice on the table, and strained the gravy, feigning more confidence than I felt. Yet if Mimi wasn't backing down in deference to our friendship, why should I? "Is Rowan mad at her?"

"No. She's not trying to take anything away from anyone." Carter rested his chin on his fist.

"That's not true," Sam replied, supporting me as always. "The budget comes from tax revenue, which means all taxpayers get a say."

As Sam took a seat and filled his plate, my phone rang. He looked up. "Leave it."

But I'd already peeked. "It's Carrie. Let me take this while you all start eating."

He nodded, so I answered. "Hi, Carrie."

"Grace, I'm here and the parking lot is full."

"Already?" It was only six fifteen. My stomach dipped to my toes.

Carrie blew out a breath. Her daughter, Phoebe, was a gifted freshman. When the superintendent first published the upcoming year's budget, Carrie had enlisted me to help her rally protesters. "That Mimi's got the booster club out in full force. I bet we're outnumbered by two to one."

Poor Mimi was damned by some no matter what she did. If she hadn't gotten involved, people would've criticized her for letting others stand up for her son's interests.

"Please don't refer to Mimi that way. She's got every right to her opinion. We knew it'd be an uphill battle. If we lose tonight, we'll send letters to the County Economic Council." Hayden Chen, one of my husband's partners, sat on that council, which had the ultimate approval rights over the budget. If tonight went badly, perhaps Sam could make a personal appeal to him—from one parent to another. I wouldn't broadcast that fact to anyone, of course. I might feel a little guilty about that if Mimi and her team weren't pressing every advantage they had as well. "I'll be there as soon as possible."

"Okay. See you soon." Carrie hung up.

By the time I sat down, Kim's chicken and rice were floating in a pool of gravy, which she dipped her finger into for a lick.

"Manners, honey." I draped a napkin across my lap.

She straightened and picked up a fork.

"What did Carrie want?" Sam asked before taking another bite of chicken.

"Apparently town hall's already packed."

"Like church on Christmas—everyone's coming out of the woodwork." Sam smiled, but my stomach lurched.

Carter swallowed a spoonful of rice before saying, "If you're that nervous, don't go."

"I'm fine." I patted my forehead with my napkin and turned to Kim, forcing myself to think of something mundane. "I made brownies this morning. You can have one tonight, but only if you promise to listen to your brother."

"Okay." She then threw Carter a mischievous smile, proving she had no intention of making his job easy.

"And," I added, "you have to eat all of your salad."

Kim heaved a sigh that could raise a hot-air balloon. "Fine."

Sam stood, rinsed his dish, and loaded it in the dishwasher, then clapped his hands and rubbed them together. "Ready to rumble?"

Carter groaned, so Sam laughed. "Just kidding, buddy." He gently batted our son's shoulder. "Lighten up a little, all right?"

Carter nodded while Sam collected my plate and Carter's and took them to the dishwasher. My kids had no idea how lucky they were to have a father like Sam. The opposite of my own in every single way. I'd known from the first time I'd seen him attentively playing with his eldest cousin's toddlers that he'd be exactly the kind of father I wanted for my someday children.

"I'm finished, too," Kim said. The salad on her plate had mingled with gravy.

"I guess you don't want a brownie." I stood, aware my exerting control here was a compensating tactic to cover my nerves.

Kim screwed up her face before forcing a leaf of warm soggy lettuce down her throat.

"Please help your dad finish cleaning up while I get ready." I kissed her head before dashing upstairs to put on my game face.

I swiped a finger beneath my eyes to clear away mascara smudges, then brushed my teeth before applying lipstick. Eyeing myself in the mirror, I imagined Mimi giving me a pep talk. Despite facing one catastrophe after another, she rallied in the face of the insurmountable. It was impossible not to admire a woman who rolled up her sleeves and worked her butt off to overcome whatever was thrown at her, which was one reason I hadn't acquiesced to the gossips and naysayers. I never wanted to alienate or hurt her, which made tonight tricky. I grabbed my purse on my way downstairs, doubts festering.

"See you later!" I called to the kids from the mudroom, where Sam was holding my coat open for me.

"Bye!" came their voices from the vicinity of the family room.

After I'd slipped on the coat, Sam hugged me from behind, resting his chin on my shoulder. "You're gonna do great."

My rock since the day we met. Friendly and optimistic. Giving and patient. Hardworking and earnest. There wasn't one thing I didn't like about Sam. He was my friend, my lover, my partner. Of all my accomplishments, I was proudest of the homelife we'd created. We trusted each other implicitly, and were aligned in most everything right down to our favorite dessert—carrot cake.

In contrast, Mimi's ex barely paid child support. She had no one except Rowan at home to keep her company, either. Such a shame, because Mimi had a lot of love to share.

When Sam passed town hall, he took a right and drove two blocks to park in Saint Anne's parking lot. From there we jogged to the meeting in the dark. The formidable brick building sat atop a sloped lawn, its windows blazing with light and the heraldic state flag flapping in the breeze.

Sam wrapped an arm around my shoulder and kissed my temple as we entered through the main doors. When I'd stammered while accepting a minor honor for my work with the middle school Service League of Boys (known affectionately as SLOBs), Mimi had smiled encouragingly from the audience. She wouldn't be cheering me on tonight, but whether I embarrassed myself at the mic or we ultimately lost this fight, it helped to know that Sam would always be by my side.

Carrie stood outside the auditorium doors. Her stout build and razor-short hair made her resemble a bouncer more than a PTC board member.

"Have you seen Mimi?" I asked.

Not that anyone had to look too hard to spot her most days. She lit up any room she entered with her smile—a trait I somewhat envied. If she was here, Carrie would know.

"Nope, but I've been too busy looking for you to notice." She raised her eyebrows while cracking her knuckles. "We've got twelve of us ready to stand up at the mic. The others are gathered together inside."

Only twelve? The weight of responsibility rested on my shoulders like a yoke.

I grabbed her hand and squeezed it for a moment. "Let's go."

With a deep breath, I entered the crowded auditorium with Sam on my arm.

Showtime.

# CHAPTER TWO

## MIMI

*January 4, 5:45 p.m.*
*Sandy Shores Care Center, Potomac Point*

"Use extra spray, Mimi. This has to last all night." Agnes Folger's wrinkled, age-worn face beamed, even in her lamplit room at the Sandy Shores Care Center. She pointed at some of the framed photographs scattered on the shelves of the slim bamboo bookcase against the wall. "My daughter's family is coming down from DC to take me to dinner for my birthday."

I grabbed her shoulders to give her a little hug. "If you'd told me it was your birthday, I would've brought some razzle-dazzle for your hair."

Agnes raised her bony hands and wiggled her fingers. "Ooh, I love razzle-dazzle."

It took so little to elicit a smile from the seniors who resided here. A little attention. A little silliness. A little hope of something different from the routines inside these walls. That's what kept me coming back twice each month to give free haircuts and blowouts. Once in a while, I threw in a perm if I had enough time and it had been a good month at my salon, A Cut Above.

Some people got uncomfortable around old folks, but a benefit of being raised by my pious uncle Tommy was that he'd dragged me around on his good deeds, one of which had involved a local senior center in Goochland County, Virginia. That taught me how a little kindness could brighten the day for a lonely senior, and how much they had to tell us if we'd listen. Those Saturday morning visits had been one of the few things from that life that I'd brought with me to Potomac Point.

"Hang on. Maybe there's a rhinestone hair clip somewhere in my bag." I spun around to rummage through the giant duffel I used to tote my products back and forth. My fingers caught on something. "Aha!"

I withdrew a crystal-encrusted clip, waving it in the air.

Agnes clapped. "Pretty!"

It was pretty, although it was meant for someone with thicker hair than Agnes had sported in at least twenty years. I combed back a section of her silver bangs and fastened it with the clip.

Agnes made grabby hands for my hand mirror and then dipped her head to get a better look at the sparkler under the lights. "I love it. What do I owe you for it?"

I waved her off. "Consider it a birthday gift. I know I shouldn't ask your age, but we don't keep secrets, right? So tell me, how old are you today?"

"Eighty-two."

"Holy Moses, you don't look a day over sixty-five. Seventy tops!" I teased the hair at her crown and began to empty a bottle of hairspray so even a hurricane couldn't disrupt the do.

She preened for a moment before handing my mirror back to me. "How's that handsome boy of yours?"

"Rowan?" He was handsome, like his father. Tall, broad shouldered, a headful of wavy chestnut-colored hair. Hopefully, he'd become a more dependable kind of man than Dirk, though. "He's all right. ADHD makes school such a struggle, but he's aces on the field. Best receiver this town's had in five or six years, Coach says. That's his ticket to college."

Thank God, because even though my salon paid my mortgage and our bills, I wasn't rolling in the kind of dough that'd pay tuition—assuming he could even get into a decent school with his C-plus average. Although I never went to college, my son deserved that opportunity.

I loved Rowan despite the fact that he sometimes cut class to work out, or broke curfew, or habitually left his dishes in the sink no matter how often I told him to put them in the dishwasher. He'd gotten only more challenging since Dirk left us—sulkier. Grace hadn't a clue how lucky she was to have a boy like Carter. Polite, smart, responsible. A worry-free teen. Simply unimaginable.

"And what about you?" Agnes elbowed my hip while I sprayed the right side of her hair. "Any romance? It's so dull around here I could use some sexy gossip to keep our tickers going."

"Men don't line up to date a single mom with a teen son." Strictly speaking, that wasn't true. Even at thirty-nine I could find a line of interested men, but they wanted only a roll in the sheets. Been there, done that, and never signing up for that ride again. "The best I can do for your ticker is to bring some Harlequin novels the next time I come."

"You're meeting the wrong men. Is that what this getup is all about—making a change?" Agnes pointed at my outfit.

Granted, jeans, Keds, and a crewneck sweater weren't my usual fashion, but I had to look the part in front of the board of education tonight. Normally, I couldn't care less if people judged me on my sense of style, but this was about Rowan's future. For him, I'd do anything—including dress like my mother, God rest her soul. And my recent efforts had earned me some respect, which was a nice change, too. Hopefully some of the women I'd been working with would remain friendly after the budget was confirmed.

"Gotta look smart so the board takes me seriously." Which reminded me to watch the time.

"I read about that debate in the paper. Town sure is divided."

"Yep." Although that made it sound more split than it was. Sure, there were protesters, but they were a small, if vocal, group. Still, Grace was savvy and organized, and would come loaded with facts and figures tonight.

When she first told me that she'd be protesting the proposal, she'd credited me with giving her the courage. That made me proud of us both, and I'd wanted to be happy for her. But dang it, part of me had wished she would stand down and let my son and me catch a break for a change. Everything I'd ever accomplished had been hard-won since losing my parents at twelve. And here I was, closing in on forty, and still scrapping and fighting for any advantage.

Not that I could begrudge Grace doing the same for her kids. It's not like she'd never tried to help Rowan and me. When Dirk first left, Rowan had been ten. Grace had watched him after school every day for two years so I didn't have to pay for a sitter. She'd helped him with his homework, too. Even got Sam to toss a football with him and be a father figure from time to time.

I stepped back and chucked the near-empty spray bottle in my bag. "All done. You like?"

I held up the mirror for the last time.

"I love." Agnes unsnapped her vintage beaded change purse and pulled out three dollar bills. "I know you don't let us pay, but please take a little tip."

Normally I wouldn't accept the money, but who could deny a proud woman like Agnes the joy of doing me a kindness? The pocket change might also come in handy at the vending machine if I got thirsty at tonight's meeting. "Thank you, Agnes. That's mighty sweet. I hope you have a wonderful birthday dinner."

It took her a while to push herself out of the chair, but I'd learned last year not to offer help. She needed to prove to me and herself that she could manage on her own, and I sure did understand the importance of those little wins. Sometimes little wins were all that got me through a rough day.

I cleaned up around the chair where I'd styled her hair before packing all my things, heaving my duffel over my shoulder, and saying goodbye.

"Good luck tonight, Mimi!" Agnes waved as I left her room.

I strolled through the lobby, saying goodbye to Clara—a care worker whose poor dye job made me suspect she did it herself—before zipping up my winter coat to brace for the arctic blast outside.

My legs froze on the run across the parking lot, so I fired up the heat as soon as the ignition turned over. The windows fogged while I rubbed my hands together before putting the car in reverse and heading home.

Even in the dark, you could see that our little Craftsman needed work. A combination of barren, overgrown, and dead shrubs surrounded the house. Warped roof shingles warned of another big expense heading my way. And a gigantic crack split the center of my driveway like a fault line. The one great thing about our house was its location, seven blocks from the shore. On breezy summer days, you could smell the salt water from the backyard. The other good thing about this tiny house was its walkout basement, which gave Rowan and me some necessary separation.

I made my way in through the side door, which led directly to the 1990s-style kitchen. Bland blond wood—ugly, to tell the truth—cream-colored appliances, and tile counters. I still hadn't found the secret to keeping that grout clean. Grace could make it sparkle, though. I'd never forget coming home after my appendectomy three years ago to find my house cleaned and organized, top to bottom, with the laundry washed and ironed, and the fridge loaded with food. Grace had even put fresh hydrangeas in my living room and bedroom. No one had pampered me that way since my parents had died. The memory could still make me a little weepy.

Sadly, neither Rowan nor I tidied up as well as Grace, but neither of us was overly bothered by clutter, either.

Speaking of my son, he sat slumped over the small oak table in the corner, eating pizza and watching something on his phone. I tapped his shoulder to get him to acknowledge my presence.

He barely raised his gaze. "Hey, Mom."

"How was your day?" I ditched my bag in the corner of the cramped space and arched my back with my hands on my hips.

"Fine," he mumbled, his focus still on his screen as he lied. I didn't need to see his whole face to read his hunched shoulders and the flat line of his mouth. Lately, his moods could whip up because of anything from a pimple to something related to Dirk. Right now, I prayed for a pimple-level crisis.

"Hey, give me two seconds and tell me what's up."

"Nothing's up," he huffed, still not meeting my gaze.

Internal mom alarms kept beeping. "Rowan, I know when something's wrong. Did you flunk that history quiz?" I held my breath.

"Got a B."

A jolt of joy made me squeeze his shoulder, although his lackadaisical attitude about it confused me. "That's great. See what happens when you apply yourself?"

I hammered the carrot approach to parenting much like my own parents had used before that car crash killed them. I could still hear my dad's advice to others. *Praise the good efforts, talk through the mistakes. Never shame a kid for being less than perfect.* On the other hand, my uncle had applied the stick—laying down punishments and consequences intended to force me to make "better" choices. Those years hadn't been nearly as happy, and I wanted Rowan to remember childhood fondly.

"It wasn't me. Carter helped me study."

"That's nice of him, but you put in the work. Well done." I'd have to remember to get Carter a little gift card to thank him. The boys' friendship had withered by fifth grade, when kids began to form groups based on interests and talents instead of classroom recess and scheduled playdates. I'd worried that their different paths would weaken my friendship with Grace, but we'd weathered it fine, which was why I knew we could handle being on opposite sides of this budget thing. Grace had proven herself to be fair, rational, and kind. Unlike so many in my life who'd taken one look at me and formed all manner of opinions, she never judged me. I daresay she even respected me. That was both rare and priceless. "So, then, what's with the mood?"

Rowan heaved a sigh. "Dad's blowing me off again this weekend."

His bitter tone and narrowed eyes underscored the constant accusation—that somehow Dirk's leaving was my fault, as was everything Rowan had failed to do since that day. Even though Dirk had walked out on us, my son's pain coated me with guilt.

Without Dirk, I wouldn't have my son, so I didn't regret having loved that man. But boy, did I wish Rowan had a better father. That part *was* my fault—indirectly, anyway. Dirk hadn't always been neglectful. He'd loved toting his young son around to sporting events and fishing outings, or to tinker with the car. But the drudgeries of parenting and marriage had never interested him, and so he'd found himself Miranda, a kid-free woman.

I'd been lucky to have started life with two loving parents who'd valued my individuality, but for the rest of his life, my son would suffer for my bad taste in men.

"I'm sorry." What else could I say? Dirk lived less than an hour away yet had steadily become less reliable with his visits these past two years. "It's his loss, honey."

"Doesn't matter." Rowan turned his attention back to the phone screen, but his father's neglect mattered more than anything—maybe even more than school.

Not that I had time to find a solution now. The clock already read six thirty. I grabbed the last slice of pizza and ate it standing up. "Come on, bud. We've got to go."

"What?"

That got his attention.

"You're coming with me." I cracked open a ginger ale from the fridge and took a few long gulps before taking another bite of pizza.

"No way. That meeting will be long and boring." His head fell back with a grunt.

"Boring? We're talking about the fate of the fields. You should care about that more than most."

"Mrs. Phillips can't win." He scratched behind an ear. "No one cares about science labs."

That dismissiveness reminded me of Dirk. Few things stank more than seeing someone you loathed in someone you loved. I gave Rowan a lot of free passes, but once in a while I had to put down my foot.

"That's not true. Plenty of folks care about the budget, so there's no guarantee. The school board should see you boys there. If you don't care, why should they? Now go comb your hair and put on a button shirt. Call your friends to show up, too. I bet Carter will be there with his friends."

"All two of them," Rowan muttered before he stood, broke down the empty pizza box, and stuffed it in the trash. "Besides, they won't show up. Trust me."

My alarms clanged again. "What's that mean?"

Rowan wiped away his smug expression, but not in time for me to miss it. "They know it won't be cool for anyone to take our money."

Entitled—another of Dirk's bad traits. Dang it, no matter how I modeled generosity, he was determined to be more like his father than me. "First of all, it's not your money. It's taxpayer money. Secondly, you'd better not encourage your teammates in that kind of BS. I thought you were friends with Carter."

"He tutors me. We aren't friends."

A shame, really. If Rowan had stayed close with Carter, my son might've been a better student. "Well, you used to be friends."

"When I was nine." Rowan rolled his eyes. As if that were a million years ago. Then again, sometimes it felt like it was.

"He helps you, so you be nicer." I mussed his hair. "Now come on and do your part tonight. I shouldn't be the only one fighting this battle for you."

By the time I hustled Rowan into the car, found a parking spot, and scrambled into the auditorium, the meeting had begun. Standing room only, with a row of board members at a long table on the stage. There were two mic stands near the front of the room, with lines formed behind each. Jillian Beckman, another football player's mom, was currently voicing support for the budget while Rowan and I picked our way through the crowd. Along the way, I scanned the throng in the back, looking for Grace, but didn't see her. Had she chickened out? That possibility produced mixed feelings.

"No one brought their kids," he grumbled.

"It's still a good civics lesson. You don't have to talk, but stand where I can see you. I'm going to get in line," I whispered.

Rowan stood along a wall, wedged between some parents he knew. I got in the line closest to me, which was when I noticed Grace waiting in the other one. Her eyes widened, most likely because she'd never seen me in this kind of getup. We smiled at each other, although she had to be strung tight. Public speaking was to Grace what discovering lice on a client's head was to me—a horrible, awkward thing you hoped to avoid. Still, her discomfort might make her less persuasive, which would be a blessing for my side.

I shifted my attention to the front of the room. One board member poured herself water from a pitcher. The others glowered, doodling on notepads and shifting in their seats. Each of them clearly dreaded sitting through this community bicker fest. Two had kids who played sports for our school, so those votes were fairly certain, but a handful of unfamiliar faces reminded me of every principal I'd never liked.

Movement caught my attention. Grace stepped up to the mic, note cards in hand, perspiration beading above her lips. The scuff of shuffling feet, a stray cough, and pages of paper being folded broke the silence. My heart squirmed while she appeared to be dying inside. As much as I wanted to win, I didn't want to see her fail. Finally, she cleared her throat.

"Good evening. Thank you for allowing us this t-time to speak on behalf of all taxpayers. My name is Grace Phillips, and I'm against the p-proposal to allot capital expenditures for improved athletic facilities rather than for upgrades to the academic facilities. Statistically, less than t-two percent of high school students go on to play Division I college sports, and only one in sixteen thousand high school students goes on to p-play professional sports. Conversely, every single student takes science and other STEM classes while in high school and college, and almost two-thirds of the thirty top-rated careers you're supposed to be preparing students for are in the sciences, engineering, and big data fields.

"Every member of this community pays school t-taxes, so those funds should be used to benefit the majority of students instead of a small minority, especially when the booster club annually raises an average of seventy-five thousand dollars through its membership dues, annual gala, and other efforts that can be p-put toward better equipment and scoreboards and so on over time. Our high school's statewide rank in education has dropped twenty spots since I moved to town. It's been more than a decade since the high school's science labs have been upgraded, despite the technological advances since then. Better academic results lead to higher school rankings, which increases not only our kids' competitiveness but also the property values for all residents. All of this should be factored into your decision to reconsider the superintendent's budget. Thank you."

Well, well. Grace did just fine once she got rolling. Maybe I shouldn't have encouraged her to be more assertive. If we'd talked about this issue instead of around it, I might understand her motivation better. From where I stood, her son made top grades, so our school's rank wouldn't stop colleges from fighting over him or from handing him academic scholarships. Not that the Phillipses needed those. Between Sam's career and the extra money Grace earned from giving piano lessons, they could afford to educate their children with very little debt.

She threw me a relieved smile before making her way over to Sam, who beamed at her. I meant to return it but wasn't sure that I did. Against my better nature, the acid burn of antagonism bubbled in my stomach.

Grace knew Rowan didn't have Carter's opportunities. He wasn't as smart, and I lacked her deeper pockets. Despite what I'd said at the market earlier, it did feel a little personal. That might not be fair, but I couldn't help it. And after listening to her arguments, even I had to concede that the proposed budget might not be the best use of town funds.

No one could miss the respectful nods she'd earned from the crowd. Not to begrudge her something she deserved, but she took general admiration for granted. Since my parents died, I'd spent lots of effort to win admiration and affection from others. Older folks liked me, and young kids, too. But my peers typically considered me a little too much. Respect was something I really wanted, yet most days I hardly even got it from my own son.

It'd be nice if fortune would break my way once. Absent that, the only sure way to lose was to quit. My mama had always said flattery would get you everywhere, so while Grace chose to attack the superintendent's decision, I would praise him and the board. When my turn finally came, I adjusted the mic down to my level. It helped to see dozens of people I'd been working with these past months giving me a thumbs-up. I supposed that would be the silver lining if we lost—at least I'd gained more acceptance from folks.

"Good evening, everyone. I'm Mimi Gillette, and I support the proposed budget. Some folks have thrown a bunch of statistics at you, but I'm pretty sure Superintendent Musgrave already considered all that before making his decision. High school isn't only about preparing kids for college. It's also about preparing them for life. Team sports help many kids learn to work as a unit, to socialize, to excel and push themselves. These things matter, too, and shouldn't get pushed aside as less important than science or math. Plenty of kids—people like me—who aren't great students need to see that they can still become successful, happy adults by leaning in to their own special talents.

"Student athletes spend up to twenty hours per week practicing. The current fields serve multiple sports and are worn down. Sharing the existing space forces some teams to practice late at night. An upgraded sports complex will alleviate a lot of those problems. So thank you, Superintendent Musgrave, for finally putting some money into them." I flashed my best smile with a perky nod before leaving the mic to go stand beside Rowan.

Across the room, Grace and Sam were holding hands, their expressions attentive as they listened to the last speaker—Jim Russo, another ally of theirs. Thank God our being on opposite sides of this would end soon. Meanwhile, I envied her having Sam on her arm. A solid guy. Clean-cut, devoted, dependable. Everything I'd always considered nice but boring until Dirk and the two bad boyfriends since him ground me down. Guess when it came to picking men, I hadn't been any smarter than my son had been about his priorities. Next time around, I'd choose someone like Sam. With my increased social acceptance, I might have more opportunities to find him, too.

"Mrs. Phillips's speech was good," Rowan said, surly. "She made it bigger than just the school when she talked about people's property values. Even people with no kids care about that."

Truth. Her thoroughness didn't surprise me nearly as much as my son's attentiveness did. Grace had always been organized and prepared. When the boys were tykes, she'd been ever ready for any situation. If you dumped out her purse or opened her hatchback at any time, you'd find first-aid supplies, extra jackets, shelf-stable snacks, and other assorted items.

"Nothing Grace said is new information. The board might even be insulted by the suggestion that they hadn't already thought of it."

My son didn't look swayed. "Can we go now?"

"It's almost over. Let's wait so we don't look rude."

Rowan whipped out his phone. A few minutes later, the audience began to file out of the auditorium. In the lobby, we bumped into Sam and Grace. Under other circumstances I would've taken her out for dessert to celebrate her personal milestone. Now we all stood in an awkward huddle beneath the weight of curious glances as people passed us on their way out.

"Grace. Sam." I gave them each a quick kiss hello before elbowing Rowan.

"Hi, Mr. and Mrs. Phillips." He shook Sam's hand.

"Rowan, it's terrific to see you participating in politics," Sam said. Per Grace's encouragement, he'd tried to be there for Rowan that first year after Dirk split, but Rowan hadn't been into it. It was almost as if he'd rejected Sam to prove his loyalty to Dirk, although no one—not even Dirk—had ever suggested that anyone wanted to replace Rowan's father. At least I'd never said it aloud.

"Mom made me come," Rowan replied.

"Well, that's smart. If Carter wasn't babysitting Kim, I might've made him come, too." Sam winked, his hands now in his front pockets.

"Carter wouldn't have come. He's already worried my speaking up will cause him more trouble at school." Grace sheepishly eyed me while she spoke, but I'd no doubt that her message was meant for Rowan.

She hadn't directly accused him, but Grace had a way of making her feelings known without getting her hands dirty. We'd practically raised our kids together, so the insinuation stung. Then again, Rowan had already hinted at some bullying, so perhaps she wasn't wrong.

"Boys talk tough, but Rowan would never do anything to Carter or anyone else, Grace," I assured her, tucking my arm through my son's.

"I know Rowan wouldn't hurt Carter," she covered, smiling at Rowan and then meeting my gaze. "It's been a tense time for everyone."

"Well, regardless, your speech was great. Even Rowan said so. Now it's up to the powers that be," I said, pretending not to care much about the outcome.

"Seems so," Grace said, but something about her expression gave me pause. Like she knew something she wasn't sharing. I hated this distance between us, yet I hadn't been willing to back down or share strategies any more than she had. Hopefully when things were settled, we'd return to normal. "We should probably all get home. I'll see you Friday morning."

"Wouldn't miss it." I smiled and waved at Sam before tugging at Rowan, who didn't need any coaxing to leave. When we got to the car, I said, "Rowan, listen up. It's really important that you and the others don't harass Carter or anyone else, especially if this thing goes against us."

Rowan shrugged. "I can't control everyone else."

That was exactly what worried me.

We were nearly home when he finally spoke again. "Mom, since Dad blew me off, can I have some friends over Saturday night?"

Oh, the guilt trips my divorce caused on a weekly basis.

"Maybe a few friends, but I'm not up for a big group, okay?" I could manage a handful of boys and a six-pack with pizza, but that was my limit. Rowan didn't respond, so I repeated myself. "I said *okay*?"

He barely glanced up from his phone. "Sure, Mom. Don't worry."

*Don't worry.* If only hearing those words actually made it so.

# CHAPTER THREE

## GRACE

*Friday, January 8*
*Sugar Momma's pastry shop, Potomac Point*

At promptly eight thirty, I arrived at Sugar Momma's. An old Stevie Nicks song rang out over the bustling, eclectic pastry shop's speakers. The café's cheery red, yellow, and turquoise decor induced a smile as usual, as did the buttery aroma of Hannah's excellent pastries. When a quick scan of the room proved that Mimi hadn't yet arrived, I made my way to the last open table.

This many years into our friendship, I'd accepted the fact that her internal clock ran at least five minutes behind. I draped my jacket and purse over the back of my chair before sitting. The tight ball of anxiety from my morning conversation with Carter as he bolted outside to catch the school bus sat in my gut. As he'd anticipated, some of the jocks had been giving him and other kids a hard time all week.

Nothing physical—more along the lines of insults disguised as jokes in front of girls and such. Antagonism—a trait I'd never understood. Who gets joy from making others squirm? A joke wasn't funny if everyone couldn't laugh. And Carter's particular sensitivity meant these antics hit him twice as hard. I didn't relish hashing this out with Mimi, given the way she'd taken offense when I'd referenced it after the hearing, but it'd help if Rowan could get his crew to knock it off.

My son's suffering for my actions mirrored how I'd felt whenever Margot's smart mouth enraged our dad. I closed my eyes, ashamed of how often I'd resented her when her behavior had backfired. My regrets changed nothing, then or now. And like all things past, the school debate had come and gone, so we'd all have to live with the fallout.

Two tables over, Trudy Miller and Anne Sullivan waved to me. I'd bought a beautiful painting from Trudy's gallery a few years ago, but didn't know her well. Anne, who was newer to town, was a local artist and an ally in the budget fight, although her daughter, Katy—currently a senior—was both an athlete and a scholar. Anne and I regularly took yoga classes at Give Me Strength and occasionally chatted afterward over a smoothie. Divorced, she now dated Dan Foley, a talented builder in town. I liked her, but with younger kids at home, I didn't quite share her freedom; thus, our friendship had plateaued at a superficial level.

"Any word?" Anne asked.

I shook my head.

"Your statistics were persuasive. I have a good feeling." She smiled, unaware of my bittersweet feelings about my involvement.

"Let's hope you've got ESP," I teased, although winning could make things worse for my son, and between Mimi and me. She was pinning her hopes for Rowan's future on his NFL dreams. With all my heart I hoped he achieved that long-held wish. Sam and I cheered him on at every game. But that didn't mean that Carter's goals weren't as important, or that Kim's education should take a back seat.

"Come join us." Trudy pulled out an empty chair at their table.

"Oh, thanks, but I'm waiting for Mimi Gillette."

Trudy nodded with a grin but didn't offer for us both to join them. Any other day the subtle slight would've upset me on Mimi's behalf.

But I wanted to speak to Mimi privately, and she'd implied she also had something to discuss, so I didn't push for a broader invitation.

I'd been so focused on Carter during breakfast I hadn't given much thought to what Mimi wanted to share. It could be anything: news about the decision, seeking advice about dealing with Dirk, or even fun gossip she'd overheard at her shop this week.

Hannah stopped at my table on her way out of the restroom. She and Mimi were kindred spirits, with their colorful hair and bold fashion choices. "Good morning, Grace. Can I bring you some Earl Grey?"

Many people know me well in our small community, which could be a blessing and a curse. Hannah had a talent for making her customers feel like close friends, but in truth she played her own cards very close to the vest. The school debate had opened a divide in town, yet I had no idea which side Hannah took. Either way, the split should knit back together once the losing side accepted defeat—provided the kids didn't make it worse by doing something stupid.

"That'd be lovely. Cream too. And what muffins do you have today?" I asked.

"Banana chocolate chip, blueberry, pistachio, and cranberry orange." She folded her arms beneath her ample bosom.

"Can you bring a pistachio with two plates? And Mimi loves your macchiato."

"You got it." She sashayed away, carrying herself quite regally.

The bell above the shop door rang as Mimi bumbled inside, having tripped over the tiny lip at the entrance.

"Oh!" she yelped, calling more attention to herself. I, too, would've lost my balance if I'd been wearing those boots—gray snakeskin ones with at least a three-inch heel. They looked painful, but Mimi swore heels put her at the right level for reducing neck and shoulder strain while styling hair. She limped her first two steps toward me. "Sorry I'm late!"

When she noticed Trudy and Anne, she flashed a smile and waved at them, too. They offered polite nods.

I stood to give her a quick hug. "No problem. I'm not the one who has to be at work soon."

She glanced at her watch. "I wish we had more time."

"Actually, I've got errands to run for Kim's birthday sleepover party tomorrow, so I wouldn't be able to linger as much today, either."

"Aw, how fun." She set her phone on the table while shucking out of her short-waisted puffy silver coat. Then she combed her fingers through her curls and shook her gobs of tousled hair. Even when worn messy, it looked terrific. "I would've loved a daughter. Tea parties and manicures and all the hairdos!" She wiggled her fingers. Each of her nails was painted a different color, which made me smile.

Mimi did everything big and loud, like how she'd dressed up in formal wear for the boys' middle school music recitals, or how she strung dozens of strands of colorful lights around her house and yard at Christmas, or how she hollered from the sidelines during football games. She had a flair that made ordinary things more extraordinary. As more people let her in, they'd want her to do that for them, too.

"Except that we're talking about *Kimmy*." I folded my hands (with their unimaginative clear polish) in my lap. My daughter's picture would not be in the dictionary beside words like "dainty," "demure," or "biddable." "God give me strength to get through her preteen and teen years. Something tells me they'll be much harder than Carter's."

I leaned back when Hannah showed up with our drinks and a softball-size muffin. The dense, bright-green, moist pistachio treat was coated with crystallized sugar and loads of crushed pistachios. Utter decadence.

"Hannah!" Mimi immediately cut into the muffin. "How's it going?"

"Terrific, thanks. You?"

"Hanging in there." Mimi scrutinized Hannah's hair. "I think it's time we touch up the pink, and maybe brighten the roots, too?"

Hannah heaved a dramatic sigh. "Being this good lookin' ain't easy or cheap." Then she cackled before wandering back to the counter, her psychedelic handmade knit sweater flowing behind her as she called over her shoulder, "I'll book an appointment next week."

Mimi gave her a thumbs-up before turning back to me. "Where were we?"

"Kimmy entering puberty," I replied ominously.

"Ah. Yes. Listen, Grace. No one—boy, girl, or gender-fluid person— would be as easy as Carter. I swear, he's all the best parts of you and Sam shoved into one body." She sipped her drink and then sucked in air, waving her hand rapidly in front of her mouth. "Hot!"

"Thank you." My son always brought a smile to my face—until recently. "Sadly, he's shy like me. More so, maybe, so he's never developed a gang of friends. He could really use one, especially now." If anyone could empathize with that, it should be her.

Mimi leaned forward, her chin on her fist. "Why especially now?"

My mother would tell me not to meddle, but Carter was suffering, and I wouldn't stand by and watch it another day, the way she'd done with Margot and me. Until he developed better coping tactics, I would be Carter's advocate.

It took two heartbeats before I spoke up. "Well, it's delicate because it relates to the budget debate, which I know we agreed not to discuss. I alluded to it on Monday night when I mentioned how some boys have been picking on kids like Carter. I feel awful because he might've been spared if I hadn't gotten involved, yet you know I'm trying to teach my kids to stand up for their beliefs so they don't have my regrets."

"Are you trying to say Rowan is bullying Carter?" She frowned.

"No, Carter's never mentioned Rowan." Rowan didn't go out of his way to be considerate of Carter, but he had never been rude that I knew of.

"Good." She blew out a relieved breath.

As much as Mimi adored her son, when she'd had a second glass of wine, she'd confide her worries that he'd turn out like his dad—a car salesman who wasn't keen on taking responsibility for much, including child support. For the most part she was a terrific mom, except I sometimes worried that she overcompensated for Dirk's absence by letting Rowan run wild. Mimi rarely lectured him. Sometimes it seemed like she'd rather be his friend than his mom. By the end of his freshman year of high school, her permissiveness was legendary—no curfew, serving alcohol at parties, not grounding him when he cut classes.

Other moms would question me or expect me to say something, as if it were my business to tell Mimi how to parent. Even though I secretly believed she should rein him in, I defended Mimi's right to raise her son as she saw fit. Every mother has that right, and Mimi's encouraging style had often brought out the best in all our kids.

She tapped a finger against her lips. "I already warned him that I won't tolerate any kind of revenge."

"I wonder . . . Do you think he could get teammates to lay off, too? He's so charismatic and a team leader, so he could make a difference. Besides, he can't be comfortable watching Carter suffer."

Mimi's gaze dipped to her coffee. "You're assuming he's got more power than is true. Rowan's only a sophomore—pretty low in the pecking order. Even if he wanted to help, I doubt he could do much. And if word gets out that Carter complained or you're fighting his battles, it could get worse for him. Maybe it's best to let the boys handle it themselves."

I'd hoped for more. If she'd asked for my help, I would've given it. In fact, I'd demand it of my son simply because bullying of any sort should not be tolerated. And frankly, Carter tutored Rowan for free, so Rowan should want to repay that favor.

I almost pressed her, but wouldn't criticize her decision. "I suppose you're right."

"I'm sorry." Mimi scrunched her nose. "I don't mean to be unhelpful. Truthfully, now isn't the best time to ask Rowan for anything. He's been in a crap mood all week thanks to Dirk. That damn man is blowing his son off again."

Ah. This must be what she'd wanted to discuss.

"I'm sorry, Mimi." Dirk could be selfish, like my father. It'd take hard work for Rowan to overcome the scars inflicted by that man's neglect. Same for Mimi.

"I swear, every day I feel Rowan drifting away from me. Whenever I offer any advice—about school, or anything—he rejects it. Thinks I'm a nag instead of appreciating how I'm looking out for his future . . . trying to teach him to be a better man than his father is. Not that I say that last part. It galls me how much he worships Dirk yet gives me a hard time." She dropped her forehead to the table for a moment before popping back up, shoulders slumped.

"I'm sorry you feel defeated, but Rowan loves you. He's a teenager, so he won't show it like he did at six. When he's matured, he'll reflect your values of kindness and caring." I reached across the table to squeeze her shoulder in solidarity. Nothing about parenting was easy, and she'd been doing this on her own for almost five years. I couldn't imagine raising my kids by myself or, worse, with a distant partner. Sam's and my parenting styles and values were in sync, which made everything easier. Of course, Kimmy would likely challenge us. Heaven help us if she really was Margot 2.0. "In the meantime, how can I help?"

"You can't, but thanks." Mimi pinched the bridge of her nose with those lengthy rainbow-colored fingernails. "Guess I'm exhausted. He'd be failing history without Carter's help. Seriously, if he doesn't get a football scholarship, he's got almost no shot at a better life than mine."

Now wasn't the time for another conversation about putting all her eggs in one basket. Rowan could be a better student with a little more effort, as proven when I'd tutored him, and more recently with Carter's help. But I knew the pain of worrying about your kids, and I hated the way she sold herself so short, so I patted her hand. "We all hope our kids surpass us, but he'd be lucky to end up like you—a small-business owner who's great at her job."

"Thank you." She stared at me, a thin smile tugging at her mouth and a sheen coating her eyes. "Listen, I know we promised to keep the budget debate out of our friendship, but I also don't want unsaid junk putting up walls between us, so can I be honest with you?"

A flash of heat hit me. I sat back, nodding with bated breath. "Sure."

"Everything you said at the hearing made sense, but Carter will have a dozen great choices by the time he's a senior no matter what shape those labs are in."

Like Rowan would have college coaches looking him over no matter what shape the fields were in. "It's not only about Carter—"

She tipped her head. "You aren't looking to move anytime soon, so your property value doesn't matter, either."

"No, but in a global market, we need our kids to be well educated, so school budgets should be weighted toward academics, not sports. I've got Kim to think about, too."

Mimi stared out the window before returning her gaze to me. "The deck is already stacked in favor of smart kids. Sports are some kids' only shot."

"Mimi, do you really believe Rowan has no other skills or talents? Because I know that's not true. I've worked with him. So has Carter. When Rowan puts his mind to something, he succeeds, so is it possible you might be selling him a little short?"

Mimi's posture stiffened. "I know you mean well, but kids like Rowan don't learn the same way Carter does. His brain is different. ADHD makes organization a thousand times harder, too." She dragged a hand through her hair, which she often did when frustrated.

This conversation had shoved me onto thin ice at the center of a deep pond.

"You're right, I don't know how hard that is to manage day after day." I'd only meant to give her hope, not to make her feel responsible for Rowan's struggles. "But even if he gets into college on a football scholarship, he'll need decent grades to stay. Wouldn't it be better in the long run if the high school allotted some of its budget to provide struggling athletes with free tutors and organizational support rather than buying a new scoreboard? It seems to me that, no matter how you look at it, academics matter most."

She waved me off again. "Athletes get tons of support at the college level."

"Exactly." I turned my hands over with a shrug. "Why not start that early so the foundation of his education is stronger?"

Mimi pushed her mug away, frowning. "Sometimes it feels like people are jealous because athletes take spots at good schools away from their kids. Maybe some athletes don't have the same grades and SATs, but they earn their way, too, giving up summers, breaks, and holidays to playing and practice. They're committed, working as hard to excel in their sport as others do with grades. And sports bring in real money to those colleges that helps pay for all the other stuff."

None of that was new ground, nor did it change my opinion. We would never see eye to eye, so it'd be better dropping it altogether.

"I promise, I'm not jealous and I'll be thrilled to celebrate when Rowan leverages his talent that way. In the meantime, if Rowan wants help with math or English, Sam and I are happy to step in." I picked a sugarcoated pistachio off my plate and ate it, concerned that my offer came out wrong. "I'm sorry you're upset. I'm not sure what else to say. You asked me to be honest . . ."

"It's okay." She checked the time on her phone and blew stray hair from her face. "You're entitled to your opinion. I'm just dealing with so much on my own, and now the one thing my son loves is being threatened."

"Mimi, whatever happens with the vote, you don't have to go it alone. I mean it. Lean on Sam and me." That also might've sounded smug when I hadn't meant it to. What we needed was something to look forward to, like the old camping trips and minivacations our families had taken when the kids were younger. "We both could use something fun to plan, so let's organize one of our family-combo trips for Memorial Day weekend . . . or Fourth of July?"

"Maybe, although I've been pinching pennies saving up for when Rowan goes to college, so it'd have to be within driving distance, like Deep Creek." She inhaled through her nose and released it in one quick huff. "What are you and Sam up to this weekend?"

"Kim's party."

"Oh, that's right. I forgot." She made a face. "When's the last time you and Sam got out on your own?"

"Meh, you know us. We're homebodies. A roaring fire, Netflix, and pizza suit us as well as any fancy restaurant." I sipped my coffee and snagged a bit of the muffin.

"That's nice. I want that—or at least I'd like that option." That's what I wanted for her, too, but before I said as much, Mimi's expression shifted as she broke off a hunk of the muffin. "I haven't gone on a date since the disaster that was Tony."

Tony Brickmont, a personal trainer who specialized in football conditioning. After Dirk left, Mimi'd first had a brief affair with a guy named Boo McDonough from Chesapeake Beach, who'd turned out to be married. She found that out only after an unplanned pregnancy made him confess the truth and end things. She'd considered terminating the pregnancy because, in her own words, she "had enough on her hands dealing with Rowan and Dirk without adding the stress of raising another cheating married man's child," but her religious upbringing made her waffle. Ultimately she hadn't needed to make the choice because she'd miscarried. At the time, she'd seemed more relieved than sad, but I sometimes wondered if she now wished she had another little boy or girl to love.

A year after Boo, Mimi had hired Tony to help Rowan build up strength and speed for eighth grade football. She could afford only a few lessons, but he'd formed a crush on her and bartered extra time for Rowan in exchange for Mimi's promise to do his sister's highlights and haircuts for free. The summer before our boys started high school, she'd felt ready to date again and gave in to Tony's pursuit.

At first it had seemed to be a good match. Tony and Rowan got along, and Mimi liked Tony's energy level. But at only twenty-seven—a decade younger than Mimi (not that she looked it)—Tony had been fit, handsome, and not exactly interested in settling down. She ended it nine months later, after getting wind that Tony had been coming on to a female colleague at the fitness center where he worked. I'd cleared my schedule to help her cope, but unlike how she'd cried over Dirk, she moved on from Tony without many tears. Maybe divorce had toughened her heart, or worse, conditioned her to be let down. That was my fear: that she'd keep settling for less than the love she deserved.

"'Disaster' is a strong word. He was too young." I sipped my tea.

She nodded again. "Rowan missed him when that ended. That's one reason I've avoided dating. It's hard enough to trust someone not to cheat, but to drag Rowan through it all with me?" She grabbed her head as if trying to keep it from exploding, then shrugged and sipped more coffee. "But I'm lonely."

The little ache in her voice hurt to hear. "I'm sorry, Mimi. You deserve a good man more than most. He's out there somewhere. In the meantime, let's plan a girls' night next weekend."

"Thanks, but I'm lonely for things you can't give me." She chuckled.

"Oh!" A flush rose in my face. "Well, I'm not sure I can help with that." I couldn't imagine going without physical affection month after month. "What if you dated casually but didn't introduce anyone to Rowan until you knew the man was worthy?"

"That's a problem, though, 'cause my radar sucks. I thought Tony was worthy. Same with Dirk. And men like Sam aren't attracted to me." Her rainbow-colored nails tapped against her coffee mug.

I raised a brow. "Finding a good man who is attracted to *you* isn't the problem."

"Oh?"

"Getting you to find a good man attractive—that's the issue. Anytime I've pointed one out, you've begged off. The truth is, you think you'd be bored with someone like Sam in five minutes. But while he might not be flashy on the surface, there's a lot to be said for a steady guy. Think of how our differences bring balance to our friendship. You might also find that with a man who is more like me than you."

She slumped. "You know I love Sam, and you two are so great together, but I'm a sucker for outrageous charmers."

"Even I've fantasized about being swept off my feet by a James Bond type. But deep down we know those guys are too self-absorbed to be good partners."

"And I'm not getting any younger."

It couldn't be easy to be approaching forty as a single mom. "You're gorgeous and you know it."

"Men don't take me seriously because of how I look—so it's a catch twenty-two. I shouldn't have to dress like my mom to be respected."

"Agreed." I sighed, unsure how to help. "Do you want me to ask Sam about his single colleagues?"

"No!" Mimi shook her head. "How awkward for him. Anyway, I've joined Bumble."

My eyes widened. "When, and why am I only hearing this now?"

"I just did it this week. It's not ideal, but between work and Rowan, I've got zero chance of meeting someone organically. I wasn't going to tell you if it didn't lead anywhere." She opened her phone and started thumbing through her apps. "But I want your opinion on this guy."

She showed me a picture on her phone of a middle-aged man in a navy crewneck sweater, with deep-set yet kind brown eyes and slightly thinning salt-and-pepper hair. "Rich Polanti. Forty-two, divorced father, fashion designer."

"Ooh, fashion! He looks friendly, too." And nothing at all like Dirk, Boo, or Tony: all alpha-male types more suited to romance-novel covers than monogamy. "Why him?"

"He seems sincere." She grimaced. "He's not my physical type, but we've already established that my type sucks. He's nice. Asked a lot of questions about me instead of bragging about himself, but"—she shivered in her seat—"I don't know. What do you think?"

"Those sound like good reasons to take a chance. You love fashion, so at least you'll have lots to talk about. What's the worst that could happen? Even if he's not 'the one,' he could become a friendly companion for dinners and movies. You can't have too many friends."

"You're my voice of reason, as usual." She smiled and then swallowed the last bit of muffin with coffee before tossing her phone in her purse. "Well, I'd better go get ready for my first appointment. Thanks for meeting me, and I'm sorry about bringing up the whole budget thing."

I stood to gather my things, too. "It's okay. I always want us to be honest with each other."

"Same."

Relief washed through me. We'd had a difficult conversation, and while I wasn't any closer to solving Carter's current problem, I was relieved that our friendship would survive this budget thing.

We tossed some cash on the table and waved to Trudy, Anne, and Hannah on our way out the door. When we parted ways on the sidewalk, Mimi said, "I'll talk to Rowan about sticking up for Carter and the others."

"Really?" Pleased that she'd changed her mind, I grabbed her into a hug. "Thanks, Mimi."

She eased away, shrugging one shoulder. "Don't get too excited. It might not turn out like you hope."

On the way to my car, I considered her earlier warning that things could get worse for Carter if I interfered. Like a boomerang, history snapped back to sting me. At thirteen, Margot had pulverized some of Mom's sleeping pills and poured them into Dad's bottle of Jack Daniel's hours before he stumbled out the door, fell asleep near the road, and got hit by a car. His death had kicked off the downward spiral into drugs and alcohol that killed her and haunted me.

Perhaps I should stop Mimi.

I turned back, but she was gone.

A sign, perhaps?

She'd be at work for hours, so I had time to consider my options. First I had to tackle my to-do list for Kim's party.

# CHAPTER FOUR

## GRACE

*Saturday morning, January 9*
*The Phillips home*

Carter stared at me from the kitchen entry while I finalized my last-minute party details checklist. I gave him a double take. "What?"

He glanced to Sam—who was still enjoying his second cup of coffee and the *New York Times* crossword puzzle—then back to me again. "Can I go to Rowan's party tonight?"

I set down my pen. "What party?"

Mimi hadn't mentioned anything yesterday over coffee. Then again, Mimi didn't make a habit of telling me about Rowan's parties, probably because she knew without asking that I wasn't a fan of adults hosting underage drinking parties.

"When I was helping Rowan with history at school yesterday, his friends came over and mentioned it, so he invited me." Carter shoved his hands into his sweatpants' pockets. "Can I go?"

I said, "I don't think it's a good idea," at the exact time Sam said, "Sure."

My head swiveled toward my husband, while Carter's gaze darted back and forth between us, then stuck pleadingly on Sam. This fall, when he'd suggested loosening some of our rules in order to help Carter socialize, I'd never imagined he'd also planned on breaking our pact about making those decisions together. Perhaps he'd forgotten about Mimi's stance on teen drinking.

"You know Mimi allows kids to drink beer." I stared at him in a way that should've signaled for him to play dumb and rescind his approval.

But he nodded with a shrug and winked at our son. "I trust Carter to go and not drink."

My lips parted. Carter was a great kid, but not immune to peer pressure. I'd been honest with my kids about my father and sister, but the more their peers normalized drinking and smoking, the less they'd fear the legacy of addiction.

"That doesn't mean there won't be trouble. What if the police come, or the party gets out of hand?" I asked.

"Nothing bad has ever happened at his parties." Carter kicked his toe against the floor. "You know it's been a crappy week. You should let me go to make up for that board meeting."

I folded my arms across my chest to defend against the guilt trip. Although unfair, my first thought was that it seemed strange that he got invited now—after getting picked on all week—when he'd never been included before. But then I remembered Mimi's promise to talk to Rowan, so maybe the invitation was a peace offering. "It must've felt great to be included, honey. And it sounds like things will get easier at school now, too. But will you really feel comfortable with all those boys at a party where you'll be the only sober one?"

"Rowan's never a jerk to me, and it's his house," Carter suggested, so willing to give everyone the benefit of the doubt. "I could've lied to you and gone, but I'm being honest. Doesn't that count for anything?"

I said nothing, still in disbelief that Sam had picked this issue to throw our rules out the window instead of asking Carter to give us five minutes to discuss this in private. This must be how Mimi felt making most every decision without Dirk.

"Babe, I think we should let him go. We've got Kim's birthday sleepover tonight, so it'll be chaotic here. He'll have no privacy with screeching girls everywhere. Plus, this is a chance for him to socialize and make new friends. Carter knows our stance on alcohol, but it's a fact of high school life. Let's give him some freedom and trust him not to overstep." Sam looked at Carter for confirmation, as if my fears would be assuaged by the two of them acknowledging their existence. "Now, don't make a fool of me, buddy. We don't get to decide which laws to break, so no drinking. If you need to take a sip or two of beer to give an appearance of fitting in, I'm okay with that."

"Sam!" My spine lengthened into a stiff rod. "Carter, I'll treat you and your friends to dinner and a movie. Or whatever. Surely you can find better things to do than sit around pretending to drink beer with boys who've been making you miserable all week."

Honestly, saying it aloud only made his request and Sam's consent sound more insane.

"No one has plans. Besides, all the pretty girls hang out with Rowan's group. Come on, I swear I won't do anything stupid. If I don't go, they'll think I don't like them or think I'm a wuss." He leaned against the refrigerator, tugging on his hoodie's strings. "What's the big deal? Most kids party every weekend."

I buried my face in my hands, my mind blank. It was hard enough to be on opposite sides of the budget issue with my best friend, but now her permissiveness pitted me against her as well. I'd seen teen drinking spin out of control with my sister. I didn't want to live afraid for my kids all the time, like I'd been afraid for Margot.

"Grace, he needs to learn how to handle himself. Better he tests some of those limits while he's still under our roof than having him go wild while away at college." Sam stared at me as if this were a conversation we'd already had instead of him sandbagging me.

"Why do people assume that every kid will go crazy in college if their parents set reasonable restrictions in high school, such as obeying the law and treating their bodies and brains with respect?" I swung my gaze to my son. "Honey, alcoholism runs in our family. I really want both you and Kim to stay away from it until your brains are more fully developed."

"I promise I won't drink. I'll carry one around and pretend to be buzzed." He blinked his round, sincere eyes. He might be six feet tall, but to me he'd always be my little boy. No matter how much he believed what he was saying, I'd seen my sister swing from one extreme to the other.

"What if they haze you or make you play beer pong or whatever boys do at these parties? Will you be comfortable saying no?" I shot a hard stare at Sam because he'd clearly not thought this through.

"He's not a baby, Grace. He'll never become a man if we keep coddling him." Sam leaned forward, challenging me.

If that was how Sam felt, he should've spoken with me about this sooner—and in private.

"Please, Mom," Carter begged.

Kim raced into the kitchen—hair in pigtails, decked out in the Abercrombie sweat gear my mom had sent her—before coming to a dead stop, wearing a scowl. "Where's my cake and balloons?"

"I'm on my way out to grab them now and could use some help, so go get your coat on and come with me." I shooed her to the mudroom so the rest of us could finish our discussion.

Honestly, I wished for more time to consider this, but there were many things to do for Kim's party, and without Sam on my side, I was adrift. Carter probably wouldn't drink, and I did feel guilty that the budget protest had made his life miserable. Maybe I was overthinking things. I didn't want a rift between us and Carter, or between Sam and me, and Carter wanted to make new friends. And even though I didn't agree with Mimi taking the law into her own hands, she'd had supervised parties before without incident. "Carter, promise me you'll use good sense and you won't drink."

He grinned—the first smile I'd seen in a week. "I swear. I'll just pretend."

"Looks like I've been outvoted." When Kim came back into the kitchen, I tore my list from the pad, shooting both my boys a hard look. "Don't make me regret this."

"I won't," Carter said.

"Regret what?" Kim asked.

"Nothing that concerns you. Now, let's go." I kissed her head. "We've got party decorations to get."

Kim clapped. "Yay!"

"See you later," I muttered to Sam, whose expression proved he knew we'd continue this conversation in private when I returned.

I barely paid attention to my daughter's yammering while driving across town to Take the Cake, which was located across the street from the longest pier in town. In July, it would be packed with fishermen and kids peering over in search of dolphins, while daredevils on Jet Skis tore through the water. Now, one lone jogger was making her way back to shore.

Kim followed me inside the bakery. While waiting in line, I reconsidered the idea that Mimi might've texted Rowan yesterday morning, which might've prompted his unusual invitation. If so, how could I be upset? Scratch that. I knew how. Because permissive parents' casual disregard for the law put out a signal that caused other kids to challenge law-abiding, safety-conscious parents like me. The result? I was forced to debate underage drinking parties with my teenager.

"Am I getting an iPhone for my birthday?" Kim asked.

"A, I'm not telling you what we bought you. B, you're too young for an iPhone."

She threw her head back and stomped a foot. "I'm not too young. All my friends have them. I can't snapchat without one, Mom. Please. Pleeease!"

The older woman in front of us glanced back at us with a raised brow before turning forward again.

"Kim, stop it." I set my hand on her shoulder. "I mean it."

"You have too many rules. Why can't you be like other moms?" she whined, deaf to my request.

Why indeed? Everything I did, from my flexible job to volunteer work to birthday parties—even the budget issue—I did for my children. So why did it feel like I couldn't win? No matter how many times I shared the chaos of my childhood, my kids couldn't understand because they hadn't experienced it firsthand. They didn't get that my rules helped prevent the kinds of tragedies I'd suffered before they were born. "Parenting would be so much easier if I didn't love you to death. Rules are there to teach you and your brother important things."

"What things? That you don't want us to have friends?" She crossed her arms with a scowl.

"If I'm not mistaken, you have a bunch of friends coming over tonight, so don't start. It's okay to learn to wait for things, to understand age appropriateness, and to keep your brain from becoming addicted to screen stimulation. When you're older, you'll get why Dad and I set limits."

My mother had been a much better grandparent than mother, so I never criticized her in front of my kids, nor had I openly blamed her failures for what had happened to my sister. But I would not make my mother's mistakes and leave my kids vulnerable. When they had families of their own, they'd see that everything I did, every rule I made, was in their best interest. I was neither mean nor a fool. I merely learned from others' mistakes.

Kim bobbled her head while making a raspberry sound with no regard for where we were, exactly like my dad and Margot. My tolerance for insolence had reached its limit, so I bent to her level. "If you keep acting this way, maybe I won't feel like throwing you a party tonight."

Kim tucked her chin as she glared at me from beneath her lashes. But she didn't say another word, so I stood upright and stepped to the counter when our number was called. Not even noon and already both my kids had made me feel like an out-of-touch failure.

———

I handed Sam another stretch of FrogTape, with which he fastened the last of the streamers to the ceiling before climbing down from the step stool. Spirals of metallic gold and pink decorations hung all around us, as if My Little Pony had thrown up all over the family room.

"You might've gone overboard." He chuckled, collapsing the stool. "But Kim will love it."

"Will she?" I tucked the tape roll under my armpit and held out my hand for the step stool, recalling her bratty behavior at the bakery.

Sam didn't hand it over, though. He leaned it against the wall. "You've been in a mood since you returned. Did something else happen, or is this still about Carter?"

"Both." I huffed. "Kim is getting mouthier, and I'm still miffed that we didn't talk things over privately and present a united front to Carter."

"I've apologized, Grace. But I've been telling you we need to rethink things. Our pact made sense when the kids were small and we were setting basic expectations. Now that they're getting older, we have to be more fluid—more flexible. Judge things on a case-by-case basis, and include them in the conversation—make them think through the pros and cons and feel like they have some say."

"I disagree. The stakes are higher now, so it's even more important to have clearly defined expectations. You know kids, Sam. Once they know they can divide us, we're sunk."

"Babe, if we're too rigid, they'll rebel. We have to tailor things to suit the occasion." He massaged my shoulder.

"Something this big could've at least used a five-minute huddle. You blindsided me."

"I didn't mean to, but I honestly think we did the right thing. He's fifteen going on sixteen. In two years he'll be making these decisions without us. He's a good kid. He listens to reason, and now he feels like he has some autonomy. That builds his trust in us. And we've got no reason not to trust his judgment."

He wasn't wrong about Carter, an eminently trustworthy kid.

"It's a slippery slope, though. First it's going to the party, and then sipping a beer. What's next? Breaking curfew? Coming home drunk? Trying weed?" That'd been Margot's path, beginning the summer between tenth and eleventh grade—right about where Carter was developmentally. And Margot had hated our dad's drinking as much as I did, so I'd been shocked by her choices. Shocked and angered, which was why I didn't intervene early on—a guilt I live with to this day.

Sam wound his arms around my waist. "Come on, babe. One step at a time, okay? Let's not rob him of a chance to be mature. He's not your dad or Margot. I know you worry about history repeating itself, but isn't it finally time to leave the past behind?"

It didn't surprise me that he knew my thoughts. He took these things seriously, so I didn't mean to be dismissive of his opinions. But an entire childhood destroyed by the horrors of drinking wouldn't permit me his confidence.

"What if this request becomes a habit? I don't want the norm to become Saturday-night drinking parties. And what about Kim? She doesn't share Carter's restraint, but now we've set a precedent that will be difficult to undo." God, I shuddered projecting the many ways she would test us in the future.

Sam dropped his arms and rubbed his chin. "I hadn't thought about that. I'll tell Carter not to mention this to Kim, and to let him know this is a onetime thing because of the rough week at school."

He meant well, but honestly, that wasn't how kids worked. I could already hear the *"But you let me before, so what's the difference"* arguments headed our way. "Let's finish blowing up all the balloons. The girls arrive at six."

Sam enveloped me in another hug. "I'm sorry, babe. I should've asked for a minute to talk privately before we worked it out with Carter, but I do think he's old enough to have mature conversations in the future. You're intent on not being absent like your mom, but remember my parents never set limits, and I turned out fine. Our home environment is nothing like yours was, so our kids aren't as much at risk. We got this, okay?"

I laid my cheek on his shoulder and soaked up the warmth of his body. It was true: together we'd created a respectful environment with solid values, much like the home Sam had grown up in. He had turned out better than fine, but my kids had my genes, too. "I hate that alcohol and drugs are such a big part of teen culture."

"Me too. Listen, I promise it'll be okay." He eased me away to give me a kiss. "Now, let's save our strength for tonight. Eight girls—it's a lot."

I chuckled. "Our girl is a lot all on her own."

Sam's eyes twinkled. "God love her."

As if on cue, Kim wandered into the family room. "Mom, what's *Breaking Bad*?"

"An old television show. Why?" I frowned.

"Jessica says she wants to watch it instead of *Mulan* tonight."

I shook my head. "No, honey. It's a grown-up show."

Kim scowled. "But Jessica says she's watched it with her brother, and now she's telling everyone about it, so everyone wants to see it."

"I'm sorry about that, but it isn't age appropriate, and it's not our place to make that decision for all the other parents, either."

Kim rolled her eyes. "They can watch it on Netflix anyway, so what's the difference?"

I shot Sam an "and so it begins" glance before answering her. "The difference is that we don't want you watching that show until you are older, and this is exactly why you don't have the Netflix password."

"But—" Kim started.

"Kim, stop it." Sam lifted the step stool and headed toward the kitchen. "No more arguing every time you don't get your way. Spoiled behavior isn't a good look. How about thanking us for the party?"

Whether or not he truly agreed with me, I appreciated the backup.

Kim seemed to be debating her next move, but she usually gave in to Sam much more quickly than she did with me. "Fine. But you're not going to take away our snacks too early, are you?"

"Not on a special occasion. You can eat until you make yourself barf," he promised.

Oddly, that wrought a smile before she skipped away.

I sank onto a chair, already anticipating the protests that would ensue when I collected the phones from—and otherwise monitored— the ten-year-olds tonight. Who would imagine that a sleepover party could create as much stress as a drinking party?

# CHAPTER FIVE

## Mimi

*Saturday, January 9, 7:30 p.m.*
*The Gillette home, Potomac Point*

The doorbell rang for the fourth time in ten minutes as Rowan's friends collected downstairs.

I checked my hair one last time and spritzed La Vie Est Belle on my wrists, then spun around to make sure the miniskirt didn't hug my butt too tightly. Rich Polanti's fashion-designer career created extra pressure. I did not want to be a walking billboard of a "Fashion Don't."

Tonight marked a giant step toward ending my lonely streak and creating a better life for myself and my son. I'd made inroads with some women these past weeks, and now I had a real date with a respectable man. One who wasn't too young for me, wasn't married, and wasn't a loudmouth. I'd call it personal growth in spades. Unlike Dirk, Rich might also be someone Sam would get along with—a real bonus for Grace and me. Granted, this was a lot of weight to put on one dinner, but I couldn't stop myself from projecting. The life I wanted was within my reach as long as I didn't screw it up.

After shoving my feet into my spiky ankle boots, I clomped down the steps to find a cluster of four boys already arguing over the Xbox remotes.

"Hey, boys!" I waved while scanning the room for my purse.

"Hi, Mrs. Gillette," a chorus of deep voices sang out as I crossed to the sofa table to collect my black leather clutch.

I'd known them since grade school. Good kids. Tough and committed to the team. Now most of them towered over me, so I could no longer lean down to kiss the tops of their heads.

"Rowan, I'll leave some money for pizza." I waited for him to look up. When he did, I gestured toward the kitchen with my head.

He reluctantly tossed Deshaun a remote and followed me. "What?"

"I'm going out, so don't do anything stupid."

"Okay." He didn't meet my gaze, so I touched his chin.

"I mean it. Don't leave a huge mess in the kitchen, and if you leave, make sure to lock the door."

He wrenched free of my hold. "Okay."

I slapped thirty dollars on the counter. "This should buy you two large pizzas and a liter of root beer."

"Thanks. Can I go back now?" he asked.

I grabbed his shoulder and kissed his cheek. "Have fun."

It occurred to me to remove the beer from the refrigerator, but I didn't want to embarrass Rowan in front of his friends. There were eight or nine cans in there. Even if they drank them all—which they wouldn't risk because it'd be too obvious that they drank without adult supervision—that was only two per person, not enough to be a real danger.

Before he left, Rowan's gaze grazed me. "Why are you so dressed up to go out with friends?"

I lied, but only because Grace was right: Rowan didn't need to know about any man until one became significant. "I'm in a fancy mood."

He made a face but didn't question me further. I grabbed my keys off the hook and went out the side door toward my car, which was parked in the driveway.

"Hey, Mrs. Gillette." Carter Phillips smiled as he crossed the yard, stopping me in my tracks. His breath fogged around him but didn't obscure the rosy tip of his nose.

"Hi, honey." I gave him a hug. He seemed taller every time I saw him. "What are you doing here?"

"Rowan invited me over." His earnest face lit up.

I blinked, trying to cover my surprise. Reflexively, I glanced at the house. My talk with Rowan yesterday must've sunk in. He hadn't been very enthusiastic at the time, but maybe he was more introspective than I realized. The glimmer of compassion in my otherwise stubborn teen warmed my heart. Grace was right about that, too; I ought to give him more credit in the future. "Well, isn't that nice. I left you boys money for pizza and soda. I think they're already arguing over the Xbox remotes, though, so good luck."

"You're going out?" Carter caught his lip in his teeth.

"Dinner plans." I opened my car door. "But I won't be too late."

His brows pinched together. "Oh, okay. Have a nice time."

"You too." I slid onto the seat and closed the door, not thinking much of it. But when I backed out of the driveway, Carter remained rooted in the yard, staring at the house. I started to roll down my window, but then he ambled up the walkway and knocked on the door.

Well, shoot. Seven forty-five. I was now officially late for my date. No matter how I aimed to be punctual, something always delayed me. Gunning it would save me only a minute or two, and I couldn't afford a speeding ticket. Rich might as well get used to my fluid relationship with time if this was going to work out.

The guy earned big points for choosing Bistro Henri. Swanky with a capital S. After handing my keys to the valet, I straightened my skirt and then drew a deep breath before opening the door. Rich stood near the maître d's station with a pleasant smile on his face.

"Wow, Mimi. You're even prettier in person." He offered his hand. Starting off with a compliment, and he wasn't grabby—no hugs or cheek kissing. Two more checks in the pro column.

And a fourth, because he'd used an accurate profile photograph. Rich's oval head shape made the most of his cropped, thinning hair. He wore charcoal-gray slacks, a white-and-pink-checked shirt, and a casual black blazer. I smiled at the pop of neon-pink socks revealed when he rocked back on his heels. Our mutual love of bright colors was a good sign.

"Thank you, Rich. It's nice to meet you in person." We shook hands; his was dry and warm. His friendly expression, colored with the slightest hint of anxiety, probably mirrored mine.

No sparks, but it was early. Sparks might come through conversation.

"We have your table ready," the maître d' said.

We followed her as she weaved through candlelit, white-linen-covered tables to seat us in the far corner, near a large window that overlooked the street. It was a classic, romantic dinner-date setting. The aromas of wine and butter and fresh bread stirred my appetite.

Rich stood while the maître d' pulled out my chair, sitting after I'd been seated, then promptly placed his napkin across his lap. Nice manners. Another check in the pro column. Grace would love everything about him so far. If only my heart would flutter a bit. But flutters or not, dating a suitable man like Rich could only bolster the social progress I'd made this month. How great would it be to live like Grace, with a partner who'd be emotionally able to discuss serious things—a smart, ambitious man in my life to help me raise Rowan? My hopes rose like soap bubbles.

"Your waiter will be right with you to take your drink orders." With that, the maître d' left us alone.

My pulse kicked from nerves. "So, Rich, this is lovely. I've eaten here once before—years ago. I remember the trout amandine to this day."

"I'm glad you're pleased. My wife—ex-wife—never appreciated French food." He looked at his manicured hands for a second before sipping his water.

Hm. Referencing his ex before we even ordered might be a check in the con column. The jury would remain out unless he brought her up again.

"My ex's favorite was KFC." I laughed. Rich didn't. Either he hadn't heard me or he didn't find it funny. My knee started to jiggle beneath the table.

A young waiter brought us menus and a wine list, then gave my cleavage a brief appraising glance before addressing Rich. "Good evening. Welcome to Bistro Henri. My name is Alan and I'll be your server tonight. Can I interest you in drinks or some wine?"

Rich looked at me. "Do you have a preference?"

More manners. Another pro to consider.

"I'm easy." I waved, then made an "oof" face. "I mean, I drink anything."

Not that that sounded much better.

Rich nodded, maintaining his composure, and ordered a bottle of Sancerre before handing the wine list over to Alan.

"Certainly." Alan affected a slight bow, this time meeting my eyes with a friendly gaze. "I'll be back to take your orders."

The downside of first dates at fancy restaurants: the slow pace that'd be perfect with a good friend or second date might be excruciating with a stranger who couldn't relax. I wanted this to work out, so there had to be some way to get Rich to unwind.

I sipped my water and decided to get him talking about his work. "I've been looking forward to this all day because I'm dying to learn more about your job. You've been mysteriously vague in email, but now you can't avoid me. Tell me all about what you do. Would I be familiar with your work?" I leaned forward, genuinely interested.

He folded his hands neatly on the table, his spine still straight. "Well, to be honest, I do love my job. I've been working in fashion since graduating from Kent State in 2000."

"You must've lived in New York or LA when you started, 'cause Potomac Point isn't a hotbed for the industry."

He finally chuckled. Good. "Yes, I worked in New York for Ralph Lauren for years."

An electric charge raced through my veins. Granted, that conservative brand wasn't exactly my style, but who couldn't appreciate its elegance?

"Oh, its Purple Label fabrics are sumptuous and the lines so classic." Not that I could ever in a gajillion years afford an eleven-hundred-dollar shirt. "How thrilling it must've been working for a major American design house." Did he work with models and celebrities? Would he share juicy gossip?

"Well, it wasn't without corporate challenges and stress. Frankly, one of the benefits of my divorce was the chance to leave New York. I moved here almost two years ago and started my own company."

I nearly clapped my hands together. A risk-taking entrepreneur— that deserved two checks in the pro column. Not only could he help me with Rowan, but we could help each other with small-business issues. "How exciting, although I know how hard starting your own business can be. I thought I could open a storefront and cut hair, but my God, all the paperwork and filings and insurance and tax issues."

"There are complications, to be sure. I mostly work from a home office at this point, although I'm considering leasing a small retail space now."

"That's super, Rich." I sat back, filled with joy. Few things were more inspiring than when someone achieved a long-held dream. It's why I hoped Rowan would be drafted by the NFL despite my concerns about injuries. "You must have an online store now. What's it called so I can look it up? I'll rally all my customers to check it out."

He cleared his throat. "I certainly welcome any support, although unless they're buying for their husbands or sons, I'm afraid you'll all be disappointed."

"So you design men's clothing?" Slightly less exciting, but still creative and cool.

"In a manner of speaking."

What did that mean? "Well, my friends have boyfriends, sons, and husbands, so what's the name of your company?"

"Foot Forward," he said, chuckling again, this time at his apparent cleverness. When I blinked in confusion, he added, "You know, as in 'put your best foot forward.'"

"You design shoes?" I loved shoes, like most women I know. Of course, to my untrained eye, many men's shoes looked alike.

"Heavens no. Socks!" He jauntily stuck his leg out from under the table and pulled up his slacks to reveal his flamingo-patterned neon-pink socks. Unfortunately, his gesture nearly tripped Alan, who'd returned with the wine.

"Please excuse me, sir," Alan said, finding his balance. His sandy bangs fell across his forehead. "Although those socks are quite something."

"Aren't they?" Rich said as he dug his hand into his jacket pocket, pulled out his wallet, and handed Alan a business card. "I have seventy-three unique designs currently available."

Meanwhile, my chest sank like a pricked balloon. Socks? Not that there is anything wrong with socks. Even that Kardashian guy had started a funky sock brand. However it wasn't the glitzy design job I'd envisioned—no one-of-a-kind sexy gowns or tops would be inspired by or created just for me in my future. It didn't make his accomplishments any less impressive—I knew that rationally. But the thrill factor? Gone.

"Thank you." Alan spared me a curious look before taking the card. For the first time, I took stock of him. Physically speaking, his wavy blond hair and high cheekbones were more my type. But Rich was obviously intelligent, polite, and ambitious. I could do worse. Heck, I had done worse. "I'll have a look when my shift ends. Now, would you care to sample the wine?"

Rich studied the label and gestured toward his glass, then swirled and sniffed and sipped like a real pro. He held up his hand, making an "okay" gesture with his fingers. "Perfection."

"Wonderful." Alan poured the wine. "May I take your orders?"

Rich looked at me. "Are you ready to order, or would you prefer more time?"

Such nice manners. If only they made him more interesting to me. The truth was that, despite my inner pep talks, Grace's good advice, and my efforts to get Rich to show some personality, the past twenty minutes had been a lot of effort. There hadn't been any true sense of connection despite him being as sincere and nice in person as he'd been in email. "No, I don't need more time." A lie. I'd barely looked at the menu but saw no point in lingering longer than necessary. Grace's and my differences did add richness and stability to our friendship, but friendship didn't require romantic sparks and energy, so her logic that those differences would be good in a love match had been off. The most Rich and I could ever be was friends. "May I have the trout, please?"

"Excellent choice." Alan nodded with a grin. "Would you like a soup or salad? We have a special lobster bisque tonight—"

"This wine pairs exceptionally well with goat cheese," Rich interrupted, "so you might like the field greens salad."

"Thank you," I said. "That salad sounds nice." It would give me something to occupy my time. "And will we get some of that bread I keep smelling?"

"Of course. I'll send a basket over," Alan said.

"Thank you."

Rich ordered *le gigot d'agneau* in what sounded to me like a perfect French pronunciation, and then Alan left us alone. Seconds later, a staff member set a small basket of fresh-from-the-oven baguette slices on our table.

I reached for one and smeared it with butter. "I noticed how nicely you pronounced your meal, Rich. Did you spend much time working in Paris?"

*"Mais oui!"* he teased. "I traveled to Paris frequently. I admit I'm a bit of a geek. I love languages, so throughout my career, I made it a point to become slightly conversant in French, Italian, and Chinese."

"Wow. I'm barely conversant in English." I laughed. Smart people made me anxious. School had never been my thing, although if my parents had lived to my thirteenth birthday, I might have approached it differently. Uncle Tommy had put more emphasis on religion than academics and didn't bother to help me with homework, which had made it easier to give up on school. Mike Mathison, the high school quarterback, had also been a pretty big distraction . . .

Rich smiled sympathetically; his brows scrunched together with more confusion than humor. A brief pause ensued as he searched for something else we might discuss. "You have a son, correct? A teenager?"

"Yes. He's at home tonight with a few friends playing some zombie video game." Rolling my eyes, I added, "I hope my house is still standing when I return."

He nodded. "Is he into socks?"

"Oh, no." I tried not to laugh in his face at the thought of Rowan—whose entire wardrobe consisted of athletic wear—being interested in designer sock patterns. If I told Grace about this, she would laugh her butt off. "He's into football, hoodies, and TikTok. If you designed games instead of socks, you'd be his new hero."

Rich shook his head. "Everything I read about video addiction is quite troubling. What will this young generation do in adulthood when all they know is how to consume things instead of creating them?"

Oh, Grace would definitely like Rich's perspective on this topic. She'd tried like heck to get Rowan to take an interest in piano. In fact, she still couldn't believe she failed. On the other hand, Carter had been a star student. Kim not so much.

"Well, they're still kids. They'll grow up eventually." I slurped my wine down quickly, which, if Rich's raised brow said anything, he didn't like.

"I tried hiring a college intern last summer, but goodness, she was useless." He readjusted the napkin on his lap. "She needed direction on absolutely everything. Not that she didn't do a credible job when given explicit instruction, but she lacked any ability to think for herself or add value with original ideas. Very disappointing."

I nodded because arguing would be useless. Now he was starting to remind me of Uncle Tommy. Not a bad man, but not an open-minded one. At this point, it was clear that Rich and I were not a match made anywhere near heaven. Grace would tell me to hold off judgment and give him a fair chance, but sometimes you simply know when it isn't meant to be. I would do my best to enjoy my meal and hear him out, but this night was a bust. Maybe Alan would meet me for a drink sometime . . .

"You have a child, right?" I asked, remembering that he'd mentioned one in our email exchange.

"Yes—Haley—but she's still in New York with her mother. I see her at holidays and on certain weekends, and for a month each summer." He glanced out the window, but not fast enough to hide his pained look. A contrast to Dirk, who didn't seem to miss his son.

"That must be hard. Do you think about moving back so you can spend more time with her before she flies the coop?"

He sighs. "I can't afford to live there, pay alimony and child support, and run my own business. Not yet, anyway. I grew up nearby, so returning was a homecoming of sorts, and Haley likes to spend July at the bay."

"Divorce is hard—on grown-ups and kids." I took another piece of bread, forcing a smile. "Let's change the subject before we both end up depressed."

Rich nodded. "Would you like to know the current trends in men's socks?"

"Why not? I'll share it with my clients so they can keep their mates in style."

He smiled broadly. "Retro. Tie-dye, neon . . . things like that. For men and women. And men, in particular, will be looking for high-quality feel and moisture-wicking fabrics."

"Who knew there was so much to consider?"

"Oh yes. I have to create tech designs and artwork, put together concept boards, track and manage seasonal patterns and colors. Then there's managing multiple product development tracks, and responsibility for technical knit design. Creating and tracking vendor files for jacquards, textures, prints, and patterns. And that doesn't touch upon having expertise in yarns, textiles, knot-and-performance products. Design details like lengths and packaging—it never ends!"

"Wow." I had nothing else to add. While his passion was admirable, his droning on did not excite me.

Truthfully, I didn't dislike Rich. He was kind and mannered and thoughtful. These were all good traits. Respectable ones. But I couldn't bring myself to care or even make myself want to care. He bored me. Grace was right. I struggled to find decent, everyday men intriguing, as proven tonight. I wanted someone who made me laugh until my belly hurt, because regular life was serious enough. Sadly, my dilemma wouldn't be fixed by Rich or his fancy socks.

Alan returned with our salads. "Enjoy."

"Thank you." Rich looked at me with a sincere smile. "Bon appétit."

I nodded and stabbed some lettuce and goat cheese.

The meal passed one long minute at a time until my phone rang during dessert. Twelve past ten? Those two-plus hours had felt more like seventeen. More troubling was seeing Rowan's name on my screen. He never called me on a Saturday night. "Excuse me, this is my son," I said before answering the call.

"Mom!" His panicked tone made me freeze. "You have to come home. Now! Come home now!"

"Rowan, calm down and tell me what's happened."

"Carter's hurt. He's on the floor in the basement and isn't moving."

"What?" Stars exploded in my eyes. "How?"

I sprang from my seat, grabbed my purse, and bolted toward the door without a word to Rich. When I burst outside, I threw my car ticket at the valet.

"Lots of people showed up—it got out of hand. I don't know what happened, exactly."

I was shaking when the valet held my car door open. I threw him a five and slammed my door shut. "Call nine-one-one now. I'll be there as soon as I can get there."

"But there's beer and stuff everywhere."

"Call nine-one-one now, Rowan. Now!" Tears streamed down my cheeks as I shook. "I need to call Grace. I'll be home in ten minutes."

"Okay."

"I mean it. Call nine-one-one as soon as we hang up."

"I will." A stab of empathy pushed through my anger the moment his voice cracked.

"Goodbye." I dialed Grace while pulling away from the restaurant, my heart rising into my throat. Please don't let it be as bad as Rowan made it sound.

"Hello?" Grace answered.

"Grace, there's been an accident." My voice involuntarily broke apart. "Carter's hurt. Rowan's calling an ambulance now, but you should meet me at my house right away."

"What?" she asked. "Hurt how?"

"I think he fell down the basement steps. I'm not sure yet. Just meet me, please."

"Oh God, is he okay?" The alarm in my friend's voice tore through me.

"I don't really know. I'm sorry. I'm so sorry." That buttery trout soured in my stomach as a dry heave formed.

"My baby," she cried out as she hung up without saying goodbye.

I swerved into my driveway as the ambulance turned onto our street. Kids scampered out of my house like ants and disappeared behind my neighbors' homes. Rather than wait for the EMTs to unload, I raced inside. The stench of teen body odor and spilled beer hit me as I stepped over the mess of empty beer cans and chips ground into the living room rug. A scream gathered inside, but there wasn't time for anger. I stumbled down my basement steps to find Carter on the tile floor with Rowan kneeling beside him, both boys crying and breathing too hard. Carter's face twisted in pain with each breath.

I held in my sob but couldn't stop the sweat from coming on. Our boys looked ten years younger and much more fragile than their six-foot-tall bodies should appear.

"What happened, Rowan?" I snapped out of my fear. "Why were all these kids here?"

He looked up, eyes swimming in contrition. "They showed up."

In the moment, it was easier to direct my horror and fury at my son than to take in what might be happening to Carter. "Why were y'all drinking when I wasn't home to supervise?" I stood over the boys, my thoughts jumbled, my heart now reaching hummingbird-wing beats per minute.

"I'm sorry. I messed up. I'm sorry!" Rowan swiped the back of his arm across his reddened face. Carter lay beside him, crying in silence. Always such a quiet boy, even now. Oh Lord, why did this happen?

Shouting at Rowan wouldn't calm Carter, and I had to help that sweet boy now.

"Rowan, go bring the EMTs down here." I crouched to hug Carter but stopped myself, afraid of moving him in any direction. I gently laid one trembling hand on his shoulder and smoothed hair from his forehead with the other. "Carter, honey, can you move?"

His head shook slightly, eyes wide and wild with panic. "I can't feel my legs!"

My stomach lurched and I nearly lost my balance.

He hiccuped from crying. "It hurts to breathe."

I blinked to hold back tears so he didn't become more frightened. A memory of him at six with his newly toothless grin, handing me a Mother's Day card, flickered. How many times had he slept here when the boys were kids? A hundred? Seeing him distressed now set my heart on fire. "Try not to panic, honey. You're in shock. That's probably why you feel numb. The EMTs will take care of you. Meanwhile, take slow, shallow breaths. You might've cracked a rib, but that will heal." I kept stroking his hair while tears spilled onto my cheeks despite my best efforts to contain them. "Can you tell me exactly what happened?"

His eyes darted around the basement, but the EMTs clomped downstairs before he answered, so I moved aside. While they assessed Carter, I tugged Rowan into a corner, thinking about whether the foot-ball team's bullying might've factored into this situation.

Out of terror, I barked, "Tell me what happened, and don't even think about leaving a single detail out. This is very serious, Rowan. I need to know everything."

My son wrapped his arms around his waist, peeking over my shoulder to see what the EMTs were doing.

My body buzzed with energy, so I squatted, blew out a breath, and stood again, shaking my arms to rid myself of my nerves. "Rowan, I'm talking to you."

He met my gaze. "People showed up with cases of beer. I tried to keep it under control, but I guess some of the guys started pushing Carter around because of the budget stuff. They didn't mean for him to fall down the stairs—he lost his balance. I don't know, he fell down the steps and then didn't move. That's all I know."

"Carter!" Grace's shrill voice rang out before she barreled down the stairs and fell to her knees, trembling. "Oh, Carter, honey. What happened?"

Her splotchy face was wet with tears. Wearing yoga pants and slippers, she'd obviously raced out of her house without thinking. Seeing them crying together made my chest seize with so much pain I had to gulp in air to make my lungs work again.

"Grace." I stepped toward her, but her tortured expression drained my blood and left me shaky.

My friend didn't look like she could deal with anything other than her son in that moment. She grabbed one of the EMTs. "I'm his mother. Please tell me what's happening."

"Ma'am," the young man began. "We're still assessing. He's likely sustained a concussion, maybe some cracked ribs, and possibly a spinal fracture. It's too soon to tell the extent of damage right now. Try to stay calm. We'll get him on a backboard with some spinal precautions. We should take him straight up to the Shock Trauma Center in Baltimore. They've got specialists and better facilities up there than the local ER."

Specialists. Baltimore. Spinal precautions. The room seemed to tilt, so I reached out to grab the first thing I could find—Rowan's shoulder—to steady myself. Another dry heave bent me forward. How had this happened in our home?

"Spinal fracture?" Grace wobbled as if she might faint, then braced herself by planting her palms on the ground by her knees. With a shake of her head, as if clearing her thoughts, she said, "Yes, of course. Take him to the best place."

Grace was whiter than snow as she rose unsteadily to her feet.

I moved behind her to catch her if she collapsed. She stiff-armed me, blinking rapidly, so I gave her some space.

"What happened?" she finally asked me, looking desperate for an answer that could magically make it all go away.

"I don't know. Rowan called and I raced right home, but I only got here a minute before you did."

Her brows gathered together as she continued to wobble. "You weren't at home tonight?"

I shook my head, my hands still stretched out to catch her if she lost her balance. "No."

"You left during the party?" Her tone sounded more confused than accusatory.

"There was no party when I left, just a few boys playing video games. I left them pizza money, having no idea it would turn into this."

She reached for Rowan, clasping his hand. "Rowan, did you see what happened? How long has Carter been like this?"

"I don't know." Rowan was still crying, trembling as his shoulders rounded. Since the boys stopped hanging out together, Rowan had become a bit submissive around Grace because of her formal demeanor. "I was upstairs."

Grace didn't seem to notice that I was rubbing her back. She dropped Rowan's hand and curled both of hers to her chest as if she needed to collect all of herself in order to wrap her brain around what was happening. She looked at me, her eyes a mirror of agony.

"Grace, we're right here, whatever you guys need." I'd never felt more helpless in my life. Or more frightened. "I'm so sorry."

She stiffened and opened her mouth, but before she said anything, two police officers male and female descended the stairs.

"Who's the homeowner?" the male asked.

I raised my hand, rendered nearly speechless by the sight of those uniforms. "I'm Mimi Gillette. This is my son, Rowan."

"I'm Officer Martinez, and this is Officer Hartung." Officer Martinez was of medium height and build, with a crop of shiny, dark hair and equally dark eyes. Officer Hartung might be shorter than me, if that were possible, and didn't look tough enough to be a cop.

Officer Martinez exchanged some words with the EMTs before speaking again. "Ma'am." He was addressing Grace. "Who are you?"

"Grace Phillips, Carter's mother." She pointed to her son. "I just arrived."

"I'm sorry. This must be a shock." He offered her an empathetic expression before turning to me. "Due to the seriousness of the injury, we'll be treating this as a crime scene with a possible felony, so I need to ask you not to touch anything until we finish an investigation."

"A felony?" I said, dazed. "It was an accident."

"An accident," Grace muttered, although it almost sounded like a question.

"Mom," Carter moaned from the ground. "I'm scared."

Grace let out a quick sob but then snapped herself together. "I'm right here, sweetheart. Don't be scared. I'll be with you the whole time. We'll find the best doctors."

He was ashen, appearing so frail on that board, immobilized with big foam stoppers around his head and sides. The sight made my brain fizzle out like our old toaster.

Officer Martinez told Grace, "Ma'am, I need your contact information so we can reach you. An officer will likely meet you at the hospital to monitor the situation and ask him some questions once he's out of danger."

Out of danger. Again, a ball of pain the size of a boulder crushed me. Carter was in danger because of my son and his friends. This terrible thing had happened in my home. A night that had started with such high hopes had been trashed, and so had my house.

Grace gave the officer the information he requested. When the EMTs lifted Carter off the ground and guided him up the stairs, my friend followed behind them without another glance at my son or me.

I couldn't blame her. She wasn't thinking about anything other than her baby's pain.

Officer Martinez turned to me. "We need to clear the area so the other cops can conduct an investigation. How about you two follow me to my squad car for questioning."

The word "felony" plowed through my thoughts again, so it took me five seconds to answer. "Are we under arrest?"

"Not at the moment. We're only beginning our investigation, but if this is an accident like you say, then your cooperation would certainly help us sort out the details more efficiently."

"Of course we'll cooperate." I couldn't change what had already happened, but I could help the officers get to the truth. I reached for Rowan's hand, pulling him along as we followed Officer Martinez out to his squad car. The red and blue lights from the cop cars and ambulances added more confusion to the chaotic scene. It took all my concentration not to trip, because the commotion and my racing pulse were making me woozy.

While we crossed the yard, the ambulance pulled away from the curb, blasting its sirens. My heart pounded violently as I recalled Carter's inability to feel his legs. Wasn't it just yesterday that he and Rowan were toddling around this yard together, pretending to be firemen? I covered my face while shaking my head, as if that could make this all go away.

"Are there any security cameras in or outside the house?" Officer Martinez asked while opening the rear door of his car.

"No." I let Rowan climb in first, then slid onto the back seat beside him. He hadn't looked this upset since Dirk walked out the door. I wrapped an arm around his shoulders. He'd gotten himself in way over his head, and neither of us could undo what fate had done. I didn't even have teen experiences to pull from because nothing close to this had happened to me. Maybe Uncle Tommy's strict curfews and rules hadn't been as ridiculous as I'd thought.

Officer Martinez got in beside me and closed the door to keep out the cold. We were cramped together, but I supposed he'd have a hard time talking to us through that divider. I scooched Rowan over farther to create some distance between the cop and myself, while the cop spoke to his partner through a walkie-talkie. "No home video cameras, but canvass the neighbors to see if there are outdoor cameras that could show us license plates or anything else to identify participants." When he finished, he leaned forward and looked at Rowan. It might not be the cop's first busted party, but I was still catching up. Half my heart was riding to Baltimore with Grace and Carter, the other half aching for my son's remorse. "So, son, want to tell me in your own words what happened tonight?"

The air inside the car crackled. I blinked, forcing myself to focus on what was happening, although my brain wouldn't cooperate. I held Rowan's hand. His grip was so strong he nearly broke my bones, which would be problematic for my job. I rubbed his forearm to ease his grip. "It's okay, honey. Take a breath."

Rowan swiped his eyes. "I don't know what happened with Carter."

Officer Martinez stared at him. "You don't know anything?"

"I wasn't in the kitchen when it went down." Rowan glanced at me, red-faced, and then back to the cop. "I swear."

I pressed on my knee to keep it from bouncing. Was he lying? Should I get a lawyer even though he hadn't been arrested? My chest squeezed so hard that breathing burned. I had options—smart choices to make, but those weren't always the moral choices. The Bible school lessons from my teens played like a tape recording. *"Blessed are those who hunger and thirst for righteousness, for they shall be satisfied."* Although I'd suffered big losses, things had usually turned out okay because I'd worked hard and done right, so I would put my faith in Him again.

Officer Martinez's voice broke through my thoughts even though he was speaking to Rowan. "Surely after it happened, someone came to get you. Someone told you something. Maybe you could identify eyewitnesses for us."

Rowan's expression grew more terrified. When I suspected he was trying to protect his friends, I, too, began to panic. What would this mean for my son, for me? Still, I held his hand and nodded so he knew he was loved and forgiven, and that I would keep him as safe as I could.

"We'll be catching up to a lot of kids and the victim, so you might as well help us rule you out." Officer Martinez remained calm and nonthreatening. Almost folksy.

I tried to find a steady rhythm for my breathing. "It's okay, baby. Be honest."

Rowan's face imploded like a badly made soufflé. "I heard that John Winters and Deshaun Jackson were giving him a hard time, pushing him around a bit—you know, guy stuff. They didn't mean for him to fall down the stairs, though. That part was an accident."

I'd known John and Deshaun for at least five years. Two great, polite athletes. Deshaun's big grin and bigger personality always brought a smile to my face. I'd even nicknamed him Teddy (for "teddy bear"). My affection for my son's teammates had let me dismiss Grace's concerns. I hadn't wanted to believe they could be cruel to someone as sweet as Carter. Even my request that Rowan get the team to lighten up had been mild. Hell, I'd been mild about most things where Rowan was concerned since the divorce. Look at where that had gotten us all. Everyone's pain could be laid at my feet.

"Can anyone corroborate that you weren't in the kitchen?" the officer asked, emotionless.

My son's cheeks and neck turned redder. "Melissa Watson."

"Where were you, exactly?" I demanded, newly mortified.

His eyes darted to me and the officer, then back to me before he mumbled, "In my room."

Not only had my son let a ton of kids trash our house and hurt his former friend, but he also had been hooking up with a girl he wasn't even dating. I elbowed him. "Rowan Michael Gillette, what the hell is wrong with you?"

Things could not get worse.

"I'm sorry," he moaned.

"Everybody calm down." Officer Martinez waited for my attention. "Where were you when all this was going on?"

"Oh God." I slapped my hand over my mouth. Rich had no real idea why I'd left. What a disaster. How amazing that I hadn't barfed up my dinner. "I was on a date. I bolted as soon as Rowan called. I should text him or something."

I'd lied to my son and ignored my intuition when I saw Carter in the yard because I'd thought some man would complete my life. Decisions like those might explain why so many women in town didn't care for me.

"A date?" Rowan's accusatory gaze scorched. Karma.

"Who were you out with?" Officer Martinez asked.

I avoided my son's scowl. "His name is Rich Polanti and he lives in town. We met online. We were at Bistro Henri when my son called. The waiter, Alan, can confirm that."

Officer Martinez's eyebrows rose, perhaps in acknowledgment of the fancy venue. "Okay. I can follow up on that later. You say your son called to tell you about the accident? About what time was that?"

"Ten twelve. I know that for sure because I'd been counting the minutes until that date was over." I grimaced at how cruel that sounded when I hadn't meant it to. Nerves always made me say the wrong things, and boy, was I nervous right now. "When I left the house tonight, there were only four boys here—John, Deshaun, Eddie, and Mason. Carter was on his way inside as I was pulling out of the driveway. I'd given Rowan money for pizza, and that's all I know." I splayed my palm across the base of my neck, my heart squeezing again as Carter's terrified young face flickered through my mind. They probably weren't even at the trauma center yet. Every minute in that ambulance must seem an eternity.

I pictured Grace straining against the seat belt to huddle protectively over her son. Imagined her leaning down to whisper calming words. She probably wished Sam and his bright-side mentality were taking that ride with her. He could pull her back from the edge of panic. I couldn't even take Kim off their hands right now because the cops could be here for hours.

Officer Martinez said, "Rowan, how did this go from being a small group of boys to a rager?"

Rowan shrugged, his eyes darting around as if seeking some escape from having to out his friends. "People snapchatted about the open house, and then others started showing up."

"I'll need a list of everyone's names—everyone you remember who was here—before I go. So no one was drinking before others showed up, correct?"

Rowan spared me an apologetic glance, cheeks aflame. "We poured some of my mom's rum in our root beer."

Every time he opened his mouth, he said something I wished I didn't know. Apparently the lessons I'd hoped to teach him about responsible socializing hadn't stuck at all. Sneaking my booze. Not saying no to people showing up with cases of beer. Sexing up some girl for fun while his friends got rowdy and picked on Carter. What kind of mother was I that my teen son thought any of this was okay? My heart felt like someone had stomped on it.

This night would change the course of so many lives, including our own. Everything would be marked by the before and after of this party—especially if Carter's injuries were permanent. I grabbed my stomach and forced that thought away before it took me under.

"Unlocked liquor cabinet?" Officer Martinez muttered.

Rowan's distress tugged at his mouth, and my heart stopped. The rum and vodka in the house hadn't even crossed my mind until now.

My son finally nodded without words.

"Okay. Unfortunately, while I can issue a summons for the underage possession, serving minors is a misdemeanor, so I've got to issue a warrant." He went on to recite those Miranda rules I'd heard on TV shows a million times, having never myself dreamed they'd become my reality. My whole body went numb with fear. Was my son going to jail? Was I? Had we completely ruined our lives?

Rowan screwed up his face again. "Am I going to jail?"

"Like I said, you'll be booked for the misdemeanor, but then appear in family court as a juvie, where you'll likely get a fine and maybe community service or sentenced to attend some classes about alcohol abuse." Officer Martinez sounded certain and calm, but my blood pressure rose. I couldn't even begin to comprehend all the ways this situation would impact my son's future, or mine, or Carter's. I wanted to know what was happening with Grace, too, but I was stuck here in the back seat of a patrol car, and my own son was starting to break down. Officer Martinez furrowed his brows. "Do you understand your rights?"

Rowan and I both nodded through our tears.

"Do you want to call a lawyer now, or can we keep talking and sort this whole thing out quickly for everyone's sake?" He looked to me now.

My mind raced. I knew nothing about juvenile laws, but this discussion felt fraught with danger. I'd been programmed to trust that telling the truth was always the right thing to do.

God's protection was great and all, but had I left Rowan unprotected from man's law? Not that I knew or could afford any defense lawyers, even if I wanted to call one. And Rowan had already confessed, so stonewalling seemed pointless. It'd probably only piss the cop off. Hiding behind a lawyer would also send a terrible message to my friend. Carter got hurt here. Someone was responsible for that, and if it ended up being my son and me, we'd have to own it.

I could be accused of a lot of things, but I'd never shirked responsibility, nor did I believe in teaching my son to avoid consequences.

Officer Martinez said Rowan wasn't going to jail, and I chose to trust him because he'd been decent and fair so far.

"Son." Officer Martinez flipped a page in his little notebook.

I thought about my own parents—my father, in particular. He'd come home from work once, having been chewed out by his boss because a coworker had messed up a joint presentation. When I'd asked why he didn't tell his boss it was the other guy's fault, my dad explained that he should've been working more closely with that guy to make sure their presentation went well, and that the best way to learn from mistakes was to acknowledge them. I'd since found that truth applied to most things in life.

"Rowan," I said, wrapping an arm around him, although who was supporting whom I couldn't tell. "You already admitted what you did, so I can't see any sense in waiting for a lawyer. Things got out of control tonight, and now we have to accept our role and make things right. It's okay to make mistakes as long as you admit it and learn from them."

Officer Martinez cocked his head. "I wish more parents had your attitude about dealing with these situations."

His expression suggested that he hadn't meant to say that aloud, making me grateful for the slip. The hint of respect made me feel the tiniest bit better, although it didn't prevent the image of Carter's fearful tears from flashing before my eyes again. Or erase the shiver of concern about Rowan's potential criminal record.

"Okay," Rowan said, wiping tears from his cheeks.

Officer Martinez asked, "Where'd the others get the beer?"

Rowan shrugged. "I don't know. Maybe older brothers or the Beer Mart in Chesapeake Beach—they don't always card kids . . . or so I've heard." He hunched as his voice trailed off.

The things I hadn't known about my son horrified me. I'd thought that taking away the mystique of drinking with a little supervised experimenting would lower the thrill and curb his enthusiasm for this kind of behavior. It sounded so stupid in the aftermath of what'd happened here. And the consequences—so much worse than I'd ever foreseen. I'd never been less happy with myself than in this moment, shame raining down like an April thunderstorm.

"So, fair to say, by the time of the incident, most kids were not sober?" Officer Martinez asked.

Rowan closed his eyes and dipped his chin, fresh tears glistening in his lashes. "Yeah."

I covered my face with my hands. I'd never intended for anything like this to happen. Not to Rowan, or Carter, or any of the kids who'd been at my house.

"Sorry, Mom," my son squeaked out. I knew he was, but suspected he mostly worried about his own hide. Had he given any thought to what Carter and the Phillipses were going through right now?

"I'd like to look at your phone for pictures taken tonight and to scan texts and look at social media accounts," Officer Martinez said to Rowan.

Rowan looked at me, terrified, but I shrugged. This had gotten beyond our control, and we deserved our lumps. "I didn't take any pictures."

"Others probably posted some and are sending you texts or chats with important details," Officer Martinez said. "If you cooperate now, I'll take it into consideration at your hearing."

Rowan moaned before he unlocked his phone and handed it to Officer Martinez. I gave my son a hug, wishing I could do more to protect him. Watching someone you loved learn a lesson the hard way was torturous.

The officer handed a notepad to Rowan. "Write down everyone's name who was at your house tonight, and phone numbers or emails that you know. Social media handles. The works."

"I don't know all that without my phone," Rowan said.

The officer handed it back. "Go ahead and write everything down, and then we'll go through your texts and accounts to see what others are chatting about now."

Tears leaked from my son's eyes, but I couldn't take away his sick feeling about turning in his friends. He needed to stew in what he'd created. The fallout. All of it. I could only pray that this night would be his rock bottom, and he'd mature as a result. As for my own guilt, that'd have to be put on ice until I got my son through this interrogation. My thoughts frayed as I sat there in silence, waiting for Rowan to finish compiling a long list of names to hand over.

Each of those kids would end up giving Rowan a hard time for this, but that didn't matter. Carter might be looking at life in a wheelchair. And as tough as it was for me to watch my baby squirm and cry when questioned by the cops, it paled in comparison with what Grace was facing. On that thought, the fear and frustration I'd been trying to contain like lightning in a jar turned to rage and broke apart.

I raised my hand like I might swat Rowan—something I'd never done—then lowered it, clasping it against my chest.

My son let out an inarticulate sob. With a creaky voice, he said, "I'm sorry, Mom. I swear. I didn't mean for all this to happen."

I'd thought—hoped—that the day my parents died in a car accident would be the worst of my life. Now this one might eclipse that loss. That had changed my life, but this one would change mine, my son's, Carter's, Grace's, and on and on. People throughout the community would all be hit by reverberating bands of pain.

Grace and I had seen each other through some tough times before, but I couldn't even begin to figure out how to help her through this. First I'd need information about Carter's condition. I dreaded making that call. That sinking feeling would not let go. Grace hated drinking, and I understood why. Having lost her dad and sister to alcohol-related deaths had to make this situation excruciatingly terrifying.

After Rowan handed over the notepad with names, he asked, "Will all my friends be arrested now?"

"It's too early to tell. We'll have to question everyone and the victim first." Officer Martinez spoke into the walkie-talkie again, and another wave of unease rose like the tide. Question the community? Any goodwill I'd garnered these recent weeks would be gone by morning. A selfish, selfish thought, but there it was. Officer Hartung showed up, shaking me out of self-pity. Officer Martinez handed her the paper. "Run down this list of guests, particularly the ones I starred, who might've been directly involved in the incident that precipitated the injury. Have dispatch send some cars and try to get those interviews tonight. I'm going to go through the host's phone now."

The distant way Officer Martinez referred to Rowan as "the host" caused my stomach to turn again. But a juvenile misdemeanor—even Dirk had had that experience in high school. Not that that was a great comparison. Officer Hartung nodded and left.

"They're gonna kill me." Rowan turned to me. Both boys were juniors on his team. "I ratted them out, and they're gonna get in serious trouble."

"You have to tell the truth, Rowan. It's not your fault that those boys behaved badly." I squeezed his thigh. Disappointment and anger tempered my sympathies, making it hard to know how to react.

"If you'd lied or conspired to delete texts, you could be facing obstruction charges, so you did the right thing," Officer Martinez said.

Rowan wasn't listening, though. Instead, he'd bent in half and was holding his stomach. "I feel sick."

"Take a few breaths. When you're ready, we need to go through your phone." Officer Martinez cracked the door open to let in some fresh air. I didn't need the chilly breeze when my bones were already frozen in panic. What if there was something more incriminating in those texts . . . something Rowan didn't know about or remember?

Rowan began scrolling through his texts with Officer Martinez, identifying the senders and providing context. He also opened Snapchats and screenshotted them for the officer. Outside the car, neighbors opened their doors to speak with the officers, and others peeked through their blinds. I knew they were thinking, *That Mimi and her son . . .*

While Officer Martinez's phone search dragged on, Grace's anguished face replayed, causing me to tense. What fresh hell was she in, and had Sam caught up yet to help her through it?

I decided to bite the bullet, like my son had, and call her. No answer. Dang it. I'd feel better if I knew what was happening and could help my friend. She was probably busy checking Carter into the ER.

Please, God, let Carter be okay so this could be a near miss—a learning experience for these boys rather than a life-changing event for everyone.

# CHAPTER SIX

## Grace

*Sunday, January 10, 12:43 a.m.*
*Shock Trauma Center ER near Baltimore*

"I have an update" echoed inside my skull as I sprang from my seat.

The doctor's somber expression weakened my knees. I reached for Sam, my gaze fixed on Dr. Acharya. My heart pulsed as if it had risen to my throat. Sam snaked an arm around my waist and tucked me against his side, his solid presence holding me together.

"Will he walk?" I blurted, terrified yet unable to withstand another minute of uncertainty.

The doctor clasped his elegant hands together. "I cannot say for sure, but there is reason to be optimistic."

The nonanswer wrenched an otherworldly sob from some dark corner of my soul. Faint from the weight of his ambiguity, I bent at the waist, my mind noisy. If we hadn't been in public, I would have screamed until my voice gave out.

Whenever another incident of online bullying or a random school shooting had sent me into a tailspin about our kids' fates, Sam and

Mimi had told me to relax. Like many others, they'd relied on the odds to assure them that nothing ghastly would ever claim one of our own.

But I'd known.

I'd always known that someday the scales would be rebalanced, because it had never seemed fair that my little family had been so fortunate when others weren't.

Mimi hadn't sympathized with my sense of dread about that invisible "other shoe" dropping, probably because she'd been ducking shoes left and right for most of her life. Well, she might dodge this one, too, but my son wouldn't.

Dr. Acharya waited for me to stand upright. I blinked, forcing myself to focus on him and his words.

"Why don't we go to your son so I can explain what's happened and what we need to do." The doctor gestured toward the doors behind the nurse station.

Dread rooted me in place. I must've squeezed Sam extra hard, because he gently loosened his grip.

"Honey, do you need a minute?" he asked. "We've got to hold it together for Carter's sake or he'll be more frightened."

I nodded despite lacking confidence, my body trembling with each shaky step. We followed Dr. Acharya as he led us toward our son's bay.

Sam hefted Kim against his chest before laying one hand on my lower back to guide me. Kim barely woke, her head peacefully resting on his shoulder, her eyes closed. I dried my cheeks with the backs of my hands before seeing Carter hooked into monitors and IV lines and buffered with immobilization braces.

Another scream threatened to explode, but I forced a smile and went to stand at the head of his bed. "Honey, how do you feel?"

He stared at us stoically, in shock or terror, or both. Probably both. I would've done anything for it to be me lying there immobile instead of my son. A backup of fresh tears burned my nose and eyes.

The nurse checked one of the lines. "It'll take time for the cracked ribs to heal, and his breathing may be a bit painful until they do, but they didn't puncture his lungs."

Might they still? How would we know? What were the symptoms? So many questions, but my voice seemed paralyzed.

Dr. Acharya nodded, confirming the nurse's statement. I returned my attention to him because he alone had all the answers.

"Your son sustained an injury to his spine. Basically, he broke a portion of the spine and injured the nerves going to his legs."

Everything dimmed, as if my vision were being compressed. I grasped the rail on Carter's bed to keep myself upright but wouldn't look at my son until I could fake the composure he'd need from me.

"What does that mean?" Sam asked, blinking excessively. My husband rarely got rattled, so the perspiration beading above his lips scared me.

"There are some urgent things we need to do now—decompression of the nerves and stabilization of the spine. Stabilization is accomplished with metal rods and screws. We'll also need to take some bone from his pelvis to help with the healing."

Rods and bone grafts and what? My son's widened eyes oozed fresh tears.

Bile rose up my throat. This night was worse than when Margot died of an overdose. The only thing I understood with certainty at this point was that Carter would have a lifetime of back problems at best, and paralysis at worst. A silent "No, no, no!" in my brain made it impossible to process anything else.

"Is his spinal cord severed?" I asked, trying to clear my head.

"It's unlikely, but the important thing is how the nerves recover after decompression." He didn't sugarcoat anything—that was for sure. But he also didn't give me the answer I wanted. "Unlikely" wasn't unequivocal. And what did "recovering" nerves mean? How would Carter's future be changed?

"So you plan to operate soon?" Sam asked, settling Kim onto an empty chair before returning to huddle around the doctor and Carter with me and grabbing hold of my hand.

"As soon as possible, yes."

"Spinal surgery . . ." I looked into Sam's eyes, unconcerned with whom I might offend: "Do we need a second opinion?"

Sam settled his palm against my cheek to calm me. "This is the best facility in the state, Grace. It sounds urgent, so maybe we shouldn't waste any time." He waited for some sign of affirmation before turning back to Dr. Acharya, despite my needing time to slow down so I could catch up. "What happens after surgery?"

"Fusion recovery takes roughly three to six months, but we mobilize patients as immediately as possible. The hope is that once the swelling subsides and the bone fragments are removed, your son will recover sensation and the use of his legs. Resulting muscle damage or weakness will make it a difficult recovery, requiring weeks or months of inpatient rehab."

"Months?" I gasped.

He nodded, like this was business as usual instead of the beginning of a whole new life for our family. "The average inpatient stay for T-level burst fractures is in the mid-fifty-day range."

Fear suffused Carter's face, striking me like a thousand needles to my heart. I couldn't crawl into the bed and hug my child with the braces and the IV and all of it, but the urge overwhelmed me.

"After that, he'll be able to walk?" I wanted to shake the doctor until he gave us the answer we needed to hear, but Sam draped one arm around my shoulders to hold me tight.

"Honey, he's saying we should be optimistic." He darted a glance at the doctor for confirmation. "The spinal cord doesn't seem to be severed, so that's the good news." Then he smiled at Carter as if we'd been given a gift.

How Sam remained calm defied comprehension. It was as if he wasn't hearing what I was hearing or taking it as seriously. Or was I the one mistaken? I searched Dr. Acharya's eyes for any flicker of positivity, but he must've been trained to avoid making false promises. To him, Carter was one of many injuries tonight. He didn't know the sweet toddler whose mood had been affected by sad songs, the big brother who'd lovingly built sandcastles with his little sister, or the dedicated student who wanted to change the world.

Dr. Acharya nodded. "We simply cannot know the extent of the damage until we get in there. Throughout my career, I've seen any number of outcomes." He looked at Carter. "There's significant swelling now, which could account for your deficits. Once that subsides, we'll know more. Some of it will be dependent on your commitment to recovery as well. Also, as with any surgery, sometimes there can be complications. We can't give a definitive answer at this point. But I have reason to remain optimistic, and you should, too."

I found the courage to look Carter in the eyes and smile so that he didn't lose hope or fall apart. "We can do this."

Carter's gaze grew distant, like it often did when he worked out a problem. If only my love could seep beneath his skin and mend his bones and nerves, I would squeeze him tight.

Dr. Acharya said, "Since he's a minor, we need your consent to operate. We'll discuss all the risks when we go over the forms. But again, we'd like to get started as soon as possible to minimize the damage."

I nodded blankly, unable to take it all in. My mind remained mired in the lack of assurances. The thought of my baby in a wheelchair for the rest of his life unleashed a bloom of hatred for the football team. Not my norm. My school volunteering meant I'd known many of them for years. Seen them win spelling bees and football championships. Worked alongside their mothers to raise money and organize activities. We'd been a constant—if small—part of each other's lives. Never had

I believed any of them could cause this kind of damage, or turn me into someone filling with rage. But there it was. Rage and fury igniting because Carter was too young to be stuck in a chair for the rest of his life.

Sam was too attuned to Carter and the doctor to notice how my entire body had gone cold and stiff. "Anything else we should know?"

Suddenly my husband's calm, collected demeanor made me feel isolated, adding to my upset.

"Let me get the forms and go through the risks so we can get your son prepped for the OR." Dr. Acharya left us without delay.

Carter stared into space, eyes watery and unblinking. To what dark, terrifying places were his thoughts veering? A soul-crushing helplessness made me woozy.

Mothers are supposed to protect their children, not feebly offer comfort after the worst happens. I'd let my guard down for one minute, and boom, his future was destroyed. The only thing I could do for him now was hide my worry to assuage his.

I stroked his hair and kissed his forehead, whispering, "This is an excellent hospital, and the doctor is very experienced. He sounds optimistic, so we need to keep the faith, okay? Dad and I will do everything possible to help you recover. Everything."

"What if he's wrong? What if I can't walk?" Carter croaked, his breath coming short and fast, which made him wince in pain.

His fear dipped my heart in acid, leaving me speechless.

Sam squeezed my shoulder before drawing closer to the bed. He leaned in to kiss our son's head, too. "Bud, he's seen hundreds of these injuries and seen your tests. He's a straight shooter, so if walking was a long shot, he'd say so. We're in great hands. I expect a good result."

Carter's gaze darted to me, so I mirrored Sam's confidence—not because I believed him but to decrease Carter's anxiety. Our son relaxed slightly, though his eyes remained misty. "What about school?"

"We'll figure that out later," Sam promised. "If you need private tutors to keep up, we'll get them. But don't worry about that tonight. Your only job right now is to stay positive and to pray."

Kim slid off the chair, grabbed her dad's hand, and tugged. "Daddy, what happened to Carter?"

Sam drew in a deep breath—the only sign that his energy levels were flagging more than he'd been letting on. "There was an accident—he had a big fall."

An accident. That's what Mimi had told the police. But could a mere accident cause this much damage? I stopped short of accusing anyone of such malice, but those boys had been bothering Carter for two weeks. Had they pushed him on purpose?

I didn't share my thoughts.

Sam continued, "Carter will have surgery, and before we know it, this will be behind us."

Life would be lived easier in his fantasy world. Had he not heard the doctor's equivocation, or considered the difficulty that months of in- and outpatient rehab posed? And that didn't even begin to cover the long-term effects of having rods and pins in one's spine. It would be hard enough for Carter to get through this, but without the certainty of Sam and me being in lockstep as usual, I was untethered.

Carter's life would never be the same. This injury—this night—would never be put fully behind us. It was like Dad's and Margot's deaths all over again—the cops, the tragic news, the mistakes acknowledged in hindsight.

Of course, that brought my mother to mind. I'd rather not share this news until we knew its full scope, but she lived nearby and could take Kim off our hands tonight. "Kim, honey, let's call Grammy to pick you up for a sleepover, okay?"

Sam looked at me with surprise.

I shrugged to answer the question in his eyes as I dialed my mother. "She's fifteen minutes away, and this isn't any place for Kim to spend the night."

He ran a hand over his hair. "I rushed here without thinking to send her to one of her friends' homes."

I didn't blame him. I'd been frantic, too.

Mom's sleepy voice answered the phone. "Hello?"

"Mom, it's me. I'm sorry to wake you, but there's been an accident and we need your help." I flushed. At forty-one years old, I'd yet to resolve our complicated relationship. She'd never been cruel, but her weakness had scarred me. Fair or not, I would always indirectly blame her for Margot's death. Like Carter might now grow up blaming me for his injury because I'd let him go to that party.

"What's happened?"

I downplayed the seriousness of Carter's fall despite Sam giving me eyes about that. If she knew the full story, she might insist on sitting with us all night. Her love for my children was true, but I didn't need the undercurrent of friction between us tonight. "Would you mind driving here to take Kim for the night?"

"Of course. I'll put on some clothes and come right over."

"Thank you, Mom. See you soon."

After hanging up, I took a deep breath to ward off the anxiety tightening my chest. Between my son's uncertain recovery and knowing I'd probably need more of my mother's help in the coming weeks, the future looked dim.

Sam said, "I'll take Kim to meet her so you can stay with Carter."

"Thank you." I grabbed Kim into a hug and kissed her cheeks. "Be good for Grammy, okay? We'll see you tomorrow."

Kim's expression seemed a mask of confusion—maybe even of fear. A first for my sassy, confident child. Until now, it hadn't even occurred to me that Carter's injuries would also affect her. "Okay."

Tunnel vision had me so focused on that thought that I jerked with surprise when Sam touched my elbow. "Call me if they come with the forms before I've handed Kim over."

"I will." I waved them off, watching him and Kim disappear beyond the blue curtain. Oddly, my breath came easier with Sam gone—something I'd never before felt.

"Mom, I'm still scared," Carter confessed once we were alone.

My watery eyes betrayed me. I cleared my throat and squeezed his hand. "It's okay to be scared. You wouldn't be human if you weren't. But you're young and healthy. There's no reason to think your body won't heal well. I trust the doctor, Carter. We'll follow every instruction to a tee. It will be difficult, but you've never shied away from difficult things before."

My calm tone belied the circus of emotions in my heart. I wanted to turn back time. To disappear and wake up anywhere else. Another scream gathered in my mouth, so I clenched my jaw to keep it inside.

"But what if it doesn't work? What if I am paralyzed?" Carter's voice cracked before he started to cry.

"Oh, honey, please don't think that way." I kept running my hand over his scalp to settle him so his shaking didn't inadvertently make anything worse. "You know the science behind the power of positive thinking. And the doctor would've been bound to tell us if there was no chance. But even if it were a remote chance, you must believe that you could be the exception."

I kissed him again, but my words hadn't relieved any of the tension in his face, so I said, "Remember that football player from Pittsburgh—Ryan what's-his-name? They thought he might never walk again, but now he can. Have his attitude—stay determined and work for what you want. The mind is powerful, so start sending healing vibes right now."

"But what if we do all that and it doesn't work?" Carter had reverted from a know-it-all teen to a frightened child, and I couldn't blame him. The terror in his heart broke mine. Relentless self-reproach—that I should've fought Sam harder about the party—pounded in my head. Why had I given in?

"If—and that's a big if—but if that's the outcome, then we'll deal with it together." I aimed to reassure us both while considering the worst-case scenario. "Think of all the people, from athletes to soldiers, who've lost the use of some part of their body and yet gone on to live amazing lives and accomplish the unbelievable. If you can't walk, it won't be the end of your life, Carter. You don't need to be able to run to be a scientist or engineer. And you know as well as anyone how rapidly science is evolving—stem cells and robotics—so who knows what treatments there might be in the future? We will never give up hope. Never. I mean it. Till my dying day, I will research every option if we must. But right now I'm putting my faith in Dr. Acharya. You should, too."

He nodded, seeming temporarily emboldened, thank God. I wanted to believe everything I'd said, but my stomach wasn't buying it.

Sam returned at the same time the doctor and nurse came in to inform us of the miles-long list of risks and have us sign a bunch of papers. We listened as they spoke, me staring at my husband, remembering the gorgeous spring day we'd brought Carter home from the hospital. Sam's fascination with Carter's tiny fingers and the scent of his tiny fuzzy head could still bring tears to my eyes. The span of time between then and now bent in half as we signed form after form.

As soon as they whisked Carter away, my torso caved in and I buried my face in my hands, crying. Sam rubbed my back, yet I felt nothing. This happened because we'd broken our pact. He'd changed the rules on me without warning, and now our unshakable trust seemed tenuous.

His eyes were wet, too, as he squeezed my hands and set his expression to one of confidence. "We have to hold it together. And whatever the final news, Grace, we cannot break down in front of Carter. If the worst comes to pass, we can't act like it's the end of the world."

I jerked my hands free. "I know. Dammit, don't you think I know that? I'm doing my best. Right now I'm terrified, so it's a little hard to smile. But I'll keep it together in front of our son."

Sam raised his hands. "I didn't mean to upset you. How can I help?"

"Only the doctor can help us now," I snapped, unleashing pent-up anger now that Carter wouldn't see me unspool.

When Sam winced, I felt nothing. No regret for sniping at him. No empathy for his pain and worry. Nothing. My own pain and regret consumed me, so I couldn't soothe him. The only person in the entire world I wanted to reassure right then was my son.

"It's going to be a long night. Let's see if we can find something to eat, and get more coffee, okay? It won't do Carter any good for us to get run-down."

Reluctantly I followed Sam out to the waiting room, where we saw a cop talking to a nurse at the main desk. When they spotted us, the nurse pointed and the cop walked toward us.

"Mr. and Mrs. Phillips?" she asked.

"Yes, that's us." Exhaustion settled in my bones now that Carter had been taken away and I had room to breathe.

"Hi. I'm Officer Jones. I've been sent to follow up on the incident that happened earlier tonight at the Gillette home. Can I talk to your son?"

"I'm sorry, but he's been taken into emergency surgery." My attention split between Carter and wondering what the police had found out. Only then did Mimi cross my mind. She'd looked as horrified as I'd felt. So had Rowan. The cops might still be at her house. I didn't know how to feel about that—my worry for Carter squeezed everyone else out of my heart. "Have there been arrests?"

"We're bringing in a few kids for questioning, but it's an ongoing investigation. Once we complete that, then, if supported, charges will be filed."

"If supported?" I glanced at Sam. "The house was filled with alcohol and my son was injured. Surely there will be consequences. It's hard to believe that Carter—who was sober—fell down a flight of stairs for no reason."

"I'm very sorry about his injuries," she said. "We'd like to get your son's version of events as soon as possible. As time passes, details get forgotten. Do you think he'll be able to talk to us in the morning?"

It would have been kinder of her to ask how he was doing rather than lament her inability to question him, although I supposed she had a job to do.

"What are those boys saying?" I asked, growing aggravated at the injustice of their able-bodied, uninjured selves crawling into their beds tonight.

"Like I said, we're still investigating. But you'll get a copy of the final report when it's done."

"Well, for what it's worth, some of those boys had been giving Carter a hard time all week." I would make an allowance for Rowan, but only him. He'd been too much a part of our lives for me to conceive that he would purposely hurt Carter. "All because of the damn budget debate, if you can believe it. I admit, it seemed a little suspicious when they suddenly invited Carter to a party this week."

The expression of disapproval on Sam's face didn't dissuade me or slow my train of thought.

The officer made a note. "Opinions aside, we need firsthand accounts from eyewitnesses."

"Like my wife said, now isn't a good time." Sam frowned. "We'll call when Carter's settled and able to talk."

"All right," she said. "Good luck to him. I hope everything turns out okay."

"Thank you." I watched her exit the hospital.

If those boys had pushed Carter on purpose, I wouldn't shed a tear upon seeing them in handcuffs. An almost vengeful glee slithered through me until I pictured Mimi panicked and dealing with the fallout on her own. A stab of sympathy for my friend pierced my chest, but the mother in me wanted everyone responsible to pay for my son's injuries. Mimi had knowingly rolled the dice by allowing boys to drink at her house since last year. My son's needing spinal surgery as a result of such a party dampened my empathy.

Sam tucked the cop's card in his jeans pocket and reached for me. Normally, his tenderness brought me pleasure, but I remained numb. Would I feel happiness again?

Sam thumbed a stray tear from my cheek.

I pulled away, ashamed and confused by my conflicting emotions.

We sat in silence, my thoughts a slideshow of our life together. Our first date—dinner at Antonio's followed by *Erin Brockovich*. The first time he'd met my mother and Margot, on my twenty-first birthday, which we'd celebrated at the Royal Sonesta Harbor Court Baltimore, much to Margot's chagrin, who would've preferred a weekend in Vegas. Our first anniversary, when he'd filled our bedroom with peonies and peppered me with kisses. Carter's brilliant grin when he'd taken first place in the fifth-grade science fair, and Kim's failed attempt at ballet. Everything had seemed to be plugging along.

We'd had a plan that kept us in sync and protected our children. It'd helped us create a happy, healthy, loving family. We had strayed from the plan, and now faced a real crisis. How could I live with this guilt? How could Sam? And who else was responsible?

Tomorrow I'd follow up with the police.

My phone buzzed, so I checked it in case it was my mother. No. Mimi again. My muscles constricted—the opposite of how I normally reacted to her calls. We always supported each other, but this time felt different. As with the budget debate, our interests in the aftermath of Rowan's party were not aligned, which drew a line straight through the middle of everything.

Laden with sorrow for all of us, I hung my head and prayed for the strength and wisdom to get my family through the crisis.

# CHAPTER SEVEN

## M I M I

*Sunday, January 10, 3:30 a.m.*
*The Gillette home*

A raccoon hissed as I unloaded another bag of empty beer cans into the recycle bin beside the garage. My backward stumble caused the critter to scurry beneath a bush, thereby leaving me blessedly alone in the darkness. I wrapped my jacket tighter around me—the tip of my nose already cold—and stared toward heaven for a sign of God's mercy.

Rowan's postarrest meltdown while we were cleaning up had broken something in me. His emotional breakdown proved he wasn't nearly as tough as he pretended to be. My guilty conscience made me shoo him to bed rather than force him to finish the task. I'd never had Grace's parenting discipline, largely because my parents' looser style had made me happier than my uncle's. Now it looked like I'd been too soft.

Thinking of Grace made me edgy. What news had the doctors given her family? Her silence was suffocating.

Overhead, the moon played hide-and-seek behind sweeping gray clouds. The universe's mysteries made me wish I'd paid more attention in science classes. My life might be better had I been more studious. But longing for a different life erased my son, my salon, and other bright spots, so I backed away from that and wished only for Carter to be okay.

When no sign of mercy or other message revealed itself, I headed inside, where I leaned with my back against the kitchen door and hung my head.

Cleaning up hadn't quieted the recurring images of Carter splayed on the basement floor in utter shock and agony. Grace had freaked out when Kim cut her own bangs, so she probably wasn't coping well tonight. Their family's misery rooted me in place as if wet sand filled my limbs.

I dragged myself to the counter to check my phone for a message. Still nothing. I'd lost track of how many times hot tears had coated my eyes tonight. Honestly, my eyeballs might melt at this rate. But whenever I closed them, a sickening mantra played on an endless loop: What would become of us all?

As I shucked out of my coat and tossed it on a kitchen chair, Rowan reappeared wearing plaid pajama pants and a Tigers football T-shirt, his arms hugging his waist. His ashen face looked years younger than fifteen, which I guessed made sense, considering he'd been fingerprinted and processed mere hours ago. "Mom?"

I set one hand on the counter to steady myself, but all I wanted right then was to fall into bed. In my fantasy, I'd slip into a peaceful sleep and wake up to good news. "I thought you went to bed?"

"My texts keep going off. Word is spreading that I ratted everyone out." Color flooded his pale face as he choked on despair. "I didn't want to, but you made me give that cop my phone even though I told you I didn't see what happened. I swear, no one wanted Carter to get hurt like that. Now they're probably getting arrested. How will I go to school when everyone hates me?"

Unfortunately, I knew that kind of dread, having long suffered as an outcast for reasons I'd never fully understood. Grace had been a rare exception: a friend from the beginning despite our opposite personalities. Because of them, perhaps.

She'd been the one who'd encouraged me to open my own shop, and on its first day, she'd arrived with champagne and let me give her any haircut I wanted—so unlike her to give up that control. It proved how much she trusted me, and her faith had meant everything. I wouldn't own that shop or be handling divorced life half as well without her.

The fact that her son got hurt because of mine and his friends planted a sharp ache deep in my chest.

Neither my son nor I could turn back time, but we could show integrity. "There's no shame in telling the truth and cooperating. When good people mess up, they take their lumps." The time Uncle Tommy accused me of stealing four dollars from his coffee can of cash to buy a sleeve of colorful hair scrunchies came back to me. There'd been so many dollar bills in that can I could hardly believe he'd noticed. But once caught, I'd copped to my crime. Like he always said, confession is the first step toward redemption. Channeling him, I said, "It's hard, but it'll make you stronger in the long run. Let those other kids and parents blame you, and me. Heck, some will even blame Carter. Crazy, I know, how people like to make excuses rather than take responsibility. But, Rowan, I'm not built that way, and I hope you aren't, either. If we could've done things differently to have prevented this, we need to own that, okay? It's called integrity, and as long as you've got that, you'll always like yourself no matter what other people say." Most of the time, anyway.

His shoulders drooped after he wiped away tears with his forearm. "Why would you get blamed? You didn't do anything wrong."

Didn't I? "I left a group of teen boys alone in a house with liquor. I should've hidden the booze, or at least let the other parents know you'd be here unsupervised."

He dropped his head for a moment and mumbled, "I'm sorry it got out of hand."

When kids are little, we teach them to apologize, like that is enough in and of itself. As an adult, I'd rarely found that even a heartfelt "sorry" did the full job. The first time I caught Dirk cheating, he'd seemed sorry, until he'd done it again. Contrition without action was meaningless.

"I keep thinking about Dad." He repeatedly bumped his butt against the refrigerator in a rocking motion.

"Dad?" I scowled because Rowan should have been more concerned with his own mistakes, disappointing me, and the fact that a boy he'd known since they were wearing Pull-Ups was in the hospital. "Why are you thinking about him?"

"He's gonna be so mad and think I'm a loser." Rowan's face crumpled. "He barely sees me now. This will make it even worse. What if he hates me for it?"

Slam! Guilt flooded my system again. I'd never escape how my divorce had hurt my son. I crossed to Rowan and wrapped him in a hug—as much for my own comfort as for his. "Honey, he doesn't think you're a loser, and he could never hate you." But Dirk would probably find a way to blame me for everything. Maybe he wouldn't even be wrong.

"He's gonna kill me." Rowan burrowed his head against my shoulder.

My son never worried about whether I would kill him or stop loving him. You'd think my dependability would be rewarded with kindness and deference. Instead, he saved his best behavior for his father and took out his worst on me. "He won't kill you, but I'll call him first thing tomorrow and explain everything, okay?"

Rowan eased away, nodding. "I only invited Carter because you told me to get the guys to back off, but now look—it's all worse and I'm getting blamed."

I rubbed my hand over my chest to loosen the gathering tightness. While I'd worried that meddling could backfire, I hadn't foreseen this unholy mess. "Honey, we all have regrets, but I'm honestly too tired for this conversation right now. Go on up to bed and we'll discuss how we can make amends in the morning." I kissed his head.

He took a step away and then stopped to glance over his shoulder. "Have you heard from Mrs. Phillips?"

I shook my head and set a hand over my stomach, which twisted again, as if the full strength of Grace's suffering had reached inside me and squeezed. "Obviously they've got a lot going on tonight. We won't know anything for a while, so say some prayers for hopeful news."

Rowan's chin wobbled. "What if he can't walk? What's going to happen to us and everyone?"

My brain ached from the uncertainty. "I don't know, Rowan. But you should be more worried about Carter than about the boys who pushed him around—or even us—right now." My tone carried a note of warning.

He jabbed his elbow back against the wall with a growl. Classic Dirk move. Genetics could be a bitch—or maybe it was learned behavior. Either way, I lacked the stamina to lecture him at this hour. He muttered something before barking, "This sucks so bad."

*Welcome to adulthood,* I wanted to say but didn't. "Fretting and crying won't change one damn thing, Rowan, so pull yourself together. When the shit hits the fan, the only way out is to dig deep and think about what you can do to make it better. Now please go get some sleep. Tomorrow we'll come up with a plan."

He hung his head, turned around, and left the kitchen. His footfalls broke the silence as he trudged up the steps. When his door clicked shut, I closed my eyes and thought about Dirk. The knot in my chest coiled tighter, but he should hear about this from me, not the grapevine. I scrubbed my face two or three times before reaching for my phone and texting.

Hey, it's me. There was an incident tonight at the house involving our son that we need to talk about. I want you to hear it from me first, so call me when you get this message.

Thinking of my ex reminded me of poor Rich Polanti. The man deserved an apology. He would probably read about the party in this week's local paper and rejoice in his narrow escape from me and my problems, but it'd been rude to bolt without explanation. I texted him a quick apology, then turned off the lights to go upstairs and rest. On my way through the living room, my phone rang. Dirk . . . at this hour?

"I didn't mean to wake you," I answered without preamble.

"I'm up. What happened?" The slight slur told me he'd been drinking. Same with that husky rasp he got after a night with the guys. The only good thing about those warning signs was how they reminded me that I didn't need or want him in my life anymore.

I slumped onto the nearest living room chair and summarized what had transpired.

"Jesus Christ, Mimi. Arrested?"

"Yep. Supplying minors. But at least he didn't get arrested in connection with Carter's injuries like some of the other boys involved might. Honestly, I'm a little worried that the push was intentional. The team has been giving Carter and others a hard time because of their parents' position in the stupid budget debate. But if Carter is permanently hurt—" My stomach clenched. "Oh Lord, thinking about it makes me want to throw up."

"And you're sure Rowan had nothing to do with that?"

I nodded even though he couldn't see me. "Pretty sure. He was too scared to lie to me or the cops. And the cops haven't come back, so no one else must've accused him. He says he was with a girl in his room when it happened."

Dirk grunted. "He'd better be using condoms."

"We've talked about being responsible and respectful to women." *Because you weren't,* I almost added. Fortunately, I kept my big mouth shut. Not that I was thrilled that my fifteen-year-old was throwing parties and having sex while other kids trashed the house. "He's made mistakes, but he's a good kid."

"He stole your rum, hosted a damn party, and had a girl in his room, so you're naive to take him at his word." Dirk cursed softly. "Why'd he do something this stupid?"

As if Dirk had never thrown a party, drunk beer, or had sex in high school—although it'd be a bad idea to spout the pot-and-kettle saying now.

"He says it snowballed. When I left, there were four boys playing video games." Five, if I counted finding Carter outside. "News of the empty house spread on social media. When kids showed up with booze, he didn't know how to turn them away."

Hearing my justifications only strengthened Dirk's point. Did I whitewash my son's faults? Still, Dirk brought out the bull in me, and his lectures were a red cape I charged at despite the chance of getting speared.

"I warned you letting those kids drink would come back to bite you." Dirk clucked his tongue. I closed my eyes, absorbing the blow. Others were also thinking it. More evidence to justify their low opinions of me even though many allowed the same thing. "When his coaches get wind of this, he could be kicked off the team."

"Football season is over." If this were in season, it'd be a different ball game—no pun intended. However, the arrest could keep Rowan from becoming a captain in his senior year. And depending on the severity of Carter's injuries, the school might make examples of every-one involved. If Rowan couldn't play football, it'd kill him. Worse, his chance at an affordable college education would die—they don't hand out Division I offers to kids who get kicked off teams. But Dirk's mak-ing this all about my mistakes pissed me off. "While you're criticizing me, remember that Rowan wouldn't have been at home tonight if you hadn't blown him off this weekend. What the hell was so important that you had to disappoint your son?"

"Don't change the subject and turn this on me."

I rolled my eyes toward heaven. "You're right—it's a waste of time to ask you to take responsibility for anything, including Rowan." Missed child support payments, skipped visits—he had some gall to scold me.

"You want me to take responsibility, you got it. Maybe we start by moving Rowan here since you obviously can't manage a teenage boy."

Yeah, right. He couldn't handle the responsibility for more than three days, and Miranda wasn't interested in raising Rowan. "Don't threaten me when you've hardly been around these past five years. Why do you think he's so insecure he couldn't turn all the partiers away? If you need someone to blame, look in the damned mirror."

"Christ, I don't miss your bitching. You'd better pray that Carter can still walk, or this will get way worse for you and Rowan. Especially since you didn't even lawyer up before cooperating. Honestly, Mimi, your knack for making things worse is unbelievable."

"Gee, thanks. And your concern for Carter is real heartwarming, by the way. Go to hell, Dirk." I hit "End" and threw my phone across the table, where it landed on the sofa, and then I bent over and hugged my legs.

I remained crouched that way for minutes, shivering as every emotion wormed through my veins.

Giving Dirk an inch felt like having my teeth pulled without novocaine, but he hadn't been all wrong. I'd been easy on Rowan these past few years, trying to lift him out of the blues whenever he'd get upset about missing his dad or when he struggled at school. Bending a rule or two had seemed harmless enough, especially when compared with the alternative—a mulish kid who never spoke to me.

Since Rowan's birth, I'd been determined that things between us would not be like the pins-and-needles relationship I'd had with Uncle Tommy. He hadn't been cruel so much as indifferent. Having been forced to move to that tiny, religious community in Virginia had been especially tough on me—with my fondness for Gwen Stefani and her belly shirts.

Looking back, I think it was even harder on my uncle. He never brought a single date home in those six years he raised me. At the time, I didn't think much of it, but as I got older, I realized he'd never talked about or flirted with women. After a while, I assumed he was gay and hid it from fear of his community's reaction or because he'd been raised to believe it a sin. It made me sad to think of him stuffing down his need for love to pacify some community bigots, but it also made his eagerness for my departure and his own privacy feel less personal.

To this day I had no idea if I was right, but he never mentioned a girlfriend when I called him. Regardless of the reasons he and I weren't especially close, it'd kill me if Rowan were counting the days to his eighteenth birthday like I'd done then.

My relaxed style had seemed to be working. Rowan didn't fear me. I'd thought that meant we were close. But in truth, he might not respect me much, either, which was a consequence I hadn't ever considered. If I couldn't even win my son's respect, no wonder I struggled to win it from others.

Dirk's warning about the football team lingered. Maybe Rowan and I should call the coach first thing tomorrow—even if I had to track him down at home. Better to meet this head-on than wait until he heard the news through the rumor mill.

Good Lord, I'd bet this had already hit the moms' Facebook group. Not that I wanted to dig for pain right now. The ugly comments would be there in the morning, waiting to stab me in the eyes and heart. Was it mere hours ago I'd been celebrating how my life had been improving? Man, that made this hurt worse.

But self-pity seemed a childish waste of energy when I pictured Carter on my basement floor.

I pounded on my thighs as punishment for my selfish worries when that poor boy might never walk again. The very idea of paralysis bounced off my brain like a rubber ball off cement. Rejection, pure and simple. I could neither accept it nor live with the guilt if it came to pass.

I pushed out of the chair, grabbed my phone, and tried Grace once more. When it went straight to voice mail again, I dialed Sam.

"Hello?" came his exhausted voice.

"Sam. It's Mimi." I braced, but he didn't bite my head off or hang up. "I've tried Grace a few times, but she's not answering. Is there any news?"

A pause ensued. "Not yet. I can't talk long. Grace will be back from the restroom any minute." He made it sound almost as if she'd been avoiding my calls, which caused a new kind of pain to erupt.

I listened, sinking onto the sofa in tears as Sam explained all they knew. "Oh God, Sam. I'm so sorry. What can I do? Can I come get Kim for you?"

"She's with Becky, thanks."

My eyes widened. After ten years of learning about Grace's childhood and watching her and her mom interact, I knew she hated having to ask her mother for help.

"Oh. Well, I can watch her tomorrow or whenever. Or drive up now and sit with you and Grace. Anything at all. Please. I need to do something."

"No, don't come here, Mimi. Grace isn't in the mood to deal with anyone. It's best if you sit back and wait it out. We won't know anything for twelve to twenty-four hours, anyway."

For the first time since Rowan had called me tonight, I realized that this incident might affect our friendship. My eyes filled with tears. "Of course I'll wait. I don't mean to push. I'm worried, is all."

He sniffled. "I shouldn't have convinced Grace to let Carter go to Rowan's party. I thought it'd get him over the hump with the bullying."

"Wait." My body turned cold as I straightened my spine. "Are you saying the party was planned?" I glanced toward the steps to Rowan's bedroom.

"Far as I know. Carter said that on Friday afternoon Rowan had invited him to a party. He was excited to hang with the 'pretty' girls."

Sam's voice faltered a second time. "I just wanted him to be happy. We assumed you'd be at home, but we got so busy with Kim's birthday party neither of us followed up. Jesus, I wish I could take it all back."

Sitting alone in the dark while listening to a brokenhearted man falling apart stilled everything but my heart, which throbbed with the load of everyone's pain. Fresh tears clogged my nose, the growing sense of Rowan's and my blame for all this deepening.

"It's not your fault, Sam. If I'd had any idea there'd been a party planned, I would've stayed home." I dropped my head to my free hand. Maybe I was the biggest idiot on the planet, always looking for the best in everyone. My son had lied to me, like Dirk had guessed. And I'd ignored Carter's hesitation on the lawn because I wanted to believe that my talk with Rowan had worked. "Sam, would you mind texting me any updates? I'm beside myself with worry. And please give Carter and Grace a big hug from me. You're all in my thoughts and prayers tonight." I might even text Uncle Tommy to put Carter on his church's prayer list, or ask him how this was part of God's plan. For so long I'd believed God had a big plan for each of us, so I hadn't worried much about my daily decisions. Maybe Grace was right, though. Maybe we did control our own destinies.

Sam cleared his throat after pulling himself together. "Listen, I've got to go now. Appreciate the call, but it's not a good time."

"Of course. Bye!" I hung up without any promise of updates.

I set the phone on the coffee table, shut off the lamp, and curled into a ball, too exhausted to take Rowan to task for lying to me. That could wait until breakfast. Was dealing with his arrest enough of a consequence for him, or should I take his phone and ground him? If tonight wasn't a wake-up call for me to rethink some of my parenting strategies, I didn't know what was.

Eerie blue light filled my quiet house. Please, God, *please* let Carter be okay. I rested my forehead against my knees, replaying the night. Self-doubts polluted my thoughts. Officer Martinez had been kind, but maybe he'd been lulling us into complacency to get Rowan to talk. It would've been smarter to have involved a lawyer before letting Rowan blab, but my conscience couldn't let us skirt responsibility after seeing Carter motionless on my floor.

Carter had to be okay. He just had to. Any other result was unbearable.

I hugged my knees tight, banging my forehead against them. My best friend might be avoiding me. None of us functioned well when heartsick and panicked, but I loved Grace and her family as much as I hated being helpless. There had to be some solution to bring us all together. Yet when I closed my eyes to think, only darkness came to me.

# CHAPTER EIGHT

## GRACE

*Sunday afternoon, January 10*
*Shock Trauma Hospital recovery room*

"Where are you going?" Sam whispered when I rose on weak legs from my seat beside Carter's bed thanks to a sum total of two hours' sleep, all of which had occurred in that uncomfortable chair.

"Downstairs. My mom texted. She and Kim are parking." I sighed, wishing my mother hadn't insisted on seeing Carter today. I had enough on my plate without her judgment piling on.

"I'll come, too." He pushed out of his seat.

"But Carter might wake up."

Sam looked at Carter, who appeared to be dead to the world. "He'll be fine for ten minutes."

I walked to the door, too exhausted to argue.

Glimpses of Sam were all I could tolerate after fifteen grueling hours of uncertainty, because instead of seeing my husband, all I saw was the face of the man who'd broken our pact. That spawned an unsettling emotional distance. It'd been twenty years since I'd handled anything on my own. I couldn't imagine coping with all these changes without Sam at my side, yet my anger intensified with every minute our son was in pain.

Sam could still stand and walk and run and jump. So could I. So could Mimi and Rowan and all the other kids who'd attended that party. But would my son, who'd never hurt a soul?

We strolled past open doors and a nurse station to the elevator, the endless cacophony of beeps and buzzing and chatter abrading my nerves. As we descended, I forced myself to study my husband. Disheveled bangs suggested he'd run his hands through his hair a hundred times. His pained face, etched with deep grooves and shadowed with purplish circles beneath his eyes, appeared a decade older than his forty-three years. In short, he was hurting as much as I.

In the past, we'd comforted each other with hugs and shoulder rubs, but not today. Yet my limbs and back ached for his touch. Mental images surfaced of him cheerfully massaging my feet when I was pregnant, bringing me breakfast in bed for days at a time after the births of our children, hugging me with a pep talk whenever my mother upset me, holding me endlessly after Margot's funeral. I grieved my shaken sense of security and certainty in our marriage.

The elevator doors opened, so we exited in silence and made our way toward the main lobby with its soaring glass walls. The flat, gray winter sky outside mirrored my mood.

"Daddy!" Kim's voice echoed off the cold surfaces as she ran to Sam's open arms.

He scooped her up and hugged her tight, as if the sheer force of his grip could heal us all. She slid to the ground as my mother caught up to us and gave Sam and me each a kiss.

"You look exhausted," she said, hand on her cheek.

I nodded, having no better response to something so obvious. "Thanks for watching Kim last night." I ran my hand over my daughter's hair, planting a quick kiss on her head.

"I loved having her. We made a candlelight breakfast this morning." She spoke to my kids like a female Mr. Rogers—such mellow tones and cadence. When I'd been Kim's age, my mother hadn't the time for or interest in whimsical treats like candlelit meals, having spent all her energy anticipating my dad's needs and blaming Vietnam for his faults. As a child, I'd never asked why she stayed with Daddy, but I'd never believed the answers she'd given Margot—about vows and God and the devil you know. I supposed that the occasional brief stretches of time that he'd stayed sober had given her hope that he'd get better. "Kim makes terrific french toast!"

"She does?" News to me. Then again, we didn't let Kim use the stove yet. Now she'd certainly leverage having gotten my mom's permission.

"Where's Carter?" Kim asked, looking around.

"In his room," I said. "He'll be here for a while, honey."

"How is he?" my mother asked, not having heard anything since the handoff in the wee hours.

"Dr. Acharya removed all of the bone fragments, including the ones that had put pressure on his spinal cord. He also took bone from the hip to graft to his spine," Sam said.

This experience had expanded my vocabulary. "Decompression" was the fancy term for removing the bone fragments from the narrow spinal canal. The hardware used to stabilize his spine—pedicle screws and rods—would be fused with bone grafts to take some of the load off the hardware.

"How did this happen?" Mom asked, fingers pressed to her temple. Thankfully, she hadn't asked the one question we all wanted the answer to: Would he walk?

I glanced at the floor. "He fell down the stairs at a party."

"Carter went to a party?" My mother's features pinched together, stunned speechless that I'd allowed him to do that given our experience with Margot's wild teen years. "How did he fall?"

"It's still unclear, but it sounds like there'd been some horseplay near the top of the steps . . . ," Sam added.

Horseplay. How many times had Mimi and others said things like "Boys will be boys" to minimize bad behavior? Why didn't anyone want to hold their kids accountable or take responsibility for the values—or lack thereof—they expressed? Kimmy never got a free pass when she acted bratty, even though punishments didn't improve my relationship with her. But in the long run, enforcing a certain level of respect and responsibility mattered.

"Were they drinking beer?" Kim's eyes were big as quarters now.

"Carter wasn't drinking," I clarified, looking at Kim. "The other boys were."

Alcohol at fifteen, as if the drinking age weren't twenty-one. Those boys and their parents walked around as if rules didn't apply to them. What is a society without rules? Anarchy, that's what.

Mom asked, "Did they push him on purpose?"

"Maybe," I said as Sam said, "I doubt it."

With my eyes closed, I shook my head. More evidence of a widening divide. Had he been pretending to agree with me in the past, and if so, why? What other things about our relationship had I taken for granted?

"There's been some animosity since the budget debate," Sam added, handing my mother ammunition. "The jocks have been harassing others, but I doubt they intended things to go this far."

My mother slapped both hands to her cheeks. "Oh, Gracie. I'd had a bad feeling."

I glared at Sam, who had the good sense to look sheepishly apologetic as soon as her subtle "told you so" slipped out.

"Can I please see him?" my mother asked me.

"He's sleeping, but you can come peek in. In fact, let's get back so we don't accidentally miss the doctor." I took Kim's hand, and we all walked back to the elevator.

On our way to Carter's room, I considered how Kim might react. His surgical wounds remained covered by bandages, but I'd seen the gruesome images when googling everything available online about his specific injury—an unstable burst fracture at the T12 vertebra—and the rigor of his surgery. Thinking of the lumpy, raised scars my son would have, like those in the photos I'd seen, made me want to rip the blinds off the rods and throw things around the hospital.

Before we entered Carter's room, I bent to Kim. "Honey, don't be nervous when you see Carter, and don't be loud. He's going to be in pain for a while, and if he's resting, I don't want to wake him."

Once she nodded, we entered. Carter's eyelids fluttered open as we gathered near his bed.

"Hi, sweetheart." My mother's voice choked.

"Good to see you, buddy," Sam said, relief flooding his eyes as Carter awakened.

"How do you feel?" I asked. "Are you thirsty?"

"Tired." He attempted to shift in the bed and then cried out in pain, his grimace making every muscle in my body taut.

Kim's chin trembled and she reached for Sam. My mother kept touching her own face, her expression fraught. The collective agony in the room closed in on me like a prison built from guilt and self-loathing. I'd never forgive myself for giving in about Rowan's party.

Whatever pain medications they'd given Carter must have been wearing off. Meanwhile, questions in my head exploded like popcorn: What had happened last night, who'd pushed him, could he sense his legs yet? I wouldn't interrogate him, so I asked, "Honey, what can I do?"

"Nothing." He closed his eyes, shutting us out. Hiding his feelings, like he often had since puberty struck. A trait he'd probably inherited from me.

As a child, I'd been trained to de-escalate conflict by withdrawing to my room, listening to music, and pretending my floral wallpaper was a field of daisies far away from the fighting downstairs. By my twenties, keeping the peace and obeying authority came as naturally as breathing. Yet Sam and I had never so much as argued in front of our kids, so Carter shouldn't have learned to swallow his feelings out of fear of reprisal.

Anxiety about my son's state of mind made me jittery.

I exhaled slowly, stroking his forehead and squeezing his hand. "It's okay. You don't have to talk. Just rest."

In truth, I didn't want answers that I wasn't sure I could handle. The unending hours of waiting for updates frayed my nerves. Helplessness cloyed, and my body sank onto the chair like deadweight.

Heightened awareness of my beating heart, of the blood flowing through my veins, of the itch of my dry skin, or a twitch of my calf—all the little bodily miracles that we take for granted—grabbed hold. My son had never been an athlete, but he'd enjoyed hiking and swimming. He'd enjoyed his independence. How would he handle losing all that if that came to pass? Without warning I began to weep silent, terrified tears. Kim climbed onto my lap to hug me, settling her cheek on my shoulder. Greedily I absorbed the affection despite not deserving a lick of it.

Sam kissed the top of my head and then filled the pitcher with water, which he set on the overbed table. Carter hadn't kept his eyes open long enough to notice the red rims of his father's eyes, but I did. He stood like a sentry on the other side of Carter's bed. Did he regret giving permission to go to Rowan's, or notice this stiffness settling between us, or have a solution to put our family back together?

I had no idea how much time had passed—having lost all sense of it since last night—when a stout nurse whose build reminded me of a bulldog appeared. Her jolly countenance seemed at odds with the ghastly injuries she witnessed every day.

I could never work someplace with such sorrow and pain, and with so many things beyond anyone's control. Then again, apparently I hadn't had nearly as much control of my own life as I'd believed.

"How are you folks hanging in?" She checked the time and made a note on Carter's chart.

I jumped out of my seat, rubbing my biceps as if I were freezing. "Okay, thanks. Anxious."

The nurse nodded sympathetically, then looked at Carter, who'd opened his eyes upon hearing her voice. "You're lucky. None of your organs were damaged by the fracture, which means you won't have any trouble controlling your bowels and bladder. That's a big win." She flashed a gummy smile while checking the IV. I hadn't remembered that those were concerns, but was relieved for any good news. "Are you comfortable enough?"

Carter nodded, although maybe he was too tired to complain. He stared at her as if holding his breath. Perhaps, like me, he dreaded the answer to the only question for which he most wanted an answer.

"What now?" I asked.

"He'll stay for four or five days so we can monitor his post-op progress and watch for any signs of possible infection or other complications. After that, we'll transfer him to our inpatient rehab facility. The doctor will give you more updates in the coming days, but usually patients with your son's deficits are there for at least four weeks, probably six, sometimes longer. When he's ready to be released, he'll go home to you, but will likely have months of outpatient rehab. A lot depends on his progress in therapy."

I nodded, taking it all in.

Kim moved on from me to hug Sam's leg. My mother stood back, her face scrubbed to that blank expression she'd worn after a bad fight with my dad or when Margot started coming home drunk, which left me guessing what she was thinking.

While the nurse moved around Carter's head and checked the lines and equipment, my mind wandered, organizing a to-do list. At a minimum, I had to cancel my piano lessons for the foreseeable future, talk to Carter's teachers, hire tutors . . . And then there was Kim. A sick pit opened in my gut as I acknowledged the best thing for my daughter would be if my mother temporarily moved in with us to help care for her in my absence. Jesus, this would be daunting even if Carter regained sensation in his legs.

My list evaporated the instant Dr. Acharya stepped into the room. "I'm on my way out, but thought the patient might be awake now."

"He is." I donned a tremulous smile.

Carter groggily cleared his throat, his voice raspy. "Hi."

"Hello, champ. You came through surgery great." The doctor threw back the blanket and sheet to expose my son's feet. "I'd like to do a quick test. Tell me if you feel anything."

I held my breath.

When Dr. Acharya swiped a metal instrument across my son's right footpad, two of Carter's toes contracted. Was that a good sign? My stomach squeezed.

Carter blinked fat tears onto his cheeks. "I think maybe a tingle."

The doctor said nothing but ran the instrument over the other foot. More toes flinched.

"I felt something—a little, but the other foot." Hope edged his voice. "Is that right, or am I imagining it?"

"No, that's right, and it's a good sign." Dr. Acharya didn't exactly smile, but his expression relaxed.

*A good sign.* A relieved sob bubbled up from inside, so I covered my face. My mother and Sam exhaled.

"Like I mentioned before, your spine has undergone trauma, so there's a lot of swelling, which can confuse the nerves and cut off sensation. I told your parents that we successfully removed all the fragments without causing additional damage. As the swelling subsides, the hope is that you'll regain all sensation and some or full control of your legs. We'll know more in the coming days, but I'm encouraged. You'll experience muscle weakness as a result of the nerve injury, but let's see what unfolds as you work with the therapists." Dr. Acharya spoke to Carter about the road ahead, and the hard work and complications that could ensue. I tried to focus, but exhaustion mingled with the tiniest relief made it difficult for me to process new information.

When the doctor finished, I followed him into the hallway. "So you think he'll walk again?" I asked.

"We're moving in the right direction." He offered a slight smile instead of an affirmative reply. "I'll see you tomorrow."

"Thank you." I swiped my cheek dry, refraining from hugging him, as he didn't appear the type who'd welcome it. He'd left room for hope, so I would cling to it.

When I returned to Carter, I silently thanked God for this small chance. My son could feel his feet. With dedication and hard work, he might walk again. And no one was more dedicated and hardworking than my beautiful boy.

"I love you so much, sweetie," I said.

"Do you think he's telling the truth?" Carter asked, his anxious gaze darting back and forth between Sam and me.

The desperation in his eyes made me equally frantic to ease his mind. "Doctors don't lie—"

Unaware of the gravity of our situation, Kim interrupted. "Can I use your Xbox while you're here?"

"Not now, Kim," I said.

My mother shot me a disapproving look before pulling Kim to her side and rubbing her shoulders. I regretted my tone, but the cortisol coursing through me had me strung tight.

Carter pressed. "Do you think I'll be able to walk again?"

His despair strangled me into silence.

Sam gripped Carter's hand and leaned close, fixing his steady gaze on our son. "I'm encouraged by what he said and what you felt. If it's possible, you'll make it happen. I've never known anyone more determined than you, son."

Carter's facial muscles relaxed. As usual, Sam's easy manner and confidence had calmed our child much the way it had always soothed me. I was grateful, if a bit envious, of that talent. For so long I'd seen my job as protecting my kids, but it would be lovely to also reassure them.

Carter fell silent, his gaze unfocused. Too soon the space between his eyebrows creased with worry lines.

"What's the matter, honey?" I frowned. He had a catheter, so he didn't need to use the bathroom. "Are you hungry, or do you want to rest?"

He worried his lip, his eyes now as wide as Sugar Momma's cookies. "The cops were there when we left. What's happening to Rowan and the others?"

"The police were at the party?" Kim's fascinated expression might have been comical under other circumstances.

"I don't know," I answered Carter. Aside from the run-in with that cop in the waiting room hours ago, I'd hardly spared a thought to any of the others since climbing into the ambulance.

Sam cleared his throat. "I spoke with Mrs. Gillette earlier this morning. She's extremely sorry about what happened and sends her love, but didn't mention what the police have determined, or if any charges are being filed."

"You spoke with Mimi?" Other than my few trips to the restroom, we'd been together all night. Why had he kept it a secret? The flash of anger turned to envy because, unlike him, I couldn't take comfort in talking with my friend today.

From the corner of my eye, I noted my mother's hand cover her mouth. She probably thought it suspicious that another woman had called my husband, but she'd never understood how intertwined my life and Mimi's had become. Since Dirk left, Mimi contacted Sam about everything from simple plumbing problems to tax questions.

"She tried me when she couldn't reach you. She's worried about everyone and asked for updates. Why don't you call her now and fill her in?" Sam projected his "please do the right thing" look my way without apologizing for keeping this from me for hours.

Normally the "right thing" with Mimi was as obvious as the sun in the sky, but now a fog of doubts descended. Why had she gone on a date and left the boys alone with alcohol? Even if she hadn't permitted this particular party, she'd been careless with other people's children. And had she ever sought other parents' permission before letting their boys drink beer? Surely no parent had the right to make those important choices for other people's kids.

"Maybe later, Sam. I'm still processing what the doctor told us." I then turned to Carter. "Honey, whatever's happening with those kids, their parents will help them deal with it. Your only job is to recuperate. Stressing out over that other stuff will hurt your recovery."

"Where's my phone?" Carter asked.

Social media chatter would only work him up. The first shots of a parental battle over this party had probably cropped up on the moms' Facebook group before breakfast. I'd been praying too hard to bother checking. "You're barely out of surgery. Let's leave the phone be until tomorrow."

"Dad," Carter begged, turning from me.

Sam's hesitation told me he didn't agree, but he said, "Your mom is right. Relax and rest. Everything will still be there in the morning."

I would've mouthed a thank-you, but everyone would've seen me.

"I'll ask the nurse what you're allowed to eat. There may be restrictions for a few days, but I'm happy to bring you your favorite meals." I held my son's hand.

"I'm not hungry." Carter stared at the ceiling. If only I could hear his thoughts, I'd know how to help him.

"Well, let me know anything else you want from home. Your laptop, comfortable loungewear, slippers . . ."

He shrugged, uninterested in such details. Even that small gesture made him yelp. A reminder of the pain and scars he'd carry around forever. The only thing holding me together was the fact that he wasn't falling apart. My mother remained suspiciously silent, but I preferred that to more of her "should've" statements.

"We probably ought to get Kim settled at home and make some arrangements soon," Sam said to me, then glanced at our son. "If you think of things you want us to bring back, let us know."

"I'm not going anywhere." I shook my head.

Sam blinked. "I suppose I could take Kim home, and you could Uber later."

"No. I mean I'm staying the night." I flashed my son a smile so he knew it wouldn't be any burden.

After catching my attention, Sam turned his hands over. "There are visiting hours."

"Then I'll ask for an exception." I gestured to Carter. "He's only fifteen and has been through a huge ordeal. I want to be here in case anything changes or if he needs company. I also don't want to miss seeing the doctor in the morning because we're stuck in traffic."

"Is that workable, though? We need to figure out all the moving pieces, like getting Kim off to school. We need to make long-term arrangements." Sam stared at me as if waiting for me to wake up. If he didn't understand why Carter's security and comfort outweighed any other consideration today, what else could I say? This new disconnect between us couldn't have come at a worse time.

"I can help with Kim," my mother offered, then promptly hunched as if bracing for a blow.

Granted, I might've bristled. But her posture irritated me because I'd never once tried to hurt her. If anything, I'd gone out of my way to repress my resentment because she was the only family I had left.

For two seconds, no one made a peep. There was no better solution, but I struggled to trust my mother to keep my children safe when she'd failed miserably with Margot and me.

"That's very kind, Becky. Could you excuse us for a second?" Sam gestured to the door, so I followed him out of Carter's room.

Sam drew a breath, tapping his fingers against his mouth while considering what he wanted to say. I folded my arms beneath my chest and waited him out, too aware of how this situation had killed our ability to read each other's minds. "Grace, I don't think it's a good idea to baby Carter. He's facing a lot of time away from home, and making him afraid of being alone or having him relying too heavily on you to make everything better won't help him in the long run."

My jaw nearly hit the floor. "You're not serious right now, are you? He *just* got out of major surgery."

"I know, and if they'll make an exception, then sleep here tonight. But you can't ignore Kim's needs all week. Once Carter is settled, we need to come up with a workable game plan."

I flinched. "I can't think about the future when I'm still catching up with what's happening now. Let's take my mom up on her offer. That gives me the freedom to see how things unfold this week. By Friday, we'll have a better idea of what to expect, and then we can make long-term plans. If you want to be more involved this week, maybe you could work from home to help deal with Kim after school."

Sam made a face. He wasn't wrong to be concerned. My mother could be spacey, and Kim was likely to take advantage of our absence and manipulate her in any number of ways. "Despite your mom's intentions, we both know she'll struggle with Kim. Mimi offered to watch her for a few days. That would take the burden off your mom, and maybe then you and I could get a hotel room up here for a few days."

"You want to hand Kim over to Mimi after what she did to Carter?" My words felt like razors coming up through my throat.

"Mimi didn't hurt Carter, Grace. You can't blame her." He crossed his arms, a signal that he was losing his patience with me. Well, ditto.

"It's hard not to, given that this happened at her house among Rowan and his friends." My body buzzed as if someone had plugged me in. For Rowan to let things go so far suggested he was becoming more like his father than Mimi or I would have hoped.

Sam shook his head. "We still don't know what happened."

"And we won't until Carter is ready to talk. Until then, maybe we shouldn't speak to anyone else involved." My heart split in two, creating a piercing ache in my chest. I loved Mimi. Every time I looked out my kitchen window at the cherry tree she'd bought me on the fifteenth anniversary of Margot's death, it reminded me of her generosity and love. She would be beside herself with regret and worry today, but I was running on empty, and the person who most needed my love and protection was my son. I'd failed him once. Never again.

Sam closed his eyes and breathed deeply. "We're both upset and concerned, so I'm trying to give you a lot of rope, Grace. But in this case, we need to follow Carter's lead, not the other way around. This happened to him, not you. You weren't there, so whatever he says goes."

"Carter is a child. You and I are the grown-ups. You don't let children make decisions that require adult experience and comprehension." I scowled. "Look at what happened when we gave in to him this weekend."

I didn't know where that urge to lash out with sarcasm had come from, but the betrayal in Sam's eyes hit me like a bullet. We'd never hurt each other before. "Sorry. I'm exhausted and on the verge of collapse. Please, let's first focus on getting through the next twenty-four hours. I can't think beyond that."

"Fine." We didn't hug or smile like we usually did when coming to a decision together. Instead, he rocked back on his feet. "Becky can watch Kim this week. I'll book us a hotel room nearby and take a few days off work."

"Thank you." I sighed at the hollow victory. His uncommon coolness proved he was still smarting. For whatever reason, I could not make myself reach for him. That scared me almost as much as Carter's injuries. Until I had a better handle on my son's status, I couldn't deal with my marriage. "Do you have that card the cop gave you? We should let them know they can come talk to Carter."

Sam shook his head slowly, then reached into his wallet and retrieved it. "Here. You call since you're so eager to assign blame."

I clasped his arm. "You think I'm being a monster, but tell me why you aren't more interested in getting justice for our son."

"If Carter tells us that those boys pushed him on purpose, then I'll encourage him to press charges. But I don't want this situation to rip apart our friendships or our marriage and family, Grace. That would make it all more tragic."

As soon as I let him go, he disappeared into the room, leaving me alone. His words repeated like a yellow caution light.

I flicked the card, debating with myself.

The cops wanted to talk to Carter—that was the law, not some extraordinary request of an overwrought mother. And by God, when we'd played fast and loose with the law about attending Rowan's party, our carefully planned world had gotten upended.

I glanced at the open door, knowing Carter needed more rest before any interrogation. The call could wait until morning, but I would make it then.

# CHAPTER NINE

## MIMI

*Monday, January 11, 6:45 a.m.*
*Mimi's kitchen*

"I don't want to go to school." Rowan wore the same pained expression he'd sported since Saturday night.

"Last I checked, school wasn't optional." Things at home had been rocky since yesterday, when he admitted that he'd planned the party—although he swore it had gotten bigger than he'd intended. Until this weekend I'd trusted my mothering instincts. All these years of being his buddy—someone he could talk to who wouldn't judge him—had landed us here. Yet playing a hard-ass did not come naturally. I'd grounded him, which hardly seemed like much punishment considering most of his friends would also be grounded.

"Mom!" he moaned, tossing his phone across the table. "Look at the hate because I talked to the cops. I'm gonna get crushed."

The phone's screen lit up with each new message like a fireworks show.

"No one said it'd be easy." I winced, remembering the ugly comments posted to the Potomac Point Moms Facebook group last night. It wouldn't have surprised me if my computer screen had started to ooze tar and sprout feathers.

It was one thing to have suspected many had tolerated me out of respect for Grace, quite another to see their disdain on display. And these women were out for blood—specifically mine. Multiple versions of accusations like All the kids knew that Mimi let boys drink at her house, so it's no wonder something like this happened hadn't been a shock, but It should've been Rowan on the floor had literally made me cry. That kind of cruelty went so far beyond the thinly veiled judgment I'd finally begun to overcome in recent weeks. Now I wasn't back to square one; I was ten paces behind it. "But we can't move out of town, Rowan. My business is here, with a lease I can't break. And playing on this high school team can get you a football scholarship."

"Just let me stay home today. Please." He pulled the phone back to his side of the table.

His suffering hurt me, especially because I blamed myself. I'd been lax about parties and imposed merely a stern discussion whenever he screwed up, creating an environment where he and his friends thought they could do as they pleased. Uncle Tommy would be so ashamed. Heck, my own parents might even be disappointed. They hadn't imposed a bunch of rules, but they'd had more expectations of me in terms of chores and manners than I'd required of Rowan.

"Putting it off will only prolong your anxiety. Own what you did, and make your friends own what they did. You didn't hold a gun to anyone's head, and you sure didn't force anyone to give Carter a hard time." That was the truth. I'd made mistakes, but I hadn't raised a bully.

My son's shoulders slouched; his jaw bulged from grinding his teeth.

After I removed a tray of cookies from the oven and set it on the stove top, I crossed to him and gave his shoulders a squeeze. We both needed a hug and some hope. Harkening back to my cheerleader days, I tried to rally him. "Honey, I hope this is the hardest thing you'll ever do in your life. Look at it like any other challenge—like building muscles. This is a character-building moment that may end up changing who you become, hopefully for the better. You want to be a captain one day? Be a leader now."

He glanced up at me, doubt in his eyes, but grabbed for a warm cookie. "Why'd you make these for breakfast?"

I'd been up at dawn, racked with uneasy energy and needing a project. Using a spatula to transfer the cookies to a cooling rack, I said, "They're for Carter. He loves my double chocolate chips. He also loves my homemade mac 'n' cheese, so I'm making an extra tray to take over to Grace's." The last thing she'd be thinking about right now was cooking, but her family needed to be fed. "Hopefully when I go over there, I'll learn what's happening. The not knowing is killing me, and the hospital won't tell me squat 'cause I'm not family."

Those folks didn't know that Grace treated me like family. Once she'd learned about my parents' deaths and my lack of close family connections, she'd consistently invited me and mine to holidays, birthdays, and even on a few vacations despite never much warming to Dirk. She'd been the sister I'd never had, and I'd filled the hole that Margot had left behind long before that poor young woman died. Our relationship was one of the biggest blessings in my life.

Rowan shook his head. "That's not a good idea, Mom. If the Phillipses aren't calling you, they probably don't want to see you. They probably hate us now."

The sting of tears gathered behind my nose, but I kept them at bay. Our differences had always brought out the best in Grace and me, so I held on to hope that this time would be no different once the dust settled. "Grace is too overwhelmed to think of us now, but I can't sit here and do nothing. Today is my only day off, so I've got to make it count. Now quit stalling and get yourself to school."

"What if everyone comes at me?" His whole face looked three inches longer from the way his mouth and eyes turned downward.

"If you get harassed, go to the guidance counselor or to your coach."

"Coach hates snitches."

I shook my head. "This isn't like telling on someone for skipping practice or pulling a locker room prank, Rowan. He's an adult. He'll be upset with everyone, not only with you."

"Great." Rowan rolled his eyes.

Ooh, I wanted to grab him by the chin for acting like he drew the short stick when it was Carter who'd ended up in the hospital. Maybe grounding him hadn't been punishment enough, because his attitude was far from what it should be. Grace would have advice about how to impose more discipline without creating a ruckus, but she had enough on her mind.

I'd be more empathetic with Rowan if fate had simply shown up and ruined things, but this time what had happened had more to do with bad decisions than bad luck. Like when I'd fallen for that sob story Debbie Winters sold me about her husband being out of work. I believed in second chances, so I'd hired her to clean my salon even after Grace warned me that Debbie had a drug habit. At first, a missing bottle of shampoo here and a hair mask there didn't faze me, but then cash went missing from the register and Debbie never came back to work. "When you gamble, you gotta handle the losses."

Rowan grabbed his backpack, snagged a second cookie, and slunk out the back door like he was being dragged to his execution.

"Love you, but come straight home after school!" I hollered as he closed the door. After refilling the baking sheet with raw cookie dough, I swiped a fingerful for myself, then set the timer and began to clean up while the last batch baked. Normally, I hated to clean, but right now anything that kept my mind occupied was a relief.

I usually operated under the "no news is good news" theory. But the fact that Grace still hadn't called with any update tied my stomach in a tangle. Still, I kept my impulses in check, giving her time to wrap her arms around whatever news they got.

After scanning the fridge and seeing that I needed some ingredients for the mac 'n' cheese, I brushed my hair while waiting to take the last batch of cookies out of the oven. Once they were cooling, I hustled to the market.

Last Monday I'd bumped into Grace. It wasn't uncommon—small town, small store. I rarely came here without running into at least one person I knew. But if I had known Carrie Castle would be here today, I might've worn a floppy hat and dark glasses.

"Mimi." She practically sneered as we crossed paths on our way to the registers.

"Hi, Carrie," I replied evenly. Carrie had kept her distance ever since her husband had paid a little too much attention to me at one of Grace's potluck parties six years ago. Not that Dirk had noticed or cared.

She looked at my cart, which was piled high. "Throwing another party?"

My cheeks got hot. Maybe I deserved that, but with the echo of the ugly Facebook comments rattling around my head, I wanted to punch back. Of course, sparring with a woman who'd never been my friend seemed ridiculous given all that had happened.

"No." I waved a hand to prove she couldn't get to me. "I'm making Grace's family dinner and picking up some extra groceries to save her a trip."

Carrie's expression shifted, if reluctantly. "That's thoughtful."

"The least I could do." The very least. In fact, maybe I could mobilize other women in town to do the same. They didn't have to like me so long as they liked Grace—and lots of people liked Grace because she treated everyone with dignity. I'd have to go back on that stupid moms' page to organize them, which meant seeing more hatred aimed my way. I supposed it was a small price to pay. "I thought I'd ask others to help out. Are you willing to make dinner one night?"

"Of course." She threw her shoulders back as if I'd uttered a slur.

"I figured you would be." A lie. Carrie was one of those women who talked a lot about right and wrong, but my mama had taught me to look at what people do, not what they say. Anyone who gossiped and judged others like Carrie did wasn't nearly as good-hearted as she thought she was. Today I extended her the benefit of the doubt. "I'll post a Meal Train link on the Facebook group to keep everyone organized and let them sign up for convenient dates. Kim is allergic to peanuts, but other than that, I think anything would be welcome."

"Hm." For a split second, she looked like she might take credit for my idea. She made as if she were about to push her cart, then paused. "I heard Deshaun and John got taken in for questioning, but you did not. How is that possible?"

An elderly lady passing by overheard her and gave me a double take before moving on.

Being forced to confront this here and now was unpleasant, but at least Carrie had the balls to say it to my face instead of hiding behind Facebook.

"I didn't break any laws. I wasn't at home during the party and hadn't given permission for it, either." It had been a relief not to be arrested last night, although the absence of legal liability hardly made me blameless. There'd been many things I could've done differently, and hopefully Rowan had been thinking about that, too. "If it makes you feel better, Rowan got charged with a misdemeanor for providing alcohol to minors. From what I understand, John and Deshaun were directly involved with Carter's fall. I'm sick about what happened—for Carter and everyone else. But Rowan wasn't in the kitchen when it happened, so he didn't get charged for that."

Carrie raised her brows as if she didn't quite believe my son.

"If Rowan had been there, the other people interviewed would've said so by now."

"Well, it's a shame that Carter was the victim of some spoiled boys' gripe."

"I agree." My tongue hurt from biting down on it to keep from making a snarky comment about how she'd whipped up animosity among parents.

"Hopefully you've learned what can happen when you encourage teens to drink," she added, her chin slightly tipped up.

I'd never meant to encourage drinking, only to make the inevitable safe. I'd give anything to undo what had happened. Absolutely anything, including enduring this tongue-lashing. "Please watch for the sign-up, Carrie. I've got to go." I pushed away before giving her a chance to insult me again.

My son was probably being mocked this way at school. Please, God, help him keep his head together, and help me deal with the bear he'll be tonight. I couldn't turn to Dirk for help, given his attitude. My mother was long dead, and Uncle Tommy would be too busy praying for my soul to offer practical advice. The one person whose advice I'd always counted on didn't have time for me now, leaving me lost and alone.

I kept my head down while bagging and paying for the groceries, then hustled to put them in my trunk and retreat to the safety of my car.

Sometimes the right music could bring on a good cry, so I went ahead and listened to my "Sad Songs" playlist on Spotify for the drive home. Within three minutes, my cheeks had turned gray from runny, half-wiped mascara streaks. My first thought upon seeing Dirk's shiny new SUV in my driveway was that I didn't need another lecture from that hypocritical jerk.

I pulled in beside him while the f-bomb repeated in my head. We both got out of our cars at the same time.

"Wish I could say this was a pleasant surprise." I loaded my arms with grocery bags.

"Where were you?" His inability to deduce where I'd been didn't shock me. Nor did the fact that he didn't offer to help carry one item.

"What are you doing here, Dirk?" I brushed past him. "It's not a good time."

"I'm waiting for Rowan to get some of his things." He followed me toward the back door.

I jerked to a stop. "What?"

"He called me on his way to school, begging me to come get him. I called him out sick and brought him here to get some clothes. He'll stay with me for a couple of nights—till things settle a bit around here."

"Like hell he will." Newly livid, I scrambled for the door, but Dirk was practically breathing down my neck. I elbowed him in the ribs. "Back up—but first open the door for me."

He did, then gave me a second to step inside before barreling in behind me.

"You can't stop him, Mimi," Dirk said, staring down at me. "He's my son, too. I get a say."

Suddenly he was interested in parenting. Did that mean I could finally count on regular child support payments, too? A welcome silver lining.

"I have a custody agreement that says otherwise, and we are not going to teach him to duck and cover when the heat turns up. Jesus, for such a 'big man,' you sure can be a wimp." I set the groceries on the counter, certain Rowan was upstairs cowering at the sound of my voice.

"You have no idea what it's like to be a boy his age. Or as an underclassman on his team after having turned in teammates. He's terrified, and I don't blame him."

I lowered my voice so my son couldn't accuse me of running his father off. "You don't get to ignore him for weeks at a time and then come in and mess with my rules when the whim strikes. He's going to school today. End. Of. Story. If you want him this weekend to make up for last, we can talk about that, but he's grounded, so it can't be all fun and games up there, either."

"You think you're such a great mom, but where were you this morning when he needed you? Where were you when you should've protected him from the cops and gotten him a lawyer? Why'd you leave him alone with alcohol in the first place?"

My ex knew how to hit below the belt, and those questions took me out at the knees. But while it was one thing for Carrie to insinuate that I was an unfit mother, Dirk had some nerve playing Monday-morning quarterback, especially when he'd left me to raise Rowan alone these past few years. It didn't matter that his points were valid. He'd lost his right to criticize me when he stopped being a dependable father.

"Get out." I pointed at the back door. "I mean it. Get out or I'll call the cops—got one on speed dial now, so I'm not kidding around."

Dirk narrowed his gaze before muttering a curse and storming past me. "Rowan!"

"What?" came our son's anemic reply.

"Get down here," Dirk said.

Rowan appeared without his bag, which meant he'd heard our argument and conceded the fight. "What?"

"Sorry, buddy, but your mom won't let me take you. Call me later, though, okay?" Dirk crossed to our son and gave him a hug and kiss on the head. "Love ya."

Rowan kept his arms around Dirk's waist extra long before releasing him. My already weakened heart hurt more to see how much he missed his father. Maybe I should've let him go, but running away from his fear felt like the wrong message. I had to hit the reset button on our dynamic now, and that meant my new rules had to stick. As his mother, I had to teach him about respect and integrity. If he couldn't face school today, then he could help me make the meal and drive up to Baltimore to see Carter. At least that would be taking some responsibility.

Dirk made a face at me on his way out of the house. My son did need a father—but this man? I didn't trust him not to put bad ideas in Rowan's head. But I also couldn't come between those two.

"Rowan can stay with you this weekend," I called after him.

"Whatever," he said as he closed the door behind him on his way out.

If Dirk wanted to fume in my driveway, let him. I spun around on Rowan.

"Okay, honey, you've got two choices. I can drop you at school now, or you can help me make food for the Phillipses and then come with me to deliver it."

His eyes grew four times their size. "Mom! You can't go over there."

"Says who?"

"You're crazy!"

"No, I'm not." I began unloading the pasta and cheese. "I care about them and want to show my love and support. This is what you do."

He shook his head. "Take me to school then, 'cause I'm not going with you."

"Well, that's fine by me, although I actually think you'll feel better once you face them."

"No way." He shook his head, paling by the second.

"Fine. Let's go—I'll write you a tardy note."

———

Two hours later, I drove across town to Grace's pristine home. It reminded me a lot of the house in that old Steve Martin movie *Father of the Bride*. Preppy and perfect inside and out, a lot like Grace.

I slung two grocery bags around my arms and then lifted the tray of mac 'n' cheese out of the back seat before making my way to the front door, knocking even though I had a key.

Grace's mother, Becky, answered. "Oh, hello, Mimi." An uncertain smile appeared. "Uncertain" seemed the perfect word to sum up that woman. Every time our paths had crossed—whether at one of the kids' birthday parties or a Memorial Day picnic—she'd been pleasant yet nervous, like she wasn't sure of herself. I assumed Becky's self-doubt was the result of years of abuse, which always made me sad for her and for Grace. "What are you doing here?"

I held up all the food in my hands. "I brought dinner and groceries so you don't have to shop and cook."

Becky set one hand to her chest—such a Grace move. "Oh, well. That's thoughtful. Come in."

I stepped inside and headed back for the kitchen. For years Grace and I had taken turns cooking and sharing dinners with our kids. It'd been fun company for all of us, and a nice break from cooking on our respective "off" days. All those dinners together meant that I knew her kitchen as well as my own, so I started putting things away. "How are you holding up? And how is Kim?"

"We're managing. I'm here for the week while Grace and Sam stay at a hotel near the hospital for a couple of nights." She touched her hair and hovered anxiously while I sorted things.

Grace had unfinished mental work when it came to her mom, that was for sure. So many of Grace's parenting decisions came from trying to be the opposite of her own, like me with Uncle Tommy. Given how much she hated having to rely on her mother for help, her turning down my offer to take Kim surprised me.

"I'm glad Grace can stick close to Carter this week. She must appreciate that you've stepped in to care for Kim." The old cuckoo clock Grace had inherited from her grandmother started to sing. My breath caught in my chest as it struck me anew why I was in Grace's house without her. I stopped and set my hands on the counter, eyes brimming. "Becky, I'm so sad about everything. Please, if there's anything I can do to help, let me. And so you know, I've asked others in town to volunteer to cook meals, too, so that should lighten the burden on you all for the next few weeks."

Becky scratched her head, her hesitant smile suggesting discomfort about accepting the help. She wasn't easy to read, but I was getting the funny feeling she wanted me out of the house. "Thank you, Mimi."

She folded her arms and glanced at the clock again.

All night I'd thought about what Sam told me—how he'd convinced Grace to let Carter come to the party because he thought it would help end the bullying. Grace regularly shouldered more guilt than the entire congregation at Saint Anne's, so I guessed the fallout from her speaking up at that hearing was probably exactly why she caved. It made me heartsick that her big step forward had backfired this way.

"So, any word?" I pressed.

"Carter's through the surgery and has some sensation in his feet." Her rheumy eyes held a dewy sheen.

Relief crashed over me, practically throwing me at Becky, whom I grabbed into a hug. "Oh, that's great news."

She patted my back while worming away and wringing her hands. "We don't know exactly what that means, and no matter what happens, he has a long, hard road ahead." She sighed. "We're praying that he'll walk again."

"I'm praying every minute for that, too." Every second. Every millisecond, even.

"I guess we all are." Becky had survived a lot of pain and disappointment in her life. Loss, too, with her husband and daughter. Grace had also suffered those losses, as had I with my parents. Not that loss was the kind of connection you liked to brag about.

The air in the room was stiff, so I let Becky off the hook. "I should let you rest. Once the calendar of meals is set, I'll drop it off so you know which days you can relax."

"All right. Thank you." She politely hustled me out of the house and closed the door.

I stood on Grace's walkway for a moment, sun beating down as if it were a summer day, then confirmed the ballsy decision to take my own advice and face Grace and Sam.

Rowan hadn't been wrong about the risk of showing up uninvited. Today might not be the best day to visit, but my friend needed to know that Rowan and I were sorry. I was one of two people she turned to in tough times. Having Sam at her side didn't mean she couldn't also use my help during this family crisis. There might have been a lot of things that other people didn't respect or understand about me, but I knew how to face pain head-on. Grace could borrow my strength again whenever she was ready to ask for it.

It wasn't often that I left Potomac Point. The drive along Route 2 wasn't all bad, but I bristled when passing the exit for Annapolis, where Dirk now lived. Normally his custody threat would have made me laugh, but something in his tone had hardened today. If he squawked about my letting Rowan drink beer, Child Protective Services might get involved.

I almost swerved off the road on that thought, like my life had become a terrible Lifetime movie. Could my history of supervised parties be deemed child endangerment? My hands began to sweat from my tight grip on the steering wheel. No pencil-pushing bureaucrat would be persuaded by my argument that my son would be in more danger drinking in the woods than when having a couple of beers at home. Carter's injuries proved that my theory wasn't exactly true, too.

If Dirk wanted to use this situation against me, he probably could. I shivered, tempted to pull over. I'd have to pray that he didn't want to be responsible for the day-to-day care of his son, which felt like an awful thing to pray for. Seemed I was more selfish than I realized. Maybe people who didn't like me saw that trait.

By the time I arrived at the Shock Trauma Center, I'd worked myself into a tizzy. After shutting off the engine, I sat in my car with a

Tupperware of cookies on my lap and blew out a few breaths. Intruding on Grace's family to hug my friend might actually make things worse.

I wavered, then exited the car and went to the patient information desk to learn that Carter was in the neurotrauma critical care unit. Each step closer to his room came slower, each breath shakier. I turned the corner, coming to a stop outside Carter's room.

A male voice rang out through the cracked-open door. It wasn't Sam's. Nor Carter's. Had to be the doctor. I waited in the hallway, straining to listen. When I peeked into the room, the unidentified man shifted position, revealing police blues instead of scrubs.

The sight caused me to step back, my ears ringing.

"I don't understand." Grace's voice rose, loud enough for me to hear her for the first time. "You're letting them all off?"

I crept closer, my heart in my throat.

"No, ma'am. Based on all the interviews and your own son's state-ment, the boys didn't intend to push your son down the stairs. Jostling him near the top of an open stairwell was reckless, so they'll likely be charged with reckless endangerment, which is a misdemeanor. But there's no felony."

"My son will suffer for months or years while those boys get off with a misdemeanor?" Each of her words snapped like dried branches underfoot. "No jail time—a fine or less if they have good lawyers. How is this fair? They all mistreated Carter for weeks. I'm not convinced they didn't lure him there to continue what they'd already started. Carter's too sweet to be jaded, but we're the grown-ups. We know better—"

"Grace," Sam's voice interrupted. "Let's focus on Carter's recovery and not worry about those other families."

Good ol' Sam, such a solid, rational man. Of course, that attitude might not win him points with Grace. He needed help, and she needed reassurance.

I pushed the door open, crashing into the officer.

"Gosh, I'm so sorry," I said, catching myself by grasping his solid arm. When I looked up, I recognized those big brown eyes. "Oh, it's you."

"Mrs. Gillette," Officer Martinez said. His gaze dropped to the cookies in my other hand, and then he smiled.

I released his arm and turned to Grace, embracing her. "I've been thinking about you all nonstop." Tears came—a mixture of sadness and relief at finally holding on to my friend. "Your mom updated me when I dropped off dinner and groceries. I'm so glad Carter can feel his feet. We've been praying all night for that news."

Grace didn't hug me back. I'd shocked her, bursting in before she was finished talking to the cop. I eased away, aware of all eyes on me, then turned to Carter. The equipment and various IVs surrounding his thin frame drew a gasp. His expression—pained and exhausted—brought no ease.

Somehow I managed to raise the Tupperware in my hand. "I brought your favorite cookies, fresh from the oven."

His forced smile made me teary.

"Oh, honey. I don't know what to say, and now these cookies seem so stupid." My hands trembled when setting them on a table.

"It's okay," he said, his voice reedy and weak. "Thanks."

Hospitals always reminded me of my parents' car accident, when I'd sat in a waiting room with our neighbor, only to get the worst news. My entire world changed that day, exactly like Carter's world was forever changed. It made me sick to realize that, like me, he'd always think of his life in terms of "pre" and "post"—and that Rowan and I would be at the center of that divide.

"It was thoughtful, Mimi," Sam said. "I'm sure he'll enjoy them later."

The question on my mind—would Carter walk?—remained stuck in my throat. I searched Sam's eyes for a clue, but he looked more exhausted than hopeful.

My gaze darted from Sam to Officer Martinez to Grace. "Sorry I interrupted your conversation. Officer Martinez and I spent some time together last night going over what happened and booking Rowan for his offense. Rowan's learning some hard lessons from his arrest, and I'm sure the others will, too."

A coldness wrapped around me in the silence that followed.

"Officer Martinez, perhaps we'll speak more with you later," Grace said. "Thank you for coming today."

He tipped his head, hand to the brim of his hat. "Of course, ma'am. We're at your service."

She made a disbelieving face, rude behavior so out of character it took my breath away. Officer Martinez wished Carter a speedy recovery and then left us, offering me another warm smile on his way out the door.

I hesitated, then turned my gaze on my friend. "Sorry I didn't call first, but you've been preoccupied and I had to come. I'm beyond devastated by all of this."

"Yet you seem relieved that no one involved will suffer any serious consequences." Grace sounded oddly detached from her own voice as she averted her gaze.

"Arrests are pretty serious, aren't they?" I glanced at Sam, whose subtle headshake warned me to be quiet.

"Why don't we all step into the hall and let Carter rest." Sam gestured toward the door, reminding us that Carter shouldn't have to listen to this debate.

Before leaving, I crossed to the bed and kissed Carter's head. "If you need or want anything—anything at all—you call me, okay?"

His gaze wandered to his parents before he gave a slight nod. "Thanks, Mrs. Gillette."

For the first time ever, he wasn't sure how to treat me. I couldn't blame him for mistrusting me after this terrible accident had happened in my house, but it hit me like a whack to the head.

When we got into the hall, I went to clasp Grace's hand, but her brittle expression—half-crazed, half-broken—warned me to back away.

Still, I was sure I could get through to her. "Rowan got fingerprinted and charged. He has a hearing in a couple of weeks and will likely be fined and sentenced to community service. Trust me, he's shaking in his shoes."

"No offense, but that's basically a slap on the wrist. We both know most of those kids will be back to bullying and partying before the semester ends. But what of Carter?" Anguish twisted her features. "His consequences aren't nearly as simple or temporary."

That punch landed hard. "It's unfair."

"That's an understatement." Grace's bitter tone sliced through the air.

For the first time, I allowed for the idea that our friendship might not mend. That we might not bounce back from this tragedy, no matter how much time passed. That realization wrenched a slight moan from me. "Grace, please."

"What do you want me to say, Mimi?" She shrugged stiffly. "My son has permanent rods and screws in his spine. A lifetime of back pain and restricted spinal movement to look forward to. We still don't know if the sensation in his feet means he'll be able to control his legs. And what about school—the thing he loves? He's got to keep up from a bed in a rehab center for weeks. Do you honestly think I should be satisfied with such weak charges for the damage caused? Those boys broke the law and hurt my son. And unlike everyone else, I'm not convinced it was purely accidental." She scowled at me. A first ever, and it smarted like the scratch of cat claws.

"Grace, honey, Mimi came here in friendship and concern." Sam gave her a level look. "Let's not attack her."

"Really, Sam? You're taking her side on this?" Grace's eyes flashed with betrayal as a flush rose up her neck.

I'd thought the budget debate would be the only time Grace and I were ever on opposite sides of anything, but I'd thought wrong.

"She has no control over the cops," Sam replied with a shrug.

"I know that, but that's not my point." Grace glowered before turning to me. "Mimi, intentions aside, you created this situation, didn't you? All the parties you hosted made underage drinking okay. I know you weren't there this time, but is it really a shock that Rowan and the others thought you wouldn't be mad if they threw another party?"

Like a fish on the riverbank, my mouth gaped as I swallowed her accusations and tried to reply. As if there were a good reply. She was right. I had created an expectation. And even though I'd thought I was making it safe, I hadn't considered all possible outcomes. Pain tapped on my chest like an angry finger.

Before I could confess and apologize, Grace burst into tears, spun on her heel, and trotted down the hallway and around the bend. I attempted to follow her, but Sam grasped my arm.

"Let her go." He released me. "She's overwrought. I don't think she's slept three hours since Saturday night. Once we have a better idea of what's happening with Carter and she gets some rest, I'm sure she'll settle down. Maybe it's best if you wait for her to come to you, though. I'd hate to see an ugly fight cause real damage to your friendship."

"Sam." My voice cracked. "I'm so sorry. She's not completely wrong. I'm sick that I had a hand in what's happened. You know how much I love Carter."

"I know." Sam squeezed my shoulder, tears in his eyes. "This is a rough time for us all. Let's breathe and regroup. You're not the only one who made mistakes. Grace knows that, and I'm sure that's as much of what's gnawing at her as anything. Go home, hug your son, and deal with what you must. If there are any major developments here, I'll let you know."

"Thank you." I hugged him so hard he probably couldn't breathe. "And so you know, I'm organizing a meal chain so none of you have to worry about cooking or shopping for a while."

"That's thoughtful, thanks." He eased away.

I nodded, sniffling. "Tell Carter I said goodbye."

"I will." He waved me off.

As I was walking away, I glanced over my shoulder in time to see Sam head in the opposite direction, searching for Grace. If she wouldn't lean on me, at least she had him to help her. Without Grace, I was on my own.

My best friend held me responsible for her son's injuries. How would I ever earn her forgiveness? My eyes leaked tears like the broken faucet in my salon's powder room. I cried so hard on the drive home the road might as well have been a river. A meal train would not be near enough of an effort to show my remorse. Someday, someway I had to atone. I had no choice, because living in Potomac Point without her friendship would be like mourning another death.

# CHAPTER TEN

## G R A C E

***Friday afternoon, January 15***
***Rehab facility near Baltimore***

"Who are you texting?" I asked Carter while unfolding his I USE THIS PERIODICALLY throw blanket emblazoned with the periodic table that I'd brought from his bedroom. He flexed his feet beneath the covers. He'd been doing that often, as if to prove to himself that he would eventually control his legs again. Although he'd regained sensation and some ability to voluntarily move them, the muscle weakness pointed to potentially permanent nerve damage. No one could promise that he would walk without assistance in the future, although everyone acted as though it was possible.

"Dad." He didn't look up from his phone.

To avoid burdening my kids with my worries, I wore a pleasant mask whenever either brought Sam up. Despite our spending the past several days being polite to one another in front of Carter, the gap between my husband and me was widening. At the hotel, we'd fallen into the habit of turning away from each other in bed. I'd stared at the wall each night to avoid the nightmares of seeing Carter at the bottom of Mimi's basement steps. My husband's embrace might've chased them away if I'd welcomed it. Instead, the empty space between us in bed only increased my growing sense of isolation.

My son's private room had a large window with a view of the city. A cascade of sunshine made the room less dismal, although it still smelled of disinfectant laced with sorrow. Tomorrow I'd bring a fir-scented diffuser and a few more things from his room to make his temporary home feel less institutional.

Bland surroundings aside, the compassionate staff helped put me at ease. "I like Leron. Do you?"

"Yeah, I guess." Carter set his phone down and used the remote to adjust his bed, then whimpered when shifting into place. His ribs and spine were still so tender. His long, lean frame looked nearly skeletal in the bed. Between his lack of appetite because of the drugs and the unappetizing hospital food, he'd probably lost three pounds this week. Another thing to worry about.

"Oh, honey, let me help." I reshuffled his pillows, but he held up an arm.

"Mom, you heard them. I need to do as much for myself as I can." Carter grunted while repositioning himself again, using his arms to help adjust his legs even as pain carved its way across his face.

"Sorry." I hugged my waist to keep myself in check, although watching him struggle with something so simple made me want to shriek.

"Have you figured out how to coordinate with the school?" His eyes seemed too big for his face today, or maybe I was losing my mind. "I don't want to repeat tenth grade."

"You won't have to repeat, honey. I'll be meeting with the principal, your counselor, and the teachers soon. Everyone is preparing materials for you and your tutor here so you can keep up. You'll get extensions on everything you missed this week, too. But your most important job now is to focus on your recovery so you can come home sooner than later." Whenever the little voice in my head whispered that "possible" full recovery didn't mean "probable," I shuddered. Projecting positivity remained my number one goal.

He rested his head against the pillow, closing his eyes. Carter kept a tight rein on his emotions, so his sense of his prospects remained a mystery.

I made myself busy by straightening his laptop and checking the charger, folding his robe and setting it on the table by his bed, and moving his slippers to within his reach. "What else can I bring you? How about your Bluetooth speaker?"

Could he tell I was procrastinating?

He shrugged. "Doesn't matter."

"Carter." I stared at him, absorbing his malaise like a sponge. "Little creature comforts could help you keep a positive attitude, which will be important with the tough road ahead."

When tears trickled from the corners of his eyes, I breathed through the tightness in my chest, sat on the bed, and stroked his head. Rather than being comforted, he cried harder, which increased my own pain. I squeezed his hands because I couldn't grab him into a hug without stressing his rib cage and spine.

"Oh, sweetheart, go ahead and cry. What's happened is overwhelming, but this is a top-notch facility, and you're getting the very best care." There had to be more I could offer my son than trite words.

He moaned, "I already sucked at sports, but now this. What if I always need a cane or walker? What girl will ever like me then?"

Worrying about girls might have sounded trivial to me, but to a fifteen-year-old boy who wanted nothing so much as to be accepted, it must feel like the end of the world. My insides splintered like cracked glass from the endless ways this injury could affect his future. My hatred of what had happened was beginning to bleed into other aspects of my life, too.

"Carter, trust me. There are girls out there who will take one look at this face of yours and be impressed with your smarts and drive, and they will love you no matter how fast you can walk. Teenage girls aren't always mature enough to appreciate what really matters. But I promise you, high school isn't forever and adults fall in love with all kinds of people regardless of their abilities, looks, or any other thing that seems so important at your age. Besides, everyone here is encouraged by the early signs of your recovery, honey. They keep saying that incomplete T12 injuries can have very good outcomes, so let's focus on the success stories. Treat these coming weeks of physical work like you would a chem lab. Push yourself with Leron. If you give it everything, I've no doubt you'll regain most if not all of your leg strength."

He eased away and wiped his face, so I handed him a tissue to blow his nose. While he did that, I drew a deep breath to loosen my chest.

An idea came to mind. "Let's plan something to look forward to . . . maybe that summer college for high school students program at Purdue that you wanted to attend?"

The suggestion sparked no enthusiasm. "I don't want to commit to anything unless I know I'll be walking."

"Please don't lose faith, honey." We sat in silence for a moment. "What if I look into some options so we can pull the trigger when you feel ready?"

He shrugged.

Sam was the better cheerleader, so I turned to my strength: comfort. "I hate to leave when you're glum. Want me to stay and order Thai takeout and play poker?"

Sam would accuse me of lingering to avoid seeing him. Maybe he wouldn't be completely wrong, either. Lately I hardly understood why I was doing or saying many things. The number of concerned emails from neighbors and friends that needed a response had reached triple digits.

"It's fine." Carter wiped his eyes before blowing out a quick breath. "I'm tired and just want to watch *Cursed* on Netflix tonight."

"Okay." I stood, knowing I should spend time with Kim, who'd been refusing to cooperate with my mom at bedtime or eat the meals my friends had delivered. "If you think of anything you'd like me to bring tomorrow, text me, okay?"

"Reese's." He wore a hopeful half smile, knowing we didn't have any peanut products in the house because of Kim.

"Okay. Reese's it is." I leaned forward to kiss him on the forehead. "If you get lonely, call me. You know how to reach the nurses, right?"

He gestured to the call buttons, so I nodded. "I guess I'll go."

"Bye." He didn't seem overly nervous, but the magnetic pull to stick by his side held fast.

"I love you." I forced my legs to move, stopping by the nursing station to make sure they had all my phone numbers in case of an emergency.

Leaving my injured son behind felt like an abandonment. Once outside, I cried while trotting across the parking lot. Inside my car, I hung my head until the tears stopped, then checked my phone for messages and scrolled quickly through Facebook notifications. The town moms' group was active as ever.

Keri Bertram wrote:

> It's unacceptable, with everything we know about teen brain development, that anyone would condone teen drinking. When you let them drink so young, you are shortchanging their futures. Plus, they aren't mature enough to make safe decisions or moderate themselves like an adult can. It's stupid, and honestly, encouraging kids to break the law should be a crime.

I couldn't have agreed more. Not to mention the statistically significant increased risk of developing alcohol-abuse issues when kids' first experience getting drunk was at fourteen versus twenty. A twinge of guilt about saying nothing to my mother when Margot first started slipping out of the house late at night to party with her friends made me wince. But this post proved I wasn't wrong to respect both the law and the dangers of teen alcohol abuse. Keri's post had garnered a lot of likes, which also heartened me.

A woman I didn't know posted about the arrests.

> In what world is it fair that drunk bullies get off easy while their victim is gravely injured? Reckless endangerment, my ass. I doubt Carter Phillips invited their touch. It's assault, plain and simple. #PotomacPoliceScrewedUp

Yes! This stranger could see the truth, so why couldn't Sam? His reaction had made me begin to doubt my own sanity. Of course, right beneath that post, Anne Sullivan, whom I knew to be fair, surprised me with her reply.

> Our community is heartsick over the terrible accident that took place on Saturday night. No doubt the boys involved are beside themselves with regrets, so let's not inflame an already difficult situation, or undermine our police officers. They investigated the incident, so we should trust their judgment regarding appropriate charges. Let the boys learn from those consequences. There are better ways to help the Phillipses and the community heal without ruining more lives.

That particular sentiment shot hot oil through my veins. Please, please . . . let's make sure those "poor" football players' lives aren't too inconvenienced by what they did. Never mind that my son would be living with this injury for the rest of his life. How could Anne echo the same lame argument lawyers used to get Ivy League frat boys off easy after they'd sexually assaulted coeds? *"Boys will be boys"*—utter horseshit, plain and simple.

Resentment toward anyone who couldn't see the injustice hardened around my heart as I pulled out of the parking lot and made my way home. To make myself feel better, I returned phone calls to those who'd expressed concern and offered help. Well, those except for Mimi.

I didn't doubt her sincerity or her love for Carter, and he'd already devoured those cookies she'd baked. But I had no idea what else to say or where we went from here. Her home—a place I'd often gone for comfort and gossip—had now become the scene of my nightmares. Her son—a boy I'd helped raise—now seemed my son's enemy.

The combination of my grief about our friendship and the hour-long slog of Friday-night traffic wore on me. I pulled into the garage and almost ran over Kim's ice skates, which were lying in front of the shelves. Irked, I hit the brakes, got out of the car, and threw them onto the wire shelf, then returned to the car to pull it all the way inside.

I sat in the front seat for a moment after turning off the ignition, letting the quiet surround me. My tightly strung body refused to unwind, even when I closed my eyes and practiced yoga breaths.

I'd wanted to remain at the hotel, but we had medical co-pays and Kim's well-being to consider. Sam had to return to work, which left everything else to fall to me. Every day for the coming weeks, I'd be making that round trip to Baltimore, coordinating with teachers, and trying to make up for lost time with my daughter. The anticipation of it sapped any remaining energy.

My mother's car was still out front. Although appreciative of her help, I was sure to pay for it for weeks to come. She loved to play the martyr, like when Margot and I were young and she'd painted herself as "holding the family together." If neglecting her kids' needs in favor of enabling her husband's dangerous behavior was holding the family together, then she got the prize. The only good to come of her failures had been how they'd inspired me to do better, which was why I would take on the whole world to protect Carter now if I had to.

Without Sam and Mimi, both of whom usually made me laugh and put things in a brighter perspective, it became difficult to shake off the ugly noise in my head. If I closed my eyes, I could picture Mimi's chipper face and hear her voice cheering on Carter's progress: he could now move his feet and bend his knees at will. If we were speaking, she would've marked each small step with a celebration.

As grateful as I was for my son's improvements, he still lacked the strength to stand, even with a walker. However, I finally allowed myself to believe that he might not be confined to life in a wheelchair.

He would not, however, live pain-free. Dr. Acharya had explained that with the rod in his back, the vertebrae directly above and below would probably wear down because of friction with the metal's rigidity, which meant future spinal fusions and longer rods as he aged. More risk, more pain, more scars. I'd never had to dig deeper to find the courage needed to help my son accept his new challenges and limitations. Doing so took everything I had, which left almost nothing for Kim and Sam.

I wished they could understand my depleted reserves without blaming me for them. If it were either of them in the hospital, they'd be getting my all. I was only one woman—and not the strongest or smartest one, at that—yet everyone wanted something from me. Sam wanted me to relax and let go of anger. Kim wanted, well, anything she could get. Mimi wanted forgiveness. The community probably wanted to hear from me, too. All I wanted was to make this all go away, which wouldn't happen, like those other things people wanted weren't happening.

With a sigh, I tossed my key fob on the dashboard and then entered my house through the mudroom. Immediately, the aroma of a roast or possibly a stew reached my nostrils and loosened the tension in my back. My stomach growled because I hadn't eaten since breakfast.

"Hello?" came Sam's voice from the kitchen.

I hung up my coat, kicked off my shoes, and set my purse on the cubby shelf. "It's me."

A wave of yearning for the simple days preceding Carter's injury arose. I'd grown accustomed to Sam's warm smile, the hugs, the sexy promise in the gleam of his eyes. I'd always looked forward to catching up with him in the evening, especially on Friday nights when I'd feed the kids early and then have us eat later in the dining room to kick-start the weekend. Often we had then joined the kids for a family game night. And at the end of the night, we'd crawl into bed and make love.

If I were being honest, I'd also missed Mimi this week. Each time I'd caught myself wanting to turn to her for advice or comfort, I'd felt like a traitor to my son.

These days I had only my focus on being Carter's pillar of strength to keep me going.

Instead of greeting me with a kiss on the cheek and a pat on the butt, Sam remained by the stove, staring at me as if I might bite him.

"Where's my mother?" I asked.

"Packing her things so she can make her knitting circle meetup. I told her she could go home for the weekend. Becky helped a lot, but she's tired, and I doubt you want to sleep under the same roof as her night after night." He turned off the stove. His instincts about my mom and me were perfect, but I hated the way we were now making decisions separately. "You got Carter settled?"

I nodded before stretching my neck from side to side. "Leron is a big guy. Seems like he enjoys working with kids. I think he'll quickly figure out how to encourage Carter."

Sam nodded. "That's good. I'm impressed with the doctors and other professionals there. Carter's in great hands."

Since we'd met, Sam's optimism had been one of my favorite traits. It offset my tendency to stress out whenever things went wrong, whether that had been learning to live with Kim's life-threatening allergy or dealing with the disaster caused when the master bathroom pipes burst and flooded that side of the house.

When it came to Carter, though, Sam's attitude provoked inexplicable bitterness. It was almost as if I resented him for not treating this with more gravity—like he was one of those parents on the Facebook group playing down what had happened so that no one else had to suffer. Sure, I projected optimism in front of Carter, but it didn't come naturally.

"Where's Kim?" I asked, changing the subject to quell my stomach acid.

"Upstairs. I was about to call her down." He ladled stew into a bowl.

I gripped the back of a kitchen chair. "She left her skates on the garage floor again."

Sam silently fixed a second bowl.

"She really needs to learn to be more responsible," I added in a prickly tone.

My husband exhaled slowly while bringing the bowls to the table. "Generally I agree, but my bet is that she's acting out because we've basically ignored her all week. Yelling about her skates won't help her feel more secure. I'm sure she's also worried about Carter but doesn't know how to handle those feelings. She's only ten. Her sleepover party got wrecked. Her grandma was the only one around, and you know how Becky can make things about herself at times. It's been a rough week on everyone. Let's not lecture or quiz her about school or anything, but just enjoy a pleasant evening. Maybe play a game?" He returned to the stove to fill his own bowl.

"In other words, I'm the problem?" I stiffened, holding back tears.

He shook his head. "I didn't say that."

He didn't have to. He'd been growing increasingly frustrated with me all week. I'd always known he was the more flexible of us, but unlike in prior situations, now he seemed to challenge my every thought.

As luck would have it, my mother entered the kitchen at that moment. "You're finally home." Her tone wasn't as accusatory as her word choice. Was it too much to have preferred for her to say something along the lines of "I'm glad you're home and hope you can relax"?

Sam crossed to the mudroom and called up the back stairs for Kim. Despite being drained, I vowed to give my daughter whatever she needed with as much love and determination as I'd been showering upon Carter.

"Hi, Mom." I gave her a quick kiss hello. "Thanks for taking care of Kim all week."

"I was happy to help. She's a hoot. Reminds me of your sister." She flashed a bittersweet smile.

I said nothing because talking about Margot with my mother brought up regrets and resentment. Instead I asked, "Are you sure you don't want dinner before you go?"

"No. I want to catch up with my friends. But if you can't get a sitter next week, I'll come back."

"Thanks, but we'll manage something. Escape while you can," I joked, hoping to hide my eagerness for her departure.

"I'd like to visit Carter tomorrow if that's okay?"

"Of course it is," Sam replied upon his return to the kitchen. "He'll welcome seeing someone other than Grace and me."

He slung an arm around my mother's shoulders and gave her a little squeeze, which smarted because he'd not shown me a scrap of affection.

She patted his hand. "You two take care of each other now."

Something about her tone burrowed under my skin, like she was sending a secret message to me or about me—I wasn't sure. "Do you need help with your luggage?"

"No, I'm not feeble." She smiled. "I'll call you tomorrow."

I followed her to the driveway and waited for her to back out before returning to the kitchen.

The stew smelled heavenly—a mixture of rosemary and red wine and something else I couldn't place. I took a seat at the table. "Where'd you get the recipe?"

He shot me a "duh" look. "Sandra Webb dropped dinner off."

"Oh." I tasted a bite. "It's delicious."

"There's also leftover lasagna in the fridge that Carrie dropped off yesterday or the day before."

"I hope my mom kept a list so I can write out thank-you notes later tonight. Our neighbors and friends have been so thoughtful to pitch in." The community outreach had made me feel appreciated and loved—like all the years of volunteering and befriending others had meant something.

Sam tipped his head, looking as if he was holding his breath. "You know this is all because of Mimi," he said. "Will you be sending her a thank-you note as well?"

It hurt that my husband had more empathy for my friend than for me. If I weren't so hungry, I might've dumped my stew in his lap. And hadn't he just said that tonight was not for lectures?

"Maybe you should, since you two are so chummy now." As for Mimi, I couldn't speak to her while I still warred between wanting to lean on her and wanting to strangle her.

He flashed a hard look my way, but then Kim wandered into the kitchen.

Our daughter took one look at dinner and wrinkled her nose. "I don't want that."

"Please cooperate, Kim," Sam said.

"Stew meat is stringy." She scowled at the bowl as if it had insulted her.

I opened my arms for a hug, glad for the chance to make up for my neglect. "Hey, sweetheart. Come here. I've missed you and can't wait to hear all about your week."

She complied but seemed more concerned about being forced to eat stew than she was happy about my arrival. "Mom, can I eat something else? Pleeease."

It would take a few days to reestablish our rules. I wasn't upset with my mother, though. She'd done us a huge favor, and Kim was not easy to dissuade.

"What's the rule?" I kissed the top of her head and released her.

She rolled her eyes. "You get what you get and you don't get upset."

I nodded and pointed to her seat. "If you eat the stew, maybe we'll go for ice cream. But let's enjoy a nice dinner together."

She plopped her butt down but then sat with a frown and her chin on her fists. "Can't I make a grilled cheese sandwich instead? Grammy let me use the stove all by myself."

Great. Something else to worry about.

"Honey, people have gone out of their way to make us these wonderful meals." I took another bite and made a mental note to ask Sandra for the recipe.

Kim chose that moment to scoop stew into her spoon, raise it, and then let the food plunk back into the bowl.

"Don't play with your food," Sam said gently.

"It looks like barf." Kim pushed the bowl away from her and then sat back with her arms crossed. I kept eating, honoring Sam's request not to lecture or otherwise escalate our daughter's tantrums.

"Did anything fun happen today at school?" I tried.

"No." She scuffed her feet against the floor.

I let the table manners slide. "Did you finish that clay project in art class yet?"

"No."

"Hm. Is there anything you'd like to talk about?" I asked.

"Can I have another birthday party since mine got ruined?" She set her elbows on the table and held her chin in her palms.

Sam and I exchanged a glance. "I'm sorry, honey, but we can't manage a party with everything going on with your brother. Daddy and I don't have free time, and we're very tired."

"When is Carter coming home?" she asked, looking suddenly anxious. She must miss having him around, too. My heart stuttered.

"We don't know." I laid my hand on hers. "Hopefully in a month or six weeks. Now, how about you eat dinner so we can have dessert and figure out something fun to do tonight?"

She sat back and crossed her arms. "I hate stew."

"If you don't want to eat, fine. But there won't be any snacks tonight, so be sure." Sam rarely lost his patience, but his snapping proved for the first time that this week had tested him, too. "You're excused from the table. After we clean up, we'll call you to play a game or pick a movie."

Kim slid off her chair and slunk away. So much for our peaceful evening as a family.

We continued eating in silence. I didn't know what to say. It'd be hypocritical to criticize him for snapping when I'd been waspish all week. On the other hand, we'd now alienated our daughter even further. I was beginning to lose faith that we'd recover our parenting mojo.

"Sorry." He scrubbed a hand over his face, which forced me to notice his fatigue.

"It's fine."

"It's not fine, but while she's gone, let's finish our conversation." He sighed. "Mimi isn't responsible for what happened, no matter how much you want to make her the scapegoat."

Now it was my turn to push my food away, even though I'd been enjoying it. "Just because she wasn't there when it happened doesn't make her innocent. We all know she rarely punishes Rowan for anything. Who couldn't foresee the perfect storm for something to go wrong?"

"Here we go." Sam stood. "Your childhood makes you the expert, while the rest of us ignorant fools' bad decisions led to Carter's injuries. Never mind things like accidents and fate. Forget that we actually can't control the future, or that one of our kids could get hurt some other way at any point."

"Stop calling it an accident," I barked.

"Even the police believe that's what it was." He raised his arms.

"I don't care what the police believe. Those boys wanted to hurt Carter. Maybe not as badly as they did—maybe only emotionally—but their intentions were cruel." I shook my hands to release the fists that I'd formed.

"Even if you're right, how does it help to dwell on it? Carter has no interest in pressing charges. And I, for one, am grateful that Mimi organized these meals for us. Isn't it nice to come home to a home-cooked dinner without having to do the work or go to the store? Doesn't that earn her some compassion?"

"Maybe she's looking for ways to ease her guilty conscience," I snapped, giving no ground regardless of how right he might be.

Sam dragged a hand through his hair, his mouth drooping. "You always talk about her big heart, yet suddenly you're a cynic. Why are you ascribing the worst motives to your best friend?"

I stammered as if he'd dumped ice water on my head. In another context it might be a fair question, but in this case, the answer was so obvious I scoffed. "Because our son is currently living fifty miles away, in constant pain, and having to relearn how to walk."

We remained several feet apart, each ensconced in our righteousness. The temperature in the kitchen dropped fifteen degrees, and our home felt unsafe for the first time in our marriage.

Sam brought his hands to his face before dropping back onto his seat and staring at me in utter disappointment. "What will it take to satisfy you, Grace?"

"I want everyone responsible for this situation to pay," I said flatly.

Sam visibly withdrew, then his posture sagged as he tilted his head. "You realize that also means me . . . and you. We let him go to a party where we knew there'd be beer."

"You think we aren't already paying for our mistake? My God, it'll be months before I can sleep soundly. Months or years of disruption while Carter recovers—*if* he recovers. We still have very little idea what he's in for now or way down the road. Trust me, Sam, I will *never* forgive myself for giving in about the party."

"It sounds like you'll never forgive me, either." His voice was soft and aching.

I glared at him, unable to answer. I'd loved my husband for two decades. We were a team—or at least we'd always been one. Being at odds was foreign and devastatingly lonely.

He continued talking in the absence of my reply. "Is this what it will be like from now on—you giving me the cold shoulder and acting like your regrets are the only ones that count? If you felt that strongly about the party, why didn't you refuse?"

He knew better than anyone that I'd been conditioned from birth not to cause ripples. Plus, he'd broken our pattern of mutual decision-making. "How can you ask that when you not only blindsided me that morning but also ganged up on me with Carter despite all my objections? After Carter pulled the guilt card by bringing up the whole budget fallout, I had no choice."

"Oh, okay. Got it." He held up his hands, shaking his head.

He was judging me—another new facet in our relationship. One that frightened me because this was how marriages began to crumble. "What?"

"You're allowed to be human—to make a mistake based on whatever justification you think is okay—but Mimi and I are not." His caustic tone—another surprising trait—made every hair on my body tingle.

"It's not at all the same thing." Was it, though? I found myself confused, whether because he'd made a valid point or scared me with his attitude, I couldn't decide.

Rather than finish our discussion, he stood and rinsed his bowl before setting it in the dishwasher, then wiped his hands on a dishcloth and folded it over the sink's edge. "This has been a devastating, stressful week for our family, so I've tried to be patient. And I know you think rules can prevent the kinds of tragedies in your past from recurring. But no one controls the world, and hating everyone when things go wrong doesn't solve anything. If you can't find a way to forgive me, yourself, Mimi, and others, how can we move forward? This distance between us is unnerving, to say the least. You've got to meet me partway, Grace. For our sake, and especially for Carter's. We don't want him to pick up on this tension."

I knotted my fingers together, tight with discomfort while I tried talking myself down from all the indignation that festered whenever I recalled Saturday morning's discussion. How could my own husband not see that I hated myself as much as or more than I resented him and Mimi? Watching Carter struggle for each infinitesimal improvement hardly put me in mind to forgive anyone.

When I didn't reply, Sam sighed. "I'll see if Kim wants some ice cream and to watch a movie. I know she didn't eat her dinner, but she's had a rough week, and I'm not going to enforce the punishment now— especially when I said it in frustration. I'm sure you have opinions about that, too, but she needs some fun. I'd love it if you would set aside your anger long enough to join us, but if not, I'll make up an excuse."

I blinked, my heart pumping its way up into my throat because I'd never been good at faking my feelings. He'd opened the door to this conversation, and when I'd trusted him with my darkest pain and fear, he'd turned on me. Part of me wanted to toss my chair on its side and scream at him for making me the bad guy. I'd assumed that blame all week—suffering until it made me sick. "Go on for ice cream without me. Tell her I have a headache. I'll work on my mood so we can all watch a movie when you return."

Without looking at him—because the disappointment in his eyes would be too much to bear—I turned and went up the back stairs.

I stopped in front of Carter's room before stepping inside and closing the door behind me. His tabletop telescope sat on his desk, where the picture of him with his Sandy Hill Camp friends sat askew. Having those at the rehab center might make him feel more at home.

I pressed my thumbs and forefingers to my eyes to stanch fresh tears. How stupid, as if objects would make him feel normal. Even when standing in the middle of my home, I felt completely separated from my normal life.

Hugging myself, I sank to the ground and cried in silence, missing my baby, missing my husband, missing my friend. Missing life as I'd known it. I wasn't functioning well in this new world, but if I didn't figure something out soon, everything I'd ever cared about might be destroyed.

# CHAPTER ELEVEN

### MIMI

*Saturday afternoon, January 16*
*A Cut Above*

At 3:05, I peered out the window of my shop to the parking lot, looking for Linda, who hadn't called to cancel her 3:00 cut-and-color appointment. Normally butterflies wouldn't go to war in my stomach when a client ran late, but I'd had a few no-shows this week.

Having been a hairstylist for two decades, I'd lost my fair share of clients over the years. Sometimes they left because they moved out of town. Those ones told you in advance, often moaning about it and begging for referrals. Other clients went in search of cheaper prices or because a friend told them about a "new" stylist in town. Those folks skulked away, never to be heard from again. But no-shows were a new phenomenon.

I pretended to rearrange the display of shampoos, hair masks, and conditioners so Vicki, my other stylist, and her client didn't ask questions. By 3:10, I called Linda, but it went to voice mail. "Hey, Linda. It's Mimi. I'm checking to make sure nothing bad happened. Maybe you're on your way. Give me a call if something came up and you need to reschedule."

I hung up, keeping my back to Vicki and her client. This did not bode well. With my hand against my stomach, I opened the Facebook app to check on the status of the Meal Train.

When people feel powerless in the face of another's suffering, doing something to ease that person's burden helps, so it hadn't been hard to get people to volunteer. I didn't regret organizing it despite the personal downside. And there certainly had been one. While twenty-two folks had signed up so far, at least half had thrown a little shade my way.

Like this new volunteer—Katrina Wellesley.

> Does it seem a little weird to y'all that Mimi Gillette is organizing this? I mean, does she think it'll make people forget this is sorta her fault?

I'd never met this woman, but she'd already decided she knew all about me and my alleged "real goal" of making myself the hero of this story. Ha! Never in my life had I tried to be anyone's hero, let alone considered myself one. Heroes didn't end up divorced. They didn't get so overwhelmed by their kid that they bent over backward to please him and still felt like they'd lost control. They didn't have a hard time making or keeping friends, either.

This past week's gut check made me admit to some questionable choices, but that didn't make the nasty comments easier to slough off. Even when I tried to do the right thing, people cut me down. This incident had whipped folks into a heightened frenzy. Now I was the devil, and no one would let me forget my mistakes.

Sure, I knew other parents who allowed their kids to drink, but I kept my mouth shut out of respect for Grace, Sam, and Carter.

I closed the app and checked the clock: 3:17. Linda wasn't coming.

While I doubted Grace had asked anyone to blow off appointments this week, it seemed pretty clear that her friends were showing their loyalty and sending me a message.

Vicki rang up Gweneth Templeman while I stared through the window at the parking lot as if I could will Linda's car into pulling up. Gweneth, a stylish woman in her late fifties, had moved to town only months ago, so she didn't know Grace, nor did she care about the budget debate.

"It's awfully quiet in here for a Saturday," she remarked while handing Vicki her credit card.

"Yeah. Been a strange week," Vicki replied, averting her gaze.

Gweneth slid a look my way and wrinkled her nose apologetically. "I read about the party and arrests in the paper. People can be small-minded, but luckily most have short memories, too. Hope things turn around for you soon."

Most residents relied on the weekly local paper to keep up with the comings and goings in Potomac Point, so her comment didn't stun me as much as her compassion did. My splintered heart absorbed her kindness, but I shrugged because nothing would change the facts, and I didn't want to talk about it anyway.

Gweneth didn't take my hint. "Most parents are probably shaking in their boots, thanking God this didn't happen in their house, because we all know that this wasn't the first teen drinking party in town. Dollars to doughnuts, in six months they'll be back to the same behavior and turn a blind eye to their kids' behavior, like this never happened." Gweneth tucked her credit card into her wallet.

Would they?

"I don't know, Gweneth." I sure wouldn't be as careless in the future. Every time I remembered seeing Carter in that hospital bed, I wanted to throw up. Sam hadn't texted any updates, either. Did that mean there hadn't been any improvements? It was too awful to consider.

"Truth is, half the people in town wagging their finger at you right now have probably left their kids alone in a house with alcohol, or just given it to them." She slung her purse over her shoulder and casually checked her hair one last time in the mirror to her left.

Gweneth was right about the hypocrisy. Even John's and Deshaun's mothers—Roni and Jordan, fellow booster club volunteers I'd considered friends—had turned on me, acting like I'd force-fed their boys alcohol and then made them give Carter a hard time.

Roni had been so eager to distance herself and her son from this that she'd posted in the Facebook moms' group:

> We never gave Mimi Gillette permission to let John drink at her house, and if we'd known about it, we wouldn't have allowed him to hang out there.

Naturally, plenty of people piled on. I'd itched to type back BIG FAT LIAR because she let John drink in her home and her opinions about teen drinking had mirrored mine. Posting the picture I had of her and John drinking Bud at her pool this past summer would only make me feel worse about myself, though.

Aside from my shame was the bigger worry that these posts gave Dirk ammunition to make good on his recent threats. Hopefully, they'd die down quickly if I ignored them, but the criminal hearings, which were sure to stir up more conversation and accusations, were still ahead of us.

It seemed unfair that after I'd raised Rowan on my own all this time, Dirk could swoop in and take him away. Maybe that's what I deserved, though. And scary as that worry was, it seemed small in comparison with Grace's.

"Actually, the *truth* is, Carter's recovery is more important than my reputation." I pretended to clean up my station to keep my hands busy but felt close to tears.

"You're good people, Mimi. Hang in there, and I'll see you both next month." She flashed a sympathetic smile.

"Thanks, Gweneth." I waved goodbye, blinking back my tears as she waltzed out the door.

Once she'd gone, Vicki sighed. "Well, boss, what do you think? Should we pack it in for the day? There's no one else on my appointment book, and I doubt Linda will show up for you."

I nodded, knowing that was true.

Not to brag, but I was the best stylist in town. From the get-go, I'd had a knack for understanding hair—which styles would work for which textures, and which ones would look best on different people. Luckily for me, most women's vanity had always overcome whatever judgments they had about me for how I looked or acted.

That might not hold true now. If we continued to lose clients each week, we'd be in trouble by March. I looked around my shop—its buttercup-yellow walls aglow with the late-afternoon sun shining through the window. I'd gone all out and bought the fancy Colombina chairs and RIO backwash shampoo stations. Grace had helped me pick the live-edge floating display shelves and hardwood flooring.

I'd poured everything into this business, and now it, too, could be at risk. I might've broken down on the spot if it weren't for Vicki. "You go ahead, Vic. I'm going to take inventory and do some bookkeeping."

I'd fight to keep my doors open. And who knew, maybe today a new-to-town walk-in would show up.

"I can stick around if you want." Vicki's earnest young face offered enough unity to make me feel better.

"No, no. Take advantage of the free time. I'll see you on Tuesday."

"Thanks." She smiled and ducked into our workroom to gather her things. When she returned with her purse and jacket, she wore a frown. "Mimi, should I be worried about my job?"

Fair question. She had bills like everyone else. I didn't want to lie, but if she walked out on me, she'd take more business out the door.

Hiding my doubts, I tapped into the can-do spirit that usually got me through tough spots. "We should probably expect a few lean weeks. We might even lose a handful of clients permanently. But new people move to town, and customers like Gweneth will stick it out. If we have to run some price specials for a while to retain clients, we can do that. But don't worry about it. I'll figure it out." I hoped my confident smile would fool her long enough to give me time to make a game plan.

"Okay. See you Tuesday." She left with her phone at her ear.

When I was her age, I'd been pregnant and working for Kathleen over at Divaz. I'd made good money there and built up a loyal following when I struck out on my own. Kathleen and I enjoyed a friendly rivalry, but there were more than enough customers in town to support us both, so it'd never caused a problem.

But the truth was that if Carter didn't get better, things would go further south for me. That'd be a boon for Divaz's employees, and I couldn't blame them if they were happy. I supposed I could cut hair anywhere, but losing my own place—something so much mine—hurt to consider. Besides, starting over somewhere new would mean yanking Rowan from a team where he shone. Then again, I might not be happy living in Potomac Point if Grace never forgave me.

The very possibility brought me low. And it was a possibility. She'd cut me out so fast, despite all we'd shared. Even here in my shop we'd made lots of memories, like on its one-year anniversary, when she'd helped to celebrate by organizing a Locks of Love haircutting party complete with delectable petit fours. She'd even asked Sam to teach me basic bookkeeping so I didn't have to spend as much on accountants.

She'd always been there with a sympathetic shoulder anytime Dirk had let me down. She'd encouraged me to join her on the middle school PTC and on another committee she'd set up as a board member for SilverRide, the senior ride-sharing nonprofit where she'd volunteered. I knew she'd done so to help me make more friends. It hadn't ever worked as well as she'd believed it would, but all those women had been more polite to me thanks to Grace—until now.

Life without my friend was bad enough, but the idea of life as the object of her hatred shattered me.

I swiped my runny nose and dried my eyes, then shook that thought off like a dog does fleas. Sam had told me to be patient, so the best thing I could do today was get to work.

An hour later, I drove home, my stomach still a tangle of nerves. When I walked through the door, Rowan was lounging on the sofa, staring at his phone. Although he'd had a rough week at school, I'd awakened him at nine before I left for work and given him a list of Saturday chores. As I looked around at the unfolded laundry, the lunch dishes on the table, and the garbage bag by the door, it appeared he'd either ignored them or given them short shrift.

"Hey, what gives?" When he didn't reply, I shoved his leg.

He removed his earbuds. "What?"

"You didn't do your chores."

"I will later."

"No, Rowan. I asked you to do them before I got home."

"What's the difference when I do them?"

I stuck out my hand. "Hand me the phone."

"Why?"

I wiggled my fingers and uttered the words Uncle Tommy had always used that I'd sworn would never pass my lips. "Because I said so. The phone, now."

He tossed the phone on the table. "Fine."

"Hey, cut the attitude. When I ask you for help, you should do it happily. I work my butt off to keep this roof over our heads, and I don't ask much in return."

He glared at me, so I cocked a brow.

"What did you do all day?" I asked.

"Lifted at the Y."

Allowing him to keep up with his regular workouts was my one exception to his grounding. "Who with?"

"No one." He followed that up with more sulking.

When your kids are little, you can pretty much cure anything with a hug, a kiss, and deflection. So far I hadn't found those methods to work as well with teen boys. And letting him manipulate me with his moods was sort of what got us here in the first place. "I'm sorry your friends have made you their scapegoat."

His jaw clenched. "I'm over it."

"Are you?" I tipped my head, hopeful.

Another defiant shrug. "They're being jerks. I'm sick of feeling bad when I didn't do anything wrong. Dad says if I'd tried to delete the texts and stuff, the cops could've found out anyway and made it all worse for me."

I nodded, wondering what else Dirk was feeding Rowan. I understood the instinct—the desire to ease Rowan's guilt—but the more important lesson in all this was taking responsibility for his own role in what happened. For Rowan to think he "didn't do anything wrong" was a stretch. "Are you heading up to Annapolis tonight?"

"No. Miranda had some other thing they had to do." He bit his lip.

"Sorry, bud." I wrinkled my nose despite being relieved. Until I knew whether Dirk was gunning for me, I'd be wary of him taking Rowan for overnights. When I shifted, I felt something poking at my tailbone.

I turned around to fish an empty beer can from behind the pillow. Oh. My. God. I held it in front of my son and snapped, "What's this?"

"A beer."

I smacked his shin. "Don't be a smart aleck. Why'd you drink it?"

He shrugged one shoulder, too lazy to put more oomph into anything. "Nothin' better to do."

"Didn't you learn anything?" My body itched like I'd broken out in hives. Heck, maybe I had. I didn't know what behavior I'd expected of him since last weekend, but this was not it. No remorse. No respect. Did any lesson I'd ever taught stick, or had he been a great puppeteer?

"You never cared if I had a beer now and then." He didn't even look worried so much as annoyed.

My mouth fell open. "Rowan, you're grounded."

"I didn't go anywhere. I've been here all day except for my workout."

I shook the empty can. "This has to stop, too."

"For how long?" he groaned.

"Maybe until you're twenty-one." I frowned, uncertainly. I'd been around enough to recognize a pipe dream when I heard one. The frequency of teen parties was the whole reason I'd tried to create a safe space for them. But the tragedy that happened here should've knocked a little sense into my son, or at least caused enough contrition for the consequences to Carter that he wouldn't push me this way.

"If Carter hadn't been hurt, you wouldn't care." He huffed.

Was he right? I set the can on the coffee table and stared at it for a minute. "That's not true. I've always cared. The only reason I've been relaxed is so you wouldn't lie and sneak and get yourself into more trouble or danger. I wish that you and your friends didn't need to drink to have fun or be cool or whatever. Believe it or not, there are more interesting ways to entertain yourselves. In any case, my big plan to keep you all safe didn't work, so maybe it's time to make some new rules."

"Great. More rules."

"Stop whining. It's really unattractive, Rowan. Especially when other people are paying a much bigger price than you."

My son flinched, his face paling. I wasn't a big fan of the ice-water approach, but it was effective.

He didn't apologize, but he cut the self-pity. "Have you heard anything about Carter?"

"Not really. He'll be in the rehab center for at least a month. He's got some feeling in his legs, but he's not walking." It'd been days without news from either Grace or Sam. I was losing patience with the waiting game, too.

Every time I closed my eyes, I pictured Grace wringing her hands, imagined the wrinkles on her forehead when she concentrated, visualized the incessant cleaning she undertook to assert control over something. No doubt she'd struggle with juggling everything while keeping a positive attitude. Keeping her from delving into her own pain had been my role.

I turned my head to look outside. Was she across town missing me as much as I missed her? Needing my advice as I needed hers?

Rowan interrupted my thoughts, which pulled me from a dark rabbit hole. "I haven't texted him since my apology that first night. I feel bad about it but don't know what to say."

"How about 'Thinking of you and wondering if there's anything I can do'?" I suggested.

He pushed himself into a more seated position, although his legs were still stretched out. "Am I a bad person?"

I frowned. Had my one attempt at discipline sent that wrong message? "Why do you think that?"

His gaze landed on the empty beer can. "Because, you know, other than football, what good do I do?"

Oh. Got it. Self-reproach was a familiar negative spiral for me since last weekend, too. We teach kids that everyone makes mistakes and deserves a second chance, but not many folks hand out second chances. For every Gweneth, there were at least two Carries.

This moment was a hard one. I didn't want to teach him to be someone he wasn't only to please other people, but he needed to learn to demand the best from himself. That's what I'd always tried to do, even if I'd failed lately.

My heart urged me to coddle him, but I let my head take the lead. "Well, Rowan, what else do you think you should be doing . . . or not doing?" I braced for learning something I might not want to know.

Another shrug, followed by rubbing his thighs. "Dunno. But I've been thinking about why I stopped being friends with Carter. I mean, he never did anything mean. He just wasn't cool, you know? Like, he didn't play sports and he was into books. He does that volunteer stuff with Mrs. Phillips and those SLOBs. That service-league thing always seemed so stupid, but they help out at that place you go to cut old ladies' hair, and they do stuff with some food bank."

My son had a conscience, unlike his father. That victory on this otherwise crappy day made my heart swell. "It's great that you're thinking about this. Can I ask what prompted it?"

"'Cause it seems unfair that Carter got hurt when he's so nice to everyone, but the rest of us are walking around perfectly fine."

It was unfair, thus Grace's righteous anger. If only there were some way to balance the scales without making my son or myself suffer more. For the moment I kept quiet, letting Rowan stew in his self-examination and crash course in injustice.

"Your guilty conscience proves that you're not a bad person. It's normal to choose friends based on common interests. It's only natural to bond with your teammates when you spend so much time together. Are you always nice to others? I couldn't say. Do you make some kids at school feel less-than by ignoring them? Maybe. But every day is a chance to be the kind of person you want to be. So maybe next week, stretch yourself. Make one new friend . . . someone you wouldn't normally get to know."

"That won't change what happened, though. Every time I think about how Carter might not walk again, I feel sick . . . like, really sick, Mom." He held his stomach, his mouth and eyes drawn by the weight of blame.

Blame I shared. The image of Carter in that hospital bed was stuck in my head. Same with the pain on Grace's face, the crack in Sam's voice, even the worry Becky had shown. And poor Kim was probably getting lost in the shuffle lately.

My house didn't feel the same, either, like it was coated in misery. I'd avoided the basement since last weekend. So had Rowan.

I grabbed him into a hug, which we both needed. "I know, honey. So do I. That's why they call these things tragic accidents. But you might begin to feel better if you text Carter. Be honest about how you feel. He might really appreciate it."

"He probably hates me like Mrs. Phillips hates you," he said, easing out of my arms.

His matter-of-fact tone sliced through me like my best cutting shears. My heart rebelled against the idea.

"Grace doesn't hate me." I couldn't accept that. We were like family. Families fight. Even when people avoided each other, it didn't erase the bond of shared memories and adventures, of wins and losses. "She's angry with the whole world because her baby is in pain, and that anger needs a target. I can be the bull's-eye for now and keep being her friend. Eventually she'll remember that I'm not her enemy."

Grace would let me back in someday, especially if Carter regained the ability to walk, which he had to do—not for my sake, but for his.

"How do you know?"

"I don't know, but I have faith." Who knew six years of Sunday service and Bible study with Uncle Tommy would come in handy? I guessed I'd paid more attention than I'd thought I had. "Time helps people get perspective. So have faith that John, Deshaun, and the rest will come around, too, after things settle down."

"I don't care if they do." Again he mirrored his father's tough-guy bluster.

"Come on. It's okay to feel hurt, but don't close yourself off. Your friends are scared about being arrested, like you are. Lashing out at you is easier than facing what they've done. Even though they didn't intend for things to go this far, they caused Carter's fall. Imagine knowing that you hurt someone that much."

Rowan stared into space. "Maybe I could help Carter with rehab. You know, give him tips about how to get pumped up and push through pain when you think you can't do one more rep."

I smiled and squeezed his knee. This was the kind of man I was trying to raise. "I love that idea, but we should check with his parents first. There are probably restrictions on visitors. Plus, the therapists might have a strict routine for him to stick to. Start with sending a simple note—maybe some of those inspirational quotes or something."

"That's weird." He made the face he always made when I served spinach.

"Well, then ask how he is and tell him you know he can do this."

Rowan shrugged, glancing at his phone.

"Okay, now get up and do those chores while I fix dinner."

———

I entered the school's south lobby at seven o'clock on the nose, my stomach tightening. When I'd first signed up to work the booster table at tonight's basketball game with Jordan and Jane, I'd looked forward to it. Jordan and I had been friendly for a while because of our boys, but I'd recently gotten closer to Jane, leading up to the hearing. Now, as I approached the tables where they were setting out sweatshirts and water bottles, it shocked me that I couldn't see my breath, given the chilly vibes coming off Jordan.

Normally, I smiled at everyone, but tonight I settled on politeness. "Looks like you guys got a head start. How can I help?"

Jordan spared me a glance. "You've helped enough."

My face got hot, but I ignored the bait to avoid a scene in front of Jane, even though her opinion of me was probably already in the sewer. I'd expected Grace's friends to hate me, but I wouldn't have pegged Jordan for a turncoat. I set my purse and jacket beneath the table and began to unpack one of the boxes, neatly folding the T-shirts and layering them on the table.

"Honestly, Mimi, Jane and I have this covered," Jordan said, one hand gripping a water bottle. "We don't need three of us here, so feel free to go."

She bared her fangs, but I wasn't trashy, so I wanted to avoid a public fight. Much as I would've loved to have stayed at home to watch a movie with Rowan, I wouldn't let her see me crumbling inside. I turned with a smile. "That's okay. I'm happy to do my part, like always."

Jordan set her hands on the table. "Take the hint, Mimi."

Jane winced but busied herself by recounting the money in the cashbox.

Thinking about Rowan sitting alone tonight, and about the damn Facebook posts, and about the only person who had a right to be upset—Grace—snapped something inside. I spoke through gritted teeth, loud enough that only Jordan and Jane could hear me. "Screw you, Jordan. If you and Roni want to pretend that your boys are victims rather than bad actors in this mess, then go ahead and stick your head in the sand. But you don't scare me. And don't think for one hot second that your new attitude erases the time last summer when we sat in your yard while the boys grilled hot dogs, drank Bud, and horsed around. You're no different or better than me—you just haven't been caught. Meanwhile, I wasn't at home last Saturday night—and I sure as hell didn't encourage your son and the others to give Carter Phillips a hard time, so you can stick your judgment where the sun don't shine."

I refrained from covering my mouth with my hand so she wouldn't have the satisfaction of seeing any regret about my mini breakdown. Jordan went still except for the subtle movement of her eyes, as if checking for Jane's read on the situation.

"Sorry, Jane," I added. "I don't mean to make you uncomfortable, but I've hit my limit of how much shit I can swallow."

"It's okay," she said. "I understand. For what it's worth, I don't think it's fair that everyone is blaming you."

Jordan whipped her head around as if stunned to have lost someone she considered an ally. Meanwhile, I nearly dropped to my knees in thanks. Praise God that not all folks saw this situation as black-and-white. That affirmation would get me through another night.

"Thank you." I opened a second box of gear to keep busy. We had to be ready by seven fifteen, when the crowds would start arriving.

Silence settled around us thickly until Jordan finally grabbed her things. "You two have this covered, so I'll take off."

Jane shot me a wide-eyed look, but I didn't make a peep. If Jordan couldn't admit that she'd mistreated me, so be it. But I would not beg her to stay or give in to her tantrum. It wasn't about my ego. It was simply about demanding a minimum level of respect.

When neither of us acknowledged her hissy fit, Jordan stormed off, phone in hand, probably typing another post for the Facebook moms' group. Once she burst through the doors and disappeared into the darkness, I sighed. "I really am sorry, Jane. I know you didn't come here tonight to referee a catfight."

"It's okay. You should defend yourself. Let's be honest, what happened at your house could've happened anywhere. I bet there are parties going on tonight. And Deshaun and John shouldn't have been pushing that poor kid around. It's crazy how these kids got so worked up over a budget debate. We all bear some blame for fighting over that field money. Some of the opinions in the paper leading up to the hearing were downright rabid."

I couldn't stop trembling as my eyes spilled over. "Thank you so much. You have no idea—*I* had no idea—how much I needed another mom to say all that to me. It's been a terrible week, but I feel awful for whining about it when no one has had a worse week than Carter."

"I dropped off dinner tonight and saw Grace. Kim had a Girl Scout thing that Grace had to attend this morning, so Sam was with Carter today."

Ah, Girl Scouts. I'd been envious when Grace and Kim started with Brownies—something I'd done with my own mother. I would've loved raising a little girl. Grace sometimes invited me over to "help" her when she hosted troop meetings. One time I did a whole lesson on different kinds of braids, and all the girls left the house with new dos. Being so disconnected from the Phillips family now physically hurt. "I don't mean to pry—but how's Grace doing?"

Jane shrugged. "She's jittery. Looks like she's lost some weight and isn't getting much sleep, either."

Made sense. Grace had never multitasked well, especially under stress, preferring to focus on one thing at a time. She'd probably been living on tea and crackers. I was willing to bet she gave up on makeup by Tuesday, and barely ran a brush through her hair by the weekend.

Two teen girls approached the table, cutting our conversation short. I welcomed the break from bleak thoughts, and studied the redhead's overgrown style.

The blonde asked, "How much are the pajama shorts?"

"Twenty bucks," I answered, smiling. "They'd look sweet on you."

"Will you guys be here after the game?" she asked.

"We'll stay open through halftime but then will start to box things up."

She wrinkled her nose and muttered something to her friend. "I'll think about it. Thanks."

"You're welcome. And by the way, I'm running a student special next week on cuts and highlights at A Cut Above, so tell your friends to stop in with their student IDs." That came out of nowhere, but maybe I could raid the teen set for new clients.

"Cool!" they said in unison as they strutted toward the gymnasium. I hoped they meant that.

I turned back to Jane, so desperate for information I couldn't stop myself from pressing for details. It was lowering, though. "Did Grace mention anything about Carter's prognosis?"

She picked at her nails, nervously. "I was too afraid to ask, assuming that if they'd gotten good news, we'd have heard it by now. I can't imagine how she's keeping it together. I'd be a wreck."

I nodded blankly, my thoughts drifting to the time when Kim had gashed her calf while we were all hiking Broad Creek Trail four years ago. Grace had flown into a panic at the sight of the blood, but Carter had the first-aid kit in his fanny pack. He'd given Kim some gum to distract her, sprayed her leg with antiseptic spray, applied butterfly bandages to close the gap, and wrapped it with gauze to keep it clean until we got her to the ER for stitches.

"Is Rowan coming to the game tonight?" Jane asked.

"He's grounded for a while." I grimaced, wondering if Jane considered that too light a punishment.

"That makes sense." Jane took a seat in one of the chairs the maintenance crew had left out for us. I envied her relaxed attitude. Her daughter, Alexis, hadn't been at the party, so she had no shame or guilt about the events that took place last weekend. Lucky duck. It'd be months or longer before my day passed without those dual feelings.

"Do you mind holding down the fort while I run to the restroom?" I asked.

"Of course." Jane took out her phone and started scrolling. I could only hope she wouldn't post something in the darn moms' group about my argument with Jordan.

"Be right back." I scooted away, thinking about Grace and her family. The memories of us and our kids made me desperate to talk to her, despite what Sam had said. It'd been days. Maybe she'd answer me tonight. As soon as I turned the corner, I stopped and dialed her number. When she didn't answer, another piece of my heart turned to dust, but hope died hard. After the beep I said, "Hey, Grace, it's me.

Rowan would like to visit Carter, and I'd love to talk to you. I miss you. You know I love you guys and want to help you through this. There's nothing I wouldn't do for y'all, so please . . . please give me a call soon."

I hung up, dabbing the tears from the corners of my eyes, and tucked my phone in my pocket, then went to the restroom. On my way back to the sales table, my text notifications pinged. Expecting it to be Rowan asking me to bring food home later, I checked and then stopped dead. Grace! A smile broke out as my heart sped up. I knew she'd come around.

> Mimi, please stop calling. I know that you're upset, but every time you ask me to let you help, you're making this about what you need to feel better. Right now, the only person whose needs matter to me is my son.

My body flushed with heat while I reread the text a second and third time. She had a point, even if I hadn't meant to make it about me. Ignoring Sam's advice by pestering Grace for information had hardly been loving or respectful. If I kept that up, I'd only push them further away. That was the very last thing I wanted, but ultimately it would be up to Grace whether or not she'd forgive me. There wasn't much I could do other than respect her wishes and wait.

"What's wrong?" Jane asked.

I glanced up, thinking, *What isn't wrong?* but said, "Nothing. A reminder popped up."

# CHAPTER TWELVE

## GRACE

*Monday afternoon, January 18*
*Potomac Point High School*

I stopped at the visitor security desk to sign out after my meeting with Carter's counselor and two of his teachers. Coordinating with them and Carter's tutor at the rehab center was yet another ongoing item on my endless to-do list spanning the anticipated six weeks of rehab.

The thirty-minute-long meeting littered with condolences had been as tough as expected. I'd kept my answers to their well-meant questions about Carter's prognosis brief and vague to avoid getting choked up. The open question of his expected recovery relentlessly gnawed at me.

"Have a good day, Mrs. Phillips," said Terrence, whose name I knew only because of his badge. Adam Eggers normally worked the afternoon shift. Terrence had to be new.

"Thanks." I offered a tight smile. Typically I'd introduce myself and welcome him to the school community, but I hadn't the energy or interest today. Every second here reminded me of what my son was missing. The school lobby, with its soaring plate glass and terrazzo floors, might as well have been a jail for how badly I wanted to escape. "You too."

While I fished for my keys and headed toward the door, a familiar voice caught me unaware.

"Grace," Roni called out. "Wait up!"

I snapped my head up as she closed the attendance office door behind her fifty yards down the hallway. John's mother in living color. Every part of my body flushed. If I could've run through the front doors, I would've, but my legs were numb. Somehow I forced my feet to move, punching open the lobby door while she signed herself out.

Wind whipped my hair around my face, and the dazzling winter sun blinded me. I'd parked at the far end of the visitor lot. Roni raced through the door behind me, moving at twice my speed. Nevertheless, I aimed for my car. What was it with people ignoring my request to be left alone?

Before I got there, Roni's hand grazed me from behind. "Grace, please. Give me a minute."

Stilled by her brashness, I closed my eyes and remained facing forward. "What do you want, Roni?"

"We haven't had a chance to talk since everything happened. How's Carter doing?"

The lack of contrition in her voice caused me to turn on her. "I don't want to discuss this with you—especially not while criminal charges are pending."

She winced, no doubt surprised by my curtness. "I heard that Carter regained some movement in his legs, so he'll walk again. Is that true?"

Had I believed her concern was for Carter rather than how his prognosis could impact John's sentence, maybe I would've been kinder. Doubtful, but that's a pointless debate. "We don't know if he'll walk again—it's too soon to tell. All we do know is that he'll be in pain for months to come, and rehab until at least late February."

Roni clutched her purse against her stomach, shaking her head grimly. "That Mimi. This is all her fault."

Wow. Lord knew Mimi played a role, but did Roni exonerate her son from what he'd done? "*All* Mimi's fault?"

"Of course." Roni's head twitched like a bird's. "Her and those parties."

My spine became more rigid than the flagpole behind Roni while my veins filled with ice. Mimi wasn't perfect, but she wasn't a phony, two-faced bitch, either. Roni had no right to criticize her, least of all to me. To my knowledge, Roni let John attend those parties, and Mimi wasn't the one who'd raised a bully. "Did Mimi force John to drink? Did she tell him to pick on my son?"

"They were joking around, Grace. Not picking on Carter," Roni said, defending her son with a dismissive hand wave. "Boys being boys. Surely you get that . . ."

"Boys being boys?" I repeated blankly, staring over her head as if a thought bubble had popped up for me to read those words again. Those damned words. "Is that what you call assault? Because Carter didn't ask them to touch him." When Roni blinked uncertainly, I added, "The week before that party, John and his teammates were harassing kids—including Carter—because you all convinced them they were owed those field house upgrades. I doubt it's a coincidence that, for the first time ever, they invited Carter to a party. I think they lured him there. Maybe they only meant to humiliate him, but your son and Deshaun are directly responsible for my son's injuries."

"If Carter felt threatened, why did he go?" Any traces of compassion in her tone vanished, replaced by something flinty. "He's not blameless. He was there drinking, too."

"Actually, the blood tests proved he wasn't drinking." I let that sink in. "Carter went because he'd naively hoped to make new friends."

The look on Carter's pleading face from that morning juxtaposed with the pained one from Mimi's basement floor replayed like a warped slideshow, momentarily distracting me. I rubbed my aching chest, almost forgetting about Roni.

She shrugged. "Well, obviously Carter doesn't think the boys purposely pushed him or the cops would've filed different charges, so thankfully the boys have a chance at a reasonable plea bargain."

She sounded proud—not merely relieved—that her son would skate by with little consequence. I knew I shouldn't say a word, but I couldn't stop myself. "By all means, plead down your son's charges, Roni. Why make him learn anything? I'm hardly shocked. John hasn't even apologized to Carter." At least Rowan had sent a text that night— not that it had changed much. The difference between Mimi's contrite behavior and Roni's could not be starker, which said a lot about Mimi (nothing I didn't already know). While I didn't think Rowan should visit Carter yet, the sincerity in Mimi's recent voice mail had been impossible to ignore. Hearing her voice had made me miss her even more, but protecting Carter and his potential claims against these people mattered more than our friendship. "Does John even care that he's created a lifetime of back problems for Carter? Do you?"

"Of course we care. We're all rooting for him. But be reasonable, Grace. Teenagers make dumb mistakes. That doesn't make them bad people." She raised her arms out wide.

My blood heated like lava as my right hand fisted. The itch to punch Roni made me hardly recognize myself. She hadn't wanted to hear anything I had to say; she'd only wanted the chance to defend her son. This was exactly why I didn't want to speak to her or Jordan.

As someone who'd never forgiven myself for allowing my sister's downward spiral to accelerate, I couldn't fathom the free passes others were quick to give themselves. Was I crazy or were they? I might begin to feel better if I let go of this blame but couldn't imagine that. Not while Carter was suffering. I turned toward my car without another word, my ears roaring as my blood pressure spiked.

"Grace . . . ," Roni called. I braced for her arm to brush my back again, but she let me go.

After unlocking my door, I fell onto the driver's seat, glad to seal myself inside, where I could block out lame excuses. In other circumstances, I might've swung by Mimi's shop to vent about Roni. Today I was on my own. I couldn't even trust Sam not to lecture me about my attitude.

Two calming breaths later, although still shaky, I backed out of my parking space. When I remembered Roni's boast about pleading down the criminal charge, my vision blurred for a second.

Everyone else cared more about protecting the perpetrators than getting justice for my son.

Ironically, echoes of Mimi's past advice bounced around my head, pressing me to fight. Ordering me not to put up with people's BS the way my mom had always rolled over. Urging me not to bow down to bullies like my dad, who'd always gotten away with whatever he wanted. With each block of my drive, my outrage became more maniacal, leading me to veer into the parking lot of the imposing three-story brick police station.

Nothing and no one would deter my mission. Officer Martinez—his name had been emblazoned on my brain since first meeting him in Mimi's basement, not to mention our debate in Carter's hospital room. A cursory glance around the lobby proved fruitless, so I approached the officer at the front desk. "Hello. Is Officer Martinez available? I'd like to speak with him about the investigation involving my son, Carter Phillips."

"Hang on, hon," she said before turning and taking a few steps away from the desk to call into some room that I couldn't see. "Yo, Rodri. Lady here to see you about the Phillips case."

I heard men's quiet laughter before Officer Martinez rounded the bend. The sudden rise of his brow suggested he'd been expecting someone else. For the first time since turning in to the station parking lot, I tensed, uncertain.

No. I had to fight for my son.

He approached me slowly. "Your son . . . how's he doing?"

I coughed into my fist. "The doctors won't make promises, but Carter's regained feeling in his legs, so we're cautiously optimistic. He'll remain in a Baltimore rehab for several weeks."

"It must be hard to have him away for so long, but that sounds encouraging . . . about his legs, I mean." He crossed his arms. While I considered how to proceed, he asked, "What can I do for you today?"

The unvarnished truth was that I wanted everyone involved to feel Carter's pain. My only regret was that group included my friend and a boy I'd helped raise. This wasn't the first time I'd faced this predicament. Margot had been like Mimi, loving me yet inadvertently hurting me with her bad decisions and behavior. Those years had primed me for my heart's current conflict.

"Can I have the police report—the whole thing, not the summary? I want to see the interview notes and whatever else you have." I gripped my purse strap with both hands, my pulse kicking.

Despite his very kind eyes, he shook his head. "I'm sorry. You're not entitled to all that evidence. But rest assured, it will be reviewed by the ADA."

My body deflated from yet another dead end. Another person protecting the guilty rather than helping me. "Why doesn't anyone care that those boys had been bullying Carter all week? Maybe they didn't plan for things to go this far, but that doesn't mean they had no intention of hurting him. And if they intended some harm, and Carter didn't start the 'horseplay,' explain again why they're only charged with reckless endangerment?"

Officer Martinez gestured toward a bench in the lobby. "Mrs. Phillips—"

"Grace." That was my name, although I didn't feel like myself lately. Being disconnected from Sam, Mimi, and even Carter had left me equally disconnected from myself.

"Grace, I understand your frustration. Unfortunately, like I told you before, our investigation—which includes statements from your son—suggests that these kids had no intention of pushing him down those stairs, thus the lesser charge."

"But those boys were drinking and have a vested interest in self-protection. How can you trust anything they say or even their memories of what happened?"

He leaned closer, speaking in a soft tone. "Do you trust your son?"

I stared in silence because he'd trapped me. I trusted Carter as much as anyone could trust a teen, but in my worst, weakest moments, I wished he would've trusted me—respected my experience—when I'd warned him about the dangers of going to that party. It wasn't a fair thought. I was the parent and should not have been dissuaded. Yet living out my worst fears brought out the worst in me.

"Yes, but he's not popular, so he doesn't want to escalate things. Maybe he's even afraid of what else they might do if he does. Did you consider that?"

He tipped his head to one side. "I tried to suss all that out when we spoke. If he wants to change his statement, I'll talk to him again. But you should know none of the texts or other accounts suggest any kind of conspiracy. Most kids were surprised to see your son there."

My eyes stung. In what kind of world should my bright, kind boy be unpopular while ruthless bullies reigned? I resented that Carter's adherence to my values made him uncool. "I don't understand why Mimi and Rowan aren't in more trouble for hosting this party."

"Rowan's got a juvic hearing coming up. As for Mrs. Gillette, she didn't give permission for that party and wasn't present, so she didn't break any laws."

"Not that night, anyway," I muttered, feeling a little guilty for throwing her under the bus. She had plenty of wonderful traits, but like my mother years ago, she'd created an environment that enabled bad behavior. I couldn't erase that from my memory as if it weren't true, as much as I didn't want to resent her as I'd resented my mother most of my life.

Officer Martinez rubbed his thighs with a sigh before offering a sympathetic smile. "In my experience, everyone makes mistakes now and then. She seems genuinely sorry. I know your family is suffering, and I'm sorry that you don't feel that your son will get justice, but I've got to go by the evidence, and in this case, it supports only reckless endangerment charges."

I swallowed, defeated again. "You know John's and Deshaun's parents will lawyer up. Their kids will get off with a fine—one their parents will pay. Meanwhile, my son is looking at a lifetime of pain." I dabbed my eyes with a tissue, my face heating from embarrassment.

"I really am sorry about that." He turned his hands over as if helpless, having probably seen worse miscarriages of justice in his career. "You can make a victim impact statement to make sure the judge knows the seriousness of your son's injuries."

I sat straighter, newly encouraged. "Is there a form?"

He shook his head. "Typically that's made in court at the sentencing."

"But what if they plead out and there isn't any formal sentencing?"

"I'm not a lawyer, ma'am. You should contact the prosecutor's office with your concerns." He drew a breath and clucked. "But, Mrs. Phillips, would you mind a little advice from someone who's seen a lot of stuff go down around town?"

"Sure." I braced because his tone suggested his opinions wouldn't be soothing.

"As bad as everything is—and I know it's bad—your family will be living in this community going forward. You might think about whether making things worse for others will help your son get better or make it easier for him to go back to school when the time comes."

He sounded so much like my husband I blinked. Carter would not want me to make things worse. In fact, my meddling might be partly to blame for how we got here in the first place. If I'd stayed out of the budget debate like he'd asked—like my mother had warned—he would not be hurt. Same with my asking Mimi to get Rowan to talk to his teammates. With so little experience asserting myself, I'd yet to find the balance between doing so safely and pushing too far.

I felt stuck, strangely unsure of right and wrong. Then I recalled the time my mom had made an excuse to Margot's teacher when questioned about my sister's broken arm. The shame of my silence back then resurfaced. I hadn't spoken up for my sister, so my dad got away with hurting her. Worse, he'd remained free to do it again with impunity . . . until he hadn't. How might she have been different if that hadn't been true?

I shivered.

I'd always believed that our choices, not fate, determined the outcome. For so long I'd kept the peace, believing that strong reactions would lead to more danger. But in truth, my mom had chosen the path of least resistance, and things still went wrong. Was Mimi right? Was fate unalterable? Was no one to blame? If so, I knew I should let go and forgive. Mend things with Sam and Mimi and put my life back together. Yet if I did that, might Carter ultimately end up disappointed that I didn't take a stand for him? As much as I missed Mimi, our friendship wasn't worth risking my son's lifelong resentment.

"I'll think about your advice," I promised, rising from the bench.

Officer Martinez stood as well. "Good luck to you. I hope your son has a speedy and full recovery."

"Thank you." No use explaining once more that a "full recovery" was impossible. This was not some insignificant boo-boo like everyone wanted to characterize it. Even if Carter eventually walked without support, he had permanent hardware in his spine, which meant years of residual pain and arthritis, and the likelihood of more surgery in the future. The harrowing reality crippled me.

I charged out of the station, my body buzzing with restless energy. Involving myself in the criminal cases wouldn't change what had happened or alter my son's future, but it might make those boys think twice before hurting anyone else. Carter might not get that now, but when he became a father, he'd understand. He'd also have proof that his parents loved him enough to champion him—something mine had never done.

Tomorrow I'd call the district attorney's office and make sure that whoever was handling this case understood the full extent of Carter's injuries.

When I finally got home, Sam's car was already in the garage. He must've left work early. Not yet ready to face him, I turned off the car and called Carter, who'd been alone since I'd left him at noon.

"Hey, Mom," he answered, his lackluster tone flattening my heart.

"Hi, sweetheart. I met with your school team and they're all set with your tutor. How was your afternoon?" Every day he would endure a few hours of therapy and a battery of checkups.

"Hard." He sounded tuckered.

It'd been so easy to comfort my children when they were little. Even if I could reach through the phone and hold him, it wouldn't help. I pinched my nose to stave off tears. "I'm sorry. Can I help?"

A pointless question with him up there and me down here.

"No. I've got to tough it out." It sounded like he might've shifted in bed. "Rowan offered to help."

"Rowan?" I frowned. I hadn't given Mimi the green light on that. Had she ignored my text, or had Rowan taken it upon himself? Hopefully the latter, because if it was only Mimi's idea, it would die as suddenly as it was offered. That disappointment would hurt Carter, who'd always admired Rowan.

That reminded me of the old tree house that Sam had built for the kids. Carter would bring jars of bugs up there to show Rowan, but Rowan had been more interested in climbing the branches above the tree house. He'd tried to coax Carter to join him, but Carter never did. I didn't know why that memory made me smile. Maybe because they'd been so young and different yet played well—like Mimi and me. Now look at us all, torn in opposite directions.

"Don't freak, Mom."

I bit down on the inside of my cheek to keep myself in check. "How can Rowan help?"

After a slight hesitation, he said, "He's an expert at training."

Expert? I rolled my eyes. Rowan might be great at training his healthy body, but he didn't know anything about the serious limitations Carter's hardware and nerve damage presented.

Carter continued, "He said he'd talk me through the low points, like when I feel I can't keep going or I'm not making progress as fast as I want to. You know, like he has to do."

For the first time since the fall, my son sounded slightly encouraged, so I could hardly raise an objection. I had to admit it was brave and kind of Rowan to reach out. Like mother, like son. I pressed my palm against my face to subdue a headache. "Well, if you think it will help . . ."

"I do."

Fresh tears brought on by the memories of better days clogged my nose, but I cleared my throat so he wouldn't hear them. "I'll be up first thing tomorrow. Anything you want me to bring? Doughnuts, perhaps?"

"I've been reading that protein helps the body heal, so maybe some pistachios and hard-boiled eggs. Hummus. You know, snacks like that."

I couldn't help but smile and thank God that my son's brain hadn't borne the brunt of his injuries, and that he usually made good decisions. "You got it. Love you. Hope you find something good on Netflix tonight."

"I've got to read a book for Lit."

"Oh. Well, then I can't wait to hear about it tomorrow. Miss you already."

"Good night, Mom."

"Good night."

After he hung up, I sat in my quiet car, dreading the evening. When I was surrounded by the rest of my family, Carter's absence struck more keenly. I let the pain of our forced separation seep in and subside before going inside to face my husband and Kim.

I wandered through the house, passing the silent piano. I'd taken the past week off from teaching, but I'd have to start back in another week. I'd always loved those hours, but now they were simply another obligation that split my focus. Like with Mimi and Sam, another comfort lost to me.

Eventually I found Sam in his office, riffling through insurance paperwork. Our carrier required co-pays, and the costs of Carter's medical care promised to be exorbitant. He looked up and shook his head. "It's staggering. I don't know what uninsured people do when this kind of thing happens."

Those poor folks were victimized twice. I tugged at my collar to cool off. We enjoyed financial comfort, so I'd hardly given much thought to this aspect of our nightmare. "Are you concerned?"

"It's hard to tell this early, but the coverage gaps are bigger than I expected. The hospital stay and surgery were a few hundred grand, and our share isn't nothing. With inpatient and outpatient rehab, these figures could really balloon. Most of the cash on hand will be used to pay taxes soon, so we might need to liquidate some investments in the future."

My whole body slumped. The last thing we needed now was more to worry about.

He rocked back in his leather desk chair, peering at me. "You look peaked. Is there trouble coordinating with the tutor?"

"No." I paused. We hadn't been on the same page since before the accident, so I hesitated to share my earlier confrontation. "I ran into Roni at school."

Sam's anxious grimace suggested he worried more about what I'd said than what she had. I missed my husband's support, but then again, he probably missed mine. "I take it that didn't go well."

I leaned against the doorjamb, arms folded. "She had the nerve to brag about how they would plead down John's criminal charge. Everyone's getting off easy. Then I hear the exhaustion in our son's voice and I could smash something. It's all so unfair."

Sam inhaled and held his breath before letting it out slowly. His eyes reflected pity—a new and unnerving dynamic between us. "We both know life isn't always fair, babe, but burning things down won't help Carter."

I scoffed. "You sound like Officer Martinez."

Sam cocked his head, looking almost alarmed. "When did you speak with him?"

"I swung by the station on my way home." *Please support me. Please support me.*

"Grace." He'd said it softly. Sadly. Almost like he was in mourning.

I pushed off the doorframe. "Don't shake your head at me. I've got every right to be furious. Why aren't you angrier? That's the real question."

My chest expanded as the air around me charged. Sam didn't shrink in the face of my accusation, nor did he rise to the bait. The only outward signs of his contained fury were his whitening fingertips pressed against his desktop.

"Just because my anger isn't eating me alive doesn't mean I don't feel it. But what good does it do to run around like a deranged bull tromping on everything and everyone? You're walling yourself off from me, from Mimi, and everyone else. What's that getting you? Or Carter?" He pushed back from his desk, letting out a sigh as if it would carry his anger from the room.

"Justice!" I punched the air with both hands, which hardly satisfied the urge to shake some sense into him.

He frowned. "How so?"

I opened my mouth and then closed it—mind blank. My body prickled with embarrassed rage because justice wouldn't make anything better for anyone other than me. I needed the scales to be balanced because I needed proof that our actions mattered. Proof that we all weren't merely fate's puppets.

Sam stood and rounded his desk to approach me but stopped short, his gaze uncertain, his hands balled into loose fists at his sides. Neither of us was used to his touch being less than welcome. Right now even I couldn't guess how I'd react if he hugged me, which buried my heart in more pain. Like layers of soil, loss and strain piled on—Carter, Sam, Mimi, and even my relationship with Kim.

"Gracie, babe." A plea. "Let's use our energy to help Carter rather than to fight with each other and everyone else."

I shivered, unable to match his calm in the face of the overwhelming tidal wave bearing down. Our son's suffering. The months of therapy. The tens of thousands or more that this could cost us regardless of our insurance coverage.

"What do you want me to say?" I asked.

He dropped his head before choosing to return to his chair, shoulders sagging. "Never mind."

I stepped forward, afraid of what I was seeing. Aware that I might be pushing him to the end of his patience. Pushing him out of love with me. "I want to know."

He regarded me, debating with himself but ultimately shaking his head. "You'll take it wrong, and we don't need any more disagreements."

"Please tell me what you're thinking." I clasped my hands in front of my pelvis to calm myself.

He closed his eyes for a moment. "Whatever responsibility others bear, we bear some, too. We let him go, after all."

His words struck like a cattle prod, shocking me with sudden, sharp pain. I gripped the back of the chair so hard it moved. Self-loathing roughened my voice, which came out almost as a shriek. "You think I don't know that? That it doesn't eat at me every single day—and every time I look at you? Why do you think I'm desperate to fix this somehow? I failed Carter once, but he'll know that I fought for him every step of the way since that lapse in judgment. Don't you see, Sam? I can't live with any other outcome *because* of my hand in this."

Instead of backing down, Sam held his course, as if his insistence would persuade me.

"But, Gracie, your inability to forgive yourself or anyone else is making it harder on everyone. On our daughter, and on me. Probably on Carter, too. I'm grieving for our son's pain, and the loss of your respect. Kim's probably more confused and frightened than she's letting on. And your friends—people are trying to be kind, but you're so bitter and withdrawn. So rigid in your thoughts. It's been nine days. Maybe if you met with Mimi and Rowan, your rage would subside."

I reared back on my heels. "Have you spoken with them?"

His reddened cheeks answered before he did. "I texted Mimi an update about Carter's progress and gave Rowan permission to reach out to Carter."

I got dizzy, as if I'd been boxed in the ears. "Why is Mimi still texting you?"

"Probably because you won't talk to her." He cocked a disapproving brow.

While I could take no comfort in my husband or my friend, they were finding it in each other. My world was turning inside out, knocking me around like a strong wave.

There was no use in us talking in circles right now. I turned to leave, then stopped with my hand on the doorjamb.

Looking over my shoulder, I said, "You know, even if you don't always agree with me, you're supposed to be on my side. Not Mimi's. Not Rowan's. Do you honestly think I don't know that they feel bad? Or that I don't miss my friend, Sam? Or you? I'm sorry I'm not handling this as well as you'd prefer. That I can't yet make room in my heart for sympathy for others. But from where I stand, it seems like you care about everyone's feelings except mine. Just like my mother, you want to silence me and my feelings instead of trying to understand them. I have never felt more alone and misunderstood in my life. You're like a stranger to me, and that breaks my heart."

He dropped his chin, replying softly, "I could say the same about you, Gracie."

He would not hear me. He would not be on my side.

Fine. "I'm sorry you don't respect my point of view."

I walked away before he could body-slam me with another unwanted response. He wasn't wholly wrong—I wasn't myself lately and wouldn't pretend otherwise. But these were exceptional times. My feelings weren't invalid. His unwillingness to allow my anger to burn for even an instant felt like he'd snuffed out a part of my soul.

Kim was in the kitchen when I got there, sneaking a bowl of Golden Grahams. Lacking the energy to fight, I pretended not to notice. Inside the refrigerator sat an unfamiliar casserole dish covered with tinfoil and topped with a Post-it note, so I pulled it out. The fact that Mimi had encouraged my friends to help rushed in like warm water sinking beneath all my anger, trying to loosen it.

This dish was Susie Chin's teriyaki chicken casserole, which I'd enjoyed at various potlucks throughout the years. It wrought a smile that she remembered that I liked it. I turned on the oven, then made a note to write a thank-you card to Susie. Mimi deserved one, too, despite what I'd said to Sam about that earlier this week. What I didn't know was why I couldn't allow myself to accept her apologies or her help. Worse, why her attempts enraged me. She hadn't done anything to intentionally hurt my family, yet I felt betrayed.

"Did you remember my Valentine's cards and candy?" Kim asked.

Shoot. Devoting myself to Carter had left Kim in the cold. I'd yet to strike a balance. Kim deserved better. "I'm sorry, honey. I'll get them tomorrow."

"That's what you said yesterday." She wrapped her arm protectively around her bowl while I absorbed the accusation.

"I know. I've had a lot on my plate. But there are still a few weeks until Valentine's Day. I promise you'll have them in time to send to your classmates and friends."

Kim stared at me, her chin tucked. "I heard you and Dad fighting."

Her comment nearly made me stumble as I crossed to the table. "What?"

"You guys were just fighting." Her worried gaze pierced me. "Lilah's parents used to fight a lot, and then they got divorced."

Weeks ago, I would've laughed at the idea that my marriage would falter. Until this all happened, my kids had never—or very rarely—heard Sam and me quarrel. A new low point: shattering my child's sense of stability. Another thing to regret.

"Oh, honey. Dad and I aren't getting divorced." A tiny prick of doubt popped my conscience when recalling Sam's demeanor from minutes earlier, which proved we weren't impervious. I hid my alarm. "When grown-ups get exhausted, they can be crabby. Dad and I haven't been sleeping well because we're very worried about your brother. I'm sorry if we've upset you. I'll try harder to be more careful with my words, okay? I don't want you to worry."

"Okay. Maybe you'd be happier if we did something fun . . . like having my sleepover party next weekend?" She shot me a cute, if manipulative, grin.

Her tenacity prompted a slight smile that pulled me back from the abyss. I envied her ability to bounce from one extreme to another. Unfortunately, the last thing Sam and I could do right now was host a sleepover party.

"Honey, now isn't a good time, but I promise we'll do something once things settle." I reached for her forearm, stroking her soft skin. "I'm sorry if my running around so much has made you feel bad. It's got nothing to do with how much I love you. But Carter is all by himself up in Baltimore, so I try to keep him company as much as possible. Do you understand?"

"It's okay." She drank the sweetened milk straight from the bowl, which proved she knew that she had me over a barrel. If I weren't bruised from the inside out, I might've laughed. But breathing hurt enough right now. When she finished, she slid off her chair and took her bowl to the dishwasher. Before leaving, she said, "I forgive you."

Her simple words produced equal amounts of relief and shame.

Alone, I folded my arms on the table, set my head down, and wept. I could see myself from a distance—a madwoman kicking her life apart like some sandcastle on the beach and watching it disintegrate with each new wave of frustration. Trapped in an unending battle to figure out the right thing to do, unable to pry my heart open to forgiveness or move forward with confidence. Without Sam to talk to, who could help me?

Not my mother.

Mimi's sunny smile sprang to mind, which made me cry even harder.

# CHAPTER THIRTEEN

## Mimi

*Thursday, January 21*
*Rehab facility*

"I'm nervous," Rowan mumbled as the thick glass doors to the rehabilitation center opened automatically.

One benefit of my having fewer salon appointments lately was being able to bring him to see Carter this afternoon.

"About what?" I asked, dwarfed by the institution that would be Carter's home for weeks or longer, the reality of which intensified my sense of gloom.

"Seeing Mrs. Phillips." His solemn gaze landed like a gut punch.

Grace had never before been unkind to Rowan, but Carter's injury had changed my friend, so anything could happen. I loosened my white-knuckled grip on the tin of homemade nut-and-granola bars. "Don't worry, honey. She won't say anything to you."

A literal truth, I feared.

So darn sad. She'd rejected my every attempt and offer to lift her up, and meanwhile, without her grounding presence, my life, my business, and even my relationship with Rowan were off-kilter. Still, determined to heed my own advice, I tipped my chin up. Grace was expecting us. Maybe she missed me and would finally accept our apology.

Sam had given me Carter's room number, so we signed in and then walked down a corridor of patient rooms. Carter's door was partway open, so I rapped on it twice. "Carter, honey, it's Mrs. Gillette and Rowan. Are you up for company?"

"Sure," he said.

A thin sheen of perspiration covered Rowan's face when confronted with a room filled with monitors and equipment needed to assist Carter's mobility. Every contraption might as well have been a condemnation of my parenting and my son's behavior, making my stomach sour.

This depressing space would be his home for a while. Granted, Grace had done her best to add homey touches with some of his personal items. Picturing her collecting these things from his room in tears, desperately doing anything she could to make this situation less lonely for her child, made my throat ache with tightness. Despite her heroic attempt, nothing hid the medical equipment or brightened the bland floors and walls.

To my surprise, Grace wasn't in the room. That she'd left Carter alone rather than face me dashed any hope of forgiveness, which produced a lump in my throat. The nearly two weeks since she'd cut me off felt more like two years. We'd never mend fences at this rate.

"Hey." Carter winced when shifting position and then managed a polite smile. He looked thinner. Gaunt, even. His cheekbones seemed sharper, too. Seeing the wheelchair in the corner of the room nearly made me stumble. This was not a bump I could wipe away with a hug and a treat, like I had when Rowan had accidentally clocked him in the head with a football at ten. The worst part was the inescapable truth that Carter would not be here if I had been a different parent, or if my son had been a more responsible, respectful kid.

"Hi, sweetie." I set the tin on the table beside Carter's bed, my guilty pulse pounding in response to seeing him wince whenever he

moved. I hadn't fallen asleep once since this happened without seeing Carter terrified on my basement floor. If it were Rowan trapped
here fighting to relearn basic skills, I'd probably shriek into my pillow
every single night. Poor Grace. "I made you some of my special power
bars—loaded with protein. Rowan chows down on these before and
after training."

Despite the chirpy description, my gift seemed pathetically
inadequate.

"Thanks." Carter glanced at the tin, appearing uncertain about how
to greet us. His gaze darted from Rowan back to me. "I'm sure they're
great."

I twined my twitchy fingers together. "Is everyone here treating
you okay?"

"I guess." He shrugged. "They push me, but they're nice about it."

Seeing him frail and alone sharpened the unpleasantness of going
home to the scene of the crime. An apt description. Maybe Grace wasn't
wrong to be disappointed in the charges passed out like "Get Out of
Jail Free" cards.

"Are there any kids your age?" I asked, hoping he could make a
friend.

"Mostly it's older people, but some are younger than me." He nodded matter-of-factly, loosening up a bit. "Two new people this week got
really messed up because of people texting while driving."

"That's terrible." I turned to see if Rowan was still with us. My son
remained frozen and tongue-tied behind me.

"Something wrong?" Carter asked, his head tipped as he peered
around me to Rowan.

"I . . . I feel really bad. This all"—Rowan gestured around the room,
his face graying by the second—"like, really sucks. I wish it hadn't
happened."

"Me too," Carter said self-mockingly. "But don't feel bad. It's not
your fault."

"My house. My friends," Rowan mumbled. I gobbled up that moment of self-awareness and maturity like the mother starving for a crumb of silver lining that I was.

"I could've left when everyone got drunk. Pretty dumb of me to stick around just so Tracy Patterson didn't think I was lame." Carter rolled his eyes.

His light humor broke some of the tension. But Tracy Patterson? Good grief, that one was trouble. Poor Carter. Everyone does stupid things in the name of love, but most get out with nothing worse than a temporary broken heart.

"I think I'll hit up the cafeteria and give you boys some time alone to talk," I said. "Your dad said we shouldn't tucker you out, so I'll come back in fifteen or so. Cool?"

Carter nodded, so I leaned forward and kissed the top of his head before tousling his hair. "I shoulda brought my scissors. Maybe next time?"

"Yeah." He chuckled while Rowan took a seat in one of the two chairs in the room.

I pulled the door mostly closed behind me on my way out.

The cafeteria's towering windows and decent selection surprised me. Caving to the siren song of caffeine and sugar, I purchased a large coffee and chocolate-covered doughnut with sprinkles, even though I suspected comfort foods wouldn't do the trick. While running my credit card through the register, I froze.

Grace sat at a table in the far corner, staring out one of those grand windows. Her back was to the entrance, so she probably hadn't seen me come in. I could slip out unnoticed.

I hesitated, torn between leaving her to her thoughts and forcing her to deal with me. The twenty yards between us might as well have been the entire Chesapeake Bay, and crossing it would be equally treacherous. Then I remembered that very first playgroup. I'd shown up late with a batch of walnut brownies—unaware of Tina Tubman's nut allergy or the group's general ban on sugary foods for the tots.

The other four ladies in the group had barely hidden their contempt for my mistakes (or my short shorts), but Grace had smiled at me as if I were a fresh breeze coming off the water, before moving seats to introduce herself and then asking me all kinds of questions about Rowan. A week later she'd surprised me by booking a hair appointment with me when I was still working at Divaz. From then on, we'd been fast friends.

I never had a sister, nor had an easy time keeping female friends, so I'd cherished Grace in ways she probably never fully appreciated. The idea that one admittedly awful incident could erase a decade of love and trust gutted me. With that in mind, I summoned my courage, grabbed a butter knife from the buckets of silverware, and crossed to Grace's table.

"It's not one of Hannah's pistachio muffins, but it doesn't look terrible." I set the plate with the chocolate-glazed doughnut on the table while sweat trickled down my back. Grace snapped her head my way, her face ashen. My stomach burned while I waited to see if my gamble would pay off. "I'll share it with you."

Her gaze darted over my shoulder as if looking to see if anyone else had come with me or was watching us. Two, three, four beats passed in silence. Her cornered expression made me feel guiltier for forcing my way in. I was about to leave, but then she gestured toward an empty chair across the table.

A bloom of hope mushroomed so fast I almost grabbed her into a hug. Fortunately, I kept my cool, took a seat, and cut the doughnut in half. I faked a smile, pretending that we were at Sugar Momma's for one of our regular coffee dates, telling myself that baby steps were better than no steps at all.

But Grace's scrutiny made me sweat even more. Her blue eyes darkened with sorrow, defeat, and regret. I set my half of the doughnut on a napkin and then pushed the plate with the other half closer to her. At first, she stared at it as if it might be poisoned.

A host of options might build a bridge back to our friendship. Another apology, perhaps? An offer to do something more? In the end, I asked the one question that had most concerned me about her since this happened. "How are you holding up?"

"Not great," she said on a deep sigh. Grace raised her doughnut half and tore off a small piece. Before she put it in her mouth, she added, "I should've thanked you sooner for organizing the Meal Train. It's certainly helped Sam and me keep some semblance of normalcy at home." A flash of distress crossed her face so quickly I almost doubted I'd seen it. Were she and Sam fighting because he'd kept in contact with me?

Regardless, that thanks had not come out easily. I understood why, too. Her baby was in pain, and she would not be okay until he was better. "It was the very least I could do, Grace."

She met my gaze—hers tinged with bitterness—then looked away. I sipped my coffee to buy time for my thoughts to settle. The silence—so unusual for us—killed my appetite. And I'd rarely let a doughnut go uneaten.

Grace set her elbow on the table and rested her chin in her palm. "I don't know how to do this, Mimi. I can't look at you or Sam without feeling angry—at you, at him, at myself. I resent you both so much, but hate myself most of all. And yet I don't have time to indulge in and work through these feelings—the anger and the missing of what was. I have to be strong for Carter, but all I want to do is crawl into a hole to cry or find a way to turn back time. Why him? Why did this happen to my son?"

With a trembling hand, she swiped away the lone tear trailing down her cheek. Amazingly—or simply in Grace's usual way—her posture remained poised and her voice steady. Meanwhile, inside, I was simultaneously dismayed that she'd admitted all that, and falling apart because of it. My mistakes hadn't hurt only Carter; they'd hurt my friend and her entire family. No wonder she didn't know what to say to me.

"I don't have any answers, Grace. I've been beating myself up for leaving those boys alone with alcohol as a temptation. In hindsight, I see how letting them drink other times sent mixed signals. Even though I wasn't home, I bear some blame for what's happened. I know that's cold comfort because it doesn't help Carter now." I pressed my fingertips to my temples to ward off a sudden headache. "I've been desperate to keep Rowan happy ever since Dirk left. He misses his dad so much, which makes me feel damn guilty. But that's not a good excuse for bad parenting."

Her expression grew more distant—almost miffed. "Dirk called me last week."

"He did?" My eyes practically popped out of my head. Dirk had never warmed to Grace, whom he'd labeled uptight almost from the get-go.

She nodded. "I didn't speak with him."

Of course not. She'd never appreciated what I'd seen in Dirk aside from his face, which I'd always thought had a Gerard Butler kind of sex appeal. "What did he want?"

"Who knows what he was really after? Probably to make sure that I didn't have plans to ruin Rowan's life. But he mentioned your custody arrangement and asked if I had any insight that would help him decide whether to revisit that."

I gulped. Literally—like a full-on cartoon gulp. My words came out on a whisper. "What did you say?"

"Nothing. I told you, I didn't speak with him. He left a message, and I never returned the call." She took another bite of the doughnut, her gaze flicking toward the window.

She'd protected me despite everything—a sign that we could salvage our friendship. I might've smiled if Dirk's agenda didn't trouble me. I slumped back into my seat. "Lord, that man. He ignores Rowan for weeks at a time and then has the gall to think he'd be a better parent than me? Thank you for taking my side."

With no bitterness or malice, she said, "I didn't do it for you. Or for Rowan. I simply don't have the interest in or patience for dealing with your ex, or any bandwidth to think about the fallout of all this on your family. Not when my own is on shaky ground."

Each of her words landed like a sharp jab, but I couldn't blame her for her honesty. If I were in her shoes, I might feel the same. I didn't know. That was the thing about trying to put yourself in another's shoes. You could never know how you'd take that walk if forced to, and I selfishly hoped I'd never have to try on this particular pair.

"I'm sorry that seeing me is painful. I'm really sorry that this situation is causing problems with Sam. And I don't mean to make any of this about me. Honestly, that's not my intention when I ask for updates, despite my own guilt about what happened at my house. You're my best friend. We all spent so much time together when the boys were young I feel like I half raised Carter. It kills me to see him in that bed. I feel helpless and desperate, like you."

"Not like me. You'll never know how this feels unless your son's ability to walk is compromised because some drunk jerks thought it funny to push him around. But even as infuriating as that is, I wouldn't wish this on you or anyone." Her mouth twitched then with a cock of one brow. "Maybe on Roni." She stuffed the rest of the doughnut in her mouth.

That was so unexpected I laughed. "I know you don't mean that."

She lifted her shoulders and frowned as if questioning her own heart, then turned to stare out the window again.

While she gazed off, I digested her words. It wasn't our normal coffee-and-doughnuts talk, but she'd opened up. She'd refused to help Dirk. All things I wouldn't take for granted. But that damn Dirk and his meddling. He made it hard to remember what I'd ever liked about him. Life had been happier without his lies and BS, so I didn't regret our divorce. Grace, however, should do everything she could to keep her marriage on track.

I hesitated before offering advice. "This might not be the right time, but since I don't know when we'll get another chance to talk, I want to say something. And, Grace, this comes from a place of love and experience, not judgment. You mentioned being resentful of Sam. Please be careful with that. Resentment kills love. None of us is perfect, but Sam's devoted to you and your family. Please work on forgiving him before your anger tears your family in two and your life becomes a series of visitations and split holidays. Don't build walls at a time when you need each other the most."

Her face tightened, then she looked at her lap in silence. Silence, silence, silence. It killed me, but I reminded myself to be grateful she'd let me sit with her. She hadn't screamed at me or told me to leave, either. Somewhere deep down she still trusted me enough to listen. I might not be able to help Carter, but I could help Grace and Sam.

"What if I take Kim on Friday night? I'll do a whole fun blowout thing with her hair at the salon—do manicures, too. Kim likes Dante's, so we can do pizza and maybe see a movie. That'll give you and Sam some privacy to talk or do whatever you need to do to close the gap." I leaned forward, reaching across the table but then withdrawing my hands when her gaze dropped disapprovingly on them. "I'd love to do this, and I bet you and Sam could use a break."

"No, thank you." She shook her head, chin slightly wobbly.

"Why not?" I asked, wishing she would change her mind.

"I don't want your help, Mimi." She closed her eyes and inhaled slowly, but her hands trembled as she dabbed her misty eyes.

"Why not?" I repeated. She was obviously conflicted. If I pushed a little more, we could hash everything out and clear the path back to our friendship.

She glanced at me, drawing herself up as if raising a shield. "Because there's too much unknown . . . issues unsettled."

"What issues?"

Her gaze grew distant—as if she'd had to detach herself in order to answer me. "Legal ones."

My eyes began to sting. Did she mean to hurt my son now to balance the scales? "Are you coming to Rowan's hearing next week?"

"No."

Her stiff demeanor lessened my relief. I was unaccustomed to parrying with Grace, and frankly, I didn't enjoy it. "Then what are you talking about?"

She set her elbows on the table and touched her forehead to her clasped hands before looking directly at me. "There's a lot of uncertainty about Carter's recovery. His future . . . things he'll need . . . and the costs . . ."

A dull headache began beating at the base of my skull. She meant a civil suit. My salon was already taking it on the chin. A lawsuit could be potentially devastating if my umbrella policy didn't cover it. Then the thought of Carter, the expenses of his care, and the pain he was in hit me like an unexpected wave. "You want to sue me and the others?"

Her shoulders curled forward, and she rubbed her arms, almost rocking in her seat. Her facial expression pinched as if I'd offended her. "This isn't about what I want. I don't *want* any of this to be real. What I want is for Carter to be happy and healthy, but that isn't happening anytime soon, so I have to settle for what I can do to protect his future. Health insurance doesn't cover all these costs, and we shouldn't have to bear that ourselves. John and Deshaun caused Carter's fall. And even you admitted that you were negligent to leave the boys alone with alcohol in the house."

I had, hadn't I? Dammit, Dirk was right. I did have a knack for making things worse for myself. The throbbing headache now consumed my whole skull. I should've expected this—people sue for everything, as if a check will make them feel better. I just hadn't considered that Grace would ever sue me. Grace! "I don't know what to say . . ."

"Neither do I, which is why it's better that we don't say much for now." Her voice cracked and tears quivered in the bottoms of her eyes. Her obvious conflict should have made me feel better, but fear blunted all other emotions.

"Grace, let's not throw ten years of friendship out the window. There's got to be a solution that doesn't involve lawyers."

Her melancholy expression pinned me to my seat. "I wish you and Sam would quit treating me like I'm making this personal when all I'm doing is looking out for Carter. These co-pays will pile up for months—maybe years. His pain and suffering are real—bigger than the pain and suffering a lawsuit will cause any of you—and we still don't know if he'll walk again. Should I ignore all that because it's inconvenient for you and Roni and Jordan?"

Another jab, this time to the jaw. Being lumped in with those two made me lose my patience. "I'm not talking about Roni and Jordan, or even about a damn lawsuit. But lawsuits can take years. How's it so easy for you to cut me out of your life?"

"Easy?" She turned on me, eyes wide with pain. "None of this is easy. My heart hardly beats most days. I'm alone in my grief because everyone I ever counted on refuses to see my side of any of it. But this is life. We've made our choices and have to deal with the consequences. Whether it was my father's death, my sister's, or this . . . loss hurts, but it happens. And when it does, we press on."

"But this doesn't have to be a loss." I gestured wildly between us. "I'm on your side. You're the sister I never had. Why won't you let me help you?"

"Can you make Carter walk again—on his own? Can you guarantee that he won't live with pain for years to come?"

I shook my head, reluctantly conceding those points.

"Then you can't help," she said, each word enunciated with perfect clarity.

I reached across the table and grabbed her hand, holding it tight so she couldn't jerk it away. "Friendship helps. Love helps. A shoulder to cry on helps, Grace. We need each other now more than ever. Just because we don't see the answers yet doesn't mean they aren't there. Don't lose faith."

For two seconds, maybe three, her chin wobbled and her eyes filled with questions. In the span of a breath, I thought I'd broken through the ice.

She stared at me, wearing the saddest smile, squeezing my hands tight before pulling hers free. "I've never had your faith, Mimi. Now, it's getting late. Please take Rowan home so I can spend a few minutes with Carter before I need to leave."

Door closed, and me with no key. Everything ached while a coldness worked its way through me. This friendship had meant everything to me. I'd thought it unshakable. Unbreakable. Would Grace come to regret this later, and if so, would it be too late to repair the damage?

I collected the plate and stood, the seeds of anger and betrayal sprouting. As I turned to go, I said, "I don't want to fight with you, but if you come at me without even trying to find other solutions, you're not leaving me much choice. I know you have to look out for Carter, but I have to look out for Rowan. My business is already taking a hit, and now I need to prepare for a lawsuit. Meanwhile, you and Sam let Carter go to my house that night even though you knew there'd be a party. A party I knew nothing about until it was too late . . . So tell me, Grace, who's really more to blame here: You or me?"

After dumping the plate and cup in the bin atop the trash can, I raced from the cafeteria before stopping to steady myself against a hallway wall. Saying such an awful thing made me dizzy and nauseated. Especially considering Grace's history with Margot. The only thing that kept me from apologizing right away was the realization that what I'd said was true. Yes, I'd made mistakes, but so had she, and I couldn't live the rest of my life being everybody's punching bag.

I didn't dare glance back. Once upright, I hustled back to Carter's room. Outside his door, I heard Rowan animatedly telling some story, and Carter's light chuckle.

My phone pinged, so I checked it before cutting their visit short.

WHOOP!!! WE WON!!!!! Full steam ahead with the athletic facility upgrades.

I reread Kayla Barker's text without glee. Grace was probably getting a much less joyful text about that decision right about now, which meant my face would be a reminder of yet another blow. Time to get out of Dodge and regroup.

I knocked as I entered. "Rowan, we've got to go. Carter probably has homework, and I'm sure his mom wants to see him before she goes."

"Thanks for coming," Carter said, wearing a brave smile. "And thanks for those snacks."

"You're welcome, sweetie. I'm thinking about you every day." I covered my heart with my hand. Right or not, I shouldn't have taken that swipe at Grace. There was no comparison between the suffering our two families faced. Carter should be compensated for what happened, and I would never begrudge him the help he needed. "If you need anything at all, you text Rowan or me, okay?"

He nodded and high-fived Rowan before we left.

When we got into our car, Rowan said, "I feel better now. Like, Carter doesn't blame me."

Unlike his mother.

"I'm glad, honey." I was, too, despite my leaving here feeling worse. "He's got a long road to recovery and can use every friend he can find. If you can keep his spirits up, that'll be a big help."

"I'll try."

The only good thing to come of the party was how it was forcing Rowan to grow up. He and I had some work to do together, but today gave me hope that he wouldn't turn into someone who blamed the world for his own failures and faults like his father.

As we passed the turnoff for Annapolis, I remembered what Grace had said about Dirk. Recent events suggested that I wasn't fully equipped to raise a teen boy on my own—not that Dirk had proven that he'd be better. If I started laying down the law more firmly, Rowan might not be so happy with our living arrangements. It'd kill me to lose my son, but it'd be worse to let Rowan grow into an entitled asshat.

"You know, seeing Carter today really drives home how we need to change some things."

He frowned. "Like what?"

"No more parties—no more drinking beer like you're already twenty-one—even after the grounding ends."

"Seriously?"

"Seriously. I can't stop you from doing things out of my sight, but I hope you'll consider the danger involved and think about the kind of person you want to be. There are more important things in life than parties. I'd hate to see you waste your talent or lose a shot at a scholarship because you get in trouble with alcohol again."

He stared ahead with a scowl on his face.

I didn't know how Dirk would handle Rowan. Or parties. Or much of anything, since he'd been less than reliable these past five years. But in all that time, I'd never once asked what Rowan wanted in terms of custody and visitation. His opinion should matter. Heck, a judge would likely ask him.

"Honey?" The word came out choked, as if something were blocking it.

"Yeah?"

I cleared my throat. "Have you ever wanted to live with your dad?"

He scowled at me. "Now you don't want me anymore?"

"Of course I do." I stared ahead. "But I know you miss your dad. Sometimes I wonder if you wish you had a man around to talk to about stuff."

Rowan put his feet up on the dashboard and sank low in the seat, staring out the front window. "I don't want to switch schools or live with Miranda."

I nodded, trying to parse those words. He hadn't said he wouldn't like to live with Dirk. If Dirk still lived in town and weren't with Miranda, would Rowan jump ship?

Rowan added, "I like living with you, Mom."

I reached across to squeeze his knee, grateful that he wasn't itching to leave me. "Well, good, honey, because I love living with you."

At least one person in town still loved me. I could make do with that.

# CHAPTER FOURTEEN

## GRACE

*The same Thursday afternoon*
*Rehab facility*

I didn't glance over my shoulder until after I could no longer hear Mimi's heels clicking against the tile floor. Cold tears trailed down my cheeks, and my chest ached as if a part of it had been scooped out. Everything I'd always loved about her had been on display—her big heart, her willingness to work hard to solve problems, her genuine kindness. Even when she'd taken that swipe at me, conflict had flashed in her eyes.

Her direct hit smarted more than she'd ever know. On the upside, that sting confirmed that I wasn't half-dead. She wasn't wrong, either. We'd all made mistakes. I didn't need her and Sam reminding me of the obvious. But there were degrees of blame. She hadn't thought it would hurt anyone to let her son and his friends party at her home now and then, but that wasn't the point. I hadn't meant to let my sister down, either, but I did. When you do something you know to be wrong and people end up hurt, you shouldn't let yourself off easy. Of course, maybe my never letting myself—or anyone—off ever wasn't the best approach, either.

I glanced over my shoulder, then frowned when she wasn't standing by the door. Not that I'd expected her to wait for me. God, what a wreck I was, pushing her away yet wishing for another option. If Carter's injuries had been less serious, my anger might've subsided by now. But here we were, in rehab hell for the foreseeable future. With so many open questions about Carter's prognosis, this wasn't the time for wistful longing for my friendship, no matter how much her pleas wormed beneath my skin and tucked themselves near my heart.

My phone rang. I checked in case Sam needed something, but it was Carrie. I set the phone down without answering, too drained for another conversation. Friends like Carrie had been kind, sending a meal and touching base by email, but none had gone out of their way to organize help like Mimi had. And Mimi'd done that despite all the online barbs thrown her way. She was much tougher than me. She must love my family to put herself in this position. How could people not notice her extraordinary kindness?

The notification for a voice mail appeared, so I hit "Play."

"Grace, it's Carrie. I'm sure you've got your hands full, but I wanted to give you a heads-up so you aren't blindsided. The board voted to uphold its original budget. I can't believe we lost to that Mimi and the rest, but we did. Anyway, hope you're doing okay and that Carter is coming along. Talk later."

I punched "Delete" before setting the phone back on the table. The light in the cafeteria seemed to dim as my fists quietly hammered the edge of the table.

Another loss. Not that the budget mattered nearly as much as Carter's well-being, but dammit, would I never catch a lucky break?

Meanwhile, others moved on and celebrated their wins—be it the budget or a reduced sentence—while Carter remained in this institution night after night thanks to that damned board meeting. Another mistake to add to my pile. Self-doubt and loathing had become my shadow companions. This newest blow intensified my desire to burn everything down.

Assuming Mimi and Rowan had left the facility by now, I returned to Carter's room, hiding my unhappiness. Every single wince, moan, and grunt he made when adjusting positions or getting to the restroom reinforced the rightness of my intentions. The only complication was the fact that his mood had improved after talking with Rowan.

"Mom, you should ask Mrs. Gillette for the recipe for these protein bars. They're really good." He broke another section off. "Not dry and crumbly like store-bought ones."

"Sure, honey," I answered half-heartedly, unfairly angry with Mimi for being thoughtful, as if she'd done it on purpose to make me feel guilty instead of having done it because she was, in fact, kind.

After he swallowed, he stole a look at me. He hesitated before asking, "Are you mad?"

"What?" I sat forward.

He wrinkled his nose, wary. "I don't blame you for being mad at me, you know."

I frowned. "Why would I be mad at you?"

He laid his head back against the pillow, eyelids half-mast. "Because you warned me about going to the party, but I went anyway. Now I've messed up everything, including our family." His voice was soaked in sorrow.

Had he carried this guilt around for the past two weeks? I scoured my memory in search of anything I'd said or done to give that impression.

"Honey, no. I'm mad at myself—I'm the grown-up. I should've put my foot down about the party. And if I'd stayed out of the budget business, those boys wouldn't have been picking on you. Honestly, if anyone has the right to be mad, it's you." My voice cracked. "I hope you can forgive me."

He nodded. "You did what you thought was right. That's what you always tell us to do, so how can I be mad? I should've left Rowan's when things got crazy. It's not your fault this happened."

This amazing kid. I tried to smile when I grabbed his hand. "You astound me. Not once have you lashed out. You're very strong, Carter. Much stronger than I am. But, honey, this isn't your fault. You didn't drink, and you didn't antagonize anyone. You're innocent, and it's okay to want justice."

"Justice?"

"Yes. John and Deshaun should pay for what they did. You can talk to the DA about the impact this has on you so that they get a sentence commensurate with the harm they caused." I could still picture Roni's face in the school parking lot—her certainty of a plea bargain.

Carter looked down as if considering my opinion, then half shrugged. "That won't help me walk. Dad says the best thing I can do to speed up my recovery is to focus on my therapy and school. That makes sense to me."

*Dad says.* His dad had also said we should let him go to the party, and look at how that had turned out.

Carter's eyebrows drew together, and he picked at the blanket. "Plus, if I make enemies, it'll be harder to go back to school."

Seeing him suppress doing what was right to avoid stirring the pot was like looking in the mirror at my teen self. I didn't want my son to be haunted by my regrets down the road. "Is letting them off easy what you want, or are you doing that out of fear?"

He sighed as if he wasn't sure how to express himself. "I'm not say-ing they weren't jerks, 'cause they were. Drunk, obnoxious jerks. But making things worse for them doesn't change my situation. And who knows? Maybe my attitude will make a good impression on people."

His wanting admiration from those unworthy of him made my insides quake, but I wouldn't shake his confidence, which he'd need to recover. I'd have to make peace with his choice. "It sounds like you and your father have made a decision." My tone might've been clipped.

Carter narrowed his eyes. "Mom, can I ask you something?"

"You can always ask me anything."

His expression turned serious. "You've been acting weird lately. Really tense. I know you're worried about me, but are you okay?"

"Of course," I answered automatically, beating myself up anew for how my personal problems created added stress.

"Honest? 'Cause you've been sort of stiff with Dad. And you avoided Rowan and Mrs. Gillette."

Observant children made parenting trickier. I loved that he cared about me, yet his concern made me want to cry. "I'm not myself right now because these are exceptional circumstances. I miss having you at home and am focused on doing everything possible to help you. If I'm acting strange, it's because I'm still figuring things out, but I'll be okay." Please let that be true. God, help me make that true.

"I want things to be normal . . ." He toyed with the sheets, folding them at his hips. "You and Dad haven't come together all week, and you both look sad."

I hadn't realized how poorly I'd been hiding my misery. "We're sad because you're in pain. We take turns visiting so you have company throughout each day."

He shrugged. "If you say so."

"Honey, please don't worry about anything other than getting stronger." I squeezed his hand again.

"Okay."

"Good." I stood before he could see through my facade—the false certainty that our family would make it through this without damage. "Sorry to leave you, but Kim needs me, too. Is there anything else you need before I go?"

He shook his head and patted the chemistry book at his side. "I've got a lab project to finish, and you can't help with that."

A bitter reminder that the school labs wouldn't be upgraded.

"No, I sure can't." I kissed his head before smoothing his silky hair. "Love you. Keep up the hard work so you can come home soon. We all miss you so much."

"Trust me, I'm trying. Who knew I'd miss my own bed and Kim?" He rolled his eyes and smiled weakly.

I couldn't tell if he was putting on an act or if this trauma was turning him into a brave young man. "See you in the morning."

Sleet fell from the sky for the entire hour-long drive home. Perfect weather for my mood, not so much for highway driving. The incessant *thunk-thunk* of my wipers beat on my nerves. My jaw ached from clenching it with each repeated memory of Carrie's voice mail and of Mimi's face as she'd leveled me. I slammed my car door closed and entered the house.

"Judy?" I called, walking through the kitchen in search of the after-school sitter we'd hired so my mother could go home. Thank God. Although we never fought, the stain of how she'd enabled my father and how we'd both failed Margot sat between us like a divider. Now I was erecting a similar barrier between Sam and me. Had I ever fixed things with my mom, I might now have the tools to forgive Sam and bridge our disagreements. I'd been so careful to avoid getting to this place with him, yet anger now thundered like an avalanche gathering speed.

I found Judy—a leggy, freckled high school senior from our neighborhood with a charming smile—on the sofa doing homework in front of the TV.

"Oh, hi." She started to pack her things. "How's Carter?"

"Doing better, thanks. Where's Kim?"

"In her room."

"Did she start her homework?"

"I think so." When she stood to go, I handed her thirty dollars. "See you tomorrow."

"Great." She tucked the bills in her jeans' pocket before I escorted her to the door.

"Have a good night." I closed the door and leaned back against it. My body felt like a dishrag wrenched dry from my afternoon conversations. If I could melt onto the floor and disappear, I might've done so. Anything to escape this constant sense of failure.

The dormant piano called to me. I hadn't played since Carter's accident—a noticeable change. My students would be resuming their lessons next week. Perhaps returning some sense of normalcy to my life would help me push forward. For now, I sat at the keyboard and softly brushed my fingers against the cool keys.

Setting my right foot on the damper, I played the opening notes of the second movement of Bach's Prelude in B Minor. A contemplative piece that put my confusion, heartache, and desire for healing to sound. The piano had always subdued the shame and pain of my dad's addiction, of my mother's unwillingness to leave him, and of Margot's slide into the abyss. But Bach wasn't loosening the chains around my heart now, so I stopped, set my forehead to the music rack with my eyes closed, and let the silence consume me.

———

Kim and I had eaten the lasagna that Missy Fletcher had sent over and finished the dishes by the time Sam came home. He'd been working later to make up for the days he'd taken off, and because tax season was coming. After contemplating Carter's and Mimi's comments about my marriage all afternoon, I'd committed to turning the tide. Thankfully, Kim had retreated to her room after dinner.

"I made you a plate. Are you hungry?" I asked, crossing to the refrigerator.

He set his briefcase on the floor, offering a cautious smile. Trust was no longer a given. "Starving. Thanks."

While his dinner plate rotated in the microwave, I poured us each a glass of pinot noir.

His brows rose. "Wine on a Thursday?"

"I thought we could set aside everything for the evening and relax." I handed him a glass, which he handled as if it might be a grenade in disguise. Fair enough. We'd been tiptoeing around each other, no longer doing the dishes together or sitting beside each other on the sofa to watch TV, or spooning in bed. "Has it been rough getting caught up at work?"

He sipped the wine, hope brimming in his eyes. "Not too terrible, thanks. The team's been supportive, and I've been able to sneak in a little work here and there while hanging out with Carter, catching up on emails and client calls while he does homework."

Picturing father and son side by side at work made me smile. Carter inherited his ambition from Sam, whereas my biggest goal had been simply to create a happy family. "That's good."

When the microwave beeped, I set the steaming plate on the table with a napkin and silverware, then took a seat opposite my husband.

"I hate to throw a wrench into the evening, but I'm curious about how you handled what Kim did," Sam said, his eyes cautious.

"What's Kim done now?" I didn't want to know, truth be told, because I needed what little remained in my tank to patch up my marriage.

He hesitated. "The email from Mrs. Astacio?"

"Her Spanish teacher?" I frowned. "So much happened today I haven't checked my email since before I left the rehab center."

Sam set his hands on the table as if bracing for me to melt down. "She caught Kim cheating on a quiz today."

"Cheating?" I hung my head. "Kim didn't say a word to me."

I couldn't believe she'd pulled this now, when we were already dealing with more than we could handle. Then again, perhaps that was why she'd done it. She'd wanted our attention—my attention. Sam had to assume Kim didn't feel safe talking to me about it. I'd been too distant. Too focused on Carter at my daughter's expense. I started to rise, but Sam touched my arm.

"Wait," he said. "She's not going anywhere. Let's first talk about what else happened today."

I hesitated, remembering my vow, then sank back onto the seat, sipped my wine, and trusted in my husband. "Okay."

He twirled his glass in a circle on the table, wearing a loving expression. "I heard about the board vote. I'm sorry, babe. You did your best, though, so no regrets."

His rationale made perfect sense. Three weeks ago, I might've agreed and even been proud of myself for taking a stand. Tonight, however, his "no regrets" comment came across as tone-deaf. He still didn't understand the pain and confusion, or guilt and blame, swirling inside me. The very things driving us apart, too.

I swigged back half my glass. "I have plenty of regrets—mostly because I put myself and Carter through all that stress for nothing."

When he finished chewing a bite of lasagna, he flashed what he probably meant to be an encouraging smile. "It wasn't all for nothing. You wrote an impressive speech and you showed our kids how to fight for what they believe in, even when it's hard and others are against you. All checks in the win column. I'm proud of you for trying. When you think about it, the final decision almost doesn't matter."

"Proud?" I shook my head. "Not when Carter asked me not to do it. When he's not here now, in part, because I didn't listen to him."

Sam set his fork down and wiped his mouth. "Gracie, it's time to stop."

"Stop what?" I slugged back more wine to smooth the slide into my guilty conscience, letting the alcohol loosen my muscles and my tongue.

"Stop blaming everyone, including yourself. We all made decisions—ordinary, everyday kind of decisions—that contributed to a tragic accident. But no one, not even you, can control the universe. We don't decide fate, nor can we predict the outcome of every decision we make. If you pick apart every choice, looking to assign blame, how far back do you go? If I had never asked you out, Carter wouldn't exist, so do we beat ourselves up for falling in love?"

"Now you're being ridiculous."

"Am I?" He shrugged and took another bite.

I topped off my glass again, frowning. "Fate didn't throw Carter down those stairs. And fate didn't let him go to that party. We did. *We* did, Sam." I could feel tears forming again as Mimi's accusation replayed. My eyes were itchy from the tears I'd cried today.

"It's a mix, Grace. Lots of other kids were at the party, and none are hurt. Kids go out and take risks. That's what we signed up for when we had them. We do our best to guide them, but they're individuals that we ultimately can't control. At some point, you need to accept that, and accept what's happened and move forward. I know that's what Carter needs most now—for us to work together and support him in a loving environment. Not a cold, recriminating one. Kim too. She senses the tension. And we're both distracted and giving Carter all our resources."

He might have a point, but all I heard was how I was failing. Failing him, failing Kim, failing Carter. My limbs and face heated. "I wish I could get over things as easily as you, but your impatience doesn't help me get there faster. Besides, it's not even been two weeks."

"I'm not impatient or unsympathetic, but this situation affects our kids, so we need to pull ourselves together." He took a breath and waited for me to raise my head and meet his gaze. It took a while because I didn't like the mirror he was wielding. "I know you don't like surprises, especially unpleasant ones. I also know why. I'm not asking you to get all the way to forgiveness now—only that you try. Take a single step."

I'd never doubted how well Sam understood me and my triggers. He might be right about a lot of things, but his lectures didn't erase my guilt. Having worked day and night to keep Carter company and on pace at school, I was more exhausted than ever. I flattened my hand on the table, gently pounding it. "I am trying. I even spoke to Mimi today."

A cautious smile emerged. "Where?"

That patronizing tone wouldn't help close the gap between us.

"She and Rowan came to see Carter after school." I polished off my wine, harkening back to Mimi's proffered doughnut and hopeful eyes. "We spoke in the cafeteria while the boys visited."

Sam sipped his wine, eyeing me over his glass. "How'd that go?"

I sighed. "Carter seemed a little happier after spending time with Rowan."

"Good!" His grin widened. "And you?"

I raised one shoulder. "I thanked Mimi for organizing the Meal Train."

"Speaking of . . ." Sam pointed his fork at the remaining lasagna, which was stuffed with three cheeses, mushrooms, tiny meatballs, hot sausage, and hard-boiled eggs. "This is really good. Who made it?"

"Missy."

"I hope there's more."

I nodded yet felt irked by his casual attitude about all this.

"I'm sure Mimi appreciated the gratitude. Did you feel better after talking to her?"

"No, Sam." I scowled. "She basically blamed us for Carter's injury."

His entire face grimaced, as if he'd swallowed a shot of cheap tequila. He set the silverware down. "Why would she say something like that?"

Maybe now he wouldn't be so quick to label me the bad guy and Mimi the saint.

"At first she was full of self-recrimination, asking how we could get our relationship back to normal—as if that would ever exist again. Sometimes when bad things happen, you can't go back, and this might be one of those times. I mean, come on. Carter's new normal might involve wheelchairs and ramps and lifelong therapy, so we can't pretend that doesn't change everything." I tapped my fingernails on the table, calming myself down, trying to stay in the moment to win Sam to my way of thinking. "Anyway, I told her we probably shouldn't talk until after things with Carter are settled. Once lawsuits are filed, the less we communicate, the better. Well, as soon as she had something to lose, she changed her tune and blamed us."

Sam laced his fingers together on the table, his expression a picture of disillusionment. "Oh, Grace. Lawsuits?"

"Yes, lawsuits. Weren't you stressing about how the costs might add up? Why should we bear all of that when so many others were responsible for what happened? Carter got hurt at Mimi's house after she left them alone with alcohol, so her homeowners coverage will kick in. And Deshaun and John—we can sue them civilly for pushing him."

"I'm not saying it's not an option, but surely there are better ways to bring that up than threats and stiff-arming friends."

"It's not a threat, it's a fact. Set aside the co-pays, we still don't know what special accommodations Carter might need going forward. We could need to retrofit the house with ramps and special bathrooms. Plus, doesn't our son deserve something for his pain and suffering?"

Thankfully he nodded, yet when he ran his hands through his hair, it looked as if he might be tugging on it in frustration, too. "But lawsuits are a formality—they shouldn't force us to push friends from our lives. Babe, you'll regret that later when Carter is better and you miss Mimi."

"I already miss her." If this had happened at anyone else's home, she would've been at my side each day. It would've halved my sorrow, too, because I wouldn't be swimming in the cold waters of grief over the loss of a friendship along with the losses of Carter's mobility and my absolute faith in my marriage. "That doesn't change what we have to do. Why don't you understand the difference?"

"Instead of looking at the worst-case scenario, I wish you could hope for the best. But even if we go with your doomsday version, everything would be easier to manage with the support of friends and the people we love who love us. Carter will thrive more quickly if you and I are on the same page than if there is distance here." He gestured between us.

"What do you think this is for?" I raised the glass of wine. "I'm trying to share my feelings, but every time I do, you take the other side. From my perspective, all I'm doing is putting Carter's needs first. Yet all I feel is how disappointed you are that I'm not coping like I should. That's not helpful or empathetic."

He set his elbows on the table and covered his face, blowing out a breath. "I'm worried about you, so I'm playing devil's advocate so you don't end up with more regrets."

"Well, that's not what I need. Can't you just hold me and tell me how much this sucks and how unfair it is that it has happened? Or acknowledge that my anger is natural instead of telling me to get over it and make peace with everyone?"

We stared at each other in silence, my heart limp in my chest, emptied of every feeling I possessed because I'd laid them all bare in this gamble to put us back together.

"I never meant to make you feel bad. I only want you to let it go because I love you and it hurts me to see you in pain. Justified or not, anger isn't helpful. Not for Carter, or you, or us."

I leaned forward, pointing my finger at him. "Are you saying these things to Carter?"

"No. Why?"

"He asked me if we were fighting."

"I swear I haven't said a word." He stared right at me, so I believed him. Sam reached across the table to cover my hand. We hadn't touched like this in days, not even by accident. It felt familiar and yet as fragile as silk stitches holding together a gaping wound. "I want to close this distance, Gracie. I miss my wife."

"And I miss you being on my side." I left my hand in place with his on top.

He squeezed it. "Believe it or not, I'm on your side."

"Really?"

"Of course."

"Then do me a favor."

"Anything." He smiled with some relief at a shot for a quick fix.

"The school budget has to be approved by the city economic council, which your colleague, Hayden, sits on. Put a bug in his ear. Convince him that new fields aren't what's best for the students or the town."

Sam's mouth fell open, and his gaze turned disgruntled. He withdrew his hand and sat back, those first stitches now popping apart. "What has that got to do with anything that matters?"

"Roni was so smug about how Deshaun and John are getting off with a slap on the wrist. Now they've also won this debate. Meanwhile, our son's future is up in the air." I popped off my chair, hands raised. "I can't stand it. At least if we overturn this budget thing—if we get money for the labs—my speaking out will have been worth something. When Carter returns to school, he'll have something to show for all this pain."

"Babe . . ." Sam hesitated, his hand aloft like he was trying to conjure the words to express himself. "That's not how this works. New microscopes won't vindicate you or help Carter walk. Let's put our energy into family therapy to prepare for whatever lies ahead rather than into rehashing the budget. Besides, Hayden's an honorable guy. I'm not going to use guilt or make some twisted loyalty play. That's not me or him, and it's beneath you, too."

"So much for 'anything.'" I snatched my empty glass from the table and took it to the sink. "You're more interested in being right than being helpful. You'd rather manage me than understand where I'm coming from. You'd rather keep the peace than fight for our rights. Well, I've been keeping the peace since I was old enough to walk, and I'm sick of it."

Sam's face reddened. "Your attitude reeks more of vengeance than justice."

"Maybe it's both. Who cares? Every time I look at Carter in that bed, I want to scream. Like it or not, we're calling a lawyer soon, Sam." We stared at each other, but he said nothing. I supposed he gave up. That didn't make me feel better, or any closer to my husband. My plan to mend fences was as much a failure as most everything I'd done these past few weeks. My brain hurt from the circular discussion, and now he had me confused and turned around. I could have thrown up from the way he now viewed me: a vengeful wretch instead of a heroic mother. "I guess I'll go deal with Kim and her cheating."

"No." Sam stood with his half-empty plate. "Let me. You're too angry."

Another flaw. More shame.

He scraped the food into the disposal and loaded his plate in the dishwasher. Before exiting the kitchen, he glanced my way, his forehead creased. "I'm worried about us. These kinds of tragedies can break families apart. I'm not a fool. I know marriages have ups and downs, but I've done things your way from the beginning. Now I'm asking you to bend a little. Please, Gracie. If I'm unable to help you, talk to someone else before we lose even more."

After he left, I gripped the counter until my hands ached. Exhaustion and loneliness coiled around me, wrenching more tears. Slowly I bent forward, elbows on the counter, hanging my head.

I stared at the floor, unable to comprehend why everything I did pushed us further apart. Was I like my mother—seeing only what I wanted to see and blocking out the rest? Sam might have been pretending to go along with me for years while secretly disagreeing. Perhaps my need to create a calm environment—and his knowing the reasons why—discouraged him from asserting himself. Or had he been like my mother, expecting me to sit back and not complain about my own suffering or watching others suffer, like Margot and Carter?

Mimi's voice began its drumbeat. *"Please work on forgiving him before your anger tears your family in two and your life becomes a series of visitations and split holidays."* I pressed the heels of my hands against my eyes as if to erase her from my mind, but her earnest expression remained. Here I stood, abandoned and confused. Even my kids didn't recognize me. Maybe Sam was right . . . I needed help. But whatever I chose next had to be my decision and mine alone.

# CHAPTER FIFTEEN

## M I M I

*Tuesday, January 26*
*Potomac Point Juvenile Court*

I stared at the computer screen, triple-checking for typos before hitting "Post" to the Facebook moms' group for the second time in as many weeks.

> Hey, gang, while many of us are celebrating the Board of Ed's decision, others are not. Given recent events that occurred in part because of the debate, I set up a GoFundMe page to raise money in Carter Phillips's name. Every penny will be donated to the high school science department so it can upgrade some of its equipment. My hope is that everyone's generosity might help heal the rift within our community, so please consider participating, whether that means donating one dollar or one hundred. Thanks!

Satisfied, I closed my laptop. Although I'd raided my spare-change jar to fill my gas tank this week, I kicked off the campaign with a one-hundred-dollar contribution. That might buy only some beakers, but it was a start. None of us could undo the conflict or consequences created by the budget debate. But whatever others might think, and whatever steps Grace took next to protect her son's future, this would show Carter that I loved him and wanted him to have something to look forward to when he came home.

With that matter settled, it was time to take Rowan to the juvenile court for his hearing—the rare meeting I wouldn't be late for. Taking time off work when I needed every appointment I could get these days sucked, but given Rowan's confession, the lawyer thought it best to plead guilty and jump on the earliest spot on the judge's schedule. Just as well, since we were eager to get this over and done. I worried about the fines—neither Rowan nor I were flush with cash.

Dirk had promised to meet us there, making me double-dread our morning. The fact that he'd reached out to Grace made my skin hot, but I wouldn't throw rocks at a sleeping bear. No one from child and youth services had contacted me yet, but the fear that Dirk would show up today with someone to question me persisted like a low-grade fever.

"Rowan, let's go!" I called upstairs. "Don't forget to make your bed!"

Perhaps a silly request, although I'd been working on him becoming more helpful.

Two minutes later, he lumbered downstairs wearing khakis and a checkered shirt, his wet hair combed into place. He ripped his thumbnail with his teeth. "I'm nervous."

I tossed him his winter coat, faking confidence. "Officer Martinez made it sound like it wouldn't be a big deal. Same with that public defender. It's not a trial. The judge will probably ask a few questions and then hand down his sentence—a fine, maybe some community service. You won't be carted off to juvie if you're humble and show remorse."

That shouldn't be too hard. Rowan had plenty of regrets, although he remained bitter about how that night had changed my house rules.

"Is Dad coming?" Rowan shoved his arms through the jacket sleeves.

I slung my purse over my shoulder, grabbing my keys from the hook by the back door. "He said he'd be there."

I never told Rowan that Dirk had called Grace. While my son hadn't jumped at the chance to live with his father, that could change, especially with my less lenient attitude.

After pulling out of the driveway, I played Rowan's favorite classic rock station to help him relax. Tom Petty's "Refugee" blared while we drove, my thoughts spinning along with the tires. Nothing beat real-life consequences for teaching you about responsibility. In a backward way, this whole experience might save my son from becoming a reckless man.

I parked in the shadow of the courthouse, my stomach in a twist. "All set?"

"Not like I have a choice." Rowan shrugged. "I just want it to be over."

"Me too." The anticipation of a punishment was often more painful than the penance, so I hoped for the best. "Have you texted Carter again?"

"Yeah. He's doing leg work to get stronger. He's not used to working out, so he gets tired fast. His back still hurts a ton, too."

My spine arched reflexively, as if grateful to be healthy and strong. Being reminded of Carter's constant pain put this hearing in perspective. The memory of Grace's teary eyes in that cafeteria and my snide parting remark had kept me awake the past several nights. "I'm sorry he's still in pain, but if he's moving his legs, it sounds like he'll eventually walk. Is that what he's being told?"

"I think so. It could take a long time, though. He hates missing so much school." Rowan made a face, shaking his head. "I think that's the one thing he's lucky about."

I flicked his arm playfully after turning off the car. "He's lucky he's smart enough to keep up with only a tutor a couple of hours each day."

We trotted across the cold parking lot and entered the courthouse lobby. It smelled a bit dusty, like an old library. People were milling around with gloomy expressions, but eventually we found Dirk. He didn't smile, but he opened his arms to Rowan for a hug. My mixed feelings about him and his relationship with our son went to war, but I was glad he'd shown up for Rowan.

Dirk glanced at me over Rowan's head, his eyes as flat as his tone. "Mimi."

His expression remained unreadable. Perhaps a bit more somber than normal, but we were in a courthouse, so his mood might not have anything to do with his hidden agenda. Whenever I got down about my dying friendship with Grace, I focused on the fact that she hadn't cooperated with Dirk. She'd denied protecting me as her motivation, but some part of her could never turn on me that way—or use my love for my son to hurt me.

"Good morning." I unbuttoned my coat, suddenly sweating like my perimenopausal clients. I then frowned at the reminder of my shrinking client base.

"So what's the deal here?" He'd worn a corduroy blazer over a plaid shirt and combed his overgrown hair back, as if dressing like a responsible parent made up for years of absenteeism. If he were truly involved, he'd know the answer because he would've participated in the prehearing meetings. That righteous expression proved he'd never get it, even if I pointed it out. Better I simply be glad the judge would see both Rowan's parents taking this seriously.

"We spoke with Rowan's public defender last week. Mr. Syme—that's the lawyer's name—said this would be handled as a quick procedural hearing, not a trial. He also said he didn't anticipate any problem getting the records sealed and expunged. We should probably head into the courtroom to find him. Let's not be late and make the judge mad."

I led the way and spotted Mr. Syme near the front of the court-room. Its cement block walls prompted a sinking feeling despite their being painted a creamy white.

At the front of the room, the judge's bench sat up higher than everything else. Behind it a big round clock hung on a paneled wall. Commercial gray carpet muffled the sounds, and there were dividers between the lawyers' tables and the seats for the rest of us.

Mr. Syme was talking to someone else, so I waved and then took a seat behind his table, with Rowan and Dirk filing in behind me.

Rowan's wasn't the only matter being heard today, so we sat through a couple of driving offenses and disorderly conduct charges. The stack of folders beside Mr. Syme proved he'd be here all morning. I imagined the mental toll of dealing with kids in trouble day in and day out, especially if handling repeat offenders. If I messed up someone's hair—which had never happened, knock on wood—it would grow back in a matter of months. If Mr. Syme messed up, the consequences could be life-changing. I shivered and prayed he wouldn't make mistakes this morning.

Officer Martinez entered the courtroom minutes before Rowan's case got called. Those dark eyes scanned the courtroom until his gaze landed on me. He nodded with a polite smile and took his seat. Funny that seeing him settled me. Rowan and I got lucky with him. Some other cops might've been hard-nosed and pious, wanting to make examples of my son and me.

The female prosecutor looked half my age. Her thick auburn hair lay flat in a french braid. I could style it nicely to frame her heart-shaped face. Until recently, word of mouth had been all I'd needed to grow my clientele. Now I'd need to market myself more aggressively, like slipping her my card on our way out. I could offer a first-timer special. Heck, I might have to start spending Monday mornings hanging out in different places, handing out business cards.

When Rowan's case got called, he went to stand with Mr. Syme, while Officer Martinez stood with the prosecutor.

Dirk sat forward, elbows on his knees, like he was watching a riveting football game. His voice mail to Grace stuck in my craw. Revisiting custody would require the kind of sustained effort that my ex simply didn't have in him. His defect could work in my favor as long as I didn't do anything to set off his temper. He hadn't brought it up again, so maybe he'd dropped the whole idea. For the moment I set it aside and kept my eyes on our son, pressing my hands to my thighs to keep them from bouncing.

Rowan stood with his hands in his pockets and shoulders slightly rounded, his face steadily losing its color as he stared at Judge Milan, who looked like a TV-sitcom grandpa—portly and balding except for the white tufts of hair along the sides of his skull and his bushy eyebrows. After the prosecutor read the charges, the judge questioned Officer Martinez.

"You were the arresting officer?" Judge Milan glanced at the papers in front of him.

"Yes, Your Honor. I questioned the defendant on the night in question. He admitted to drinking from his mother's supply and to providing it to friends." Officer Martinez flicked his gaze Rowan's way. "I'd like to add that he cooperated fully and showed contrition, which greatly aided in our investigation and led to other relevant arrests in the matter."

I smiled, grateful for his attempt to soften the judge.

Judge Milan turned to Rowan and his lawyer. "I see you're asking for these records to be sealed. I assume the prosecution has no objection?"

"None, Your Honor," she answered.

"Young man, I understand that someone suffered a significant spinal injury at this party, so I assume you understand the seriousness of your actions?" The judge's bushy eyebrows pinched together, emphasizing his unforgiving tone. My stomach dropped.

Rowan paled even more. His voice squeaked, "Yes, sir. I'm sorry about what happened and have been helping Carter motivate for his physical therapy."

"Mm." Judge Milan shuffled the papers in his hands as if contemplating the world's secrets. He cleared his throat and stared at Rowan. "Given your age and cooperation, I'm going to impose a fine of five hundred dollars per violation, for a total of one thousand dollars, plus twenty hours of community service overseen by the Department of Juvenile Service, and eight hours of counseling at an outpatient drug and alcohol facility to be completed by May thirty-first. We'll seal the records, and once you fulfill your sentence and if no future charges are filed against you, your record will be expunged when you turn twenty-one." He slammed his gavel down. "Next case."

Dirk made a "clutch" signal with his fist. No blazer would fool anyone paying attention into taking this guy seriously. I slouched as relief slackened my muscles. Mr. Syme said something to Rowan while handing him some papers. Rowan then came back to sit with Dirk and me, a relieved smile on his face. "I guess we can go after we pay the fine. Mr. Syme said he'd call later to connect us with a probation officer who'll oversee the other stuff."

His nonchalance made me think of how upset Grace was that none of the boys were being punished enough. "I'm glad things went well, Rowan, but you'd better appreciate how easy you got off. Carter is still in that rehab center, so don't celebrate skating out of this."

Rowan frowned. "Way to be a bummer, Mom."

"I'm serious. You got arrested, fined, and sentenced. Don't treat that like detention."

"I know, but can we get out of here now?" He looked to his father.

"Fine," I said. "Let's not miss more school than necessary."

Dirk and I stood and quietly shuffled out of the courtroom behind our son. I glanced over my shoulder to toss Officer Martinez a silent thank-you, but he was speaking with the prosecutor and didn't notice.

Once we were in the hallway again, Dirk caught Rowan by the elbow. "I'll pay the fine, but you have to get a job and pay me back by the end of summer, okay?"

His showing up, his outfit, and this gesture all prompted uneasy tingles—like he'd been coached to lay some groundwork for hauling me to court next. Then again, at least I wouldn't have to come out of pocket for the fine, and right now that was a huge break.

Rowan's gaze slid from me—he was trying not to look stunned—to his dad, and then he nodded.

Dirk took the papers from Rowan and clapped a hand on his shoulder. "Come with me and we'll get this done."

"I'll wait here," I said.

With the hearing behind us, I took my first easy breath of the day. The only thing tainting it was knowing that Grace was probably up at that rehab center this morning—as she would be for weeks to come—praying that her son would walk on his own. Or she could be at a lawyer's office, preparing civil suits against all of us. Or squeezing in both visits . . .

Footsteps and voices echoed off the courthouse's tile floors. I took a seat on a wooden bench and checked the GoFundMe. It had reached five hundred dollars in two hours. Hopefully, we'd raise the two-thousand-dollar goal I'd set. To my surprise, Anne Sullivan commented, This is a wonderful idea, Mimi. Thank you for thinking of it, and for your consistent efforts to help the Phillipses during this time. And even Keri Bertram wrote, While this doesn't undo the damage done, it's a really great thing to do, Mimi. I nearly got teary. Perhaps my show of good faith would mean something to Grace, too, although a couple of grand was nothing compared with the budget funds being directed to the fields.

While I fished around my purse for some gum, Officer Martinez wandered over.

"Good morning." He smiled at me. Up close his masculinity—the strong line of his jaw, roughened with the slightest stubble—aroused an unexpected flutter. I might've reacted this way in that squad car had he not been reading Rowan his rights. Even with his hair so short, it looked thick and possibly wavy. A less military-looking style would complement him more.

"Oh, hi!" I grinned, suppressing the urge to hug him for going easy on Rowan. If I were a decade younger, I might've been tempted to flirt—assuming I remembered how. "Thanks for helping Rowan today. I mean, it seemed like you tried to help him with that judge, anyway."

"Just telling the truth. The job is to protect and to *serve*."

"Well, I'm sure there's been some pressure to make examples of the boys, so thanks for not throwing Rowan under the bus. It's been a rough few weeks, so I'm grateful this went smoothly. Maybe now my son and I can start to move forward from what's happened."

What would that look like, though? For my business? With Rowan? With Grace?

"I hope so." Officer Martinez nodded. "How's the other boy—Carter—doing?"

"Slowly improving—moving his legs." I bit my lip, holding in a sigh. "His muscles are weak from nerve damage, but there's hope he'll walk again. He still has a lot of back pain, though. That should lessen as the graft heals."

"His name's been on the weekly prayer list at our church." Officer Martinez sat down so we were eye to eye. "And how are you coping with the fallout?"

"Me?" I looked around, feeling suddenly shy. "I'm okay."

"I know folks can be judgmental."

I flushed because he'd obviously heard rumors. The empathy in his eyes invited me to unload all my feelings and regrets without risking judgment. Lucky for him, being in a public space spared him that awkwardness.

When I took too long to answer, he added, "I told you before, most people I meet don't step up like you did. I really respect that."

My face must've turned bright red when his praise flooded my heart with warmth. "Thank you. It's kind to say."

He cleared his throat. "So listen, I was wondering, actually—now that my part in this is over—if maybe you'd like to go out sometime?"

I blinked, my heart thumping. People would have lots to say about me if I started dating the cop who arrested Rowan—the very hot, young cop. "Oh. Uh, well. I think I'm a little old for you."

"I'm almost thirty-two." When he grinned, a cute dimple formed on his left cheek.

Seven years younger. So much like Tony, which hadn't worked out well for me. "I might not look it, but I'm almost forty. You might want to rethink your offer, Officer."

*Please take away the temptation.*

"Call me Rodri, please. And considering your teenage son, I figured you were a few years older than me. It's just a number. I don't care if you don't."

Did I care? I had been lonely, and as nice as Rich Polanti had been, he was not the answer to my prayers, as confirmed with his "Good luck with that" text the day after our date. Rodri looked like he could answer all kinds of prayers. But the age gap . . . the gossip. If I weren't smart, my business could take another hit.

He held up a hand. "Before you nix me based solely on numbers, come out on one dinner date."

Being pursued by a handsome young man gave me the best feeling I'd had in weeks. It was exactly the kind of thing I would've loved to share with Grace over muffins at Sugar Momma's. The very thought squeezed my heart, but I covered that pain. She'd probably raise an eyebrow at his age, but she'd admire his profession. Grace loved following rules. We'd forever debated fate versus free will. I'd never been convinced that our will dictates our future, but maybe she wasn't all wrong.

241

It figured Rodri's offer came right smack in the middle of my personal crises. Anne's and Keri's replies had been rays of hope that the momentum I'd gathered throughout the budget debate might be restored. Yet was that respect worth passing up a chance at love? "How about a friendly lunch instead of dinner?"

He sighed, resigned. "I work all week, so how about Saturday?"

"I work on Saturdays, but I'm free on Sundays."

"Okay." He grinned.

"It'll have to be a Sunday when Rowan is with his father."

From the corner of my eye, I saw Dirk and Rowan heading our way. Rodri must've also seen them, so he rose, tipped his head, and said, "I'll call you."

He nodded respectfully at Dirk and Rowan before walking down the hall and out the door.

"What did he want?" Dirk asked, staring after him.

"I was thanking him for helping Rowan." I stood and gripped my purse strap, hoping my poker face held. "Are you all squared away?"

"Yeah," Rowan said.

"Guess we'd better fill out some job applications after school, but let's get you back there so you don't miss too many classes today." With one arm around his shoulders, I looked at my ex, pretending he'd never threatened me. "Thanks for covering the fine. Is Rowan still able to come to Annapolis this weekend?"

"If you drive him up on Friday, I'll bring him back Sunday night."

Rowan smiled, so of course I agreed, letting the assumption that I had nothing better to do on a Friday night go. "I'll drop him later in the evening because I'm open until seven on Fridays." Then again, I didn't have a full slate of clients, not that I wanted them to learn that.

While we filed out of the courthouse, I texted Grace, still shame-faced about my bitchy parting remark. Civil suits were a necessary evil. It wasn't personal—like the budget debate hadn't been personal. I'd be a hypocrite to blame her for doing what she was entitled to do, so I pushed aside how it could take me under, hoping to give her a small bit of the justice she needed to move forward.

> Leaving the courthouse. The judge fined Rowan $1000 and sentenced him to eight hours of drug and alcohol counseling and twenty hours of community service. We'll make him get a job to repay the fine, which Dirk paid, if you can believe that. I know Rowan isn't suffering like Carter, but he has learned something from this and is remorseful.

I had no idea what John and Deshaun expected, or whether their parents would treat the situation seriously, but this sentence seemed fair. Rowan hadn't been directly involved in the accident. Surely Grace would realize that eventually.

Rowan hugged his dad goodbye at our car. "See you Friday."

"Bye, son." Dirk then looked at me, gesturing with his head. "Mimi, can we talk for a sec?"

My stomach hardened as I slipped my phone in my pocket. I'd known he was up to something.

"Sure." We took a few steps away from my car. "What's with the cloak-and-dagger?"

He scrubbed his palm over the back of his neck. "I talked to a lawyer about custody."

With the exception of my rising eyebrows, I remained absolutely still. How had I ever loved a guy who could kick me when I was already down? Who'd be so deluded about his own parenting that he'd think he could do better? Who'd be so insensitive to his own son's need for stability that he'd threaten to upend everything? "Why?"

"Up until now, I figured you're his mom so you know best. But with the arrest and the drinking getting out of hand, I'm not so sure." He shrugged almost apologetically. Lord, he was sincere—this wasn't some act to jerk my chain. Sweat collected beneath my shirt, but I kept my cool.

"I see." My heart pumped its way up into my throat. "And what did this lawyer say?"

"Not a lot yet. He's looking over our custody agreement. But lawyers cost money, so in the meantime, how 'bout we save time and money by coming to our own agreement? Beats some snoop from CPS getting involved, right?"

Child Protective Services. Would he really do that to Rowan? Nausea bubbled. Lawyers cost money, something I didn't have much of. Neither did Dirk, which was why he wanted to scare me into cooperating. "Did you mention your irregular child support payments and how you cancel Rowan's visits as often as you keep them to your lawyer? And let's not forget your favorite hobby—barhopping."

Self-defense mode might not have been my best move. His gaze and demeanor swiftly hardened.

Dirk gestured to the courthouse behind him. "You don't really have the upper hand right now, so maybe rethink your snooty attitude."

I folded my arms beneath my breasts. "So what, exactly, do you want—full custody? That means ripping Rowan from his team, unless you're planning to move back to Potomac Point."

"I'm thinking he stays with you on school nights, but on nonschool nights and vacations, he stays with me so I can make sure there isn't more of this party nonsense. He can't afford to lose his shot at a Division I school."

In a voice much calmer than I felt, I said, "It's great that you want to get more involved, but hardly shocking you want me to deal with the hard stuff like school while you get all the free time. Rowan doesn't need more upheaval right now, so instead of revising the schedule, how about we start with you finally living up to the one in place? Every Wednesday for dinner, and every other weekend."

"I see you want to do it the hard way." He shook his head as if dealing with a tedious child.

If I mentioned that I'd already tested the waters with Rowan, it might drive a wedge between them. Rowan also might change his tune if Dirk pressed him, which would level me. "Honestly, think about Rowan. He's got to do community service and alcohol training and get a job all while keeping his grades reasonable. He doesn't need us at war or more big changes to his homelife."

"Have it your way, but this isn't over." He waved dismissively and shuffled toward his car.

"Bye," I called in a sweetly sarcastic voice. When I got back to my car, I sank onto the front seat, hoping that final plea got through Dirk's thick head.

"What did Dad want?" Rowan pulled out his earbuds.

"To make sure you've learned your lesson and won't be hosting more drinking parties." I forced a smile, hating myself a little for lying to my son. I told myself it was in his best interest, but that wasn't the whole truth. Another of Uncle Tommy's sayings drifted back to me. *Sometimes you'll get away with lying to others, but you'll never get away with lying to yourself.*

Rowan glanced out the window toward his dad. "What'd you say?"

"That it's under control." I turned in my seat. "Look at me, Rowan. We have it under control, right? No more drinking. No more parties. I know I was loosey-goosey before, but things have to change."

He paused, then nodded. "I get it."

"Good." My heart rate resumed its normal pace. Ten minutes later we drove up to the high school's entrance and my son lugged himself out of my car. "I already called the attendance office to explain your tardiness, but check in there first. Have a good day."

He ambled inside, but before pulling away from the curb, I checked my phone to see if Grace had replied. Nothing. I couldn't tell if she'd read it or not; her privacy settings were maxed out. Dirk's threats still had me rattled. I wished I could ask Grace for advice, but that door was closing on me, too. My shaming her hadn't helped. Wrinkling my nose, I fired off a second note.

> P.S. Rowan says Carter's doing lots of leg work this week. I hope that means he'll be on his feet soon. And Grace, I'm sorry about what I said before leaving the cafeteria. Totally uncalled for. I know you're only trying to protect your son.

My thumb hovered over the "Send" button for three seconds before hitting it. My apology might not make a difference to her, but my breathing came a little easier now. Lately, that was the most I could hope for. Then again, Anne and Keri appreciated my way of handling this whole mess, so maybe I wasn't doing everything wrong.

When I got to my shop, Vicki was highlighting Celeste Winslow's hair. I had only three appointments this afternoon. Rather than panic or whine, I'd use the free time to brainstorm ideas for driving new business. The student discount had netted a handful of young clients, but I couldn't count on them to be regulars.

I clicked through a few online articles for ideas but kept getting distracted constantly checking my phone. By five o'clock, Grace still hadn't replied.

# CHAPTER SIXTEEN

## GRACE

*Friday, January 29*
*Law Offices of Bergen & Hardwell*

While I thumbed through a *Time* magazine, Sam glanced at the contemporary wall clock in the glass-and-chrome waiting room of the law firm we'd retained. It read 11:43. He had to get back to work by one, not that he even wanted to be here. "Premature," he'd said, but at least he'd come, even if only to "understand the landscape and our options." With the others already protecting their interests, I preferred to act rather than sit in a chronic state of limbo. Rowan's sentence had been reasonable, but John's and Deshaun's parents' high-priced lawyers were gunning for cushy plea deals. I'd bowed to Carter's wishes and not contacted the ADA, which hadn't been easy.

My thoughts swam like the fish circulating around the massive built-in tank. Neither of us had any personal experience with lawsuits, so my empty stomach burned.

"What time does Carter finish his rehab session?" Sam asked.

"Around one." I flattened the magazine on my thighs.

Sam's refusal to discuss the school budget with Hayden still hurt me on principle. The fact that my own husband didn't understand how much I needed a win added to the tension between us.

Then there was Mimi's latest attempt to make peace. Considering how we'd left things at the rehab center, I'd hardly expected her to set up a GoFundMe page for lab equipment. Carrie insinuated that Mimi had done it for selfish reasons—like it might make me back away from filing a lawsuit. That wasn't Mimi's style, though. More likely she'd felt bad about the swipe she'd taken at me, and about Carter's needs. No matter what else was going on between us, I didn't doubt her love for my kids.

Sam hadn't mentioned the fundraiser, but he had to know about it and probably thought I owed Mimi a thank-you note. For all I knew, he'd already texted her one himself.

He wasn't wrong, of course. Not that it mattered.

I didn't know how to react, honestly. The fundraiser would never raise enough money to update the labs, but that wasn't the point. I'd never needed proof of Mimi's goodwill—that was a given—but her efforts didn't undo the damage caused or pay the medical and therapy bills, nor could they patch together our friendship so soon. This lawsuit had to go forward, and that meant that my family remained on the opposite side of everyone involved at that party.

Interesting, though, that her latest move had won Mimi new admirers, unlike Roni and Jordan, who kept trying to distance themselves from what had happened. I didn't begrudge Mimi any respect. It made me happy that others finally saw what I'd always recognized in her—a truly good person. But you could love a lot about a person—like with Mimi and Sam—and still suffer a rift when something like Carter's injury tore through your life. The limbo and consequent longing were suffocating.

They say to err is human, to forgive divine, but apparently I was not godlike. I'd read about families who forgave their children's murderers—something I could not wrap my head around. They swore forgiveness sets you free from grief, but they never told you how to do it. I'd yet to figure that out. I wished I could so I could shed the phantom ache of Carter's pain and fears. No matter how much easier my life would be if I could let go of mistakes and trust that others (or myself) wouldn't make another catastrophic or careless error in judgment, I could not.

A shame, too, because having no one understand my feelings isolated me as much as I'd been when hiding in my room, drowning out my father's screaming.

"Grace?" Sam appeared to be waiting for an answer to a question I hadn't heard.

Now he'd think I didn't care about what he had to say. "Hmm?"

"I asked if you were going to see Carter after this?"

"Of course. I'd like to spend at least an hour with him."

"Who'll get Kim after school?" He frowned, glancing into space. "I thought Judy couldn't come today."

"My mother said she'd come down, remember?" It was unlike him to forget little details, let alone big ones. A rare sign that his stress levels might match mine.

He scratched his jaw. "I wish my parents lived closer so they could help."

I liked his parents but didn't need company right now. "Let's invite them to come once Carter is back at home."

Sam nodded. "Okay."

An outsider would think nothing of that exchange, missing everything it lacked. Normally, he would've ended that conversation by patting my hand or kissing my cheek. His warm touch had always settled me, which made its absence more painful. But the most frightening thing was that he was getting used to not touching me.

I went to reach for his hand but stopped myself. It would seem stilted, and it would hurt me if he withdrew. So instead I sat there, trying not to cry.

Our marriage might require therapy to get on track, and who had time for that? Not Sam, who had to split his focus between work and our family. Not me, who barely managed to get through the day without wishing I could curl up and sleep for ten years.

"Mr. and Mrs. Phillips?" a young woman in a gorgeous garnet wool dress asked.

"Yes," we answered simultaneously as we stood.

She stepped forward to shake our hands. "I'm Callie Ridgeway, the associate who'll be working with Mr. Bergen on your cases. If you're all set, you can come with me to the conference room."

"Thank you." Sam and I fell in behind her, strolling past several offices before being led into a glass-walled conference room with a gleaming burled-wood conference table. On the wall behind it hung a striking modern impressionist painting of the Baltimore harbor.

"Can I get you any water or coffee?" Ms. Ridgeway asked, pointing toward the credenza where a carafe of ice water, a silver coffee urn, creamer, sugar cubes, and cups had been set out.

"No, thank you," we both replied, taking seats. I unbuttoned my cardigan and tried to get comfortable in the stiff leather chair.

"Let me grab Peter so we can get started." She smiled before ducking out to hunt down her boss.

Sam didn't look at me or say anything soothing. Instead, he opened his briefcase and removed the copies of medical bills and other papers we'd accumulated in less than a month, stacking them on the table and neatening the edges of the pile.

I inhaled slowly to settle my nerves. Papers hardly told the whole story. Surgical and therapy descriptions and dollars didn't convey Carter's pain and tears, or the hours of time wasted in my car, or my daughter's confusion and frustration. And they certainly didn't reveal the subtle but steady tearing apart of a marriage, or of a friendship.

In no time at all, Ms. Ridgeway returned with Mr. Bergen, who looked nothing like I expected a prominent trial attorney to look. His tie hung loosely around his neck. He'd left his suit jacket in his office, I imagined. From the look of his hair, he must've run his hands through it more than once today. But his vivid blue eyes shone with intelligence, which put my mind at ease.

He reached across the table to shake Sam's and my hands. "Mr. and Mrs. Phillips, thanks for coming in. I'm very sorry about your son's situation, but rest assured, we're here to make sure he's compensated."

"Thank you," I said, grateful for an ally for the first time since finding Carter on Mimi's basement floor.

Sam remained silent, wearing a businesslike expression, avoiding making eye contact with me. Message received: he was here under protest. He slid his stack of papers across the table. "Here are all the bills and other medical papers to date that you requested. Obviously, this is only the beginning, though. His care will go on for months . . . maybe longer."

"Thank you." Mr. Bergen handed them to Ms. Ridgeway, who sat beside him with a fresh notepad and pen. "As I explained to you over the phone, you'll file the suit on your son's behalf because he's not legally old enough to file on his own. We've got a complicated set of facts but foresee negligence suits against the homeowner and her son, and possibly gross negligence suits against the two boys in the physical altercation."

"Can you explain why we're filing claims against children?" Sam frowned. "That doesn't feel right to me."

"The teens caused the injuries." Mr. Bergen glanced at Sam. "We'll file one suit and name all the defendants. They'll be jointly and severally liable, meaning that a judgment can be shared equally by all or collected from one, who then would have to go after the others for their share. Our goal is to cover your son's expenses plus compensation for pain and suffering."

I smiled, feeling vindicated until my husband leaned forward, unpersuaded. "I understand that, but our son isn't eager to sue fellow students."

"With all due respect, your son is a minor with a serious injury. You and your wife understand what's needed to protect him and offset the costs of his care. What he wants is not as important as what he needs, is it?" Mr. Bergen paused.

"It's not," I said before thinking about how Sam would take it. A sideways glance proved he didn't appreciate my tone, which may have been a little smug. I prayed that Mr. Bergen's walking us through this case would convince Sam of its necessity so he'd stop being mad at me for initiating it.

Mr. Bergen continued, "We'll be conferring with medical experts, but my experience with similar matters suggests the hospital and rehab bills will reach seven figures. Your share of that number could involve a significant sum. Your medical insurer will probably want to exercise its rights of subrogation to recoup what it can, too. Not to diminish your son's concerns about his classmates, but you can see now that this is bigger than that."

I nodded, doing a mental cartwheel to celebrate being validated. "Those boys got light criminal charges because of the lack of specific intent, but we don't need that for a negligence suit, right?"

Sam turned on me directly, tapping the table between us, his voice almost curt. "What about our negligence in giving Carter permission to go to the party?"

I groaned, tightening my fists at the reminder of being talked into that. "We didn't know Mimi wouldn't be home."

"We didn't check, either," Sam snapped. We stared at each other like two boxers squaring off.

Mr. Bergen held up his hands. "Folks, if the defendants raise that, sadly, in Maryland, we're dealing with pure contributory negligence law." He rocked back in his chair when confronted by our confused expressions. "Basically that means that if the plaintiff is even one percent responsible, then he cannot collect damages."

When I gasped, Mr. Bergen made a calm-down motion with one hand. "These facts are murky. I don't think what you two decided is as relevant as what your son chose to do is. Yes, he went to a party, but he didn't drink. The question of whether attending an underage drinking party is, on its face, negligent would be up to a jury. But that doesn't mean we don't bring the suit. That said, preparing for trial is a lengthy and costly endeavor. We'll balance that against the idea of a negotiated settlement. All that is a long way of saying that the contributory negligence law affects the value of your case. Your son is a good kid, and his injuries pose the threat of a very substantial verdict. But that open question about his own negligence puts pressure on us to settle before a jury can weigh in."

I frowned. "Settle for less than he could win at trial?"

"*Could* being the critical point," Mr. Bergen said before exchanging a look with Ms. Ridgeway.

Reading between the lines, what I heard was that Mr. Bergen didn't want to spend a lot of money up front preparing for a trial that could net zero income, especially since plaintiffs' attorneys work on contingency fees. Alone in my sorrow, I couldn't turn to Sam to confer privately. Meanwhile, my husband's relieved expression deflated me further.

"We understand, and I have no problem with a quick, fair settlement," Sam said without consulting me.

"I'm not convinced," I countered. "How can we make that decision before you review all the evidence, interview people, and talk to the doctors?" I shut my mouth to stop my emotional babbling.

"We won't," Mr. Bergen assured me while checking his own notes. "This incident happened recently, but you have up to three years to file a claim. We often wait to allow latent injuries and such to come out."

"But then we'd have to liquidate assets to cover all these costs now and get reimbursed later, which mitigates my only real motive for doing this," Sam interjected.

"True."

Sam frowned and turned to me. "Our case is weakened by the law. Bills are piling up now. I say we file and settle quickly on something fair, not push for a windfall. The doctors should be able to provide a good estimate of the average costs."

"I can't believe any jury would deny Carter a recovery. And what if there's a new medical complication after we settle?" I turned from Sam to Mr. Bergen.

"We can discuss your options as we get up to speed," Mr. Bergen replied, and then went on to talk about homeowners policies before asking for more detail about Mimi's history with hosting parties, and about the bullying that had been happening leading up to the party. Every answer I gave only deepened Sam's disapproving glare, even though I'd been nothing but honest. Had he forgotten that Mimi made it clear she wouldn't hesitate to point out Sam's and my negligence? Why was she allowed to protect her interests, but I couldn't protect ours?

Still, a hard lump formed in my stomach. I'd heard through the grapevine that some of my friends had canceled appointments with Mimi. This lawsuit wouldn't help with that. Her insurance premiums might also go up.

"Okay, so let Callie and me dig into this information, the police reports, and make some calls to your son's doctors. Once we have a better handle on things, we'll regroup and draft a complaint."

"While all this is happening, what do we do . . . or not do?" I asked.

"Go about your lives and take care of your son. Given your small community, I recommend you minimize contact with the defendants until this matter is settled. Definitely don't talk about the incident or the case with anyone."

"That's not a problem." I speared Sam with a look. His jaw tensed, and everything about his expression said that he didn't like me much today. Was this the look my mother had spent her whole marriage avoiding? Would she say it had been worth it, given how much it had ended up costing Margot and me? A year or two from now, would I say the damage to my relationships had been worth it if Carter got compensated? "We won't do anything to jeopardize Carter's case."

"Well, unless you have other questions, why don't you let us get the ball rolling. We'll be in touch once we are ready to file the suits." Mr. Bergen stood up, so the rest of us did, too.

"Thank you so much," I said, shaking his and Ms. Ridgeway's hands.

Sam followed behind me by several paces, as if coming too near would burn him. We said nothing to each other until we hit the elevators. Sam stood opposite me, his back to the wall, his eyes on the overhead number display.

Oddly, I didn't feel as good as I'd hoped I would after this meeting. Even a big win wouldn't change the work we had to do with Carter, or with each other. And this move practically guaranteed the loss of the dearest friend I'd known. The pain of that hardened like a kidney stone and would surely be as painful to pass.

"I wish you could bear to look at me," I said softly.

His gaze fell to mine. "I've got nothing more to say. We don't agree on how to proceed, so I think we wait until Mr. Bergen does a little digging. Maybe once he has a better handle on things, his advice will change, and then we'll have something new to discuss."

"Fine, but in the meantime, please don't make me out to be the bad guy."

He swiped a hand over his face. "Just answer me this. Is this really about what Carter needs, or is this about what you need?"

His words were razors at my wrists, draining me of blood. I could barely find my voice. "Everything I do is for our kids. All *I* need is for you to show me a little support." I turned away and faced the elevator doors as they opened. I bolted out, rushing my steps while fishing for my keys, holding back my tears.

"Grace . . . ," he called.

My first instinct was to run, but I made myself stop. "What?"

We stood two feet apart, neither of us smiling or speaking. Finally, Sam said, "Tell Carter I'll call him after his therapy session."

"Sure, but I'm also going to tell him that the lawyer said he shouldn't keep texting with Rowan. He's probably already tried to make Rowan feel better and said things like 'It's not your fault,' which could be used against him now. In retrospect, we probably shouldn't have allowed Mimi or Rowan near Carter." Another thing Sam had done unilaterally.

He looked at me with genuine dismay. "But Carter's attitude has improved since he started texting with Rowan. Isn't keeping him upbeat about therapy more important than how we pay for it?"

"Carter is working with world-class therapists. Do you honestly think his recovery depends on a few texts from Rowan Gillette? And what was the point of paying lawyers for advice if we don't plan to heed it?"

He looked at me for what seemed like a long time, but I didn't see any hint of him reconsidering his position. If anything, he looked defeated, which wasn't my goal. I'd hoped logic and the lawyer's opinions would put us on the same side. Wrong. Again. "I hope this mess gets settled soon so we can focus on bringing our son home and reconnecting as a family."

The only thing we did agree upon.

"So do I." I did reach for his hand this time, but his remained limp in mine, so I released it. My heart fell to the ground, too.

The mistrust in his eyes was another punch to the gut. We made it to our cars without speaking. Normally, he kissed me on the cheek before parting, but today he simply said, "Give Carter my love. I'll see you at home tonight."

I nodded, watching him get into his car and drive away while an icy wind raced up my legs and made me shiver.

# CHAPTER SEVENTEEN

## MIMI

**Friday, February 12**
**A Cut Above**

"Hey, Mom." Rowan showed up after his first day of work at Stewart's Grocery Mart while I blew out Madison Albright's hair. He'd ditched his overnight bag by the door and slumped onto one of the chairs near the register.

"Hey there." I turned off the blower. "I need five more minutes."

He nodded and promptly opened his phone without asking about Vicki's whereabouts. She'd left early, claiming she didn't have any appointments after four o'clock. I prayed she wasn't putting feelers out for a new landing spot before I could shore things up around here.

Madison said, "Your son's so grown-up."

"Time flies." I finished spraying her hair and then handed her a mirror so she could see the blunt swing of the back. "Gorgeous as always."

"Thanks, Mimi." She smiled appreciatively.

I whisked the stray hairs off her cape before removing it. When she went to grab her coat and purse, I turned to Rowan. "How was work?"

"Boring." His mood matched the flat gray February sky.

"That's surprising. Didn't you see a lot of people you know and keep busy bagging groceries and collecting carts from the parking lot?"

"Exactly." He barely raised his head. "Boring. And one lady yelled at me because I didn't notice how she'd organized her groceries on the belt. Like it matters what stuff goes in whatever bag."

It did matter, but I had to pick my battles while we were still feeling our way through new rules and expectations. "This is why it's important to study hard so you can find a job that isn't boring."

"I don't need As to play football."

"Football careers only last so long, honey." Assuming he made it to the NFL. I hoped so, but anything could happen. "Speaking of school, how's your history research paper coming?"

He held the phone down for a second. "Fine."

Hm. Since Grace had put the kibosh on the boys' conversations, I wasn't so sure.

Madison came out of the coatroom and handed me her credit card. "Any plans this weekend?"

Valentine's Day was this coming Sunday. I flushed, thinking about Rodri. The age difference still made me squirmy, and I had no interest in giving anyone something else to discuss behind my back. "Quiet time at home."

"Maybe next year you'll meet someone special."

I handed her back her card after running it through the reader. "Maybe."

Madison was putting a cash tip on the register when a thin young man with crooked teeth entered the shop. I didn't often cut men's hair, but I'd take anyone these days. He glanced at my son before speaking to me. "Are you Mimi and Rowan Gillette?"

"Yes." His asking about Rowan threw me. I narrowed my eyes, systems on alert.

He whipped out two envelopes and laid them in my hand. "You've been served."

With a brief bow, he quickly backed out of the salon and disappeared.

Madison made the kind of face you might expect of someone embarrassed to catch you naked. "Oh gee."

A flush spread quickly through my entire being while I stared at the envelopes. The Law Offices of Bergen & Hardwell. The envelopes might as well have been pistols for how uncomfortable I was holding them. My friendship had come to a lawsuit. Objectively, it made sense: the American way of dealing with injuries. But friends suing friends broke a little piece of my faith in everything.

"What's that?" Rowan's sharp gaze stuck to me.

I didn't want to get into it in front of a client. With a forced smile, I said to Madison, "Well, I sure hope you're headed out tonight to show off your hairdo."

"Yes, I should get going." She waved nervously. "Good luck with . . . everything."

I nodded, tears looming behind my eyes. "See you next month."

Stupid chirpy reply. Although barely treading water, I couldn't crumble in front of a client or my son.

"Okay," she said before leaving us alone.

I slipped the envelopes into my purse to read later. "Let's get moving, Rowan."

"Are you being sued?" He sat straight up in his chair.

This was not the conversation I wanted to have right before dropping him with his father for the weekend, but it couldn't be avoided. "Apparently we both are."

"Both?" His eyes flew open and shone with confused anger as he rose off the seat. "Why am I being sued?"

I made a "pump the brakes" gesture. "Probably negligence for hosting the party where Carter got hurt."

"But I'm already paying for that with the dumb job and fines and stuff." His attitude needed further adjustment, but I didn't have another lecture in me. This was a lot for anyone to process, let alone a teenager.

"This is different. It's a civil suit, not a criminal one. The Phillipses are hoping to recover some of the expenses of Carter's care." The calmness of my tone came from my expecting this but belied a sudden queasiness. Hopefully, Carter would be coming home in another two weeks, if the original six-week rehab schedule still held.

"Why is Mrs. Phillips being such a bitch?"

"Whoa, Rowan!" I frowned. "No cursing. And don't disrespect Grace, no matter how mad or confused you feel. Her family is in a world of pain, and Carter's care is superexpensive."

Not that I agreed with this solution, but I understood where she was coming from. And I expected my son to respect my friend—former friend? My stomach tightened.

He glared at me as if pissed off that I wasn't angry on his behalf. "I don't have any money, so why sue me?"

Neither did I, not that I said so. "Our homeowners policy will cover us." Assuming the payout didn't exceed my policy limits. "I'm sure they sued everyone involved. I'll know more when I read the paperwork, but right now let's go so your dad doesn't chew me out for being late. But, honey, this lawsuit is exactly why you shouldn't drink anymore. Do you understand?"

He grunted and grabbed his bag. "I hate this."

So did I, but not for the reasons my son did. "At least you get to spend the weekend in Annapolis."

Thank God Dirk hadn't canceled. Rowan would escape the inferno of Potomac Point for two days. Of course, John and Deshaun would be texting him soon enough.

We got in my car and headed toward Route 2. Dirk would probably gloat about my getting sued. To think that we'd been in love once upon a time . . . Now he got off on threatening me and making me feel like crap. Meanwhile, he'd been the cheater, not me. I didn't deserve the way he talked to me, and I was as sick of it as I was of the gossips. "Rowan, can I ask a big favor?"

"What?"

"Can you not mention this to your dad?"

"You want me to lie?" His brows shot up.

"No." Yes, actually. "I need a day to get my arms around this before he questions me." As soon as I said that, I knew it was wrong. If my son needed to talk to his dad about being sued, he should be able to do so. "On second thought, never mind. You go ahead and talk to him if you need to."

I considered mentioning Dirk's custody threat so Rowan wouldn't inadvertently answer probing questions in a way that could hurt me. But Rowan was upset enough now, so I wouldn't add to his burden. Another mistake, probably. Damn, I really had no instinct for self-preservation. I hoped someday Rowan would understand how much I've always loved him and tried my best to do right by him.

I could picture Dirk's smug smile as he added this lawsuit to his pile of evidence against me. If I'd been alone in the car, I would've pulled over and bawled. How much more humiliation, expense, and rejection would I face before this situation was all said and done?

———

On Sunday, I sat in my car in front of the East Beach Café, debating the wisdom of this lunch date. Life had been tossing lemons at me left and right.

Friday night, Jordan's frantic Facebook rant seeking recommendations of good lawyers made this mess public, adding another layer of humiliation to my life. Meanwhile, I'd accept whomever my insurance carrier suggested, while hoping my annual premiums didn't increase much.

I had no reason to believe today's Valentine's lunch would go anywhere but south. I would have blown it off if Officer Martinez hadn't been one of the few people who'd been good to me—who'd seen good in me—since this whole mess started.

Shaking my head, I then glanced in the rearview mirror to reapply a little lip gloss. The boardwalk was empty; the blustery day whipped up tiny whitecaps across the turbulent bay. My hair got tossed by the breeze when I hauled myself out of my car. I stared at the front door and sighed.

Pasting a smile that I didn't quite feel on my face, I swung the door open and nearly tripped over Officer Marti—er, Rodri—who was waiting for me near the hostess stand with a single red rose in hand.

"Oh, hi. Sorry to make you wait." I tucked the loosened curls behind my ears. "Even when I'm looking forward to something, I always seem to run a little late."

He smiled, handing me the rose. "No problem. I'm just glad you showed up. I was starting to wonder . . ."

"Oh, heavens no. I'm not rude . . . only tardy." I grinned with a helpless shrug, my stomach a tangle of flutters. I dipped my nose into the bud. "Thank you for this. It's lovely."

"You're welcome." Rodri turned to the hostess. "We're all set. Can we have a table by the windows?" Then he looked at me. "Unless that makes you chilly. My friend Erin isn't a fan of window tables in the winter."

"We might as well enjoy the view." The bay glittered amid stark surroundings on sunny winter days. Maybe its fierceness would energize me for the fight on the horizon.

The young hostess was making cow eyes at Rodri and nearly giggled as she led us to our table. Lord, it was like being with Tony again. Grace wouldn't encourage this, not that I should care so much about her opinions anymore. But I'd been burned before. If this went anywhere, I'd be competing with girls half my age while also baiting the gossip mill.

The hostess handed us our menus before sashaying away.

"What's wrong?" Rodri asked as we took our seats. Being a cop made him observant.

"Oh, nothing. My mind wandered." I recovered with a smile and scanned the plastic menu, stealing little peeks at him while he studied his.

"How's your son?" Rodri leaned forward after he set down his menu.

"Better than his mama." As soon as those words left my mouth, I wrinkled my nose. It might've been wiser to reschedule this date to a time when I had a better grip on my life. And if Dirk found out about Rodri, Lord help me.

"Sorry to hear that. The repercussions will take a while to quiet down. I wasn't a saint in high school, but as a cop I've seen teen drinking end up badly too many times. It's a shame alcohol is always a big part of the high school social scene."

"Preach. One reason I'd been permissive is because I didn't want to be a hypocrite."

"I hear that a lot, but there's a difference between being a hypocrite versus having matured and come to recognize the danger involved." He offered another warm smile. "It'd be hypocritical to tell your kid he should never drink if you party every night. But teaching him to respect the law and the risks of teen drinking isn't hypocritical."

"I never thought of it that way. But in any case, I should apologize right now because I'm usually pretty sunny, but the squeeze of this nightmare is wearing me down. Carter's injury is the worst of it, for sure. Rowan's criminal hearing was a little scary, but then on Friday I got served with a negligence suit. On top of that, I'm losing customers over this, so I'm stressed to the max." When he didn't run for the door, I added the most painful part of all. "And underneath all that, I miss my friend." I didn't bring up Dirk because dating rule number one was "don't discuss your ex."

Rodri regarded me for a moment, like he was really listening to and processing what I'd said. With a slight tilt of his head, he said, "I might not have answers, but I'm happy to be a new friend you can talk to."

My heart swelled a little. I almost reached for his hand, but that seemed too bold. "You're sweet. Thanks. One way or another I'll dig myself out of this mess. It feels extra hard, though, because Grace has been my go-to person for levelheaded thinking. She keeps my worst impulses in check. Now it seems our roles got reversed, with her spinning out of control and me buckling down."

He nodded thoughtfully. "It's probably better that you two don't talk much with a lawsuit pending, right?"

"Doesn't make it easier, though." Until Grace withdrew from my life, I hadn't realized exactly how much I counted on her, having always seen myself as the one she needed for fun. "And I'm desperate for good news about Carter's recovery."

Rodri sighed empathetically. "Sorry I brought up a sore subject. I figured it'd be weird not to acknowledge it, considering how we met. Let's talk about something else."

"Good idea." I forced a grin, determined to enjoy a one-hour break from my troubles. Rodri had such kind eyes—soulful, even, although that sounded so Harlequin. Agnes would love to hear about this when I went to the care center next week. Gosh, if only I could go back to the last time I saw her and get a do-over. "So tell me something about yourself. Did you grow up around here?"

"I did. My parents are still in town, although my older sister moved to DC after college, and my baby brother is in Winchester, Virginia, with his new wife." His entire face beamed when he talked about his family. It pressed on one of my tender spots—the fact that my son had no siblings.

"Do you fit the middle-child mold?"

"What mold is that?" He tilted his head as if he'd never heard of birth-order traits. Guys didn't obsess about such things, but surely he'd heard the basics.

"You know, do you like to keep the peace and make people happy. Sociable, loyal . . . all that? Sort of fits with your job, I guess." I winked.

He snickered, scratching his head. "Well, what do you know? And here all this time I thought I was simply a great guy."

I laughed. "So that's a yes?"

"Busted." He shrugged one shoulder. "In my defense, it was never a conscious response to my birth order. What about you? Any siblings?"

I sipped my water, pushing the image of Grace's face from my thoughts. "No, sadly. I always wished for a sister, though. Does that count?"

"Don't think so." He rested his chin in his hand. The intensity of his attention made me tingly. "Did you grow up here in town?"

"Sort of. I was born here, but then my parents died in an accident when I was twelve, and I had to go live with my uncle in Virginia. Came back when I was eighteen. Been here ever since." Somewhere along the way I'd learned to spit that all out quickly so people didn't feel a lot of pity, and to avoid reliving the more painful parts. Yet Rodri seemed like someone who would treat other people's pain with great care. It made him a terrific cop.

"I'm sorry you lost your parents so young." His gaze softened, giving me the sensation of being held tight. "You've had more than your fair share of tragedy."

"I don't dwell on it. I mean, in a way, losing my parents and moving in with my uncle taught me to adapt to change and to count my blessings to get over the hump whenever stuff like my divorce happens." Of course, Grace and Sam had helped me through that mess.

"And again we bump into an unpleasant topic. Sorry." He stretched his long legs out and crossed his ankles right near my feet. I could almost feel the heat coming off him. "Let's try something else. What do you like to do for fun?"

He earned lots of points for rolling with the punches, but I suspected this would be our one and only date. A guy his age didn't need someone with all my baggage when there were plenty of younger women who weren't single-parent orphans in the midst of a lawsuit. I allowed myself a moment of self-pity.

"You realize I'm a single parent of a teen boy, so I'm not swimming in free time," I teased. Truth was, other than going to Rowan's games and shopping or eating with Grace, I hadn't invested in new hobbies or other outlets for myself. "How about we start with what you like to do for fun?"

"Fair enough." When he smiled broadly, his toothy grin set off another round of tingles. He held up a thumb. "One thing I love is to drive my motorcycle along the rural coastal routes on sunny days." Then he began using his fingers to mark each successive reply. "I play basketball in an adult league at the Y. I'm a decent cook—especially when I steal my abuela's recipes. And once in a while you might find me in the back of a Zumba class."

"Zumba?" I laughed while trying to picture it. "Aren't those classes pretty much filled with women?"

"Why yes they are. That's actually how it all started." He chuckled without blushing. "One of my buddies thought it would be a great way to meet women, so a bunch of us went to a class together. Who knew it would kick my a—sorry, my butt that first time? I lift a few times a week, but Zumba is great cardio."

"You must like to dance." A brief daydream about his hips swiveling ensued. It'd be fun to work up a good sweat on a dance floor with him.

"I wasn't much of a dancer before, but now I've got some moves." When he stared at me, my whole body flushed.

I gulped more water. "Well, I confess, I'm on my feet most days and am a naturally busy person, so I've never been big into formal exercise, although Grace managed to drag me to yoga a few times a month." I hadn't been since the accident, and doubted Grace had found time, either. "I do like to dance, though."

"Noted." His warm gaze melted more of the protective ice that had encased my heart since Friday.

The waitress chose that moment to stop at our table. She barely looked at us as she turned over a new page on her order pad. "Ready to order?"

Rodri gestured for me to begin.

"I'd love a Blue Moon with an orange slice, and the crab cakes, please." I handed her my menu. When you live in Maryland, you eat crab in every form—steamed, in soup and omelets, and of course as crab cakes. It's a thing, like hanging the state flag somewhere in your yard or buying clothing with the flag in the design.

"Make that two," Rodri said with a cheerful smile.

"Got it." She promptly turned away to head to the kitchen, failing to put the "friendly" in her service.

"Okay, where were we? You like to dance," he said. "What else did you do before you became a single mom?"

I scanned the memory banks to remember what I did before motherhood and my shop ate up all my time. "I used to be a pretty good bowler."

"With those nails?" His brows rose.

I splayed my hands on the table, displaying navy glitter nail polish. "They weren't always this long . . ." I withdrew them and narrowed my eyes while thinking about what else brought me joy. "Oh. This might sound weird, but I also love to paint walls."

He laughed. It was a great laugh—a deep chortle, and that's not a word that rolls off my tongue. "Most people would call that a chore, not a hobby."

I chuckled. "I know, but I love it. The smell of a freshly painted room screams 'clean start.' A new color can change the whole mood of a room. It's the cheapest way to redecorate, that's for sure. And really, it's sort of meditative. Paying careful attention to those up- and down-strokes with the roller and being neat around the edges shove your problems aside for a while."

For a second, I wondered if a fresh coat of paint might help clear away the memories of Rowan's party. I still avoided the basement except when doing the laundry.

"Maybe it's time for a home-reno project." It was like the man could read my mind. Exciting yet slightly dangerous.

I sat up straighter, encouraged. "You know, maybe you're right. It's been a while since I spruced up the house, and I could really use a fresh start right about now."

"Well, if you need an extra hand, I'd be happy to help." He leaned forward, folding his arms across the tabletop. He had great forearms with a sprinkling of arm hair. Surprisingly light, considering his thick crop of hair.

I was about to tease him when someone's shadow darkened our table.

"Grace?" My heart stopped as if I'd been electrocuted. "What are you doing here?"

"Picking up crab legs to take to Carter." Her confused gaze darted back and forth between Rodri and me, and landed on the rose. Hiking a thumb my way, she asked Rodri, "Did you go easy on Rowan and the others to get in her good graces?"

I gasped at the accusation.

Rodri's pleasant smile evaporated, replaced by a sober-as-shit expression. "No, ma'am. I told you already, we conducted a thorough investigation and filed appropriate charges based on the evidence. I had no personal interaction with Ms. Gillette until after her son's hearing."

"Appropriate charges? Hmph. All these guilty kids are running around as if nothing ever happened. I'd bet they'll be back to the same nonsense any minute." Grace's face flushed and a sheen coated her eyes.

Then she looked right at me. "Well, Mimi, I know how much you love the crab cakes here. You be sure to enjoy your lunch date while I spend Valentine's Day driving up to visit my son after another of his grueling mornings of physical therapy."

She spun on her heel and stormed off, a takeout bag in hand. Through the window, I watched her march to her car, her face drawn with a mix of dismay and pain. Seeing that—knowing I continued to cause her such agony—stomped out any bit of joy from this lunch.

I set my elbows on the table and buried my eyes in the heels of my hands. "Oh, dang it."

Rodri reached across the table to grab my wrists and gently pry my arms away from my face. His hands were warm and rough on my skin. "You okay?"

"I'm sorry. This can't be the way you wanted to spend your afternoon." I let loose one heck of a sigh, thinking again that coming had been a mistake.

He sat back and stared at me with such tender compassion I almost cried. "Mimi, I told you before. I come across all kinds of people in my job. It's so rare to meet someone who worries about everyone else more than about saving his or her own skin. I know this isn't the best time in your life, and that you think I'm too young, but I also know when I'm interested in someone genuine and kind and caring . . . and pretty. So I'd like to get to know you better—however slow that has to happen. I can be a good friend right now—someone to listen to you when you need a shoulder." He shrugged, wearing a sheepish grin. "That's it. That's my pitch."

His words bathed my heart in silky, warm water and then wrapped it in soft cotton.

"You're very kind, but maybe you should run while you can. I mean, what kind of friend goes on a date when a kid she helped raise still isn't walking?" My voice was shaky, which made me flush.

"From where I sit, you're doing everything you can for that family. And don't forget, you've gone through something traumatic, too. It's okay to take care of yourself now and then—or let someone else take your mind off your troubles for a while."

I sucked my lips inward, torn.

"Besides," he continued, a grin forming. "I was getting jacked to paint your place. Judging from your hair and your clothes, my guess is we wouldn't be using beige."

I laughed at that, which felt damn good. He would never know how much his kind words had helped me today. Seeing myself through his eyes gave me the boost I'd needed to press forward despite the lawsuit, my business woes, and Dirk's BS. "No, we would not. More like coral or lemon."

Rodri opened his mouth to say something, but the waitress showed up with our drinks and meals.

"Anything else?" she asked, as if she hoped we'd say no.

"No, thank you." After she walked away, I glanced at Rodri. "Grace was right about one thing. I do love these crab cakes." Of course, my appetite had waned in the face of Grace's look of betrayal.

"Then dig in." Rodri gestured with his fork. "If you love crab, someday I'll make you taste-test my crab sofrito."

"What's sofrito?" A man who could dance and cook? Jackpot.

"A traditional Spanish sauce of tomatoes, onions, garlic, bell peppers, cilantro, and hot pepper. You can eat the crab in a taco shell or with rice and plantains."

"Sounds yummy, but hanging out while you cook could lead to weight gain. I'm not known for denying myself, and none of what you said sounds like diet food." I took a bite of the town's best crab cakes—totally worth the mediocre service.

Rodri appeared to be waiting for me to swallow and give him my attention, so I did.

"There are lots of ways we can burn those calories, like . . . paint-ing." He winked, sending a zip of sexual tension straight to my inner thighs.

I didn't trust myself not to say something stupid, so I took another two bites of my lunch and enjoyed the view. Yes, the bay sure was beau-tiful, but so was the man in front of me.

"Thank you for getting me out of the house today, and for being sympathetic and accepting. Like you, I see lots of personalities and gos-sip in my work, too. Rarely have I met a man as nonjudgmental and sincere as you."

He grinned. "Does this mean you'll answer my future calls?"

"Heck yeah." I chugged a bit of the beer, enjoying its refreshing citrus note. "Free labor doesn't come around often, and it's past time to update my living room," I teased, which prompted a smile from Rodri.

It still felt wrong to enjoy the fact that something good had hap-pened to me as a result of something terrible happening to Grace, but I couldn't make myself give it up. This budding relationship was worth exploring, although I'd keep it from Rowan until it had real legs. Grace was already jumping to conclusions. Too bad, because under other cir-cumstances she might've liked Rodri. A little pinch of guilt held tight when I recalled the look on her face thirty minutes ago.

Yet I shouldn't have to apologize for being selfish in this regard. I'd made mistakes as a mother and a friend, but I always tried my best to be a good person. That should count for something, too.

# CHAPTER EIGHTEEN

## GRACE

*Monday, February 22*
*Rehab facility*

Sam had taken the day off work because, after Leron told me yesterday that he planned to have Carter attempt unsupported steps today, I'd taken a page out of Mimi's playbook and asked my mom, Kim, and Sam to come surprise him with a little celebration. Hopefully Carter would be pleasantly surprised by the red velvet cake—his favorite.

Since our first meeting with the lawyers, Sam had been spending more time at home closeted away in his office. I saw him when depositing the daily mail, in which the bills continued to pile up. He hadn't said another word about those, though, probably because they supported my argument for filing a suit.

I knocked on the door before peeking into his office. "We should get going so we can pick up my mom and decorate Carter's room before his therapy session ends."

Sam scrubbed his scalp, glancing at the paperwork to his right. "Let's hope he does better than expected. The sooner he comes home, the better."

For many reasons, I thought, praying he'd be home in another week. But seeing uncommon worry etched on Sam's face made the hairs on the back of my neck tingle. With a hand over my stomach, I asked, "How bad are things financially?"

He hesitated. "You don't want to know."

"I do actually."

Sam pressed his lips together as if debating whether he could trust me not to freak out. "Well, between this and property taxes, we've drained most of our bank savings account. We can tap the money market for the next round of co-pays, but after that we'll need to liquidate some investments, which will mess with our retirement portfolio and trigger capital gains taxes."

From the beginning, we'd saved and planned with an eye toward our kids' educations and a comfortable retirement. That one bad incident could reverse our fortunes made me want to throw up. "A big verdict would help, right?" I tried not to sound righteous.

"*If* we win . . ."

Before we got into a debate, Kim raced in. "I made the sign!"

She held up poster board that she'd decorated with hearts, glitter, and gold sticker letters that spelled out CONGRATS.

"It's perfect." I squeezed her shoulder, wishing hearts and glitter could make us all feel better. "Thank you for making something special for your brother."

Sam stood and closed his laptop, forcing a smile for his daughter. "Guess it's time we get the party started."

"Who else is coming?" Kim asked as we filed into the garage.

"Gram." I held the car door open for Kim, who scooted into the back seat with her poster.

Kim grimaced. "That's not a party."

Maybe not, but I didn't want to overwhelm Carter with visitors.

Sam turned on a country station and then remained quiet the entire drive, not even participating in Kim's lively conversation with my mother about *Dolittle*, which we'd watched together last night. "Together" might be a misnomer, given that Sam had sat in the easy chair rather than beside me on the sofa, and Kim had plopped onto the floor with a bowl of Cheetos. Throughout the film Carter's absence had loomed large in my thoughts, so much of what Kim was telling my mother about the movie was news to me.

Throughout the drive, I could feel my mother eyeing Sam and me from time to time. When he pulled into the parking spot, Kim swung open her door without paying attention.

"Carter's coming home soon, right?" she asked. Sam barely kept her door from dinging the car beside us.

"Maybe this coming weekend," I answered, smiling. I could not wait to have him under our roof.

"So that means I can have my birthday sleepover finally!" She waved the poster board in the air.

"One step at a time, Kim." Sam closed her door and locked the car.

"Hold my hand in the parking lot, Kimmy," my mother said, grabbing her free hand.

They walked ahead of Sam and me. We, however, did not hold hands. Sure, I was carrying a cake platter, but Sam didn't even settle his hand on my back.

"Is everything all right?" I muttered quietly.

"Fine." He shrugged. "Just preoccupied."

What could be more important than Carter's progress? With the prior weeks' accumulated apprehension wedged between us, I wouldn't push for answers he didn't offer. The inability to share in any joy about our son's progress hurt, though.

By now I knew nearly everyone at the center, so I flashed friendly smiles and introduced Marcus, a guard, and Emily, a therapist, to Kim and my mother as we wound our way through the building to Carter's room. His therapy would end in fifteen minutes, which gave us time to hang the sign and "hide" to surprise him.

"Can I tape the poster in the window, Mom?" Kim raced to the window, hauling herself up onto a chair.

"Careful, Kimmy," my mother said.

I set the cake on the table and was fishing for the roll of tape in my purse when suddenly Carter came into the room on his walker with Leron trailing behind. My son's splotchy face was the first sign of trouble.

"You're back early!" My grip tightened around the tape as my mother's nervous gaze bored through me.

"What's going on?" Carter froze.

Kim held up her sign. "Mom made cake because you're walking and coming home soon."

He grunted, finishing the route to his bed before shoving the walker aside and collapsing on his mattress. "You shouldn't have assumed that."

"Isn't this nice? Carter, cut yourself and your sister some cake while I chat with your folks," Leron said in his upbeat way, then gestured to Sam and me to follow him into the hall, where we stood about a foot apart. "Don't be alarmed, but Carter had a little trouble today."

Don't be alarmed? Naturally, my entire body tensed. I'd been so hopeful—more the fool. Dread strained my words. "What kind of trouble?"

"I pushed him hard. He struggled and couldn't quite take steps on his own yet. Don't worry, though. The only thing hurt was his pride. I told him it was normal, but he shut down, so we ended the session early."

I brought both hands to my face. My son's disappointment—his frustration—created a dull ache in my chest. "Is this a bad sign?"

"No. It's just hard to rebuild strength and balance when you've got nerve damage. I'm confident we'll get him to a near-full recovery over time if he doesn't give up."

Finally, the kind of certainty I'd been craving. The relief working its way through my limbs felt foreign and unreal because my hopes had been dashed too many times in recent weeks. "That's great news."

"How much longer will he be here, do you think?" Sam asked, his expression still uneasy.

"It's hard to say. We were aiming for a week or so, but it'd be best if he could stand on his own before we release him. His progress will depend on his attitude."

"I'm sorry he was rude," I said.

Leron waved my apology off. "It's not the first time I've dealt with a moody teen. But Carter's attitude has taken a turn recently, which could slow his recovery. Dr. Spotts is digging into it during their sessions, but maybe you two could find some answers or inspire new motivation."

My stomach felt like a fist beneath my skin. Dr. Spotts was the psychologist working with Carter.

I'd noticed my son's recent quietude—his putting me off more— but when I pressed, he'd told me he was preoccupied with schoolwork. I should've dug deeper. "We'll do our best."

"No doubt. See you tomorrow." Leron waved and strolled away.

"Grace." Sam caught my arm before we returned to Carter's room. "Let's make a game plan."

He'd finally touched me, but not with affection. Another slam to my soul. "What do you mean?"

"Let's not run at Carter with a bunch of questions right now."

As if I'd planned to grill him in front of his sister and grandmother. "Of course not, but I'd like to get back in there."

Sam gestured for me to go first and then closed the door behind us for privacy.

"No one cut the cake?" I smiled, pretending that things were going according to plan rather than acknowledging that Kim was sitting on a chair, hugging her knees, while my mother sat on Carter's bed, rubbing his shins.

"There's nothing to celebrate." Carter crossed his arms, tears welling in his eyes.

My gut tightened. My mother made room for me on the bed.

"Sure there is, bud," Sam said. "You've made steady progress since checking in, and Leron's certain you'll be walking on your own. So what if today's attempt didn't go exactly as you hoped? One day at a time . . . that's all you can do."

I nodded, counting on Sam's optimism to work its magic.

"It's not just one day. It's every day. I'm sore and tired and weak, like some freak show . . . It's so embarrassing. And the tutor isn't as good as my teachers. I miss my classrooms and friends and the house and your food. I miss our family being normal instead of stressed, and now I've let everyone down again." Once the dam broke, he kept crying. Big cracking sobs that somehow strangled my throat. "I just want to be normal. What if Leron's wrong? What if I never walk without help?"

The edge of desperation in his voice made me want to scoop him up and run away. Gritting my teeth to keep myself from crying, I rubbed his shoulder and kissed his head. "Let it all out, honey. All the pain and worries are normal. You don't have to be strong all the time."

My mother went to sit with Kim, who'd begun crying in the face of her brother's pain. I held my son for what seemed like an hour before his sobs dissolved into sporadic hiccups. Sam's and my gazes locked for a shared moment of guilt and sorrow.

Self-reproach pricked my conscience like hundreds of needles. Not only had I let him go to that damn party, but he'd now taken on my worries and sensed our marital trouble. All these years I'd thought I was so much better than my own mother. But the first real crisis in my family had me crumbling and spinning in circles much like she had done.

By the time Carter had finished crying, his face was swollen.

I poured him a large glass of water. "Stay hydrated, honey."

Begrudgingly he took it and chugged about a third of its contents before setting it aside.

I wiped my cheeks dry and glanced back at my mom and Kim. "It's been a long month for all of us. Let's celebrate being together for the first time in a while. Mom, can you take Kim to the cafeteria and bring back a little ice cream to go with the cake?" I wanted Kim out of the room so we could have a few minutes alone with Carter.

"Good idea, Mom." Kim's eyes lit up as she slid off my mother's lap. She crossed the room to give Carter a hug. "Don't be sad. I'll get vanilla and chocolate."

Carter closed his eyes, accepting her hug, before she followed my mother out of the room. He looked at me, heartbreak written all over his face. Would that look, which I'd seen many times since finding him on Mimi's basement floor, ever stop haunting my dreams?

"Sweetie, the uncertainty must seem like a big black hole. I'm sorry it's so hard, but you can do this. And whatever Dad and I can do to help make it easier, say the word."

His face crumpled again. "I'm lonely."

The only thing worse than the pain in his voice was my own helplessness to make any of it better. I would sleep here with him every night if I could, but even that wouldn't restore the life he'd lost. "Would you like me to call Mrs. Daniels and Mrs. Shin to see if Ted and Ollie can come up this week?"

Carter shrugged.

Sam pulled a chair up to Carter's bed. "Bud, does us cutting off communication with Rowan have anything to do with your being so down?"

"A little." He averted his gaze.

I worried my lip as more guilt piled on.

Sam said, "I think it's okay for you to text him as long as you promise not to discuss anything related to the night of the party."

I barely had time to react to that pronouncement when Carter shrugged and said, "We've already talked about that night."

"You have?" I raised my brows, heart thumping. "When?"

"When he visited." Carter stared at his lap, picking at the blanket and then glancing at us, as if afraid we might blow up. My body grew cold, but given what had happened today, I wouldn't express shock or disappointment. Carter needed to be able to tell us things without worrying about how we would handle them.

"Did he bring it up?" I asked evenly, despite Sam making eyes at me to stop.

"No. He was upset by all this stuff in here, so I told him not to feel bad because I could've left the party when things got out of hand." In the face of my silence, he added, "You and Dad always tell us to be honest and have integrity."

My pulse pounded. Dear God, he'd admitted negligence. That could bar any recovery. Mimi hadn't mentioned Carter's confession. Maybe he'd said those things to Rowan while she was with me in the cafeteria. Would Rowan have thought to mention it to her?

What did it say about me that I hoped he hadn't?

I struggled to keep my expression blank. It'd break Carter if he thought he might've cost us our chance at getting reimbursed. If he realized that, without some financial recovery, we might have to raid his college fund to pay for his ongoing care.

Sam squeezed Carter's shoulder, offering up the first smile he'd worn all day. "It's never wrong to be truthful."

Sweat beaded all over my scalp. "Dad's right, honey, but in this case, I disagree with your conclusion. Just because you feel that Rowan had no responsibility doesn't make it so. And attending that party doesn't make this your fault. You didn't drink. You didn't antagonize anyone. You're not responsible for what happened. Please promise you won't talk about that night with anyone, okay? That's really important, Carter."

Already my mind raced ahead, wondering whether Rowan had shared Carter's confession with John and Deshaun. Roni and Jordan wouldn't hesitate to use it against him.

I blinked to clear my blurry vision, choosing to change the subject. My son was lonely and missing normal things, some of which I could rectify. "What if I ask Principal Davies about virtual classrooms so you can connect with school friends and classroom discussions?"

He frowned. "I don't want everyone to see me like this."

Sam jumped in. "No one would think less of you, and you might really enjoy the change of pace, so give it a little more thought. You could sit in a chair instead of the bed during class time."

"Maybe."

My poor baby. How would he cope with being othered if he couldn't walk without assistance? How would his access to things be more difficult? How would life with chronic pain change him? The endless list of concerns embittered me, especially because I couldn't discuss any of it with anyone.

My mom and Kim returned too soon, stopping our conversation. I retreated to a corner of the room to think while Sam cut into the cake. All the excitement I'd felt icing it this morning had evaporated. Not only hadn't Carter taken solo steps, but he also might've shot a big hole straight through the center of a financial recovery, too.

"I want a big piece," Kim demanded as she scooted onto the end of Carter's bed.

"Oh, Kimmy, that's too much. You'll get sick," my mother said.

"It's fine," Sam said, slicing a piece for Carter while Kim dumped some ice cream on her plate.

My mother then came to stand near me. Her piteous stare made me itchy.

"Honey, things have been tense since you picked me up. Sam is so quiet," she murmured.

"We're under a lot of stress." I wouldn't begin confiding in my mother now, or here. Especially knowing that she, like Sam, would prefer to whitewash everything and pin our hopes on prayers.

"I know, I know." She patted my shoulder. The way she cupped her cheek told me she had more to say.

"What, Mom?"

"Maybe it'd help if you did some things around the house like you used to. You know, brighten it with flowers. Play with Kimmy, even though you're tired. Find a way to reconnect with Sam. Your marriage is the bedrock of your family. You have to make it as important as everything else or you'll all suffer."

If I'd had a glass in my hand, it might've broken into a million pieces. "I'm doing my best."

"Of course you are." She shook her head. "I wish we could turn back time."

She left the rest unsaid, but I knew she was thinking about the school board hearing. Or maybe the fact that Sam and I had let Carter go to that party. Or even all the way back to the mistakes we'd both made with Margot.

"I know you mean well, but this isn't helping, and now really isn't the time."

"I'm sorry. I want to help. If there's anything you need, please ask." My mother forced a smile, but the weight of her concern reflected in her eyes. I ached because of our strained relationship, as well as my deteriorating one with Sam, and even with my kids. I should've known better than to plan a surprise—or to let my hopes rise.

Sam remained beside Carter, doing his best to stay engaged with both kids. I listened as Kim peppered her brother with questions about other kids at the facility, but Carter's confession to Rowan kept breaking through my thoughts. Surely the lawyers could neutralize an offhand remark by a teen who was trying to make his friend feel better.

---

I was putting Kim's clean clothes in her drawers when Sam's voice bellowed from downstairs. "Grace, we need to return Mr. Bergen's call soon."

"Coming!" I closed the dresser drawer, taking a deep breath. Sam and I hadn't had a second to ourselves since leaving Carter's side this afternoon. We'd come home after dropping my mother off, at which point Sam caught up on client work while I prepared dinner and did laundry. He'd shot our lawyers an email earlier, suggesting we talk ASAP. Other than that, I had no idea what was going through his mind when I finally took a seat in front of his desk.

Sam's expression held all the worry he'd covered with optimism these past several weeks. It hurt to realize how much better we might've helped each other through this if we'd allowed ourselves to be more vulnerable. "Let's get this over with."

I sat in silence while Sam told Mr. Bergen about Carter's emotional and physical setbacks, which would increase the medical care costs, as well as Carter's slipup with Rowan.

"I'm sorry to hear all this. Despite your reasons for wanting to let him text with that boy, I strongly advise against it. Kids don't always realize when they've done or said something that can hurt a case, so let's not take more chances." Mr. Bergen's voice boomed over the speakerphone.

Sam shook his head almost as if he were angry at the lawyer. I shared his desperation to make our son happy, yet wasn't sure we could trust Carter not to further damage the suit.

I stopped myself from incessantly rubbing my thighs. "Is our case dead in the water?"

"I'll get a better sense of where things stand when we get answers to the complaint. If they raise his admission, it'll put more pressure on us to seek a settlement."

Once again, justice—real justice—might elude us. I wanted to stomp around and throw something. "Can't you argue that it was a throwaway comment from a kid who was trying to make his friend feel better?"

"Sure, but we can't control what a jury will decide." Mr. Bergen coughed on the other end of the line. "If we're lucky, maybe the other boy won't think to mention it."

Sam put his finger to his mouth in a silent plea for me to keep quiet. "We understand and will wait to see how they respond."

"Okay. I'll be in touch."

"Thanks. Bye." Sam punched off before I could raise another objection. "Grace, I know it's been a rough day, but he's giving us his best advice. If he thinks we should settle, then we should even if it doesn't satisfy your need for revenge."

Revenge? My heart splintered like fine crystal from the blow of Sam's harsh words and judgments. It was as if he didn't know me at all, which heaped more pain on my already-broken spirit.

"Stop calling it revenge. I'm allowed to be furious that those boys got plea deals and Mimi gets a new boyfriend, but Carter is crying himself to sleep at night in Baltimore, frustrated by and afraid of his own body, and you and I have to liquidate investments." My body heated at the idea that Mimi and Officer Martinez might be canoodling while my marriage was falling apart.

Sam tipped his head. "Not long ago you would've been thrilled for Mimi to have met someone decent. She's still the friend she's always been, Gracie. Look at what she's done with the food and the fundraiser, and even with taking Rowan to see Carter."

I didn't want Mimi to live her life alone, but I detested how her good fortune came from my son's injury.

Sam prodded. "She loves you and Carter. Come to think of it, I doubt she'll go out of her way to share Carter's confession if she believes we'll settle within her policy limits."

I scowled, snapping my head up at that pronouncement. "How can you say that after what she said to me in the cafeteria?"

He shook his head above a shrug. "She probably snapped at you because you hurt her with the legal threat, but she's a businesswoman who understands how insurance works. I doubt she wants to rob Carter of all compensation. You might want to think about that when you're making decisions about how to treat her."

My body turned cold and my throat closed. Once again, he was taking her side over mine. Every time he did that, I questioned myself and our relationship, which uncertainty pushed us further apart. "You seem to admire her more than me these days."

"That's not true. Grace, I don't know how to talk to you anymore." Sam scrubbed his hands over his face as if exasperated. Hot tears built up behind my eyes because I no longer knew how to talk to him, either.

I couldn't bring up the possibility of couples counseling and add to our growing stack of bills, although it also seemed like we couldn't afford not to get help. I was paralyzed—terrified and lonely. "I'm sorry. I don't know what else to say. I'm so tired . . ." My voice cracked.

Sam held still; his eyes looked misty. Did he feel as fragile and defensive as I? If I cried or told him I missed him or asked for a hug, would that help, or would it make the gap between us more obvious and painful? I couldn't move, too afraid of the truth to try any of those options.

"We're all drained." Sam sighed. "For now, let's focus on Carter's emotional crisis rather than the litigation."

I nodded, preferring a goal I had some chance of meeting. "I'll call some of Carter's friends' mothers to see if their boys might reach out to him this week."

I stood because I had to get out of the room before I burst into tears. It was after eight. I ached for a hot shower, a sleeping pill, and a pillow. Ached to close the door on this day and hope for something better tomorrow.

"Where are you going?" Sam laid his hands on the desktop, surprise on his face.

"Upstairs."

A slight frown formed as he turned his hands over. "I thought we were talking."

I dropped my chin. Nothing I did or needed was right these days. I teetered on the edge of a massive breakdown, using all my strength to speak. "I'm exhausted, Sam. Truly bone-tired."

"Too exhausted to brainstorm ways to help our son?"

"That's not fair," I cried, gripping the back of the chair I'd been sitting in, my knuckles turning white. The tears came, but I no longer cared about being strong. I wanted him to see my agony—this torment he was adding to as if I deserved it. I didn't even bother to keep my voice down. "All I've done for weeks is worry about how our son is lonely and isolated and scared that he might never walk on his own. Seeing that pain pour out of him today broke my heart. Add to that my mother, Kim, the bills, the slipup, Mimi, the lawyers . . . all of it. I literally can't process one more thing now, but don't you dare make it sound like I don't love my son. He's all I've been focused on for weeks."

Sam held up his hands, looking chastened. "I'm sorry. I know you've been handling a lot on your own."

"That's not the problem. I know you can't keep taking time away from the office when we need every penny. It's being made to feel like I'm not doing a good job—that everything I do is wrong—that hurts me." My bones actually ached, and I still couldn't tell from his confused expression if he understood my point. "I'm at my absolute limit today. Please, Sam. Let me have a hot shower and one decent night's sleep—hopefully one uninterrupted by nightmares—without being made to feel guilty."

He leaned forward, his expression cautious. "You might sleep better if we worked through some of our issues. We've hardly touched each other all month, Grace."

Now he brought that up, after choosing to sit across from me last night, and keeping his distance today? "You can't possibly think I'm in the mood for sex while our child is probably weeping by himself as we speak."

His face fell. "I said touch, not sex. Hugs. Back rubs. Affection in general." He sounded affronted, yet his eyes remained round and sincere. "We're so distant. It's never been like this, and I'm struggling with that."

"Me too. I hate the gulf between us each night, but now you're foisting this conversation on me despite my crying about what a terrible day it's been, putting me on the defensive. Our marriage seems so fragile now, like every decision we make has the power to destroy us. I don't want to be the wrecking ball, but I also can't muster up affection and trust when I feel like you abandoned me weeks ago. I'm not superhuman."

In the face of my tirade, his chin fell. His hands balled into fists on the desk until he released them. "I'm sorry, Grace. Go have your shower. I hope it helps."

He shuffled through the bills on his desk without meeting my gaze.

I supposed he, too, had bad days piling up like rocks. Awash in new shame, I backtracked. "I'm sorry I snapped. I'm sorry I'm too weak to talk about this now. It doesn't mean it isn't important to me or that you aren't important . . ."

He glanced up. "It's fine. We've both got a lot of pressure to deal with. Let's see what tomorrow brings."

I nodded, lingering as if I might circle his desk for a hug. But I couldn't. Not after confessing how it would feel like a pretense. "Good night, Sam."

I left his office feeling the worst I'd felt since this trauma began. Would a good night's sleep be enough for me to summon the will to offer the warmth he needed in the hopes of saving my marriage?

# CHAPTER NINETEEN

## M I M I

**Wednesday, February 24**
**A Cut Above**

"That was nice of you to start the GoFundMe page for Carter." Cassandra Lenox continued to scroll through her phone while I snipped the back of her hair.

"I hoped to bring the community together." I raised another hank of hair to cut, thinking about my meeting with Mr. Richards, the science curriculum leader, set for early tomorrow morning. The phone rang, but Vicki answered it.

"Haters still be hatin' . . . on both sides." Cassandra looked at me in the mirror. She wasn't wrong, although some of Grace's friends voiced appreciation of my efforts.

"It's Rowan," Vicki said.

"Excuse me a sec," I said to Cassandra, then took the phone from Vicki. "What's up, bud?"

"My grounding is over this weekend, right?" The lack of greeting and obnoxious tone of his voice grated on my nerves.

He'd been on me about ending his punishment, but I'd been dragging my feet, knowing Dirk was watching my every move. "Can this wait until I get home? I'm at work."

"Tim Johnson's taking a few guys to his place in the Poconos. Can I go?"

"You don't even ski."

"There's other stuff to do, like sled and skate. I haven't hung out with the guys in forever. Please."

He'd been living up to the terms of his sentence and my grounding, and I knew how much he missed his friends. I wanted to make him happy, but how would Grace feel if she got wind of Rowan being off on a vacation while Carter still hadn't come home? "Who else is going?"

"John and Deshaun and Gary."

Oh man. Thinking about how Jordan treated me at the basketball game made me shudder. "I don't know, Ro. The Johnsons aren't exactly strict, and we don't need more trouble right now."

"I won't do anything stupid."

"I'll think about it and call Betsy." This would be dicey. I didn't want Betsy to know about Dirk's threats, nor did I want Grace to think that Rowan and I weren't sensitive to Carter's situation. If I told Betsy that Rowan wasn't allowed to drink, would that ostracize him? Would she even listen? This must be exactly how Grace and some other parents felt about dealing with me all these years.

"Fine," he grumbled.

"I suggest you change your attitude if you want me to agree. I'll call you later." I hung up and returned to Cassandra's hair, already exhausted by the prospect of the uncomfortable conversation and decision heading my way.

"Trouble with your son?"

"It's been a bumpy road enforcing new rules."

"Honestly, Mimi, telling kids no doesn't actually stop them from doing anything. It only makes them hide their behavior. Better to provide safe spaces for drinking and make your kid feel safe talking to you about stuff rather than making them afraid of getting in trouble."

"That's what I always thought, but it's not clear-cut. Lately I've wondered if I've sent the wrong message these past two years, like I've been saying you need to drink to have fun. I haven't figured out the answer but wish I could steer Rowan to healthier outlets so that every weekend isn't about the next party."

Cassandra cackled. "Be serious. Every time moms sponsor some 'healthy' teen activity—like paintball or dances or carnivals—it fails. Those things aren't 'cool' enough. At this point, the genie is out of the bottle, so the best we can do is supervise the party scene."

If Cassandra's home had been ground zero for a catastrophic event and her daughter arrested, she wouldn't have been so cocksure.

For weeks I'd been combing through my past and my mistakes. While I accepted some responsibility for Carter's injuries, I wasn't wholly responsible, nor was I the worst parent on the planet, despite what Dirk might want me to believe. I wouldn't keep beating myself up for not being perfect. "All I know is that it backfired for me."

"Well, yeah. It's pretty terrible about Carter Phillips." She said the right words, but they lacked real feeling. Carter Phillips might as well have been some Joe Blow from another town. Who knew, though? If our roles were reversed and some kid I didn't know well had gotten hurt at someone else's party, I might've still had her attitude. "But I also heard you might have snagged yourself a silver lining."

"Oh?" I held my scissors in the air, confused.

A sly smile crossed her face as she raised one brow. "Rumor has it that you were seen out with one of Potomac Point's finest."

The temperature in my shop climbed ten degrees. The last thing my reputation needed was for people to think I was chasing men while the rest of my life was burning to the ground. And I hadn't forgotten the look of betrayal on Grace's face at the café. "What?"

"Don't play dumb." She chuckled. "You know I'm talking about that hot cop."

"It was one date." I waved dismissively to throw her off.

She fanned herself. "If I weren't married, I'd be jealous. Heck, who am I kidding? I am jealous."

She hooted. Normally I joked with clients, but not about this. If others started talking, Rowan might hear about it from someone other than me.

"I told him this isn't the best time for me to start up a relationship." A literal truth.

I set the scissors down and grabbed the dryer, which effectively ended the conversation. Her disappointed frown released the tightness in my chest, because at least she wouldn't be fanning the flames of this particular gossip any longer.

I'd barely finished styling her hair when the phone rang again. Would it be too much to ask that it be a new customer?

Vicki called out, "It's your lawyer."

My stomach dropped to my toes as Cassandra's curious gaze met mine in the mirror. "I'll let Vicki check you out, if you don't mind."

"Sure, sugar." Cassandra toyed with her shiny bob while handing Vicki her credit card. "Looks terrific, as usual. See you next month!"

"Thanks." I smiled, then grabbed the phone from Vicki and went into the back room for privacy. An unexpected call from Dina Ellers probably wasn't good news. While I stood surrounded by magazines and product, panicked tears stung my eyes. "Hi, Dina. What's up?"

"I called to discuss a new development. The other defendants have filed cross-complaints against you and Rowan."

"What's that mean?" My foot started shaking. How could those boys sue me when they were the ones who pushed Carter? The whole world was going mad. "I thought we'd all band together?" I closed my eyes to focus.

"The way this works is that each defendant is jointly and severally liable for whatever damages get awarded to the plaintiff."

My eyes popped open. "I don't understand what that means."

"It means that Carter can collect the full judgment from all of you in equal proportion, or get it all from any one of you."

"And that's legal?"

"Yes. It's to protect plaintiffs in case one of you is uninsured or bankrupt or otherwise unable to pay. But don't worry, we're filing cross-claims against them as well. After all, they were the real proximate cause of the fall."

I planted my forehead into my palm with my elbow on my desk, my body heavy with defeat. I could end up responsible for the full boat. If that amount was more than my coverage, I'd lose my shop and my house. Hell, I might also lose Rowan to Dirk. The back room got stuffier by the second. "Doesn't all this cross-complaining make it harder for everyone to work out a fair settlement?"

"This is actually typical. Everyone starts at opposite ends, but once we start negotiating, things will come together. We'd rather avoid the risk of a big jury award, despite the possibility a jury might consider his attending the party to have been negligent, barring any financial recovery."

Barring *any* recovery?

I sat up straight. Carter had pretty much admitted his fault for staying after things got out of hand. "What's that mean?"

Ms. Ellers launched into another legal explanation about contributory negligence and more mumbo jumbo.

"I see." My thoughts spun. I could end this all right now by sharing what Carter himself had confessed.

Then I remembered how he'd winced in pain whenever he'd moved in his bed the last time I saw him, and how Grace hadn't helped Dirk with his custody nonsense. Something in my chest snapped when I thought about how cold Grace had been otherwise. An ugly little part of me wanted to strike back. She kept insisting that this wasn't what she wanted, but her refusal to talk to me and trust me hurt worse than when Dirk betrayed me.

Still, I couldn't share what I knew if it meant Carter might not be able to afford the best care. And especially not when I knew he'd said it mostly to ease Rowan's conscience.

"Well, that hardly seems right. Carter will need ongoing medical care for some time. I don't want him to suffer any more losses or setbacks. I just want to be fair."

"A jury might be inclined to agree with you, especially given the fact that he hadn't been drinking. That said, it's my job to reduce the recovery, so we need to go over the facts again to make sure I've captured all possible defenses."

My spine curved as my shoulders rounded forward. Whittling away Carter's recovery felt sinful. Not that I could afford my insurance premiums going up any better than Grace could afford to pay for Carter's care. The only difference was that Carter hadn't done anything wrong, whereas I had, so I decided to keep quiet about his admission. Maybe Grace and Sam would be reasonable in settlement talks, given our personal history. "Okay. Hit me with whatever questions you've got, although I don't know what else I can tell you that you don't already know."

Yeah, I had my fingers crossed behind my back while telling that lie. Dirk would have a field day with that one.

———

"Good morning." I gave Adam, the security guy, a big smile, proud to have arrived early for my appointment despite a restless night. Maybe this marked the beginning of a new trend. "I'm here to meet with Mr. Richards."

I signed the sheet while he printed out the visitor sticker with my photograph. "Thanks."

Before heading toward the main administrative offices, I wiggled my fingers in a friendly wave goodbye. To this day, I still dreaded meeting with school faculty. Like my son, I hadn't been a stellar student, so teachers and principals gave me the willies.

Donna, the main office secretary, greeted me. "Hi, Mrs. Gillette. Let me put you in the small conference room. Mr. Richards is on a call but will be right with you."

I followed her into a windowless room with a table big enough for eight people and flopped my purse onto a spare chair before taking a seat.

"Would you like some water?" she asked.

"No, thanks." I'd already chugged a giant mug of coffee on my way over.

After she left, I took out my phone to take one last glance at the GoFundMe page. Final total of $2,975. Not bad for a spur-of-the-moment idea. If only all my impulses had that kind of ROI.

I looked up wearing a smile when the door opened, expecting Mr. Richards. Instead, Grace entered the room and then froze. I didn't move, either, like a rabbit facing a hawk.

She'd lost weight since the cafeteria run-in. The bags beneath her eyes proved she still wasn't sleeping. The notion that things had further deteriorated for her caused a little twinge in my heart.

"Why are you here?" She glanced around as if she'd been punked.

"Mr. Richards asked me to come talk about the GoFundMe money."

Her hands clasped her purse strap so tightly they were changing color. "Me too."

"Well, this is a pickle, given the lawsuit." I couldn't keep the snark from my voice. Since being served, my compassion for her had started to sour.

"I won't defend myself to you and Sam when all I'm doing is following our lawyers' advice and taking care of my son." Her weary expression showed no hint of regret as she took a seat at the opposite end of the table.

I had half a mind to throw my phone at her head. Maybe a good knock to the skull would break my old friend free. Not that she knew that I was protecting Carter by keeping my mouth shut, but you'd think she knew me well enough to guess it. That she didn't get that throbbed like a toothache. Then again, maybe she didn't know what Carter had admitted. Given her mood these days, he'd be a fool to mention it. Since I, too, was advised not to discuss the case with anyone, I'd have to stew in my own juices.

Mr. Richards entered the room before either of us said something more we'd regret later. "Good morning, ladies."

His friendly smile gave his rather narrow, horsey face a more attractive look. He took a seat and opened a slender green folder. "Well, we are very grateful for the donation to the science department. Our faculty met to discuss the best use of the funds but decided it would be nice to get input from you about whether you had specific requests."

I glanced at Grace, whose distant gaze suggested her thoughts were elsewhere. It wasn't like her to lose focus in a meeting. Something big had to be bothering her. If things were different, I would know what it was and help. Instead, I remained handcuffed by the silence. "I don't know anything about science equipment, so I have no suggestions. Sorry."

"No need to apologize. That's why I called this meeting," he said. "We could do any number of things. For instance, we could buy a bunch of new smaller items, like updated microscopes, and scales and balances. Or we could buy one or two bigger-ticket items, like a small fume hood or mobile lab unit."

I grimaced and shrugged, feeling like I was listening to that lawyer again with all the jargon. "If it were up to me, I might vote to do a big item and put a plaque on it with Carter's name . . . something that would last." Plaques and recognition had always seemed so posh, probably because I'd never received any. "But, Grace, why don't we ask Carter what he'd prefer since he's the science wiz?"

Hearing her name snapped her back to attention. "Sorry. Um, I'm driving up there after this meeting, so I can talk to him about it today." She turned to Mr. Richards. "Would it be possible for me to take your list of items so he can see all the options?"

"Of course." He slid the folder toward her. "As you know, we have around three grand to work with."

"Do the teachers have a preference?" She leafed through the pages, as if any of that equipment meant something to her. Meanwhile, it was so obvious to anyone who knew her well that something was wrong. My stomach burned with concern. "I ask because Carter might also like to know that."

"I'm glad you asked, actually." He smiled. "Other countries are doing more advanced microscopy work in the classroom. This coming summer and next, we're running our teachers through some extra coursework on how to better incorporate that into our curriculum so our kids aren't left behind in the global STEM education arena. There are some newer digital microscopes that might be great, but that said, we're open to anything if Carter has a strong feeling about it. This is, after all, a gift in his name."

"One we are very touched by and grateful for." Grace flushed when she looked at me, her eyes glistening with unshed tears, prompting some of my own. As hurt as I'd been, if Mr. Richards weren't here, I would cross the room, hug her, and force her to tell me what was going on, lawsuits be damned. She cleared her throat. "Okay, then. I'll take this and give him your recommendation, then call you later, if that's okay with everyone."

"Of course." Mr. Richards paused. "Do you mind if I ask how he's doing? I'd love to give his teachers some good news. He's very well liked, as you know."

Thank God he'd asked what I was dying to know.

"Thank you." Grace's gaze flicked my way before she finished. I remained still, as if I could make myself invisible so she would feel free to answer him. "It's been hard. He had a setback recently, which will prolong his stay up there, but he's working to get back on track. We don't know yet when he'll be released, but they keep reminding me that progress is not always linear, so we have to be patient."

My heartbeat became uneven and heavy. A setback? How big? What had happened, and how was he coping? Good grief, and here I'd been mad at Grace for not being nicer to me. I felt selfish and disturbed. "Grace, I'm sorry to hear that."

She nodded, saying no more.

"As am I. But he's such a determined kid I've no doubt that he will overcome and push forward," Mr. Richards said. "Please give him our best and keep us posted. If he needs additional accommodations, don't hesitate to reach out."

"Thank you for being so flexible. We really appreciate it." She forced a polite smile, but her movements were still nervous—birdlike, fidgety. It bruised my heart to see her this close to the edge.

He nodded, then raised his hands. "Well, thank you both for coming in. It's nice when we can be brief and get about our day." He stood and reached out to shake my hand. "Thank you, Mrs. Gillette, for organizing the fundraiser." Then he turned to Grace, offering her his hand as well. "Mrs. Phillips, best of luck to your family as you manage through this crisis."

"Thank you. If Carter wants to participate virtually in classroom discussions on days when he feels up to it, you may hear from me."

"We have the technology, of course, but I'd need to check with policies and procedures. There are always laws and safety aspects when dealing with kids and technology. I'll get back to you soon."

"I appreciate it." She nodded.

"Ladies, have a nice day." He opened the door and waited for us to file out ahead of him.

"Bye," we said in unison and then awkwardly walked out of the office and toward the check-in desk, side by side yet several feet apart.

Despite everything between us, I wanted details about Carter's setback, so I blurted, "Grace, what's going on with Carter? I'm concerned." Tears backed up behind my eyes.

"Mimi." Grace drew herself up with a deep breath while slowing her pace and meeting my gaze. "Out of respect for his privacy, I'd rather not discuss it with anyone right now."

Privacy? The word felt like a door slammed in my face. We'd always shared all our parenting worries. Then again, I supposed his progress or lack thereof could affect the lawsuit and thus was taboo, but I hated it all the same.

"All right." I kept walking toward the desk, sluggish with self-pity.

"I meant what I said earlier. The GoFundMe was very thoughtful," she said. "I know you did it because of the budget vote and to cheer Carter up, so thank you. It doesn't change our situation, but your heart is in the right place, as usual."

Her cheeks turned hot pink. Finally, confirmation that my friend's heart still beat somewhere beneath all her agony and exhaustion. Mine leaped at the idea that she might be starting to see that I was not the enemy and sole cause of her pain. I wanted to hug her, but she averted her gaze.

"You're welcome." I said nothing more. Until Carter came home and showed signs of a real recovery, the gulf between us could not close. I hoped things turned around quickly, because Grace looked too fragile to take more disappointment. "I hope Carter comes home soon. You must miss him."

"We do." When an unexpected sob rushed out, I reflexively hugged her. I needed it so much and hoped she wouldn't push me away. Two seconds, maybe three passed before she started pulling away, quickly dabbing her tears.

I felt bereft as she stepped up to sign herself out.

"Have a good day, Mimi."

The end of our first halfway-kind conversation in weeks landed like a soft jab to the ribs. "Thanks. You too."

She scurried through the doors to the parking lot. My chest throbbed with a yearning to change the past and fix the present. Each week that passed chipped away at my bond with Grace. The damage might be irreversible.

"Good meeting?" Adam asked.

"As good as possible, I guess." Swallowing the bittersweet lump in my throat, I signed out and walked to my car, wishing Grace and I could've gone to Sugar Momma's and had ourselves a good long cry together before heading our separate ways. I might've gone by myself and cried to Hannah had I the time.

When I got to my shop, there was an envelope with my name on it taped to the front door. Please, God, don't let this be some kind of landlord notice of a rent increase.

I opened the letter.

*Mimi,*

*Is it time to plan a painting party? If you're not ready to spend a whole day together, maybe we could graduate from lunch to dinner soon. Call me if you're interested.*

*Rodri*

I pressed the sheet of paper to my chest, savoring the little jolt of happiness. A painting party might break through my doldrums, but I wasn't ready to introduce Rodri to Rowan.

On top of that, there was Dirk's reaction to consider. One would hope that, since he'd left me for another, he wouldn't begrudge me happiness with someone new. Yet Dirk had been snide about my relationship with Tony throughout its duration. Now I had the added concern of whether he'd use Rodri as more evidence of bad judgment and push harder to modify our custody arrangement. I couldn't afford to fight a custody battle, which left me in a pretty weak position.

Surely Dirk wouldn't risk getting Child Protective Services involved in Rowan's life. Yet he'd never gotten this worked up before, so he had to honestly believe I was a bad mom. His trying to be a good father made it harder to hate him.

Business woes, lawsuits, custody threats, and friendship rifts—each of which had been hits to my self-esteem—scrambled my thoughts. Lunch with Rodri had been the only bright spot in weeks, and even that had come at a cost because of how it had hurt Grace.

I fanned myself with the note. My house could use some freshening up, and I'd love to spend a little time with a grown-up who didn't consider me the devil. Maybe the next time Dirk took Rowan for the weekend, Rodri could help me paint my living room without everyone in town finding out. After all, I wasn't an awful person, and I deserved good things, too. If we kept it quiet, what could it really hurt?

# CHAPTER TWENTY

### Grace

*Friday, February 26*
*Girl Scouts meeting*

"Come on, Kim. We don't want to be late," I called up the back stairs after hurrying to put the few grocery items away. Another day of rushing from here to there, running late and barely present for anyone except Carter. Sam and I had never found the time for that honest discussion about our relationship, so each night the temperature in our bed dropped another degree as I silently cried myself to sleep. Daily failures deadened my family life bit by arduous bit.

Kim stomped down the stairs in her junior sash, replete with its many badges. "It's not my fault if we're late. You just got home from Carter's again."

As if I weren't already laden with guilt about giving her too little attention this month. She was too young to sympathize or realize I was one person trying to support a sick child, teach my music students, walk a tightrope with my husband, and preserve some energy for her at the end of each day. That discussion wouldn't make either of us feel better, so I said nothing. "I'm sorry. I'm here now, so let's get going."

"Did you remember the sticky notes and markers?" She eyed me skeptically. My heart sank even further in response to her expectation of being let down.

"I did." Barely. Not that she needed to know. I had to pretend to be excited about this meeting, so I smiled. "They're in the car, so let's go."

I dashed off a note for Sam, reminding him that I would pick up takeout on our way home from the Girl Scouts meeting. Maybe later tonight we could find time for a discussion that didn't revolve around the kids.

Ten minutes later, Kim and I arrived at Tami Zaffino's house, where we would be discussing leadership.

"Leadership is a silly topic," Kim said as we strolled up the walkway.

"It's actually really important." If I'd learned it young, so much might be different now.

"I'm already a leader. People listen to me all the time. I don't need lessons on it."

I didn't have the patience for this today. A terrible, selfish truth, but my God, I was running on empty. Never before had I wished for my kids to be older—I'd enjoyed doing these activities with them—but chronic stress had my bones as brittle as icicles and my nerves sharply bristling.

"A truly good leader always wants to listen and learn." I knocked on the door.

Tyler Zaffino, the troop leader, answered. "Hey, so glad you guys could make it. Come on in. We're about to get started."

Kim flashed her a big smile and then dashed ahead of me while I set down the bags of supplies to take off my coat, dreading the inevitable questions that would come.

"I've been thinking about you all. How's Carter?" Tyler asked, putting my coat on a hanger in the hall closet.

Even this many weeks later, well-intentioned questions made my throat clog with tears. The women here were all perfectly lovely people whom I considered friendly acquaintances, but they were not my confidantes. Mimi and Sam had been mine. And like with every reminder of what I'd lost, it seemed a little harder to breathe.

Tyler didn't actually want to know about Carter's daily sessions with Dr. Spotts or my family's steady disintegration. "He's progressing, thanks."

"I'm glad to hear it." She waved for me to follow her to the large family room, where eight other mother-daughter duos sat gathered beneath its vaulted ceilings, surrounded by bowlfuls of M&M's, Cheetos, and pretzels.

If Mimi had had a daughter instead of a son, troop meetings would've always had more flair. She'd loved the few times I'd let her crash the ones I'd hosted. My favorite was when she'd brought craft paper and sparkly stickers and had all the girls create handmade cards for the old folks at Sandy Shores Care Center, which Mimi then delivered when she went to style their hair. Would there ever be a day when I didn't feel a pang from some reminder of how much happier my life had been with my friend?

"Okay, everyone. Before we make our collages, let's talk about this year's theme—leadership. Who can name some qualities in a good leader?" Tyler asked.

Kim raised her hand, full of self-confidence. "You have to be smart and confident."

Tyler smiled. "Yes, those are important. But what about things like resilience? Has anyone had to try to face something really hard and overcome it?"

Not to be easily dismissed, Kim said, "My brother's fall has changed everything and my parents are always busy with him, so I've been alone a lot. It's been scary, but I keep going." She took a giant bite of a cupcake after her pronouncement. Despite the discomfort of watching the other women pretend not to feel sorry for me, I had to admire my daughter. She had "kept going" pretty well despite being somewhat neglected. I should praise her finer qualities more often instead of trying to fix her troubling ones. I would, too. Starting now.

Tyler replied, "I'm sure you've been very brave and helpful while your brother recovers. It makes me think of another leadership trait—empathy. Leaders need to be able to understand how other people feel. For instance, at school, if you ever see someone be left out, you might think about how lonely they could feel and then include them in your activity."

I rubbed the ache from my chest. If Carter required a walker in the future, some might discriminate against him. Exclude him. Make assumptions based on that single fact of his life. He worried about that, yet I had no idea how to help him care less about other people's opinions when so much of my life had been driven by them.

"Accountability is another key trait—taking responsibility for your actions, including your mistakes." Tyler looked around the room at all the girls. "It's important that, when you are a leader, you don't take all the credit for the good things and lay blame for all the bad on your team. So let's talk about what it means to be fair . . ."

Fairness. We routinely teach kids this concept in a way that sets them up for false expectations. Life hadn't been fair to me as a kid, or to Carter. What we should have been teaching kids was how to cope with unfairness.

My phone rang, so I checked it, as I'd done with every call since the night of Carter's accident. My pulse skipped ahead when Dr. Spotts's number appeared. "Excuse me. It's Carter's doctor."

I stood to walk away from the group, but not before first seeing Kim's face fall. There'd been nothing fair about what she'd been asked to put up with lately.

When I got to the front entry, I sat on the cushioned bench, my knees jiggling in anticipation of more bad news. "Dr. Spotts, how are you?"

"Fine, thanks. I'm sorry I missed you earlier today but wanted to touch base about Carter. How are you finding his mood?"

"Unchanged. I did bring two friends to visit yesterday, which gave him a temporary boost."

"He mentioned that. Leron says he's hit a plateau with his physical progress, so we're looking at modifications to get him over this hump. Carter and I talked about how everything in life is temporary, including this plateau. We've reminded him to listen to his body's signals—sometimes it needs a rest. We've also talked about balance and patience. I'm recommending a meditation app to help him pull out of negative thought spirals and fears. It would be great if you and your husband could echo these ideas, maybe even join him in meditation when you visit to create a habit of it."

As expensive as the rehab center was, I couldn't have been more grateful for the world-class doctors' advice and support. "We'll certainly follow whatever you recommend and support him however we can."

"Great. I'm also encouraging Carter to take advantage of any virtual classroom activities the school can provide. Socializing will help, although I know he's hesitant about people seeing him looking weak."

"That's why I didn't push. I'll talk to my husband. He's often better at getting Carter to see things through a more positive lens." The back of my neck prickled because I'd been relying too heavily on Sam to carry that burden. Perhaps I'd been letting myself off the hook too easily, as if no one were suffering with regret as much as I.

"Terrific. Well, unless you have other questions, that's it for now. We're keeping a close eye on your son. This is nothing we haven't come up against before, so don't worry too much."

"Thank you. I'll be back tomorrow. If anything changes, please let me know."

"Of course. Have a pleasant evening."

After we hung up, I sat like a lump of clay on the foyer bench while happy chatter played in the background like a twisted soundtrack to my life. The girls were probably laughing and shoving fistfuls of candy in their faces.

Normally, I'd be eager to teach our girls how to look beyond their own experiences and be leaders. But with Carter's recent regression, I'd become preoccupied with big, important worries that made these exercises seem like a colossal waste of time. And yet my daughter needed her mother, and Sam and my mother couldn't fill my shoes. She deserved my attention and love and guidance as much as Carter, even if she wasn't in a rehab center.

I tapped into any remaining energy before pushing myself off the bench and painting a smile on my face. I had to do one thing well for a change. Kim would be scrutinizing me, and I didn't want to disappoint her again.

"Is everything all right?" Tyler asked with perfect sincerity.

"Yes, thank you." Lies, lies, lies. Until recently I'd abhorred lies, which corroded everything from the inside out.

Kim was sprawled on the floor, pen in hand, thinking.

"Can I help?" I asked.

She speared me with a look. "You missed the instructions, Mom. I can do it by myself."

Ouch. Punishment for my taking that call. Instead of self-pity, I took in all four and a half feet of her. My baby was ten—a birthday that came and went with little joy. In eight years, she'd go off to college. Between now and then, there'd be fewer opportunities to bond, so I couldn't waste this one.

"Maybe you could be a good leader and repeat them to me quickly so I can participate."

She peered over her shoulder at me, her expression dubious. "Okay."

She proceeded to tell me that we'd be writing out all the different roles women can have—like nurse, mom, daughter, coach, scientist, CEO—on sticky notes that would go into a pile from which we could choose ones we'd like. After that, we'd discuss why we chose that role, and how you can be a leader in that role, and so on.

"Thank you." She might be embarrassed by a public show of affection, but I leaned forward to kiss the top of her head before spreading out the notes she'd already written. With a determined shove, I set aside all other thoughts. "Well, I see you already wrote mom, daughter, volunteer, and teacher down. Let's think about what other kinds of things interest you . . ."

She speared me with a "duh" look. "Soccer player and veterinarian."

For the first time all day, I smiled in truth. "You want to be a vet?"

We didn't even have a pet. Maybe we should, though. It could've helped her feel less lonely these past weeks.

"Yes. But only for dogs."

I covered my laughter. "Well, I love that you want to be a pet doctor. It makes me very proud."

With a quick, mischievous smile, she asked, "Proud enough to plan a makeup sleepover party?"

I chuckled. She was nothing if not tenacious, exactly like my sister. Two toughies. I wanted to make her happy, but getting Carter strong enough to come home would require more of our time, not less. Despite my intentions, I was already breaking my promise to give her my best. "I'm sorry, honey. Not yet, but soon. I promise."

"Because of Carter."

I nodded, rubbing her back, but she flinched, which made me want to cry.

"But he's up there and we're here."

"That's the problem, because Dad and I are on the road hours each day. We miss spending time doing things you like, and really appreciate what a patient and loving sister you're being while your brother recovers."

"All you care about is him." She pouted.

Her expression and words were like knives to my heart. "That's not true. I love you very much. That's why I'm here with you now."

"It is true. You're always too tired, and you're always late, and no one cares that my party was ruined."

"We do care, Kim." Each of her accusations hammered me with more guilt and shame until I felt bloodied. Beside us Tyler and Tami smiled at each other while talking and adding sticky notes to the bowl. All the other moms were engaged and fully present. Sure, none of them had an injured child miles from home, but if I kept using that crutch to justify neglecting Kim's needs, I'd be no better than my mother.

I noted Kim's tight face. What if her snark wasn't toughness at all, but rather a withdrawal similar to how I'd hidden in my room with my records at her age? The sudden epiphany made it hard to catch my breath. In that instant I was a little girl again, closeted in my room, listening to music and pretending to be anywhere else.

I leaned close and rested my cheek on her head, hoping she could feel my sympathy. "Kim, I'm very sorry that you've been neglected. Let me try to do better, okay?"

She grunted as she wrote down "vet" in big block letters.

For weeks I'd been telling everyone I was doing my best. Sam, Mimi, Kim, Carter. But was it true? Was this my best? Because if it was, my best wasn't nearly as good as I thought. Another crushing blow that bruised my heart.

And yet, even as I acknowledged that, I didn't know how to achieve a true change of heart. How to rebalance my priorities with Carter still in a backslide, or shut off my worries so I could sleep at night.

I'd never before felt this inept—a fortysomething woman who'd yet to learn how to work through negative feelings. My mother had taught me to bury them. Sam couldn't help because he didn't struggle with pessimism. Mimi overcame obstacles faster than anyone I'd ever met. Without her and Sam firmly at my side, I was flailing like a newborn tossed into a pool. God had not gifted me a magic heart that was quick to forgive, quick to heal, quick to move on.

No matter how much I admired others' incredible resilience, I hardened against the potential of more pain, wallowing in the past with almost no faith in a brighter tomorrow. It was as if my father's and Margot's ghosts refused to let me believe that things would work out.

If I didn't figure out how to make them disappear, there'd be more loss in my future. A shiver spread through my entire body.

I reached out to stroke Kim's head. "Kim."

"Huh?"

Leaning closer, I said, "Could you look at me for a second?"

With a sigh, she tipped her face up. "What?"

"I hate that I've made you feel like you don't matter as much as your brother. Please forgive me. I promise I love you just as much as him." I held my breath.

"Okay, Mom." A slight smile spread. "Can we finish writing the notes?"

"Yes," I said, releasing the air in my lungs. Her easy forgiveness warmed its way through my limbs and loosened the tension in my back.

Maybe I should try that direct approach with Sam, too.

———

An hour later we entered our home through the mudroom. Kim ran ahead of me, calling out for Sam to proudly show off her leadership knowledge, while I turned on the oven to reheat the pizza we'd picked up. I wandered through the house, finding them in his office.

Sam greeted me with a cordial smile before pulling Kim onto his lap and listening attentively to her explain in excruciating detail the traits of leadership and how she demonstrated all of them. I studied them together, a simultaneously reassuring yet bittersweet image of casual comfort and trust. Things Sam and I had shared until recently. My limbs ached to go hug them both, but I felt too fragile and uncertain.

When she finally finished and took a breath, he squeezed her tight. "You learned a lot today. I'm proud of you. I hope you continue to be a leader, Kim, and use that power to help others."

"I will, Daddy." She smiled sweetly, nestling against his chest.

The scene wrought a pang in my chest. Not only for how lucky my daughter was to have a father like Sam, but because I, too, missed burrowing against my husband for security.

"Kim, why don't you go put away your sash before dinner?" I suggested. "The pizza will be ready in five minutes."

"Okay." She slid off Sam's lap and skipped out of his office. I'd achieved a small breakthrough with Kim today, which encouraged me to try with Sam.

"Looks like you had a pleasant Scout meeting," he said.

"For the most part, yes. Dr. Spotts called, though." I recited what she told me, then added, "She'd like help convincing Carter to try virtual classroom time to help connect him to his normal life."

"Okay. I have to be in Baltimore tomorrow midmorning for a client meeting, so I'll swing by to see him early, before his morning PT."

"Maybe we could go together?" I noted a hint of pleasant surprise in his gaze. A hopeful sign that we hadn't completely destroyed our marriage. That the security and safe harbor of love we'd created hadn't been an illusion but was waiting beneath the surface of all this pain for a chance to bloom again, like daffodils in spring. "If he gives the green light, I'll call Principal Davies. We could suggest starting with one class—chemistry, since it's his favorite."

"Sounds good." He smiled, casting a hesitant glance at the papers on the desk.

"What are those?" I asked, working my way up to my apology. I didn't know why my nerves had me quaking inside. Perhaps from fear based on the many times this month that my words had come out wrong or been misinterpreted.

"More health insurance forms. It's never-ending." He shook his head, looking wary of my next move.

"Thank you for taking care of all that. I know it's a lot, and I know you've tried shielding me from the worst of it."

"You don't have to thank me for looking out for our family, Grace. But you're welcome." He grinned.

My heart warmed, reassured by the softness in his gaze. "Sam?"

His brows rose. "Hmm?"

"I know I've been distant and difficult—bitter, even—and that's made everything harder on you and Kim. You're right when you say I need to forgive us both for what happened to Carter. I want you to know that I'm working on it." I stopped short of apologizing for pushing the lawsuit, because I still believed it was the right thing to do for our son. But when my husband's eyes glowed with compassion that I hadn't seen in weeks, all the tightness around my lungs released, freeing me.

"Thank you, babe. The apology is appreciated and accepted. I know you're harder on yourself than on anyone else, so I hope you'll give yourself a break, too." He rose from his desk and crossed to me, reaching down to pull me out of my chair. Without a word, he wrapped his arms around my waist and tucked my head against his shoulder to hold me. Little by little the numbness inside faded. I could feel his heartbeat against my chest, its slow, steady rhythm like a soothing hymn. I allowed myself to be comforted, and to believe that this marked a reversal of the damage we'd done to our marriage. "It's good to feel like we're back on the same side."

I nodded, hoping with all my heart that this was more than a mere truce, and that our love would survive the lawsuits and Carter's therapy. The moment would have been perfect if only the inner voice that wondered why he didn't or couldn't acknowledge all the ways he'd left me feeling abandoned and irrational had been silent. I held him tighter, as if I could literally squeeze that thought from my head before it destroyed our fresh start.

# CHAPTER TWENTY-ONE

MIMI

*Sunday, February 28*
*Mimi's house*

Rodri rolled the final stroke of "Crisp Cantaloupe" paint on my living room wall while I edged around the picture window. This cheerful color—so much more me than the forest green Dirk liked—replaced all traces of the mess this room had been the night of Rowan's disastrous party. My mood had also brightened immeasurably, thanks, in part, to the way Rodri's muscles flexed as he bent and stretched his way around the room with that paint roller.

He set the roller in the nearly empty paint pan. "I confess I worried the room might end up looking like an Easter egg, but it looks fresh. Suits you."

"Thank you." I laid the paintbrush in the empty pan as well, then stepped back to admire our handiwork. "The great thing about that old floral sofa is that it pretty much goes with everything."

He smiled. "Should we move the furniture back in place?"

"Nah. You've worked hard enough. My son can help me once the walls dry." I glanced at the clock, guessing Rowan would return from Dirk's in another hour or so. My ex's renewed commitment to Rowan had helped lift our son's spirits lately. Yet I'd caught myself wandering the empty house more than once last night, missing him and worrying about whether he'd start preferring Annapolis to Potomac Point. Having Rodri here today had been a great distraction. No, that wasn't fair. He was more than a mere distraction. His interest and compassion—his lack of judgment, despite how we met—gave me much-needed confidence and, like the paint, helped erase much of the shame I'd felt since the night of that party. "How about a beer to celebrate our hard work?"

"I'd love one." He grabbed the paint pan and things. "Do you have a laundry sink where I can clean this stuff off?"

"Oh, no. I'll do that later."

"I don't mind. Best to do it before everything dries."

"Okay. The laundry sink is in the basement—" I winced at the reminder of where we'd first met. "Sadly, you know where that is. In the meantime, I'll scare up a little snack."

After he disappeared downstairs, I raided my cupboards for chips and salsa, then popped the tabs of two Buds.

Rodri appeared a few minutes later. "I left everything down there to dry."

"Thanks." I gestured to a kitchen chair and cracked open the window, despite the chilly late-February weather. "Let's stay in here. Less fumes."

He raised a beer to his lips and chugged a healthy amount. "Ah. That tastes great."

I sipped some, staring at him. He'd been chatty—unlike my ex. I'd learned about his family, his childhood friend Erin, and his best friends on the force. I couldn't remember the last time I'd spoken so little in a day. Rodri didn't make me not miss Grace, but he proved that, if she and I continued to drift apart, there were other good people out there who could enrich my life. A bittersweet thought, but one that helped me feel less hopeless.

"What?" he asked, leaning forward with his elbows on the table.

"Thanks for taking one of your days off to help me. It certainly was a unique way to get to know someone . . . although I'm still a little nervous about agreeing to get on that motorcycle when the weather breaks."

"I won't hold you to that if you're uncomfortable, but I'm a safe driver." He smiled and nabbed a chip, dipping it in the salsa before crunching into it. "Today was fun. And who knew my rocker soul would connect with Ashley McBryde? Erin will have a field day with that one."

He'd been a good sport about my musical tastes, never once groaning about the countless female country singers and occasional Christian rock song. Dirk had never been religious. While I'd never warmed to Uncle Tommy's punishing view of Christianity, my faith had always been part of my life. The fact it was prevalent in Rodri's life had been a surprisingly nice connection.

"Well, now I owe you a favor or a freebie in return." My gaze homed in on his thick black hair. "How 'bout I style your hair?"

He scrubbed a hand over his shorn head. "I do this myself. Clipper setting number five."

I could tell, but I didn't say anything. Apparently, I didn't need to.

"Ha!" he laughed. "Guess I should leave it to a professional."

I raised my hands. "I didn't say a word."

"Exactly." He grinned. "If I grow it out, you'll be the only person I let touch it."

"I'd love to get my hands on it." I blushed at my husky tone.

After a beat or two, Rodri cleared his throat and changed the subject. "So when's your son due home?"

"Around five . . ." I trailed off, unsure how to politely ask him to make himself scarce. "I hope you aren't offended that I don't want to tell

Rowan anything yet. When my last relationship ended, it was harder on him than me. Given everything else he's going through now, I don't want to overwhelm him."

"I totally understand, Mimi. No worries." He raised his beer as if toasting my good parenting choice—another welcome show of support. "Did he finish his community service?"

"Not yet, but he's bagging groceries at Stewart's three days a week, so he'll be able to pay his dad back for the fine and maybe learn some responsibility to boot." He'd grumbled a lot at first, especially after I nixed the Poconos trip. But I hadn't coddled him, and now he was finally rising to the task without complaining. Growth, for both of us.

"He's learning from this experience, which will help him in lots of ways."

"I almost feel guilty about that, considering that Carter's recovery isn't going great." Anytime I recalled Grace's mood during that meeting with Mr. Richards, I got sad. Often I stared at my phone, thinking to leave a message, but then stopped myself because of the damn lawsuit. "He's had some setbacks."

"That can't make things easier between you and your friend." He offered a sympathetic smile. I had to admit, I was digging how this young, sexy cop was such a softy.

"No, it doesn't. It's been a long, lonely several weeks that has made me reevaluate a lot of things. I never imagined my letting Rowan and his friends have a few beers now and then snowballing like this. Sometimes I understand why Grace can't stand the sight of me, but other times I'm furious at how she's cut me out. If she'd storm over here and let me have it, maybe we could finally work through it all."

"Have you told her that?"

"It wouldn't matter. Grace learned to repress every unpleasant emotion from the master—her mother. I don't think she knows how to deal with healthy conflict and recover."

"That's the opposite of my family. Everyone's quick to share their opinions, anger, and joy. Sometimes all in the span of one meal." He chuckled, fondness coating his tone.

I smiled. "I like that—knowing where you stand, and knowing that a little trouble doesn't mean you walk away."

"We've got a lot in common, Mimi." He swigged more beer. "Although the timing isn't great, I'd like to see you again."

The bubbly feeling I'd had all day was worth the risk. "Me too, as long as we keep it quiet awhile longer."

"Understood. The next time your son's with his dad, maybe we'll take that ride up the coast if the weather breaks."

"I'll psych myself up for it," I promised, letting my shoulders relax.

Before I knew what was happening, Rowan blew in through the back door thirty minutes early. I froze like a teen caught having sex. My son came to a dead stop, dropping his bag on the floor.

"Honey, I didn't expect you home so early." I aimed for a nonchalant smile and tone.

His face turned pale as milk. "Officer Martinez. Am I in more trouble?"

Oh gosh! I almost jumped up to hug away the terror in his eyes.

"Not at all." Rodri waved his hands.

Rowan's posture relaxed, but then he frowned when his gaze landed on the beer and chips. "Then why are you here?"

Rodri looked to me, wisely allowing me to do the talking. My whole body broke into a sweat; I wasn't prepared for questions today.

"He helped me paint the living room. Wait until you see it." I rose from my chair and slung an arm around Rowan's shoulders, eager to distract him from more questions. Not that I honestly thought I'd get away with this trick, but it would buy me another minute to gather my thoughts.

"Why?" Rowan asked, pressing the point while shrugging free from me. Then his face screwed up in horror. "Are you two dating now?"

The guilt of sneaking around caught up to me even though I'd done it to protect him. "We're getting to know each other, that's all. It's nothing serious."

Not yet. And if I kept this behavior up, maybe not ever. A quick glimpse of Rodri suggested he hadn't taken offense to my remark.

"Whatever," Rowan mumbled. "I'm going upstairs."

"Okay. I'll need your help to move the furniture back in a little while. Maybe we can get Chinese takeout for dinner." I couldn't tell if he heard that last part. I hugged myself to keep the early seeds of panic from rising over how he and Dirk would react to this bombshell. Turning to Rodri, I wrinkled my nose. "Sorry. I didn't mean to be dismissive—"

"I get it." He waved a hand. "I don't want to make your life harder, so we can pump the brakes if this is too much right now."

The old me would've jumped on that and turned myself inside out to make Rowan happy, no matter what. But my needs mattered, too. There was nothing wrong or shameful about my having a date. I wasn't exactly sure how to handle things now, and I had even less of an idea how Dirk would react when Rowan told him, but Dirk couldn't exactly use my dating a cop against me when he was living with an adulteress.

I would continue to look out for my son while also allowing myself to hold on to a scrap of happiness. "No, let's not. I deserve a life. I'll call you when I confirm Rowan's next weekend with his dad."

"Okay. I'll make myself scarce now." Rodri leaned in nice and slow and kissed the corner of my mouth. His warm, soft lips heated the air between us. "Talk soon."

I touched my lips. "Bye."

He smiled and went out through the back door. The loud rev of his motorcycle vibrated in my chest before he pulled away.

With a sigh, I wandered toward the stairs and trotted up to Rowan's room. He was in bed, glued to his phone, tinny tunes radiating from his earbuds. For some reason that pissed me off. Probably because he'd been rude to Rodri and me. When I snapped my fingers in front of his face, he yanked an earbud out. "What?"

"You were pretty rude downstairs. When we have adult company, I expect you to say hello and take five minutes to offer basic pleasantries."

"Sorry." His sarcastic tone and expression piqued my anger. It always took him an hour or so to shed Dirk's influence after his visits, but I wouldn't abandon my mission to grow as a parent.

"Have you done all your homework?" I stood, hands on my hips.

"Yeah." He started to put the earbud back in his ear.

"Really? You finished your history paper?"

"Yeah, Mom." He rolled his eyes. "Why are you acting so crazy?"

"Since when is asking questions crazy?" I sat on his mattress, frowning. I didn't raise my son to call women things like crazy, irrational, or emotional when they asserted themselves. The fact that my patience had run thin due to the stress in my life made me normal, not crazy.

"It's everything. Dating the cop. Being all over me about homework and my dumb job. Not letting me go to the Poconos." Teen pushback was normal, but it pressed on my last nerve.

"Gee, I don't know, Rowan. Maybe I'd relax if you realized that it's wrong of you to run off and have fun while Carter's still in rehab." I gritted my teeth.

He groaned. "Come on, that's totally *not* fair. I've been working to pay Dad back, keeping up with school, and I was trying to help Carter until the whole lawsuit stuff happened. You can't punish me forever."

I sat back, thinking. He had shown some growth these past weeks, even though he bristled now and then when I held the line. We were a work in progress, both of us learning to navigate a healthier relationship with each other. Like Grace had said, maybe I should give him more credit instead of assuming he'd turn out like his father.

And if I wanted Grace to stop blaming me for everything, I couldn't keep casting up his big mistake without being a hypocrite. "You're right.

I shouldn't keep reminding you of your mistakes. I'm sorry. But in the future, I want you to be more polite to guests."

"Is that what you're calling your boyfriend?" He threw me a look that said he thought I was whitewashing.

"Rodri is not my boyfriend. Not yet, anyway. I didn't mention him before because I don't know where it will go. I didn't want to involve you until I was sure it might turn into something."

"Will it?"

"He's very nice. He makes me feel good about who I am, which I could really use lately. But I'm taking things a lot slower than I did with Tony."

"Maybe I should go live with Dad so you can do what you want and I don't have to be part of it," he grumbled.

That threat landed like an elephant on my chest. Part of me knew he needed reassurance, but the part that worried about Dirk's threats froze with fear. Rowan and I had rarely fought, mostly because I'd rarely denied him much. Would my new attitude end up costing me my son?

Lately life seemed like a series of forks in the road. I felt like a blind man, feeling my way along the right path. I had two choices here: live in fear of Dirk's threat for two more years or confront it straight up.

"Well, if that's what you want, I won't stop you. It might be good for you to learn to cook and do your own laundry, since I doubt he or Miranda will do much of either for you. Hopefully, you won't have competition for your position on that high school's football team. Can't tell you much about its coach, though, or guess how much playing time you'll get." I stood and headed for the door, feeling a little shaky but determined. I hooked my hand on the doorjamb and glanced over my shoulder. "And not for nothing, but your smart-aleck comment sure sounds ungrateful. For fifteen years I've given you all I've got, yet you mutter threats instead of being happy that someone kind has given me a little bit of support during this difficult time." I shook my head. "Dinner will be delivered in half an hour."

I left the room, praying that he wouldn't come downstairs in thirty minutes with his bags packed. Thankfully he didn't, but dinner was a quiet affair. I decided not to harp on the things I'd said earlier. Maybe this quietness was his way of processing everything.

After dinner, he helped me move the living room furniture back into place.

"What do you think of the color?"

"Kinda girly, but I guess it's okay." He pushed the heavy mahogany coffee table back in front of the sofa.

"I thought we could use a pick-me-up in here. A clean slate for us both."

He nodded but didn't seem all that interested in sharing an HGTV moment or exploring my metaphor. "Can I go play Xbox?"

"Sure." Before he left, I grabbed him around the waist. "I love you, honey."

He gave me a brief squeeze before squirming free and taking the steps two at a time.

Rowan was growing up and would be gone before I knew it. I loved him with my whole heart, but I couldn't make my entire life about him. Another reason to let myself explore a relationship with Rodri.

I sat in the kitchen and made a to-do list for tomorrow, which included a grocery run and the unpleasant task of doing my monthly finances and budgeting for the salon. Maybe I'd treat myself to a muffin and coffee at Sugar Momma's. It wouldn't be the same without Grace, but that didn't mean I shouldn't try to enjoy it all the same.

———

"You look like you need seconds on your macchiato, Mimi," Hannah called from the counter.

I looked up from my computer, welcoming a break from studying the losses on my spreadsheet. The longer I gave discounts to drive business, the harder it'd be to return to normal pricing. "Actually, yes, that sounds terrific."

Hannah scooted out from behind her counter to get my cup. "How've you been? Haven't seen you or Grace in here for a spell."

I sighed, having begun to accept that we might never come here together again. That hurt, but my shame and guilt had lessened. "I'm hanging in there, hoping for the best outcomes for Carter and the rest of us. It's been tough, though, I won't lie. Not sure anything will ever be the same. I only hope whatever the new normal looks like, we mend fences."

"Me too, Mimi. Wish I had some answers for you. It ain't much, but how about a pistachio muffin on the house to give you a little boost?" She grinned.

"Oh, that helps plenty, Hannah. Thanks." I filled with gratitude.

"Coming right up." She took my empty mug and returned to her counter.

Before I dug back into my spreadsheet, the bell above the shop door jingled as Sam walked in. He stopped upon seeing me, then nodded with the kind of smile one gives an acquaintance before he proceeded to the counter. I knew he was only obeying his lawyers' orders, but it stung a little anyway.

My legs started to jiggle. I stared at my laptop while debating begging him for news of Carter's progress. My gaze kept darting to his back. Did I dare? After he paid, I couldn't stop myself. "Sam!"

He paused before stepping closer to my table, yet remained stiff and at a short distance. "Good morning, Mimi."

"Hi." Despite a cold sweat, I aimed for a neutral expression. "Listen, I know we aren't supposed to talk, but I've been praying for good news about Carter ever since hearing about his setback. Is he getting better? I'm hoping he'll be coming home soon . . ."

Sam's face fell and his grip tightened around the to-go bag. "Well, an emotional setback affected his physical progress. We've taken some steps to address it, so we're hoping for the best, but it could take a couple more weeks. It's been hard."

He was blinking more than normal, probably staving off tears. I couldn't hide mine.

"Oh, Sam. I'm sorry. So, so sorry." I hung my head. Poor kid was probably depressed, frustrated, and lonely as hell.

"I know you are," he said quietly.

I looked up in surprise.

"Thank you." I stared at him. Like with Grace, the weight of his worry had aged him. It would be tough to bear up under that pressure. I was scared about my finances, but at least my kid was healthy and reasonably happy. Carter's setback probably upped the costs on their end, too. Sorrow filled my chest until it hurt to breathe.

Did he or Grace know what Carter had said to Rowan, and that it could kill their case? I couldn't lessen Carter's pain, but I could offer Sam a little hope, so I chose my words carefully. "I know we aren't supposed to talk about the lawsuit, but . . . well . . . so you know, I didn't tell the lawyers about Carter's and Rowan's conversations." I kept my gaze even and as friendly as possible, despite every muscle in my body contracting in anticipation of his reply.

His brows rose before he glanced around as if checking to see who might overhear us. Fortunately, it wasn't crowded. "I appreciate that, Mimi. I suspected as much, to be honest. What I most want is to settle things soon so we can all begin to heal. Grace seems to be coming around, too."

"Really?" My heart burst open to think she took my advice about Sam. I wanted her family to survive. And maybe if it did, the door would remain open to me, too. The possibility brought fresh tears to the surface. "I'd love for that to happen. I've missed her."

"I know she's missed you even if she hasn't shown it." He glanced at the clock over the door. "Are you okay?"

"As good as can be, I suppose. My business took a beating this month, though."

"Did it?" He frowned.

"Yeah. I'm trying to figure out how to stop the bleeding and buy myself time to find new customers." I shrugged and made a weak gesture toward my screen.

He set down his to-go bag on my table. "Let me take a quick look. Maybe I can come up with some creative accounting suggestions."

"Really?" Before he had a chance to change his mind, I turned the screen toward him. For a few seconds it felt like the old days, when asking Sam for help came easy. "Thank you."

He nodded and narrowed his eyes, clicking through various line items.

I let myself daydream that by summer I'd be sitting here with Grace again, which filled me with nostalgia that wrought a tender smile. Then the bell above the door jingled again, and in walked Grace. With the rush of hope I'd conjured, I smiled.

Her gaze darted from me to Sam's back and stuck there. Her cheeks got red as she stared at him, positively crestfallen, although he had no idea. The bubble of hope that had been rising inside popped, leaving me on the verge of new tears. I felt even sorrier for Sam, who'd apparently been deluding himself about her attitude.

"Um, Sam," I mumbled. "Grace just walked in."

He whipped around. "Grace."

"How could you?" She shook her head before marching back out the door.

My body went cold. Once I pulled the daggers from my chest, I stole a quick look at Hannah, who pretended not to be paying attention.

Sam grabbed his to-go bag. "Sorry, Mimi. I can't stay. But if you email this to me, I'll take a look and send you any recommendations."

"No, thanks, Sam. I don't want to come between you and Grace any more than I have, but you're sweet to offer." Watching my friend take a hammer to her marriage crushed me as much as her killing our friendship did.

He nodded before dashing after his wife.

I covered my face with my hands and inhaled slowly. Hannah showed up at my table and set a fresh latte and pistachio muffin in front of me, although my appetite was now gone. "You gotta give it more time, is all."

"Thanks, Hannah." I forced a big bite of muffin to stave off a crying jag brewing from the whiplash of dashed hopes and Carter's lengthy recovery. "These sure are delicious. Someday you need to tell me your secret."

"Only when I retire, Mimi. Only when I retire." She smiled and wiped down an empty table on her way back to the counter.

I covered my face as if closing my eyes would erase what had just happened with Sam, Grace, and me. Nothing I'd done since that fateful night had made a difference. Given the severity of Carter's injuries, I'd been kidding myself to think that we would someday return to normal.

Unable to focus on my damn spreadsheet, I checked my email. My breath caught for the second time this morning when I saw Dirk's name in my inbox. Ever since he'd first threatened me about this custody stuff, he'd taken to writing to me, as if I wouldn't realize he hoped to create a record of our conversations to use against me in court.

Mimi,

Dating the cop who arrested our son? Didn't see that coming—not real sensitive to Rowan, is it? Under the circumstances, you really ought to cooperate with me. I'm planning to pick up Rowan on Friday after school and will return him Sunday night. We can do a trial run of my proposed custody modifications this spring and then make decisions about summer. Given the drinking party debacle, recent arrest, and your new boyfriend, it seems like the less of Rowan's free time you need to monitor, the better. Don't make me file a petition. I'd hate to bother people like Grace to testify, and I don't think you want to cause that family more trouble, do you?

Dirk

I set the phone facedown and took three shaky breaths, drowning in defeat. How many times would I get kicked in the teeth? How big a price did I have to pay to make up for my mistakes? If I were at home, I might've thrown my cup against a wall and screamed to release my frustration and fear.

Rowan must've been more upset about Rodri than he'd let on. That surprised me, because we'd always been honest with each other. For his sake, maybe I ought to cooperate with Dirk. It'd be awful to make Rowan a pawn in our fight. I couldn't afford to fight Dirk in court, and although Grace had previously said she wouldn't get involved in my family drama, that was before Carter's setback and her catching Sam talking to me. Now all bets were off.

The weight of losing everything—my son, my business, my friend—pressed from all sides, cornering me. Rowan's face flickered—at four, at ten, and now. I wasn't ready to be less of a mother to my son already. And Dirk's dig at Rodri made me bitter about the idea of caving in.

My indignation ignited. No matter how this turned out, Dirk had no right to insinuate that I hadn't been a good mother these past five years while he'd stood on the sidelines. I also wouldn't pretend I didn't deserve a love life after he'd run off with Miranda in the middle of our marriage. Sure, I'd made mistakes, but so did every mother I'd ever met, including my own. Dirk had started to take a serious interest in his son only this past month, so screw him.

Dirk,

Your newfound enthusiasm for fatherhood is heartening. Unfortunately, Rowan and I have tickets to a Capitals game on Saturday, so you can't have him this weekend. I'm sure he'll be happy to spend time with you next weekend as scheduled and, of course, on Wednesday for dinner. As for revisions to our custody agreement, I suggest you talk to Rowan before moving forward with court hearings or taking other steps to pull him away from his friends.

P.S. His work schedule might require us both to be a little flexible with his time, so I'll make sure he emails you his schedule every week.

Mimi

I ignored his quip about Rodri, but reread the note twice, my finger hovering over the "Send" button, my lip caught beneath my teeth. Daring Dirk to bring up custody with Rowan was a calculated risk given my son's current mood. But I was so done being made to feel like I was something stuck to the bottom of a shoe. I hoped Rowan would choose me, but if he really preferred Dirk—if that's what would make him happiest—then the unselfish, loving mother's choice would be to let him go.

And that's the kind of mother I was . . . or at least the one I wanted to be.

Satisfied, I sent the reply, then shut down everything and drank my latte. As the minutes passed, I reconsidered my hasty response, which had sounded tougher and more confident than I felt. Didn't it figure that when I needed Grace the most, she was completely lost to me? Her approval had always made me feel more certain. Would she be proud of my standing up to Dirk? Of my realizing that part of being a good mother might require me to let my son go?

Maybe Sam would tell Grace that I didn't tell the lawyers about Carter's confession and it would soften her. Maybe he could even convince her that the time for blame had passed and we needed to work together. *Yeah, sure.* I rolled my eyes. *And maybe I will win the lottery.*

# CHAPTER TWENTY-TWO

## GRACE

*Monday, March 1*
*Outside Sugar Momma's*

"Grace, wait!" Sam called. The scuff of his footsteps raced to catch up behind me, so I stopped. The gray sky threatened rain, but thunder had already gathered in my head. I flashed back a few nights to our bedroom—those tentative first kisses that had quickly stoked passion. Coming together in love and vulnerability from all the suffering we'd endured. Waking the next morning spooned together as before—and each night since turning to instead of away from each other, I'd let my guard down bit by bit. The tension between us had been melting, and I'd even begun to believe that we were united on the lawsuit. Now this?

Whirling around, I cried, "I thought we've been rebuilding our trust, yet I find you sitting with Mimi despite what the lawyers said."

Not only did that jeopardize Carter's case, but it felt like a personal betrayal. That stung like hell, especially when he knew my dearest friendship was another casualty of that party. When he knew how much that loss cost me.

His shoulders fell. "I didn't plan to run into her. Would you have me be rude?"

I growled with frustration that he was making this my fault . . . again. "A simple 'good morning, Mimi' should've sufficed. Sharing coffee and fiddling with her computer goes way beyond basic politeness." Were they discussing the case, or me? My stomach grew queasy in protest.

"She mentioned a downturn in business, so I offered to look over her budget for suggestions for stretching her finances until things returned to normal."

*Normal.* I was starting to hate that word. Why did he and Mimi and others keep talking about "going back to normal" as if it were a given? What once had been normal was an impossible goal. This catastrophe had irrevocably changed our family the way my father's death had changed my relationship with Margot. We'd been on the same side before he died. Afterward, she'd slowly followed in his footsteps— whether from guilt or anger or both, I would never know—betraying everything she'd fought against before. She'd left me on my own long before she'd died. Now, similar to how my sister's behavior changed everything, even if Carter could run cross-country next year, this experience had transformed all of us. Whatever the future held, it would not be like our past.

"Carter's barely getting back on track. Our financial security is pinned on this lawsuit. I'm not out to bankrupt Mimi, but her business isn't our primary concern, and you're not the only person she can turn to for help."

"She didn't turn to me. I offered after she mentioned that she didn't tell her lawyer what Carter confessed to Rowan." His expression hardened as he crossed his arms. Relief should've sunk in, but "didn't tell" didn't mean "would never tell." "Given that, the least I could do was help her shift some things around to buy a little time to recover."

"So you *were* talking about the lawsuit?" My brows rose.

"No." He shook his head, then grimaced. "I mean, yes, she mentioned that one thing, so I said that I hoped we could settle things quickly, move forward, and heal."

How did he not hear how that statement did, in fact, give her lawyers helpful information?

I pressed my fingertips to my temples while beginning to pace in a circle, my mind racing through all possible scenarios. "What if she brought up Carter's confession to persuade you to settle for a low figure? Or maybe her lawyers are coaching her to trip us up or admit something that could help them? Maybe you fell for it, suggesting we'd settle quickly."

"Jesus, Grace," he spat out, making me flinch. He raised his hands from his sides, the bag of goodies hanging in midair, his brow pinched together in disillusionment. "Do you really think your friend is so devious?"

I felt ashamed. Not usually. Never, really. But everyone, including someone like Mimi, defaults to self-preservation when backed against a wall—everyone but Sam, apparently. "The point is that I thought we were aligned. That we agreed to support each other through this and follow our lawyer's advice."

"Fine, but then you can't cherry-pick which advice to heed and which to ignore." His face was turning red.

"What does that mean?"

"Our lawyers are telling us to adjust our expectations and aim for a reasonable settlement, yet you continue to clamor for a trial." He tipped his head, looking at me as if we'd only just met. "Honestly, I thought that you'd turned a real corner. That you were coming around to forgiving us all, but now it feels like a pretense. Did you think you could fake your way into being your old self? Hell, I wish that would work, because I don't recognize this version of you. And I'm tired of kowtowing and being made to feel bad because I'm not as angry and bitter with myself and the world as you are. Stop criticizing me for keeping my focus on repairing our family instead of seeking vengeance on some kids for their mistakes. And I really don't appreciate being dressed down in the middle of town." He turned away for a moment, rubbing his forehead, before facing me again.

My entire body smarted, as if each of his statements had been a lashing. Me criticizing him? Talk about the pot and the kettle. All he'd done since this happened was dismiss my feelings and refuse to validate a single one of my concerns. The hypocrisy balled up in my throat, ready to explode.

He covered his mouth with one hand, staring at me, before letting his arm fall and saying, "Maybe we need some space from each other, before we say or do things we can't take back."

"Space?" My heart thumped wildly. "What's that supposed to mean?"

His expression shifted to something defeated and serious. "I can't live with someone who jumps to the worst conclusions about me and everyone else. I hate to upset Kim and Carter, but I'm afraid we're on the brink of permanent damage to our marriage if we don't take some time apart." His voice cracked a bit and his eyes got watery.

My body heat drained away, leaving me shivering. I'd not only lost control of this conversation, I was losing the family I'd invested everything into building. I could barely speak, so my words came out as a whisper. "Where would you go?"

"I don't know." He scrubbed a hand over his face. "We need to protect Carter's emotional state. Maybe if you stay with your mom for a week, we could tell the kids you wanted to be closer to Carter so they don't get alarmed. It'd let us hit pause and catch our breath."

Panic prickled, hot and razor-sharp, as it rushed up my body. He was serious. "Wow. You've got it all planned out—almost like you've been thinking about it for a while." I took that possibility in.

There on the sidewalk, in the middle of town, I was the most alone I had ever felt in my entire marriage. Not only alone, but maligned and misunderstood. Blamed for all of it as if nothing I'd said or felt were valid. In that second, indignation grabbed hold. "I feel foolish for believing that you were trying to meet me in the middle. I know I'm far from perfect, and slow to forgive everyone who hurt our child, but I didn't realize I was on a deadline. If this is what you want, I'll pack a bag today."

I turned toward my car so he couldn't see my tears.

"Grace, slow down," he called. I could hear him catching up to me. "This isn't the end of everything. Just a little break—breathing room for us both. Maybe we should go to counseling."

After unlocking my car, I stared at him over its roof. Everything inside was dead. Beaten down by failure and fear. Vaguely, it occurred to me that this emptiness must've been what my sister had felt—what had driven her to drinking and drugs. To giving up on life. Those weren't options for me, but in this moment I couldn't shoulder any more sadness, blame, or disappointment. "Sure, we'll squeeze that in between your work, Carter's visits, Kim's homework, and my students. I'll research therapists as soon as I finish packing. We can add that cost to our growing stack of medical bills."

Before he could reply, I slid onto my seat, slammed my door, and screeched out of the parking spot, leaving my husband standing on the sidewalk while onlookers strolled past.

Hot tears washed down my cheeks. In less than two months, my carefully constructed life had fallen apart. The years I'd spent ensuring that my children's lives didn't mirror my childhood destroyed in mere weeks. In the silence of my car, I couldn't even channel Mimi's advice without conjuring more pain.

My heart lay lifeless inside my chest, kicked around too many times to bother beating again. When I got home, I sat in the garage, crying inside my car. For a fleeting second, I flirted with the idea of leaving the car running with the garage door closed. It sounded easier than the daunting task of reassembling my family, and given how far I'd pushed everyone, they might not miss me much.

Ten seconds, maybe fifteen, passed before I turned off the ignition. I couldn't leave my kids motherless, or hurt Sam or my mother, or even Mimi, all of whom might assume some responsibility for my deteriorated mental state.

I needed help, clearly. My support system no longer trusted me.

But first I had to pack my suitcase.

Sam might be right. A little distance from him and our home might help me sort myself out.

Any other time I could've gone to Mimi's. We'd often joked about how much fun we would've had as roommates. There'd been evenings in her backyard with wine and country music when we'd talk about the future—side-by-side rooms at Sandy Shores—and she'd laugh. If she weren't at the root of my current mess, she would've made up her guest room, baked up a storm, and handed me a pinot grigio with a hug upon my arrival. Even in the midst of this crisis, she'd tried to warn me about pushing Sam too far. I should've listened. She'd always had good instincts about people's emotions. Much better than mine.

Having to turn to my mother, who no doubt had opinions about how I've mishandled everything, made me break out in hives. For most of my life I'd been critical of her, yet I had not handled my family crisis any better than she had. Maybe worse, which broke me to acknowledge.

Once inside, I popped a Benadryl pill before calling her.

"Hello," she answered.

"Hey, Mom, it's me." My voice was raw from crying.

"How's Carter?"

"The same. That's not why I called, though. I have a favor to ask."

"What, honey?"

I closed my eyes, hot with shame because of the lie I was about to tell my own mother. I could pretend I was lying to ensure that my children never got a mixed message, but the truth was that I couldn't stand to let her know she'd been right. "The daily commute is really wearing on me, so I wondered if I could bunk with you for a few days, maybe a week. It would make it easier to put in time helping Carter over the hump."

"Of course you can stay. How can I help with Carter? Would my apple turnovers help cheer him up?"

"Probably." A month ago I would've viewed her using baked goods as a salve for big emotional problems. A reminder of the batches of walnut brownies she'd always made after another round with Dad had left Margot and me upset. But maybe that was the only way she knew how to show love and offer comfort. I could hardly get upset at her for doing the best she could. "I'll be up in a little while to drop my bag before I go to the rehab center."

"I'd better get cracking on the turnovers. See you soon." She hung up.

I went to my bedroom and laid an unzipped suitcase on the bed. Tears formed as I folded a few things and grabbed my toothbrush. I hadn't made real progress this week. I'd let the agony and fear Carter's injury inspired affect every relationship that mattered to me. No wonder Sam didn't recognize me. I didn't, either.

———

"Hey, honey. Look what I brought, still warm from the oven!" I set down the paper plate on Carter's bedside table and peeled back the tinfoil, revealing four perfectly browned apple turnovers. Notes of butter and cinnamon floated up with the steam, which should distract him from noticing my unusual mood. "Gram sends her love."

Carter's heartbreakingly blank expression morphed into a genuine smile as he reached over to take one. I'd have to give my mother credit—baked goods were good comfort. "They smell great."

"She dropped everything to make these today." I poured some water and set the glass near him, remembering the care with which she'd slid them onto the plate and covered them with foil. "Maybe give her a call later to thank her."

"Okay." He took a bite, then licked his greasy lips, nodding. "Mm."

His teen appetite bubbling back to life hinted that his sadness might be lifting. One hopeful sign in an otherwise terrible day. I hung my purse over the back of my chair and took a seat, scooting close to the bed. "Did you have a good session with Leron this morning?"

Carter shrugged, concentrating on the turnover. "He wants me to try the multipoint cane tomorrow."

My lungs ballooned with much-needed hope. "That's good, right? You must've increased your leg strength this week to move off the walker to a cane."

"I guess." He nodded, eyeing a second treat. His lack of enthusiasm diminished mine.

"I'm happy. It's a great step forward, and toward your coming home." I bit my lip, aware that "home" might not be what he expected, and how that might cause another setback. My lungs felt leaden. After a mental shake, I added, "I'm glad you're working hard again. Has Dr. Spotts's advice been helping?"

"Not really. I'm sick of this place, so I decided to do whatever I could to get out of here." His gaze caught mine; he looked much younger than fifteen. "I miss home."

Warm tears collected in my eyes. "We miss you more. Dad and I even talked about throwing a little party or something when you get released, if you'd like that." I forced a smile, although now those plans might die off. Mimi's warnings about broken families filtered through my conscience. For weeks I had blamed Sam and then myself, but today blame seemed pointless. Confusion and defeat broke me down until every cell in my body hummed with remorse.

"Is Dad coming later?"

I glanced at my lap to hide our marital discord. "I'm not sure. We're balancing a lot with Kim and his work and you."

"I miss family dinners. Could we all do a pizza night this weekend?"

My lungs deflated like empty bellows.

"I'll talk to Dad." I didn't want to promise when I wasn't sure Sam wanted to spend time with me. Carter was too smart not to notice something, so I came a little clean. "I'm actually staying at Gram's for a few nights."

He stopped eating and stared at me. "Why?"

My cheeks trembled from holding a false smile in place, but I had to sell this so he didn't spend one second worrying about our family. "The daily commute's exhausting. This way it'll be easier to spend extra time with you while you're making a final push."

He made a disbelieving face. "That's weird . . ."

"Is it?" I pretended to laugh at myself, hoping my perspiration wasn't noticeable. "Well, considering your progress, maybe it will be very short-lived. You must be eager to get back to school, too."

Rather than agree, he looked at his lap, brow knitted. "Mom, can we talk about something?"

"Anything." Relieved for the change of topic, I leaned forward.

With solemnity, he said, "I swear I haven't texted Rowan, but other kids still text me. First it was the budget stuff. Now some kids are mad about the lawsuit. They're saying stuff about our family, and about me."

The anger I'd been trying to tamp down reignited. Since when was it okay to berate the victim? "Like what?"

"That we're being uncool and greedy."

Greedy? My body turned hot with indignation. "I'm sorry you have to deal with that. People always have opinions, but we're merely protecting your future."

He twisted the sheets around his finger. "How long will the lawsuit last?"

"I don't know." Was this feeding his recent despondency? "If it goes to trial, it could be a year or two."

He groaned, his expression tightening like he was fighting nausea. "It'll be weird to go to school with kids I'm suing. And Rowan is in my history class, so I won't be able to avoid him. Do we have to sue them, really?"

Like father, like son—and me left defending myself again. Consulting lawyers had been a logical response, but the constant resistance from my own family left me doubting myself.

"Yes, honey. The surgery and all this therapy cost a lot of money." I gestured around the room, trying to explain things without increasing his concerns.

He chewed on the inside of his cheek for a moment. "Why can't you agree on the costs and settle it?"

"It's complicated because the costs depend on the speed and fullness of your recovery, which are two things we don't yet know."

Carter flung his head back into his pillows, whining, "I don't want everyone fighting over what happened to me. Now people either hate me or feel sorry for me. I just want to be normal. Please, Mom. Talk to Dad and try to end it."

"Try to relax." I rubbed his thigh, wishing I could make this easier on him while battling the voice yelling about how I was screwing up as a mother—that protecting him shouldn't cause him this agony. "Honey, no matter what other kids say, you deserve to be compensated for everything you've lost and suffered."

"Mom, you don't get it. You keep telling me to focus on therapy, but I care about my reputation, too. I care if people don't like me. They're already saying I shouldn't have been at that party. What if no one wants to do anything with me after this because they think I'll sue them if I get hurt?" His voice cracked as he rubbed his eyes dry.

His ache ripped through me as sharply as any razor. "Honey, it hurts me to see you suffering, but you're smart. Do you really think it would be fair that we be forced to pay all these bills ourselves rather than require the people responsible for your injuries to cover them?"

He frowned and turned his head to stare out the window. "This sucks."

"It does. For everyone, but mostly for you. I'm sorry. What else can I say?" A dull headache began pounding at the base of my skull. Giving him what he wanted while also getting him what he needed was a quandary I couldn't solve. And it was costing me a dear friend and a husband. Was it worth it?

"Promise me you'll convince Dad to use his actuary stuff to figure out a fair number instead of going to trial." His pleading eyes pinned me to my seat, leaving no wiggle room.

"I'll talk to your father, but I don't want to make a false promise. I don't know that we can control the final outcome." I poured Carter more water, although my hands trembled. After all, Sam and I could end the lawsuit quickly if we walked away from it. Carter would get what he wanted now, but in two years, when he couldn't attend the college of his choice without massive student loans, he might regret being so quick to give in to the very kids who put him here in the first place. Giving in to bullies leads to other problems, as I knew well from life with my father.

On the verge of a breakdown, I fought to redirect my thoughts. "Why don't we focus on something we can control right now. You have a history test tomorrow, right? Would you like me to help you study?"

"Sure," he conceded, handing me some stapled pages. "This is a practice test with an answer key. Can you run through the questions and let me know when I get something wrong?"

"I'm happy to." I smiled, although I knew neither of us was at peace.

———

Two hours later I pulled into my mother's driveway, body limp from the emotional chaos of my day. I entered my childhood home through the side door. The house smelled of my mother's powdery scent mingled with warmed butter. But my memories, particularly in this kitchen, weren't as lovely. The dent in the cabinet beside the sink—a reminder of the time Dad threw a metal beer stein at her.

"Did Carter like the turnovers?" Mom was sitting at the speckled Formica kitchen table playing solitaire, comfortable amid the bad memories in a way I could never manage.

I hung my purse over the back of a kitchen chair. "He did. I'm sure he'll call you later to thank you. We got busy. I was quizzing him for tomorrow's history test."

She smiled, pleased by his reaction. I crossed the kitchen to fill a glass with tap water.

"I saved you some potpie. Would you like me to reheat it?" My mother stood and made her way to the refrigerator. She preferred to keep busy when it was only the two of us. I supposed it made it easier to ignore all the things we never said to each other.

"Thank you." I grabbed a plate and silverware.

"Honey, you look exhausted. Take a seat and let me fix your plate." She patted my shoulder, so I set the things on the counter and obeyed. The awkwardness of accepting her help without resentment hit me. The last time the two of us sat alone at this table had been not long after Margot's funeral. Mom had packed up my sister's things to donate, but had pulled aside a few mementos for me. I'd been miffed because she'd held on to Dad's things longer than she had Margot's. At the time, her choice had felt like a slam to my sister—like she couldn't wait to get rid of her. But now I realized that maybe the reminders of her daughter had simply been too painful. My already-weak state collapsed at that revelation—how uncharitable a daughter I'd been.

While my mother scooped a portion of the potpie onto a dish, I opened my phone to scroll through missed messages, hoping for something from Sam. Nothing. I might've sighed aloud.

"I'm worried about you, Grace." She took the dish to the microwave, her features pinching together. "I know this situation is difficult, but you're getting worse, not better. Are things still tense between you and Sam? Is that part of why you're here?"

I ached to unload all my pain, but my mother had never protected me as a kid, so I'd never learned to trust her. "I'd rather not talk about it, if you don't mind."

She sucked her lips in, nodding and waiting for the microwave to finish its cycle. After it beeped, she brought the dish and silverware to the table, then took a seat.

We sat in companionable silence for the first minute or two, with me testing the heat of the potpie. Mom had always been a great cook. Flaky crust, delicious gravy. For the first time in weeks, someone was pampering me, and that did feel lovely. So much so that my eyes got teary. "This is delicious."

"I'm glad you like it." Mom worried her lip and went to the counter to get me a tissue, then chose to bring the box over. "You might feel better if you opened up."

My heart thudded—one beat, two, three.

"I don't know where to start." I dabbed my eyes before blowing my nose.

"How about with Sam?" She folded her hands on the table and waited patiently, her face a picture of empathy.

My mother was all I had now, and I'd begun to realize that maybe I hadn't been fair to her, so I took the leap of faith that, despite our tangled history, she might have something to offer. "We haven't been on the same side since the morning of Carter's injury because he talked me into letting Carter go to that party. But I've been trying to let go of the blame. I apologized, and thanked him for all that he'd been handling since then. I thought things were getting better, but this morning I caught him helping Mimi. It felt like such a betrayal, especially when he's never once apologized to me for the countless times he's invalidated my feelings. This has all been such an awful time—I've never felt so confused and lonely and scared and starved for affection." Even as a child, I'd had Margot.

I looked down, as if home-cooked nourishment might somehow feed me what I needed.

My mother stared at me with misty eyes. "Gracie, if anyone understands how hard it is to be a wife and mother when navigating trauma and tragedy, it's me. Let me help."

I might've flinched at the comparison, even though she'd been fair. "Thank you, but I'll be fine with a little peace to let me think." I couldn't meet her gaze, having never been an adroit liar.

Mom leaned forward, shaking her head. "Don't withdraw now, honey. I know that habit is my fault, always coaxing you to make the best of things. To not make a fuss. I've been thinking about that a lot since Carter got hurt—all the old memories dredged up."

Each of her words pressed on the tender spots of our attenuated bond, making me ache more, not less. Nothing I had to say about our history would make her feel better, so I avoided eye contact and continued eating.

She didn't take the hint. "I was a young, ignorant mom. Definitely not prepared to handle what my marriage and life became after the war changed your father. We'd been married only a month when he got drafted. He came back different, but I'd thought my love and starting a family of his own would heal him. But by the time I realized he'd permanently lost something in that war, I hadn't the heart to rip away his family, too. Maybe if I'd been more worldly or educated, I could've gotten him the help he needed, or left him and spared you girls so much pain and shame. So much shoving things down." Her hand-wringing and fuzzy gaze made it clear she was reliving some of our unpleasant past.

The echo of old arguments and smashed household goods clanged around inside my head, making my ulcerated stomach burn.

My eyes stung. "It's in the past, Mom. It doesn't matter anymore."

"Doesn't it? I wonder, Grace. I really do. I'll always be sorry about your childhood. About what happened with Margot. I should've done a better job of protecting both my girls." She dabbed her eyes with a trembling hand. "If I could go back and do things differently, I would. Those regrets are with me all the time, which is probably why I'm worried you're making those mistakes with your family. I know it's long overdue, but I hope someday you can forgive me for all the ways I failed you and Margot." She choked up.

I sat, barely breathing from shock, yet nearly shaking from her unexpected confession.

She gathered herself, hands now palm up on the table. "And yet we don't control the outcomes of all our decisions. Sometimes bad things happen for no good reason. And sometimes people put themselves in a bad situation, like when your dad stumbled out into the dark, drunk. I didn't go after him because I wanted you girls to have a few hours' peace. In that moment it'd seemed like a reasonable decision, but then we ended up at his funeral days later. Sometimes I still feel guilty about that, but fate had its way. And then Margot spun out of control yet refused to let me help. Maybe I gave up too soon, or maybe she would've gone down that dark path for some other reason. We don't know. But I do know that blame doesn't change the past. I can only try to do better in the future."

My insides quavered. All my life I'd tried to avoid being like my mother, yet here I was, exactly who I'd not wanted to emulate. Tears spilled over as memories of my mom, Margot, and my father converged. "But it's not fate, Mom. Not with Margot, and not with Carter. I could've told you about her drinking back in high school, but I didn't.

I was too mad at you both. And with Carter, Sam and I made a decision, and that decision had terrible consequences." If I had a knife, I might jam it into my chest so I could never repeat my mistakes again.

My mother's eyes were wide as she grabbed my hands. "Honey, you were still a child when your sister started acting out. You couldn't know how to handle that."

"I knew she hadn't really been okay after the sleeping-pills stunt, but it was easier to be mad at her rebellion than to deal with it. And maybe if I'd warned you about what she'd done that night, Dad wouldn't be dead."

She shook her head, frowning. "Your father got himself killed. Hell, he tempted fate all the time with his drinking." She set her hands on the table, like she was getting down to business. Even her voice turned emphatic. "I let him wander off drunk. Do you blame me?"

I stared at her, saying nothing.

"He chose to go instead of staying home. He made the decision that got him killed. Whatever small amount of sleeping pills your sister managed to put in that one bottle did not kill your father. I wish I would've told her that before it was too late." Her eyes teared up again, but she blinked them back and looked at me with a determined expression. "And, Grace, the hard truth is that Carter chose to go to that party and Carter chose to stay when things got rough. He didn't deserve this horrible thing to happen to him, but he isn't blameless in it, either. No one is. That's part of why it hurts so much. But if you let that pain corrode you, then the losses get bigger."

Oh God, he had, and the cost of his mistakes was far too dear. I sobbed, a gush of tears bursting forth for my mom's sorrow, my lost youth, Margot's hard life, my dad's addiction, and my son's injuries. I cried for Kim and Sam and the ways I'd made things harder on them just as my mom had made things harder for Margot and me. I even cried for Mimi, whose helpful hand I'd slapped down too many times.

I hadn't known how badly I'd needed my mother's apology—her acknowledgment of her own mistakes and her absolution of mine—until this moment.

"There, there. Let me fix us some tea." When she patted my hand, I clasped hers, standing and pulling us into a tight hug that surprised us both. I couldn't remember the last time we'd really hugged—perhaps Margot's funeral, or maybe on my wedding day. When we eased apart, Mom swiped her eyes before she went to fill the kettle. While she was up, she grabbed an open bag of Lorna Doones and set them on the table.

The energy in the kitchen had shifted, tension giving way to contemplation. My heart rate resumed a steady pace that didn't ache. The gravity of our cathartic revelations had somehow disconnected me from my body. And while the weight of the past felt lighter, that alone didn't solve my current crisis.

Mom set a cup of peppermint tea in front of me and took her seat. A shy smile emerged, as if she too felt the shift. "I'm glad we got a chance to clear the air between us, Gracie. That's something, I suppose."

I nodded, dunking a cookie in the sweet tea. "But it doesn't save my marriage. My family. I've hurt Sam, and Mimi, who has offered many olive branches. Even Carter is upset because the fighting is affecting his friends. But how does one not think and feel the thoughts and feelings that occur—how do I let go of the anger and blame?"

I let the soggy cookie melt on my tongue. A simple pleasure at a bleak moment.

My mother sighed, stirring more sugar into her tea. "Well, maybe you begin by forgiving yourself for being human. We're fallible. We feel anger and hate sometimes. You can't beat yourself up over and over, Grace. Forgive yourself, and forgive Sam and Mimi." She squeezed my hands. "The people you love are reaching out to you. Isn't your life better with them in it than when you're all alone? Don't be like Margot. She fought with the world thinking she was slaying dragons, but she isolated herself as if that would keep her from feeling pain. She made life harder. I wonder if she would admit that now, if she could?"

I'd always considered Margot and Mimi to be similar because both boldly met challenges. But in truth, Mimi was much stronger than Margot because she met hardship with love and faith rather than anger and defiance.

My mother's logic had yet to take root in my heart. "Margot's ghost lingers like a reminder of what could go wrong if I fail to protect my own kids as I failed her. I let my guard down once and catastrophe struck, yet now my vigilance is costing me everything and hurting everyone, so I'm not really protecting anyone from anything."

My mother nodded as if she'd found a lost puzzle piece. "It sounds like it's time to stop fighting everyone and start remembering why you love them in the first place."

Such simple advice. The clarity of it shone like a too-bright spotlight, making me wince. I let the peace it promised soften my spine. With my head tipped, I asked, "Is that how you stayed with Dad? You kept remembering what you'd loved about him?"

She donned the saddest smile I'd seen in ages as she nodded silently. "We didn't really know about PTSD back then, and we didn't have a lot of resources. I took my vows to heart and kept hoping, with time and love, he'd settle back to himself. In retrospect, I was naive and careless, especially when your father kept repeating his mistakes. But you, Sam, Mimi, the kids . . . It seems like everyone has learned from this and wants to do better."

I nodded. Everyone but me. The inescapable truth bore down, fusing me to the chair with no small amount of shame. I unfastened the top two buttons of my shirt to keep from overheating.

With a purposeful sigh, Mom met my gaze. "Honey, if Carter can let go of the pain and forgive others when he's the one who's been most hurt, surely you can follow his lead." She dunked a cookie in her tea before biting into it, as if she hadn't just dropped the mic on me.

These past weeks I'd been assuming my son was stuffing down his feelings out of fear, like me, when, in fact, perhaps he'd been more like Sam than I gave him credit for: a strong optimist who could focus on pragmatic solutions and higher goals. With no small measure of bittersweet nostalgia, I acknowledged the fact that Mimi's helping to raise him had also given him something I could not.

Could I learn those skills? And even if so, had I gone too far off the deep end to find my way back? "What if it's too late?"

"I don't believe it's ever too late to apologize or to forgive. After all, you forgave me for a decades-overdue apology." She looked at me, her eyes glowing with love and hope.

I drank it in like a bee does nectar. For so long I'd resented her for the chaos in my young life. For the tears I'd cried when Dad had embarrassed us, or when Mom or Margot sported a new bruise. But she'd also taught me how to cook and sew. She'd read to me and sat in the front row for my piano recitals. She'd loved Sam like a son she'd never had, and had been a kind grandmother to my kids.

"I do forgive you." I truly did, though now my limbs were heavy with the weight of regret that I'd been unable to feel any empathy for her crises until I'd experienced some of my own. "I'm sorry it's taken me so long to understand you, Mom. Can you forgive me for that?"

"I never need an apology from you, but I'm happy that you trusted me enough today to talk." Mom's warbled words and dewy eyes produced a lump in my throat. "Maybe you could use some time to yourself now to consider how to do the same for yourself and the other people you love."

A lifetime of misunderstandings, of never saying the real things, undone in less than an hour.

She rose and took her cup to the dishwasher, leaving me to sit in silence and process how our past had hurt us for too long, and what I needed to do to make sure it didn't destroy my future.

# CHAPTER
# TWENTY-THREE

### GRACE

*The next evening*
*The Phillips home*

I finished cleaning up after dinner with Kim, shaking my hands out each time I glanced at the clock. Sam would arrive soon. While Kim had welcomed my return, Sam might not consider it a pleasant surprise.

Sam's place setting looked incomplete, so I set a glass of pinot noir by the plate. My stomach fluttered impatiently. After tapping my toes for a few seconds, I readjusted the pink roses I'd put in the table vase and then went to the powder room to fix my hair and apply lip gloss.

On my way back to the kitchen, I passed a dozen family photographs in coordinated silver frames hanging on the wall. From christenings to holiday meals to my favorite candid images, my most beloved faces smiled at me, looking like a perfect American family. The nearly sixteen years spent providing my kids exactly the kind of upbringing that I didn't get—a safe, respectful, loving home—seemed evident in each image.

And yet in less than two months, I'd nearly destroyed it by compounding my mistakes. Now I could only hope Sam and I could start over—this time striving for openness and acceptance rather than perfection and safety.

With nothing to do but wait, I sat with my hands folded on the table and watched the clock. My stomach flipped when the garage door rumbled open. Sam would see my car, which would give him a moment to compose himself.

Perspiration caused my shirt to stick to my back. It seemed like forever before he came inside.

"Grace." He looked at me with an uncertain gaze, looking sharp in his navy suit and pink pinstriped shirt. Although it had been only thirty-six hours, seeing him brought on a rush of love and longing. "Where's Kim?"

Not a warm welcome, but I wouldn't condemn him. He had no idea what to expect. My recent track record was inconsistent, to say the least.

"Upstairs. She finished her homework, so I let her have some screen time." I rose on unsteady legs. "I made that orecchiette you like, with the sausage and broccoli rabe. Are you hungry?"

"Yes, thank you." He set his briefcase down, which was when he noticed my suitcase by the wall. He paused, offering no sign of his feelings about that. "I didn't expect to see you tonight. Has something happened with Carter?"

No smile. No open arms. It occurred to me that, while I'd spent the past day evaluating myself and missing home, perhaps he'd been relieved by my absence. That knocked the wind from me, but I had to take the chance that he hadn't fully closed his heart to me.

"No." I plated some pasta and set it in the microwave before meeting his gaze, trying to project my love through my eyes. "I missed Kim, and you."

Sam's responding smile looked almost bittersweet. "Kim must've been happy to see you." He sat at the table, maintaining a somewhat wary expression. "You look good, Gracie . . . rested."

"I'm feeling clearer." I set the hot dish in front of him. Rather than force a hug or kiss hello, I took my seat, my body buzzing with nervous anticipation.

"This smells delicious. Thank you." He hesitated. "Did you have trouble with your mother?"

"No. In fact, we had a breakthrough. After all these years we finally spoke openly about my dad, Margot, and my childhood. We spilled our regrets and . . . just everything." I held my breath, still marveling at how freeing it had been.

His eyes widened exponentially above a cautious smile. "I'm happy for you. That was long overdue."

I nodded. "All my life there's been a hard knot in my heart—one tied tight with resentment and guilt. I resented her for not protecting Margot and me, I resented Margot for putting Mom and me through the same stuff my father had, and yet I felt guilty that I'd never once done anything to combat any of it. But Carter's situation has made me realize that my mom had been living in crisis mode and doing the best she could, as I've tried my best these past several weeks yet failed in many ways."

Sam's gaze remained glued to me. He spread his hands flat on the table. "That's a little harsh. Making mistakes isn't the same as failure."

"Maybe not always, but I've struggled. What's happened was one of my worst parenting fears. Seeing him lying still and frightened on the ground—that image still haunts me when I close my eyes. Watching him labor with pain or to walk is grueling to endure, and knowing that we might've prevented it with one or two different decisions still guts me. That broke something in me, like a dam where all my childhood sense of injustice, guilt, and helplessness poured out and fused with this situation. I felt I'd failed to keep my vow to protect our kids. I can't go back and save my sister, but I think I thought that I could rectify all wrongs where Carter was concerned and that doing so would make what's happened hurt us all less." I stopped rambling, taking a breath.

Sam had leaned forward, intently watching me and waiting. He seemed deep in his own thoughts, his expression more pensive than emotional.

I fought my doubts, determined to convince him to trust in us again. "I spent last night in my old bed, missing you. Thinking about motherhood and marriage, humanity and mistakes, forgiveness—and fate. Since the accident, you all kept saying that we can't control the outcomes of our decisions, and we have to learn to roll with it. I resisted that because I've been fixated on preventing history from repeating itself."

"That makes sense." He smiled encouragingly, more focused on me than his favorite meal. A good sign. "So how does that affect us now and in the future?"

I drew in a breath, shaking my hands out beneath the table. "I now accept that many things contributed to Carter's injury, including his decision to stay despite the bullying. But if he isn't holding grudges—against us or those boys or himself—how can I?" I looked straight into Sam's blue eyes. "You were right. My attitude—my anger and vengeance—has hurt his recovery and hurt people I love, but I'm determined to change. From the day we met, you've been my touchstone, and I'm so sorry I've hurt you. But mine aren't the only feelings that matter, so I'm curious about what you think. How do you see us moving forward?"

He crossed his arms as if holding himself. His eyes were dewy, his expression conflicted. "First, I'm sorry I didn't put myself in your shoes sooner. You saw Carter on the ground and terrified, I didn't. You felt pressured into letting him go to that party because I broke our pact, not the other way around. I could've been more patient and less demanding while you worked through all this. I've been so afraid of everything slipping away I panicked. For all that, I'm sorry. I know you've been scared and doing your best, even when we didn't agree. I love you, babe. I'll always love you, and I'm sorry if my actions made you doubt that."

Warm tears pricked my eyes because he'd finally acknowledged that. For the first time since we sat down, I let myself believe we would find our way forward. "Thank you. It really helps to hear you say all that."

He wiped a tear from his cheek. "The thing is, Gracie, what if our apologies and love aren't enough? Can you honestly look at me without blame and resentment? I did, after all, push you that morning. Biggest regret of my life, but it's irreversible. I still don't know how I'll make it up to our son." His voice cracked, piercing my heart. All this time he'd carried his guilty burden so stoically I'd missed it. Sam leaned forward, his cheeks and eyes reddened. "Last week we tried putting this all behind us, but then we fought on a sidewalk in the middle of town. Could that happen again weeks from now when, perhaps in the heat of some other disagreement, you think about my letting Carter go to that party?"

My throat was so tight it hurt to speak. "I can't prove how I'll behave in the future. I can only ask for your faith, because I've been trustworthy for most of our relationship. I overreacted yesterday. Seeing you with Mimi made something snap. It seemed like you went behind my back and took her side. I'm not proud of myself for it. I want things between us to heal, Sam. I love you and I need you. We have built this beautiful family, so I think we owe it to each other and our kids to start with a clean slate." I trembled, but if we were to fix the damage, we had to be completely honest.

He reached for my hand, squeezing it tight. "I didn't mean to hurt you by helping Mimi. I never mean to hurt you."

"Deep down I knew that. That's why I'm here. I still believe in us. In fact, I believe in us so much I came to another decision. After giving a lot of thought to how the lawsuit is contributing to our problems and Carter's stress levels, and how it's hurting Mimi, I think we should withdraw it." I paused, letting myself absorb the hardships that would

follow that choice. "Somehow we will make it all work financially—
tighten our belts, clip more coupons, give up some vacations. Maybe I
can get a second part-time job in the mornings to supplement what I
make from piano lessons." A patchwork plan at best, and even still, it
would set back his retirement several years. "I don't have a plan, but I
know if we stick together, it will be okay. I'd rather be broke with you
than win a big settlement and lose our family."

With a surprised gleam in his eyes, Sam brought my hand to his
lips. "That's a huge change of heart, Grace. It means everything to me
here." He patted his chest, then made a rueful expression. "But ironically I've come to realize that you were right to insist that everyone
involved contribute to Carter's care. We shouldn't be the only ones
taking a financial hit, especially when we're also dealing with all the
emotional fallout. But now it sounds like you'd be on board to tell the
lawyers to float a reasonable settlement. If that's in motion before Carter
returns to school, it's a good compromise."

When Sam tugged me onto his lap, my heart jumped around like
an excited child at Christmas. Both of us spilled happy tears while I
held on tight, taking in the scent of him, the warmth of his body, the
strength of his arms. This was better than last week, because I'd begun
the hard work of tackling my own demons, and he'd apologized, too.
This reunion would stick. Our marriage would heal. Our family would
survive, no matter what. I closed my eyes. All traces of doubt and sorrow fled, and I let myself breathe.

I raised my head off his shoulder and gently touched his cheek. "I
love you so much."

He smiled amid new tears. "Love you, too, babe."

We kissed right as Kim came tromping through the kitchen.

"Ew," she groaned on her way to the pantry, where she stared at the
large container of jelly beans.

I wiped my eyes while watching my daughter, who I'd come to realize wasn't nearly as tough as she pretended to be, plotting how to get her

hands on that candy. She needed a big show of love, so I whispered my idea to Sam. When he nodded, I said, "Guess what, Kimmy? It's time we plan your sleepover. You've been really patient, so let's do it right away. Would you like your friends to come on Saturday?"

"Really?" She brightened considerably while sinking her greedy hands into the container and grabbing what she could.

Sam smiled. "I can't think of anything better to do."

"Yay!" Sensing our pliant moods, she shoved a fistful of jelly beans in her mouth.

"I'll call your friends' moms and set it up," I said.

"Can we watch *Breaking Bad* this time?" Her words were garbled by the gummy candy.

I gestured for her to join our hug. "That's still a hard no."

She wrinkled her nose before dive-bombing us. "Okay."

In the wake of forgiveness, holding on to my husband and daughter made me happier than I'd been in weeks. "Carter asked if we could all come and have pizza with him one night. How about we surprise him on Sunday?"

"Ice cream too?" Kim begged.

"Sure," Sam replied.

"This is the best day ever," Kim announced before leaving the kitchen with a second fistful of jelly beans.

"I'm surprised you let her have that candy," Sam said.

"Today feels like a day for celebrating." I smiled.

He kissed me again. "I'd like to celebrate, too."

"What did you have in mind?" I kissed him back.

"It'll have to wait until we put Kim to bed." He squeezed my bottom.

"Maybe I ought to go rush her along?" I winked and then made my way to the back stairs as love flooded my heart and washed away resentments and blame.

# CHAPTER
# TWENTY-FOUR

## MIMI

*Tuesday, March 9*
*The Gillette home*

I closed my salon and ran to my car, knowing I didn't have much time to throw something together for Rowan's dinner and get over to the high school by seven o'clock. The prospect of attending a PTC meeting without Grace left me a bit uneasy, but I had to face the public at some point. Tonight's meeting would introduce tenth grade parents to the college application website Naviance, so I couldn't skip out. Apparently, even sophomores start making up wish lists and taking personality tests that help them decide what to study and where to do that. I hoped Rowan would make the most of it.

Grace was still PTC secretary, but given everything going on in her life, she might not show. Her friends would be here, though, so while I expected to be subjected to more than one stink-eyed glare, I refused to be intimidated. I'd owned my mistakes and learned from them, and set a new direction for myself, my business, and my son, so I deserved a second chance.

I drove home belting out Adele's "Turning Tables," letting all my feelings come out, then nearly slammed my brakes upon rounding the bend to my house. Grace's car sat parked at the curb. My pulse skipped as I turned in to my driveway. After two deep breaths, I killed the engine and stepped out of my car on somewhat weak legs.

The scent of wet grass and pavement greeted me thanks to an early-evening March rain shower. Grace strode up the driveway, stopping two feet or so from me. An invisible armor locked around my chest to protect against more disappointment.

"This is a surprise." I folded my arms, gloomy about the lack of joy from seeing my old friend. My heart flattened like it'd been thrown against a wall. All this time I'd thought I'd talked myself into not needing her. I guessed I still had some work to do.

"If you'd rather I go, I will." She held her purse in front of her hips, her eyes beseeching.

I shrugged one shoulder, pretending not to care either way. "I'm not the one who's been pushing you away." When she remained still, I asked, "Is this about the lawsuit or the thing with Sam the other week?"

"Maybe both, indirectly. It's not bad news, though. I hoped we could talk for a few minutes."

I nodded, trying not to think about that lawsuit. "Well, I'm going to the PTC meeting, so I don't have a ton of time, but if you've got something to say, maybe we should go inside."

She glanced at my house with some trepidation, which was when I remembered the last time she'd been here: the night of the accident. My home represented her worst-ever memory. How callous I must've sounded, acting like it should be no big deal for her to cross the threshold.

She appeared to brace herself before saying, "Sure."

Uncertain about her motives, I gestured toward the side door. With a timid smile, she followed me into the kitchen. Rowan must've been upstairs, but he hadn't left any open snack boxes or dirty dishes lying around. Little by little he was starting to follow the new rules and be more helpful, which made me proud.

On my way to the living room, I paused in the middle of the kitchen. "Do you want water or soda or anything?"

"No, thank you." Grace then followed me out of the kitchen. I felt strange, like we were meeting for the first time, but also like I'd known her forever, both of which were sort of true seeing as how her personality had taken some twists and turns these past weeks. Maybe mine had, too.

When we got to my living room, she stopped, her head swiveling on her neck like a periscope. "New paint?"

Might as well confront the elephant in the room. "After everything that happened here, I needed a change." I warmed at the memory of that day with Rodri, and at how cheery the room looked with the crisp, bright color. We had plans for a real date next weekend, so I figured I might as well come all the way clean. "Rodri helped me."

"It's pretty," she said, tactfully not bringing up how it had looked on the night of the ill-fated party. "I assume Rodri is Officer Martinez?"

"Yes. Rodrigo. I'm sorry it hurt you when you saw us together, but I didn't go out with him to spite you. He's sweet, and kind, and didn't go easy on anyone because of me. But I'm taking things real slow so that no one gets hurt."

"I'm glad . . . I mean, that you met someone nice." She rubbed one hand over the other. "I'm sorry about what I said to him at the café. You deserve to be happy, and you deserve someone kind."

"And hot," I teased, forgetting for a moment that we weren't friends as before.

Grace chuckled, her eyes sparkling with the relief humor brought. "Yes, that too."

Heartened by her reaction, I gestured for her to sit on the sofa while I took a chair. "So, what can I do for you, Grace?"

"Nothing. You've already done a lot for Carter and my family." She crossed her legs, smoothing her slacks and the hem of her sweater before making eye contact. We'd sat in this room together hundreds of times and never once had it felt so stiff. I wanted to scream and cry and shake her all at once. Having her right here was like picking at a scab before it fully healed. "I don't know if you've heard that Carter is coming home this weekend. He's getting around with a cane now, and we're hopeful that he'll be off it by summer."

Relieved tears clogged my throat, but I kept myself together. A big part of my pain had been my inability to support Carter during his rehab. I felt a stab from not being with Grace's family when they got that good news. There'd always be a little twinge whenever forced to acknowledge that that part of my life was over. When it hurt, I focused on something positive in my life, like getting to know Rodri. For now I had to tiptoe through a conversation with my former bestie.

"I'm so happy for you all. I prayed every day for his recovery." I blinked back those tears, thinking of the days when the boys would be here on the floor with their toy cars and trucks and Grace and I would be gossiping over coffee. Now look at us—close yet so far apart. "I can only imagine how much you missed having him at home."

Grace nodded, her eyes misty. "It's been the worst time for my family."

She hadn't said it in an accusatory way, but I'd had a hand in her pain, so that stung. Despite all the conflict in my heart, I would always regret what happened here and all the ways it changed our lives.

"I've said it before, but I'll say it again, Grace. I'm so sorry, for all of it." The need for her absolution pressed on my heart even though she'd let me down, too.

"I know you are. You've said it a thousand times and shown it as often. Now it's my turn. Mimi, I'm truly sorry for treating you like the enemy."

Surprise pushed me deeper into my seat and made me lose my breath. Had she just apologized to me?

She continued. "This situation brought out the worst in me, but ironically, it's ultimately ended up freeing me, too." Her expression proved she was still in disbelief.

This was interesting. "How so?"

"Well . . ." She knotted her purse strap in her fingers. "It's a long story that involves a breakdown in my marriage and an honest discussion with my mother, but I've finally confronted my past and am now finding it easier to let go of pain and blame instead of carrying them around like invisible chains."

"Wow." I didn't know what else to say. Her and Becky sharing a "come to Jesus" milestone was major. Having encouraged that for years, I indulged another instant of self-pity that I hadn't been part of her watershed moment. "Sounds like what you're saying is that we don't have to be enemies."

I should be happy about that, because I'd hated being the object of her pain, yet the loss of our friendship still smarted.

"I hope not. I'm ashamed of how I treated you, and I wouldn't blame you for politely sending me on my way tonight." She sucked in her lips, her eyes filling with tears. "I know we don't have a lot of time right now, but I have to ask, Can you ever forgive me?"

Her begging for my forgiveness was surreal. It'd be easy to say yes, because I'd made as many mistakes as anyone and I missed my friend. But she'd basically shut me out for two months, so I didn't know how to trust in her. "Of course I forgive you, Grace, but I'm not sure what that means in terms of our friendship."

"I miss you." Her voice shook. "Not having you to lean on is part of why I melted down. I don't expect to pick up where we left off—it'll take time to work through everything. But aside from Sam and my kids, there isn't anyone in this town who means as much to me as you, so I'd like the chance to repair what's been damaged." She stared at me, her heart in her eyes.

This was the apology and sentiment I'd been yearning for, yet I didn't have full faith in it, which burned like salt in an open wound. "What about the lawsuit?"

The words slipped out before I thought them through. I held my breath, wondering if I'd ruined the truce.

"It's still pending." She made a pained expression. "Thank you for not telling your lawyer what Carter said to Rowan."

"I would never cheat him out of the help he needs."

"I know." Another pause, during which Grace stared at her lap before raising her head and meeting my gaze. She looked as if she had more to say, but Rowan bounded down the stairs, interrupting us.

"Mom, what's for dinner—" He came to a sudden stop, eyes wide, expression uncertain. This was the first time he'd seen Grace since she'd been in our basement. "Oh, hi, Mrs. Phillips. How's Carter . . . or am I not allowed to ask?" He looked at me, scared.

"Hi, honey. Thank you for asking. He's coming home this weekend." Grace stood and crossed to him. "Rowan, I need to apologize for not thanking you sooner for trying to help Carter while he was in rehab. I'm sorry that had to stop, and I'm sorry about how poorly I've handled things with you. I've been so frightened, but it's no excuse for how I ignored you. You'll always be a special person in our family's eyes, so I hope you can forgive me."

He shrugged, his expression nearly dazed. "It's fine. I'm really sorry he got hurt here and glad he'll be home soon."

"Me too." When Grace opened her arms to him, another small part of my heart found some peace. "Can I have a hug?"

Rowan obliged, which was a big deal for an awkward teen boy. When they eased apart, he went into the kitchen, presumably to figure out what we should do about dinner.

"Well, you should feed him before the meeting, but maybe we can talk again soon?" Her face filled with hope.

I stood, nodding, almost glad she was leaving so I could have a few minutes to process my own feelings before having to face the crowds at the school. "Will you be at the PTC meeting, too?"

She nodded. "Yes. It's time to get back into the swing of my normal life, and I want to learn more about that website."

"Well, then I'll see you later."

I walked her out without reaching for a hug like I normally would. I couldn't say why. Didn't know what kept me from embracing this opportunity. Maybe it was the lawsuit still between us, or maybe I simply needed some kind of proof that the friendship I'd thought we'd had had ever been real.

———

An hour later, I signed in at the front desk, my guard still up.

Grace might have come to me privately to make amends, but her friends didn't know that. This was my first PTC event since the party, so my stomach churned as I approached the auditorium.

I scanned the crowd for a friendly face and an empty chair.

"My daughter's hair has never looked better, Mimi." Annika Duncan gestured to an empty seat to her left.

I pressed a hand to my heart, grinning wide. Maybe that student special might be worth offering on a permanent basis.

"Thanks." I took her gesture as a good sign that the evening wouldn't be a disaster.

It seemed as if the worst for the salon had passed, as some of the no-shows recently had made appointments to fix whatever someone else had messed up. I'd lost a few customers, but in a way the shake-up had forced me out of complacency. I'd created new promotions to grow my customer base, which could lead to my hiring a third stylist next year. Better yet, last time I bought groceries, Jeb Stewart stopped me to tell me what a hard worker Rowan was. Grace always said I didn't give him enough credit, and Jeb's bit of praise helped me believe that if football didn't pan out exactly as Rowan hoped, he'd still have a good life. I guessed Mama had been right when she promised that even in the darkest times, there would always be opportunities for those who didn't give up.

"Did you see what Carrie posted in the Facebook group?" she asked.

A couple of weeks back, I'd stopped spending so much time investing in all that gossip and looking for validation that might never come. Haters pounce on people, no matter the issue. Universal approval was an impossible, overrated goal. I didn't need those women to teach me right from wrong. I trusted my heart again, a welcome relief. That said, I braced for whatever she was about to share.

"I've been so busy I haven't kept up," I said.

"Carter's coming home this weekend." She smiled. "Carrie says he's still using a cane, but he'll continue outpatient therapy and possibly be off that by summer."

"Oh, yes. Grace told me." Relief for Carter flooded my system again, loosening my shoulders.

"Oh? That's great." Annika stared at me, stunned, then her brows gathered as she pointed toward the aisle. "Isn't that your ex?"

There was Dirk, looking for a seat. He'd never once come to these things when we were together, but lately he'd been determined to insert himself more fully into Rowan's life, which meant I had to deal with him more often. Our gazes met, so I nodded politely while bracing for him to lay down another threat, seeing that we'd yet to come to any agreement.

Suddenly a strange buzz wafted across the crowd as all heads turned toward the door.

Grace and Sam had arrived. She clutched his arm, an anxious smile on her face as they made their way toward the front row, where the PTC board members were seated.

All around me folks whispered and shot me sideways glances. My cheeks warmed, but I kept my smile in place and ignored the lookie-loos. They had no idea that Grace and I had spoken an hour ago, and many might be hoping for more gossip for the Facebook group.

Sondra Billings, the PTC president, strode to the mic and motioned with her hands for everyone to quiet down. "Good evening, and thank you all for coming. I know we're all anxious to learn more about how to help our kids maximize the benefits of Naviance so that they have a smooth college application process down the road. It's an amazing tool, and I'm super excited to run through all its features. But first, your secretary, Grace Phillips, asked if she could take a moment to address everyone. We've all been praying for her family and are thrilled she could make it tonight. Grace." Sondra gestured to the podium.

My heart galloped. Grace hated public speaking. What on earth did she plan to say? I tensed, tempted to leave to escape the weight of everyone watching, but curiosity glued me to my chair.

Grace carried a single sheet of paper with her to the mic. She glanced at Sam, who gave her a thumbs-up sign, before she read from the page.

"Hello, friends. Thank you for indulging my wish tonight. I'll do my best to be brief." She paused, then folded the sheet of paper in half and took a deep breath before speaking from the heart. A shock! "As many of you know, since early January, I've been p-preoccupied with my son's injuries. We are pleased to share that he's coming home this weekend. He's been eager to return to his school community, having missed his friends and home-cooked meals." She paused to smile briefly. "He's getting around well with a cane, so he can move on to outpatient rehab. With continued work, the doctors feel certain he should walk again, unassisted, maybe as early as summer."

She paused for the clapping and cheering to settle, wiping a tear from the corner of her eye.

"I want to again thank all of you who contributed to the Meal Train and/or the G-GoFundMe campaign that was started in Carter's name. In particular, I want to thank Mimi Gillette for initiating both of those efforts to help my family, and to help our community heal. It could not have been easy for her, given how many people, including myself, were laying blame at her door." Somehow Grace zeroed in on me, holding my gaze while smiling. More of the ice around my heart thawed, despite how many people turned around to pick me out of the crowd.

Grace continued. "Many factors contributed to what happened to Carter, but pointing fingers helped no one. I'm sorry that my attitude contributed to additional tensions in town. P-perhaps what's happened can serve as a starting point for finding solutions to prevent something like it from happening to someone else in the future, but for now all I want is to apologize for things I did and said to Mimi and others these past several weeks that caused further division within our community. I hope we can all p-put this behind us and move forward together with compassion. Thank you."

Amid clapping, Grace abandoned the podium for the security of her seat next to Sam.

I couldn't quite catch my breath. Her being a private person meant her public apology couldn't have been easy. She'd chosen this forum on purpose, mostly to help me, I suspected.

My body grew restless during the rest of the meeting. I hoped Dirk took good notes, because my attention had splintered between Naviance and what else Grace had wanted to say at my house about the lawsuit before Rowan had interrupted us. When the meeting ended, I said goodbye to Annika and made my way out the door quickly to avoid a run-in with Dirk. Any good-luck streak I'd enjoyed these past days died when I heard him call my name.

"Mimi." Dirk waved me to his side of the hallway when I came through the door.

I crossed to him, determined to play nice for our son's sake. "Please tell me your being here means we can work together to help Rowan get into college instead of fighting over custody and visitation."

His expression remained on the cold side. "Rowan didn't tell you?"

My stomach dropped. "Tell me what?"

"After a big talk, I'm not going to push on the custody stuff. He's got a good thing going with his coach here, and making him come up to me three nights a week creates too much stress."

Miranda might have pushed back on Dirk, too, so this reversal probably wasn't all coming from a place of consideration for our son's needs. But I was no dummy. I'd take what I could get. "Thanks for putting him first and being more involved. Rowan has been happier seeing you more regularly."

"I know. So if you don't mind, I'd like to be the one to take him to the summer showcases up at Villanova and down in Texas and Florida this summer."

"That's fine by me." Sitting around college stadiums watching Rowan compete with other athletes for coaches' attention would not be my forte. As much as I would do anything to help Rowan achieve his dream, I worried about injuries, and that worry would probably get worse after what happened to Carter. "I can't really afford to miss all that work anyway."

"Cool. Well, that's all I had to say." Dirk stuffed his hands in his jeans pockets.

He didn't take any digs at me or Rodri—a shocker. "I'm glad we're on the same page."

"Sounds like Carter's doing better, too. Rowan will be happy. He's felt guilty about all that." Dirk nodded thoughtfully.

Rowan's sharing his feelings with his dad surprised me. Maybe there was more to Dirk's parenting than I gave him credit for. "We're all really happy for the Phillipses."

As if summoned, Grace and Sam came through the door with the last stragglers. Those folks had probably been peppering Grace and Sam with congratulations and questions. When she saw me, she tugged on Sam's arm to stop him.

"Well, I'd better get going," Dirk said, wisely sensing his exit cue.

"Bye." I waved absently, my gaze still stuck on Grace.

She whispered something in Sam's ear, to which he nodded, smiled at me, and then kissed her before leaving her behind.

She crossed the hall to me. "If you're not in a rush, maybe we could finish our conversation after everyone leaves?" She gestured to the auditorium.

"Sure." My nerves danced.

We took seats at the back of the auditorium, and when the last person left, she said, "Sam and I spent a few days looking for ways to offset the costs of Carter's surgery and care so we could drop the lawsuit but, after running the numbers, confirmed we can't totally walk away without major financial repercussions. However, we've instructed our lawyers to make a reasonable settlement offer in the hopes that we can all share the burden of what happened and finally put this chapter behind us."

A sob lodged itself in my throat—I was so happy to see fairness and integrity restored in my friend, and relieved that the legal battle might end soon. "I don't know what to say, except I'm glad and will do what I can to get my lawyer to accept the offer."

"I know the insurance companies could drag things out a bit, but if we agree not to talk about the case, maybe we could work our way back to being friends in the meantime."

I touched my breastbone, amused and moved. "My word, Grace Phillips, you're bending the rules?"

"Only for you, Mimi." A wobbly smile appeared. "Only for you."

That did it. I leaned across my chair to really hug my friend for the first time in too long. We cried and laughed in that strange, relieved way one does after the worst is over. I held on tight to make up for all the times we hadn't been able to comfort each other these past weeks. For all the fear and pain we'd both experienced. And to celebrate the ways in which this terrible tragedy made us both more aware of how much we needed each other. After weeks of misery, my heart rejoiced and found its normal rhythm.

When we broke apart, Grace said, "I'm so relieved. It's been awful not to be able to talk to you."

"I know. So many times I wanted to pick up the phone and ask advice—about Rowan, about Rodri, just everything."

"Now we can start to lean on each other again." She smiled, then looked startled. "Oh! I forgot about Sam. He's waiting in the car."

"Then we should get going." We both stood and made our way to the school entry.

Grace turned to me. "Can we meet at Sugar Momma's soon?"

"I never turn down an opportunity to eat her muffins." I smiled.

Grace held the door open for me. "Maybe we can plan a double date soon, too, so Sam and I can get to know Rodri."

"Maybe in a bit. I told you, I'm taking it slow. My focus is Rowan—he and I are still working out the new rules around here, so I don't want to push anyone on him until I'm sure it's someone who'll stick."

She cocked her head before we parted for the night. "Looks like we've both made some important changes these past weeks."

I grinned at my friend. "I guess we have."

# EPILOGUE

## GRACE

*July 4*
*Deep Creek Lake*

While rinsing the lettuce, I glanced through the window to the dock, where Sam and Rodri were fishing with the boys and Kim.

"I want to make candied pecans for the salad. If we chop grapes and throw in this goat cheese with a soy-lemon dressing, it's terrific." Mimi tossed two fistfuls of pecans into a bowl of sugar water before dumping them into a hot sauté pan.

"Think they've caught anything, or will it be burgers for dinner?" I grinned.

"I'm starving, so let's cook burgers. If they caught anything worth eating, we'll have surf and turf. That way no one gets offended, but no one goes hungry, either." She shook the pan to keep the nuts from burning.

I pumped the salad spinner to dry the lettuce, pausing to sip my iced tea. "It's a beautiful evening. Clear skies should make for a great fireworks display."

"Remember how Kim hated that noise when she was a baby?"

I laughed. "One of the few things she was afraid of as a toddler."

Mimi turned off the stove and came to stand beside me and peer down on our families. "Everyone's growing up so fast now."

"Rowan seems to get along well with Rodri," I said, happy for her to have a good man who seemed to want to make her happy.

"Rodri's easy, like I've told you." Mimi looked at me. "I worry, though, about the age difference. He's only thirty-two, and he'd be a great dad. He's still got time for that, you know? But I'm forty next month and have a kid who'll be driving soon."

My heart went out to her. Nothing she'd ever earned had come easy, including love. "Does Rodri even want kids?"

"He's from a big family, so I assume he does, but he hasn't said that. We haven't talked about it, actually. I'm afraid to broach it because I enjoy his company and am not ready for it to end." She poured herself an iced tea, seeming lost in her thoughts.

It healed me to be trusted with her worries this way. When she set the pitcher down, I reached for her hand. "You know, you could have another baby if you wanted. Who knows, maybe you'd finally get the daughter you've always dreamed of."

She smiled broadly, her eyes glistening. "You don't think it'd be too risky? Too . . . weird?"

"You'd have to ask your doctor about the risks, but it wouldn't be weird. You're a good mother. Besides, there is more than one way to build a family—assuming you want that, and that you could see doing it with Rodri."

"Thanks, Grace. It's been nice the way you and Sam have made Rodri feel part of us so easily." She glanced out the window at the boys. "Maybe I shouldn't be afraid to talk to him about the future."

"Since when have you been afraid of anything?" I teased, bumping our hips.

"Well, I'm afraid of the time when we'll have to say goodbye to the boys. I can't believe they'll be upperclassmen in September."

367

I nodded. "Soon they'll be off to college."

The idea of it sent competing waves of excitement and sorrow through me. My son would invest in his education and make us proud, but the thought of him leaving tugged at my heart.

"I sure hope so. The University of Maryland coach has his eye on Rowan. Same with University of South Carolina. Don't tell anyone, but I wish those teams had better names. 'Terrapin' and 'Gamecock' aren't fun to scream. If only Clemson would come calling, we could still say 'Tigers!'"

"Be patient." Ironic that I would counsel that, considering I'd learned patience only since Carter's accident taught me how little control I had over most things.

"I know." Mimi took the bowl of lettuce and added nuts, grapes, and goat cheese, then whisked together her soy-lemon dressing. "I love eating on the screened porch. This rental rocks. Imagine having a second home on a lake."

"When Rowan becomes an NFL star, maybe he'll buy you one," I teased.

"I like that dream." Mimi winked. It had taken a few weeks for us to find our natural rhythm again, but now life seemed better than before. I certainly felt stronger and less haunted by my past.

I gathered plates and flatware, and Mimi brought the salad with napkins out to the screened porch. We set the table, then she whistled— a shrill sound that pierced the air and echoed across the lake. "How's it going down there? Should we fire up the grill?"

Sam waved and called, "Hold up. We need to clean the fish—bass and perch!" Behind him, the top of the lake glittered with golden-orange light. The sun hung low in the sky, casting pink and orange swaths along the horizon.

"Well, hurry up! We need to eat and get rolling over to the Wisp Resort before all the best spots are taken," Mimi hollered back, then tipped her head. "Life's pretty great now, isn't it?"

"It is." I hugged my friend.

Down below, the dock crew began packing up their things. Rowan and Carter were laughing about something as they carried the rods and tackle box up the stairs to the house. It was too soon for Carter to wakeboard or water-ski, but he could walk and swim and dive off the dock without risking injury. By next summer he should be able to attempt other water sports. My nightmares had become infrequent as his physical and mental health were restored. His accident made me grateful for so many things and made me more present, two unexpected blessings.

My mother came to the porch door. "Should I make brownies to take with us to the fireworks?"

"Heck yeah. I've got leftover pecans if you want to add those," Mimi offered, making her way back inside.

I remained on the porch, watching my family and Mimi enjoy the evening while listening to her and my mother chatting in the kitchen. Despite all that had happened, I'd never felt more content, or more certain of what and who mattered most to me. The only thing about life's ups and downs that I would ever try to control again was how well I'd enjoy the ride.

AN EXCERPT FROM

*THE HAPPY ACCIDENTS*

# PROLOGUE

*Late October, thirty years ago*
*Brandman's Funeral Home*
*Norwalk, Connecticut*

This is already the worst day and it's not even lunchtime. Our mother takes Lizzie and me by the hands after Richard, our driver, drops us in front of the funeral home. I'm not afraid to see Marta's dead body because I've seen one before, when Grandfather died three years ago. That time was different, though, for lots of reasons.

First of all, Dad isn't coming today. This morning he told Mom he had a "conflict," his code for some important meeting. He always has them, even on the weekends. I don't really know what a hedge fund is except that it has nothing to do with actual hedges. Those are shaped like eggs and tall swirlies by a group of men who come every week with their giant lawn mowers and shears. Whatever my dad does at his job, he doesn't seem to like it very much. He complains a lot about the SEC—whatever that is—and red tape. I've seen clear, brown, and blue tape, but even when I snoop in his office, I never find any red tape.

Another difference is that Grandfather's funeral happened in our town, Greenwich, in a three-story brick building that looks like other houses in our neighborhood except for its small front yard. Marta's funeral home is only half as big (although it's a sunny yellow color), has no yard at all, and is on a street crowded with stinky buses. Thinking about her here makes my stomach hurt because she would rather be in our garden than here.

A breeze blows a bunch of red leaves across the sidewalk. That's something else that's different today. Grandfather died in July right after my fourth birthday, but Mom made me wear a navy blue dress, a matching hat, and white gloves to his funeral. Those gloves made my hands sweaty, so I'd taken them off when she wasn't looking. Later that day I got in trouble because I'd lost one of them. Today is much colder, but Mom didn't make us wear gloves or hats, although we are all wearing navy blue. Navy blue is an unhappy color, so I guess it makes sense, because I am very unhappy that Marta won't ever hug me again.

When Grandfather died, Lizzie had been only two, so she'd stayed at home with Marta. Back then I felt grown-up going to the funeral, but also jealous that Lizzie got to be with Marta. Marta had been our nanny only a little while at that point, but she'd already become my favorite person. Every night when she left our house after dinner, I'd secretly wished I could go home with her. Now I will never be able to live with her.

My chest suddenly feels like it did that time Sandra Scott whacked it with a softball. Breathing hurts so much more than when Grandfather died, and I liked Grandfather. He smelled like sweet smoke and cinnamon, and always sneaked me ten-dollar bills. Grandfather was sixty-eight when he died, with gray hair and wrinkles, but Marta was only thirty-six. Still pretty old, but younger than my mom.

Could my mom die soon? I look up at her pretty face, frowning. Could I?

When we go inside, there are a lot of strangers standing or sitting and talking. Some kids are even playing hide-and-seek or something in and around the rows of chairs. I hold my mom's hand tight, surprised by all the confusion. Grandfather's wake was hushed, and I'd stood beside my parents while they'd shaken everyone's hands.

Now people are looking at us the same way Lizzie and I stared at that peacock at the zoo. We don't look like we belong here, with our white-blonde hair and fancy shoes, but I love Marta, so I know I belong. She would want me to come say goodbye. Lizzie's eyes are like giant circles as she looks all around. She's five, and this is her first dead body.

Somehow my mother figures out which person is Marta's mother even though there are lots of older ladies with teary eyes sitting together in a group. Marta told me stories about her six aunts and dozens of cousins. I can't imagine that, because I have only one aunt, two uncles, and four cousins, all of whom live in California, where my mom was born. Dad doesn't have siblings, but I don't think he minds.

My mom offers Mrs. Sanchez her "condolences." I don't like that word. It's too cold to match the hot pit of sadness in my stomach. Mom doesn't look too sad, but she's used to death because she's a heart surgeon who even operates on babies with bad hearts. Talk about unfair. Her job sounds terrible, but she smiles more than my dad, although not as much as Marta did.

Mrs. Sanchez's bright lips wobble when she smiles at Lizzie and me. "You must be Elizabeth and Jessica."

Our names sound prettier the way she pronounces them. She sounds a lot like Marta, which makes my eyes sting. We hadn't seen Marta for a few months because she was too sick. I miss her laughing and telling me that I'm funny, and how she never minded sitting on the back veranda with all my crayons and paints, or helping me clean everything up.

She always smiled and patted my head and wiped up spills without complaining about how much the patio furniture cost or how I'd stained another outfit. *"You're a little talent, Jessie. When you grow up, I will come to your gallery and buy a painting for my house."* I frown thinking of it.

Our new nanny, Bridget, doesn't cook as well. She is pretty patient, but she never makes me feel special.

Mom steps back, pushing us forward. Lizzie has better manners than I, so she sticks out her hand. "Nice to meet you, Mrs. Sanchez. I'm sorry about Marta."

All of a sudden, my throat squeezes tight. This is real, not a movie or a story or anything like Grandfather's funeral. This is the end. Marta didn't beat cancer and will never come to our house and play with me again.

I burst into tears, but crying only makes my throat hurt more.

"Oh dear." Mrs. Sanchez throws her chubby arms around me and gives me a hug, just like Marta used to do. I feel safe snuggled in there, so I let her hold me even though she's a stranger and my mom is probably embarrassed by my behavior. Then I remember the scroll in my hand, so I ease away.

I look up at Mrs. Sanchez and my words come out in a rush. "I painted this picture of Marta surfing because she told me that when she was my age, her favorite thing was visiting her grandparents in Costa Rica and surfing in Tamarindo. Can I put it in her casket?"

All the ladies start crying and speaking Spanish. Lizzie probably understands them better than me because I never pay as close attention to those lessons as I should.

With tears shining in her eyes, Mrs. Sanchez says, "That's very sweet of you. Marta will be happy to have it with her."

"Thank you." Relief sweeps through me as my mother says something else and then scoots us away so that others can talk to Marta's family.

Lizzie lags behind, almost on purpose, as we approach the casket. My mother makes us all kneel on the padded bench in front of Marta and make the sign of the cross before bowing our heads to say a prayer.

I don't pray, though, because I'm peeking at Marta. She looks like she's sleeping but has a lot more makeup than usual. She's there, but not there. While Lizzie has her eyes squeezed shut, I lay the scrolled painting across Marta's belly and then put my hand on top of hers. It's cold and hard, so I snatch mine away, sorry that I now can't count our final hug as the last time we touched.

I close my eyes, making myself remember what she told me when she was leaving our house on her last day with us.

*"Every day is a blessing, chiquitina. Do not waste a single one."* She'd hugged me tight in our foyer and kissed my head.

I know she meant for me to listen to my parents and "make the most of my potential." But if babies and thirty-six-year-olds can die any old time—so I can die anytime—then I don't want to be like my parents, who don't laugh out loud and always take everything seriously.

Kneeling in front of Marta's casket while listening to her family's sniffles, I decide *"Do not waste a single one"* was a warning. As long as I'm alive, I will never settle for a boring day.

# ACKNOWLEDGMENTS

There are so many people to thank for helping me bring this book to all of you—not the least of whom are my family and friends for their continued love, encouragement, and support.

Thanks, also, to my agent, Jill Marsal, as well as to my patient editors, Chris Werner and Tiffany Yates Martin, who take the lumps of coal I submit and help me turn them into diamonds. In this case, their insight helped me stay on track with the story I wanted to tell. And none of my work would find its way to readers without the entire Montlake family working so hard on my behalf. I'm indebted to the PR and marketing staff, the art department, the editorial staff, and the sales team for playing an invaluable role in my career.

And then there are the many people who gave their time to help me research various aspects of this story. For the sake of dramatizing the story, I took some liberties with the medical and legal research timelines, but cannot thank enough Jason Nascone, MD, of the University of Maryland Medical System in Baltimore for his help in crafting a plausible injury and recovery for Carter. Attorneys Herb Cohen and Karen Hardwick generously shared their expertise so that I could understand the legal options and obstacles the Phillips family faced in bringing a personal injury lawsuit against the others. I also am grateful to Dionna Carlson, a local friend and board of education member, for sharing her insight about how that body makes budget decisions. And last but not least, a big thank-you to Bill Scrima, a New York police officer who answered my questions regarding the actions and arrests that might follow in the wake of a party like Rowan's.

I also want to thank my critique partners, Linda Avellar, Barbara Josselsohn, and Ginger McKnight, for their guidance. Additionally, a big thanks to my beta reader, Jane Haertel, for her feedback on the early draft, as well as hugs for my Fiction From the Heart sisters (Tracy Brogan, Sonali Dev, Kwana Jackson, Virginia Kantra, Donna Kauffman, Sally Kilpatrick, Falguni Kothari, Priscilla Oliveras, Barbara O'Neal, Hope Ramsay, and Liz Talley), who inspire me on a daily basis and who are always there to talk through plot knots and provide feedback on a chapter or two. Every book I write really is a group project!

I couldn't produce any of my work without the MTBs (Regina Kyle, Gail Chianese, Jane Haertel, Jamie K. Schmidt, and Megan Ryder), who help me plot and keep my spirits up when doubt grabs hold.

And I can't leave out the wonderful members of my CTRWA chapter. Year after year, all the CTRWA members provide endless hours of support, feedback, and guidance. I love and thank them for that.

Finally, and most importantly, thank you, readers, for making my work worthwhile. Considering all your options, I'm honored by your choice to spend your time with me.

# BOOK CLUB QUESTIONS

1. Teen drinking is an issue in most communities. Which parental position do you more closely identify with: Grace's or Mimi's? Why?

2. Each year kids in high school and college get gravely injured or killed during underage drinking parties. Do you think parenting has any impact on these outcomes? Do you think the legal drinking age should be changed, and if so, why?

3. Have you found yourself on the opposite side of a good friend on an important issue? Did it affect your friendship?

4. Have you and your significant other ever clashed when it came to a parenting issue? How did you handle that?

5. Exclusion and bullying continue to be issues in middle and high schools across the country. Did you ever feel excluded or bullied? Did any of your children? How did you handle that?

6. Grace and her mother share a tricky relationship. Have you let childhood resentments affect your adult relationship with a parent or sibling? Why do you think it is so hard to apologize for and forgive old injuries?

7. School budgets are increasingly squeezed these days, and examples of our country's public school shortcomings abound. Do you feel your children or grandchildren are getting a better or worse education than you did? Do you have any thoughts on how the system could be improved?

# ABOUT THE AUTHOR

*Wall Street Journal* and *USA Today* bestselling author Jamie Beck's realistic and heartwarming stories have sold more than three million copies. She is a two-time Booksellers' Best Award finalist and a National Readers' Choice Award winner. *Kirkus, Publishers Weekly,* and *Booklist* have respectively called her work "smart," "uplifting," and "entertaining." In addition to writing novels, she enjoys hitting the slopes in Vermont and Utah and dancing around the kitchen while cooking. Above all, she is a grateful wife and mother to a very patient, supportive family. Fans can get exclusive excerpts and inside scoops and be eligible for birthday gift drawings by subscribing to her newsletter at https://bit.ly/JBeckNewsletter. She also loves interacting with everyone on Facebook at www.facebook.com/JamieBeckBooks.